D0436611

THE HUNT

Novels by Tamas Aczel

The Ice Age
Illuminations
The Hunt

THE
HUNT

Tamas Aczel

Little, Brown and Company

BOSTON TORONTO LONDON

First U. S. Edition

The characters and events in this book are fictitious. Any similarity
to real persons, living or dead, is coincidental and not
intended by the author.

Library of Congress Cataloging-in-Publication Data

Aczél, Tamás.
    The hunt : a novel / by Tamas Aczel. — 1st U.S. ed.
      p.   cm.
    ISBN 0-316-00896-6
    I. Title.
    PS3501.C84H86   1991
    813'.54 — dc20   91-6558

10 9 8 7 6 5 4 3 2 1

RRD-VA

Printed in the United States of America

For Tomi and Julia,
my son and my daughter,
with love

A-hunting we will go
A-hunting we will go
We'll catch a fox
And put him in a box
And never let him go.

Old nursery rhyme

BOOK ONE
ARRIVALS

ONE

FROM where he stood at the window of his familiar room in the west wing of the ancient Széchy Manor, General Wulf could see the huge trees shiver on the hillside in the late-October wind. He wondered why he had been invited to the hunt. He had not been invited to any official—or for that matter unofficial—function of the State or the Alliance since he'd been forced to resign from his posts as secretary of the Alliance and minister of defence more than a year ago. Then, the day before yesterday, the leather-clad messenger of the Secretariat drove his enormous Harley Davidson up to the front door of his villa on Lilac Hill and delivered the official invitation on the official stationery, bearing Singer's official signature, 'with warm regards'. General Wulf was as much surprised as curious. The hunting season had now been on for several weeks, and everybody in the Secretariat knew well how much he loved the ceremonies and rituals of the hunt. If they'd wanted him to come to the annual October 'bloodbath', as, perhaps only half-jokingly, it was called by the participants, he would have been notified in August, when the large embossed envelopes were sent out to those fortunate enough to be on the Secretariat's select guest-list. Surely Singer, general secretary of the Alliance and prime minister, didn't want him to come to shoot rabbits and after a sumptuous dinner sip Martell, amid laughter and gossip, sitting in comfortable armchairs and plush sofas around the library's baroque fireplace.

'Wulf, you must come,' Singer had said on the phone, soon after the messenger had disappeared, the sharp report of his motorcycle as he turned the corner and started down the slope towards the river still reverberating in the air, like a shot in the back of General Wulf's head. 'We want you to come. We are worried about you, Wulf. You lead an unhealthy life. You haven't been outside your garden for months.' Singer sounded dry, dyspeptic and well-informed, as he had ever since General Wulf had first met him under the big acrocomias and doum-palms (straight from Cuba and Tanganyika) of Berlin's famous Botanischer Garten. There Singer (straight from Moscow) had told him everything about the latest plan to destroy the Social Democrats, the dagger of the bourgeoisie aimed at the very heart of the proletariat as a new Kollwitz poster was soon to transform Singer's stammering metaphor into a powerful vision of the class struggle. Singer had always been the bearer of good news—in Berlin, at Teruel, at Archangelskoe—that invariably turned into cosmic calamities.

'Don't be an ass, Wulf,' Singer had continued in his most amiable manner. 'A friendly reunion won't hurt your pride. It'll do you good. I'll have a car sent for you. Thursday, at one o'clock sharp.' Singer also sounded peremptory. General Wulf wasn't surprised. Since Copass, that wily old boss of the Alliance—Moscow's trusted agent, until they decided otherwise—had been swiftly and painlessly evicted in early summer from his spacious office in the Secretariat's old, secessionist building overlooking the river and the Avar hills, and sent packing to Moscow together with his withered little Uzbek wife, Singer was fully in control. But then, had there ever been a time when Singer wasn't in control? As far back as

General Wulf could remember, Singer was in control, the only fixed point in a ramshackle universe. No matter how much General Wulf hated him, his hatred was tempered with a respect akin to admiration: Singer was, after all, his best friend.

All his life, General Wulf had wanted to be fully in control, but had never achieved it. Among the delicate lilacs, flaming geraniums, red tomatoes of his garden he often thought about the successes and disasters of his rise to power. When, after Jarek's unseemly demise, Wulf was made colonel-general and minister of defence, he was, metaphorically speaking, only three steps from the top. When, a year later, at Singer's suggestion, Copass decided to have him elevated by the Congress of the Alliance to the post of secretary, he was virtually *there*. But Singer had other plans, and Copass, as usual, played along, his smiling pumpkin face radiant with the gratitude and trust he was about to betray. They'd let General Wulf review his troops at the May Day parades, standing erect in his black Mercedes-cabriolet, his epaulettes golden in the morning sun; they'd allowed him to kick his officers, still asleep in their tents, at his famous impromptu pre-dawn inspections; they'd permitted him to mete out punishment and reward, like some Olympian, invulnerable and immortal, while they had been setting him up for the moment when they would make *him* responsible for all *their* perversions. But there was no use blaming them. He only got what he deserved—what fools always deserve.

The fragrant pine-logs in the fireplace were almost burnt to cinders, yet it was getting hotter in the room, as the central heating, installed some years before at General Wulf's orders, had started up full blast. General Wulf opened the window and instantly the cold wind penetrated the room with the raw scent of sodden leaves and damp earth. It was the room General Wulf used to occupy when he was still in charge, his favourite room in the west wing, facing the sunset. The large brass bed, the desk under the window, his armchair in front of the fireplace, his drinks cabinet in the corner next to the last Countess Széchy's ancient *prie-dieu* were all still there, but the photos on the walls, the trophies on the mantelpiece were gone, only the dust-frames remaining, ineradicable, on the wallpaper. They had taken his job, his uniform, his car, the guards at the gate of his villa on Lilac Hill, and now they had taken his mementos too. General Wulf closed the window. The drinks cabinet was empty. He rang for a cup of tea, and when nobody answered, decided to take a bath. Maybe they'd left him some hot water.

On Thursday at precisely one o'clock a tall, thin chap, with a flat nose and the cauliflower ears of a boxer, had picked him up to bring him to Széchy Manor. Despite the driver's stiff military salute, when General Wulf moved to sit next to him on the front seat (as he always had in his time), the boxer steered him politely but firmly, without a word, towards the back seat. They drove, in silence, on winding, empty roads, beneath dusty poplars, past unkempt fields, through empty towns and villages. It started to drizzle, then stopped, started, stopped again. Once or twice they came close to the flat, grey river which reflected the flat, grey sky. Now and then General Wulf saw people—a man chopping wood, a woman with a dripping clothes basket, a pack of urchins staring at his limousine, that looked like an old Packard, but was in fact only a new ZIM. It dawned on him that he had no idea where he was. He had made this trip from his villa on Lilac Hill to the Széchy estate in

Krestur many times, reading staff reports or having a nap, exchanging old hunting stories or saucy jokes with his guests in the back seat, yet he could not remember ever having seen those towns and villages before. He felt a slight pressure in his chest, but, unlike the one he had experienced before his seizure a few months before, it quickly passed.

After a sharp bend a level-crossing loomed up so unexpectedly that the boxer had to step hard on the brakes and swing the car to the left to avoid hitting the gate. For a moment, the boxer sat motionless, both hands on the wheel, then he cut the engine and, without asking permission, lit a cigarette. General Wulf could hear the boxer's quick breathing and the train's slow, distant whistle. Staff-Sergeant Kell, his old driver, the best, most reliable driver in the world, would have recognized the danger, negotiated the curve, anticipated the gate, and stopped if he needed to; but he never needed to. In General Wulf's time, the train would have been halted at a safe distance, made to wait until his convoy of guards and guests had sailed past the crossing. But that was a long time ago. Now, General Wulf wanted to get out of the car, stretch his legs, take a whiff or two of cold air and watch the engine chug along with its interminable row of dirty box-cars and tankers. But the car doors were locked.

When he went to take his bath, General Wulf found some of his old-time favourites, things he hadn't seen since his resignation: a bar of Yardley lavender soap, genuine Gillette blades, a blue jar of Nivea cream and a small, milk-white bottle of Old Spice after-shave lotion. There was plenty of hot water, too. Cautiously, he lowered himself into the huge tub that he had had installed in place of the old countess's little bath and luxuriated in the fragrant water.

Suddenly, he heard himself singing. Why the old song should come back to him now, he had no idea, but he sang it with the same elegiac cadence that had brought tears to his eyes when he'd first heard it sung—by a young East London garment-worker, whose name he couldn't remember, in the barracks of Villanueva de la Jara, before being sent to the front at the Guadalquivir.

> *Ich came nach Spain in Januar—*
> *Yo hablar seulement English—*
> *But jetzt I say, Comment savar—*
> *Wie gehts, que tal, tovarisch!*

With tears in his eyes, General Wulf laughed out loud. Jarek had loved the song and jotted it down in his little notebook for future reference—he was collecting material for a novel whose opening was already quite clear in his mind, though he had some trouble with the ending. Singer hated it.

'Good afternoon, General Wulf,' a slight, pale woman in a white dress and tennis shoes addressed him pleasantly, as he came out of the bathroom in his dressing-gown. 'I'm Sybil Wald, the new housekeeper, at your service. Welcome to Széchy Manor, General. I hope you'll have a pleasant stay here. If you have any questions, please don't hesitate to ask. My number is nine on the house phone. This is a most interesting place, as I'm sure you know. The main structure of the manor was built early in the sixteenth century, a few years before the battle of Sentelek in 1526—we are about twenty kilometres from the battlefield, General.

'Just under your window, behind the bushes, as you'll see tomorrow morning, runs the brook in which the young king was drowned, betrayed and defeated. Some historians maintain that the battle could have been won and the king saved if Count Széchy's forces had joined the archbishop's army before sundown. That had been agreed two days earlier in the War Council presided over by the archbishop, whose battle plan called for a coordinated attack against the janissaries of the left flank precisely at sundown. Others argue that the archbishop's scheme was flawed because even if Count Széchy had arrived in time, the king's army would have found itself faced with the full power of the sultan's cavalry and artillery, and been wiped out just the same.

'However, that is all academic. Count Széchy never showed up. He vanished. But why? Why would he betray the king, his best friend, the archbishop, his mentor, Prince Toromy, who was like a father to him, his real father having died when the count was still a toddler? And where did he go? What happened to him? Legend has it that he . . .'

She stopped abruptly, a faint, apologetic smile on her pale lips.

'Please forgive me, General, I'm sure you know all that. But I find the story so fascinating that I can't resist telling it, over and over again, to our esteemed guests. Dinner will be served at seven in the green room—the one on your right as you come down the stairs, next to the library. We hope to see you there, General.'

She bowed, then vanished, leaving a bottle of Black and White and a siphon of soda on the table next to General Wulf's armchair: she knew exactly what he liked! The archbishop's strategem may have been flawed, but Singer's plan seemed to be working perfectly. It deserved a toast.

General Wulf poured himself half a glass of whisky, filled it up with soda, and took a sip. Singer was testing him, tempting him. In the wardrobe, among the hunting paraphernalia, General Wulf had found a brand-new, full-dress uniform, complete with medals and ribbons, and four gold stars on the epaulettes. Was that an offer or a provocation? Probably both. But, though he longed to put on the old uniform after his year of banishment—even more, perhaps, than he longed to take a woman to bed after his year of abstinence—General Wulf resisted. The only way to find out what Singer really wanted was to refuse to play his sly games or let oneself be overawed by his slippery indirections.

He dressed formally for dinner, in a dark-grey suit with a white shirt and a tie Inge had packed in his pigskin suitcase. When he examined himself in the wardrobe mirror, he liked what he saw. He was still a good-looking man, attractive to women, despite the few unwanted kilos around his waist he had picked up during his year of forced retirement, without a single grey streak in his raven-black hair. His deep-green eyes looked at the world with curiosity and love, fury and rage: the lamb and the lion side by side in his soul and in his destiny, as poor Inge would paraphrase her favourite Isaiah to anybody willing to listen. General Wulf, as he was fond of saying, was coeval with the century. He had been born fifty-five years ago, the day the century was born, and, according to an old gypsy hag at Albacete, he was fated to die the day the century exploded in some millennial cataclysm.

Perhaps the old gypsy had known something nobody

else knew. General Wulf had already outlived his father, who died with a bullet in his heart on the Italian front at the age of thirty-five. General Wulf had survived several wars and was in the pink of health, as Dr Asklep assured him when he sent him home from his private room in the Old Beggars' Hill Hospital. As a retired Alliance official, he was no longer eligible for such treatment, yet Singer himself had made it available the moment he was notified of Wulf's heart attack. General Wulf still had forty-five years to go.

It wasn't yet six, so he sat for a while in his old armchair in front of the glowing embers, comfortably enveloped in the darkness that filled the room. Legend had it that, on the eve of the battle, at Christ's command, a host of angels had swept Count Széchy up to heaven, so as to spare him from certain death and prepare him for the future, when he would return in glory to save his tormented nation from the ultimate Enemy from the East. Legend also had it that, during the night before the battle, devils, in league with the sultan, had spirited him away to hell to impose the supreme humiliation on the Christian phalanx and assure the victory of the infidel. But legend said nothing about Count Széchy's little group of scouts, who on his orders had successfully penetrated enemy lines the *day* before the battle. To their amazement, they had seen the sultan's cavalry and artillery lying in ambush on the northern edge of the battlefield, hidden by a grove of oaks, elms, and birches, behind the janissaries, the main target of the archbishop's thrust. Stealthily, the scouts slipped back to Count Széchy's command-post, where they were put to death as soon as they had made their report.

But what happened to Count Széchy? He left behind no sign, no explanation, no evidence. Did he really vanish from the face of the earth? Looking into the embers in the fireplace, General Wulf suddenly saw Count Széchy in his black armour on the evening of the battle and the answer that had escaped him for decades came to him.

Count Széchy went to confession, received absolution, took Holy Communion, had supper, inspected his sentries, as was his habit every night during the campaign, then disappeared, faded into the darkness. The only alternative to a meaningless death was a meaningful escape from it. The sultan received him with the great respect and honour befitting his station and rank, accepted him as his friend and confidant, and, many years later, sent him back to his native land as the sultan's personal emissary.

Selim Pasha, as he was now called, became governor-general, fully in control of the life of his slaves and serfs, yet fully aware of their needs also. The new *beylerbey* turned out to be a brilliant administrator, a vigilant commander. He quickly put an end to the unbridled despotism of the *kadis, defterdars* and *sipahis* in towns and villages, gave the land back to the peasants, the shops and workshops back to the merchants and artisans, built new roads, imported new tools, opened schools, encouraged self-government and the development of healthy self-interest which, in time, would coincide with the interests of the community. Under his enlightened administration, the soil produced more grain, vineyards better wines, workshops more commodities. Peasants adored him, priests prayed for him. Criminals feared him, for he never hesitated to have a black-marketeer hanged in the marketplace, or a thief's arm chopped off in front of the townspeople, not only because he well knew how much they enjoyed such spectacles, but because he wanted everybody to know that order resides in obedience. From being their worst enemy, Selim Pasha became the people's best friend. He turned sedition into fidelity, infamy into honour. True or not, it was a story worth pondering.

General Wulf walked down the old, creaking steps to the front hall, and stood there in the silence. The great hall was empty, and except for a silent scullion setting the table for three, so was the green room. General Wulf knew that most people would only come tomorrow, some not till Saturday morning, so he did not expect to find a crowd, but he had expected the small group of regular early birds. Old devotees of the hunt, like himself, obsessed by its ceremonies and rituals, they would always arrive a day sooner to enjoy an evening of *bonhomie*, drinks in the library and dinner in the red room, where Aunt Elsie offered them her famous venison. Her inimitable *sauce à la chasseur* was a lingering memory of that French restaurant in Chicago where she'd spent years as a scullery-maid before returning to her native Krestur and opening The Waldhorn.

Instead of the excited hubbub of the regulars, the hall echoed with their absence. Singer wanted him to be there alone when he came . . . *if* he came. Singer loathed hunting. He came only when it was absolutely unavoidable—an insistent guest from the West, an influential visitor from the East—and even then would usually find a good excuse to remain behind in the house. He would read or play chess with one of his flunkies, though he always dressed for dinner and offered his clipped toasts, which, from a man who spent so much time reciting boring statistical data or lifeless ideological axioms, sounded almost poetic. But if Singer wanted to be alone with him, who was the third place for? A friend from Moscow? General Wulf hated Singer's Moscow friends.

The rain still came down like bursts of a semi-automatic from behind the bare poplars of the service road. General Wulf stood under the large portico of the entrance for a while, then put on a long, coarse habit he'd found hanging on the huge antler-peg by the door, covered his head with its cowl and stepped out into the rain. The manor was silent, dark. No cars in the driveway, no smoke from the big chimneys that in the old days would have belched their thick columns up into the sky. Stepping cautiously on the narrow path of beautiful blue basalt from the neighbouring hills, which he'd had laid, General Wulf circled the manor. On the far side of the house, facing the hills and the woods, a single light shone in the kitchen, the bulb shivering in the draught from the open window. But General Wulf saw no people, smelled no mouth-watering aromas. He turned back.

In front of the portico a small, black Skoda was being unloaded by one of the boys from the manor. It wasn't Singer's car, because Singer travelled only in ZIMs, Mercedes or Cadillacs; it was a private car belonging to one of the very few private citizens permitted to own one. Vaguely, General Wulf remembered having seen the black Skoda before, but had no recollection of where, or when. Or, for that matter, whose car it might have been. In any case, the second card in the dinner's tierce had now arrived.

'General Wulf,' Sybil Wald said from inside the hall. 'Where have you been in this weather? We don't want our guests to catch cold while in our care, now do we?'

General Wulf returned the habit to the antler-peg, and started towards the staircase. Except for his muddied shoes and socks the good old habit had kept him dry.

'Dr Krolthy will be down in thirty minutes,' Sybil Wald continued. 'In time for dinner.'

'Did you say Krolthy?' General Wulf stopped at the stairs. 'Adam Krolthy?'

'Yes,' Sybil Wald said. In the opalescent light of the hall's big glass dome she looked frail and transparent. 'Justice Krolthy. The famous judge. You must know him, General. I'm sure you know him.'

'I know him,' General Wulf said, starting up the stairs. 'I want my dinner in my room. Breakfast as usual, at seven. And I don't want to be disturbed until then.'

It was a good, solid meal, nothing fancy or spectacular, but everything done with care and attention to detail in the best tradition of Aunt Elsie's country cooking, which Justice Krolthy always preferred to the fancy concoctions she had learned to whip up in that famous French restaurant in Chicago in her youth. Served by a buxom young maid under the all-seeing dark-shadowed eyes of Sybil, first came an exquisite soup of the giant morel mushrooms that grew wild in these woods; then a superb *tocani*—a savoury blend of beef, veal and pork cut into small pieces and cooked slowly for an hour or so with bacon, black pepper, paprika and sautéed onion—with home-made *halushka* and lightly buttered potatoes; followed by a bland chestnut torte with a thin chocolate glaze and skimpy whipped-cream topping (probably made by one of Aunt Elsie's less gifted disciples). Accompanied by mellow Green Friars and pungent Steer's Blood in crystal decanters, it was a dinner that left Justice Krolthy satisfied. But he greatly regretted that old Henryk refused to join him to eat, drink and be merry *tonight*, because one never knew what *tomorrow* (let alone *yesterday*) would bring the reveller, especially now that Gerogen's arrival was imminent. Justice Krolthy liked and missed old Henryk, once the very heart of such feasts, whom he hadn't seen for at least a year now. A pity. Justice Krolthy sipped his Green Friars.

Justice Krolthy stood at the window and looked into the darkness, suddenly dispersed by a giant half-moon that hung precariously, as though on a thread, above the woods. Late at night Gerogen's secretary had called him, about a week ago, and asked him to stand by. Charming and sprightly, she had chatted away as if it was ten minutes to noon, not ten to midnight, though he knew that after so many years she was still seething at having been dropped into the famous oubliette of Justice Krolthy's memory—as he called it among friends—to end their short but intense affair.

Justice Krolthy had no longer needed Bellona Hagen to gain access to Gerogen's second-rate mind and third-class secrets: he knew everything he wanted to know, and the risks of dumping her became fewer than the advantages of keeping her. He remembered her last theatrical exit from his apartment—the way she touched the bed, the mirror in the bathroom, and went out to the balcony to bid a tearful farewell to the river and the hills beyond, as if she were going to the scaffold rather than back to her comfortable villa on Saxenberg, and to her husband, the minister of transport and a veteran of the Spanish Civil War.

Thinking about it five years *post festum* made Justice Krolthy feel free again, delighted, almost happy. Then Gerogen, long-winded, mealy-mouthed and sanctimonious as usual, had come on the line to make sure *personally* that Justice Krolthy would not miss the weekend festivities on the Széchy estate. Gerogen, who for conspiratorial reasons called himself Singer (old Henryk's favourite chum in the Berlin years), offered to send a car for him, but Justice Krolthy politely declined. He couldn't stand being driven by Gerogen's mute boxer-types—one never knew if one would arrive at one's destination—whereas he loved driving around the country alone in his own little Skoda. Gerogen hadn't seemed to mind.

There could be several reasons why Gerogen had insisted so emphatically on Justice Krolthy's presence at Széchy Manor. A man with his unique legal mind might be needed to prepare, posthaste, the general line of attack and sweet details of a new trial of heretics, always a mouth-watering proposition. A clerk of the first order (like himself) might be required to review the final draft of the reorganization of the criminal justice system, already hailed by the press as the ultimate triumph of the people in castigating their enemies: the new *contrat social* to ensure that one could escape the guillotine only with one's head in one's hands. Or, as a Thespian of some merit, fluent in several languages, he might have been asked, as he had been many times before, to entertain visiting foreign dignitaries with his amusing tales, accompanied by practical demonstrations, on medieval cooking. He was an expert on the subject, and his bestseller, *The Plover Egg in History and Other Intimacies*, was generally regarded as the definitive treatise on medieval food.

As he watched the clouds scatter and the giant half-moon rise, Justice Krolthy decided that none of those reasons was convincing: after the dethronement of Copass and the retirement of poor old Henryk, a new trial of heretics was unlikely; he could review the final draft of the criminal justice system—his own handiwork, anyway—

much better in his office; and last, there was no sign of foreign dignitaries here, nor sign of indigenous ones, no sign of anybody. The manor was empty, the kitchen cold, only Sybil hovered above the corridors and landings. Justice Krolthy lit a cigar. Gerogen's predictability, like God's, had reached new, transparent heights: he called at midnight, as if to emphasize the importance and urgency of his message, but everybody knew that this was one of his oldest tricks, to take his victims by surprise and make them feel guilty and humiliated for being asleep in their warm beds, while Gerogen, that guardian of virtue, was at his silent, lonely outpost still burning the midnight oil. Gerogen's midnight call was a sham. Old Henryk's unexpected presence might have suggested something of interest, had Justice Krolthy had the curiosity to puzzle out its meaning, but it was too late and he was too sleepy.

He had no idea why Gerogen had summoned him here at such short notice, but whatever Gerogen's reasons or motive, Justice Krolthy didn't really care. As far as he was concerned, their old compact, which for many years had bound them together as well as keeping them apart, was still in effect. It was a perfect indenture, unprejudiced, foolproof, no human element involved. Only the mechanics of existence. *Pour passer le temps.* Was there anything more important?

In the distance, Justice Krolthy heard the battered bell of the small Krestur church strike midnight. Sitting on the edge of his bed in his silk pyjamas, he waited for a minute or two for the telephone to ring. It didn't.

When General Wulf awoke a few minutes after six, the drizzle had stopped, and the sun was rising swiftly in a pale-blue sky. General Wulf opened the window. After yesterday's wet and cold, the air was balmy, almost spring-like, and in the dawn mist the birds spied him with arrogant curiosity.

General Wulf was hungry. He had been hungry ever since he'd returned from his walk around the dark, empty manor yesterday evening and hunger, like an assassin from behind the door, had stabbed him with his long, sharp stiletto. He had eaten everything Sybil Ward had brought him—a lukewarm mushroom soup he quite liked, a hot goulash he loathed, and a chestnut torte with whipped cream he enjoyed tremendously—but he remained hungry. He asked for more. Without a word, Sybil Wald left, and soon returned with a huge plate of cold meat, hard-boiled eggs, cheese, spring-onions, tomatoes, green peppers and a loaf of fresh rye bread with a deliciously crunchy crust. In all his long years of exile—in concentration camps, prisons, on battlefields and secret missions—he had longed for a piece of fresh, home-made rye bread with a crunchy crust more than anything. He ate it all and washed it down with a bottle of dry white wine and plenty of soda water. Yet, he was still hungry. Sybil Wald came back later to see if he wanted more, but General Wulf chose to go to bed with hunger's sly, low pain in his stomach and took two tablets of Morpholomin, double his usual dose.

On the table in front of the fireplace, cold now, he saw the remains of yesterday's feast: empty bottles, broken eggshells, dry pieces of bread and salami and green pepper, and his hunger struck again, like a devious boxer, with a blow at his solar plexus. It was only quarter past six. He swept the remains of the food on to a sheet of newspaper he found on his desk, and quickly threw it all to the birds, then watched them gobbling it up with gusto and without gratitude. He was still hungry.

He sat in his armchair, motionless, eyes closed. It was as if he were being slowly drained of his warm, natural energies, and then filled, equally slowly, with some cold, alien substance that flooded his veins and infiltrated his brain. It was a strange transfusion which made his mind intensely alert, but his body almost stiff. With some effort he got up, went to the bathroom, shaved, then washed with great care the hidden cavities and crevices of his rigid body that were beginning to smell of age, listening, with indignation and disbelief, to odd sounds inside his system he couldn't understand, yet somehow knew augured ill.

Later, dressed meticulously in his brand-new hunting jacket, soft riding boots and Tyrolean hat with a little bunch of colourful feathers, he walked out of the empty house as silently as he could.

The stars and the moon were fading fast, and the frayed blue-grey rags of mist above the poplars lining the service road, once a long avenue of shadows and weeds, were quickly mopped up by the sun. It was unseasonably warm, and the manor and woods scintillated in the early morning sunshine. Not far from the main entrance, General Wulf stood on a little mound where the best beaters from Krestur and neighbouring villages used to gather around a huge bonfire of straw and wet twigs in their fur-lined short coats and fur caps. Enveloped by the smoke, shifting their weight from one foot to the other, slapping their shoulders in the cold, they would wait for Staff-Sergeant Kell's whistle to open the 'bloodbath'. Today, there was only a black smudge on the muddy ground, the memory of old fires; there were no beaters and no cars in the drive, except for that scoundrel Krolthy's black Skoda; no hurly-burly in the kitchen, no smoke from the chimneys. General Wulf knew that Singer had deceived him again. There would be no hunting, no friendly reunion here today, tomorrow, or the day after. General Wulf headed towards the woods. His hunger had vanished.

After the morning's scary stiffness in his joints, he moved with ease among the trees and bushes. He knew every turn, every path, every clearing where deer congregated, every thicket where foxes holed up and rabbits bred. He stopped, once or twice, to quiet his racing heart with deep, long breaths of the fresh morning air, but the bitter-sweet smell of decay made him not only melancholic but angry. These days, he often dreamt of being lost in vast, unknown forests, attacked by wild animals. Now he realized that never before had he walked alone in these woods; he had always been with his entourage, led by his guides, watched over by his guards, applauded by his pals when his shot hit straight between the eyes of a stag that tottered and collapsed, its commanding antlers lifeless in the wet grass. Among them, he felt as safe and secure as one could ever be in this world. How much he missed them now! He had always hated to be alone, yet now he was left completely alone in his villa, in his garden, in his woods—no matter what Singer had said and done, these were *his* woods—as if Singer had decided that public disgrace must be buttressed by private degradation.

At the foot of the hill the path forked, one track leading to the village, the other going deeper into the forest. General Wulf climbed the hill briskly, but it proved steeper than he remembered. There was an inexplicable elation in his heart, its beat now regular and painless, as though its engine had been warmed up, ready for the effort. Still, it took him almost twenty minutes to reach the top of Crazy Hill, where the ruins of Count Francis Széchy's infamous gazebo stood. It was known popularly as Crazy Tower, because the people on his estate—his serfs, retainers and fat, young wenches—considered him not only a ruthless, evil lord, but also a crazy old fool. Shortly before his death he had had the gazebo built so that he could take a good, long look at his domain; and there he did indeed die, in his sedan-chair, his eyes on his forests and fields, surrounded by his family and servants, who, according to an eyewitness-account, watched his death with glee and fear.

Sitting on a moss-covered rock, his back against the rotting planks, General Wulf laughed loudly. There could be little doubt that the count was an evil man, but a fool he was not. Moments before he died, he put a curse on the hill and the gazebo, foretelling that anyone who went there after his death would surely die within the hour, and so created a legacy of superstitious fear that still held people firmly in its power. Very few inhabitants of Krestur or the neighbouring villages dared to come up here, and if they did, they wouldn't dream of touching the decaying posts and planks of the gazebo. Whether or not the rumours of sudden illnesses and inexplicable deaths were true, it was a superb subterfuge: the view remained undisturbed by the curious, untainted by the blasphemous. After 160 years, the count was still very much in control.

And what a spot he had chosen to die in *and* survive his own death! From here the estate could be seen stretching towards the river in the east and the mountains to the west. Down below lay the manor with its conglomeration of mansions, cottages, towers, chapels and gardens. Its turbulence reflected history's chaotic profusion yet also mirrored some of life's incomprehensible order, as Professor Weiskopf, famous architect and past president of the Academy of Sciences, had once written in an essay. Singer, at the last moment, had managed to prevent publication of the essay, because he believed that to write about history's 'chaos' as the reflection of life's inherent 'order' was dangerous bourgeois propaganda and religious absurdity. Arrested, Professor Weiskopf disappeared behind the gate of the Krechk Labour Camp and the copies of his essay into Singer's safe, but thanks to the divided loyalties of Bellona Hagen, General Wulf had succeeded in getting hold of one copy. It had lain unread until his retirement, but then, in his loneliness, in his degradation, how delighted he was that he had that copy! A magnificent piece of writing, a profound insight into history; he read it over and over again, until he knew it virtually by heart. And now he was here once more, enjoying a long look over his estate, an opportunity he had so much hoped for but had thought would never happen again.

To the east, General Wulf could see the remains of a little thatched cottage built by the first Széchy for himself and his family before the king made him a margrave to watch over the borders of his domain. From there, the manor grew in utter confusion, yet in such splendid, inner harmony that it made General Wulf's eyes fill with tears. How irrefutable Professor Weiskopf's argument had been! Round Romanesque vaults were followed by Gothic arches, then by the high, slender tower of a minaret (the legacy of the famous Selim Pasha, who had reportedly visited the place for reasons contemporary accounts could not clarify, whenever his tours of inspection as governor-general brought him to this part of the country). There stood the white simplicity of a chapel, with a richly orna-

mented clock tower next to it, a curious throwback to the
thirteenth century, yet somehow part of the whole
manor's irresistible progress towards perfection. Surrounded by the remnants of fortifications against maraud-
ers of all kinds, centuries of conflict were compressed into
congruence, and resisted the invasions of time. The heavy
central portico was supported not only by some elabo-
rately decorated *fin de siècle* pillars, but also by an original
Le Corbusier fragment, the last addition of the last count,
shortly before he fled the country pursued by the Red
Army and the ghosts of his past. Such were the contours
of a villa whose incompleteness remained symbolic of the
manor's unfinished yet timeless totality, order in chaos.

General Wulf had first visited the manor soon after the
war in the course of an election campaign (in those prehis-
toric times before the Alliance of Workers, Peasants and
Intellectuals had seized power there were elections). He
had found a mess. Escorted by a young forester whose
anxious face he still remembered—the man's anxiety was
so painfully understandable—General Wulf stood in the
middle of some minor maelstrom. After the hasty departure of the last Count Széchy and his family, the local
zealots had taken control of the manor and estate in the
name of the Alliance. Singer would have valued and
praised the zealots' ideological purity and down-to-earth
practicality, but General Wulf didn't like what he heard,
much less what he saw. Zealots were always a pain in the
ass. So many screaming obstacles in the orderly conduct of
power, they wanted everything done in an instant. Here,
they were in the process of turning the manor into offices,
nurseries, classrooms, storehouses. The priceless furniture was thrown into huge piles in the great halls, the
landscapes and portraits of ancestors gathered dust in the

old wine-cellars, from which, General Wulf noted, the wine had already disappeared. The brilliantly illuminated codices were removed from the library and left on the terraces to waste away in the wind and rain.

Instantly General Wulf knew he'd found the place he'd dreamed of for years, his great *trouvaille,* as poor Sébastien used to say when they talked about such a place before the Condors shot Sébastien's antediluvian Nieuport out of the dark skies of Teruel. General Wulf wanted the manor and the estate, he wanted it badly, and before those idiots ruined it altogether. But Jarek, who, as minister of the interior, was in charge of classifying and utilizing such abandoned properties, was himself a zealot, unconvinced and impossible to convince of the theoretical rectitude and practical feasibility of General Wulf's planned 'rest home'—as he repeatedly and with heavy sarcasm referred to it at meetings of the Secretariat.

Only after Jarek's death, when General Wulf became minister of defence, was he able to lay his hands on his dream castle, and by then it was almost too late. Yet he managed to salvage some of it, restored what he could to its former grandeur, turned it into what that rogue Krolthy once called a garden of earthly delights. Now, after more than a year of absence, as General Wulf watched it sparkle in the warm sunshine, he saw something unexpected, mysterious and overwhelming—something he had never seen before, not only because he had never had the time or the patience to look, but because he never knew what to look for. The manor was beautiful simply because it was there, without purpose or reason, a link that did *not* connect, a puzzle whose solution did not interest him at all.

Later, descending the steep hillside towards the manor,

he thought of old Professor Weiskopf and wished Weiskopf could be there with him today. But the professor had died in a quarry in Krechk Labour Camp, where he, a master-builder, had been sent to cut flagstones for the new Sports Palace. Inge had told General Wulf this after she met Professor Weiskopf's wife at one of the séances she nowadays frequented. How Mrs Weiskopf got the news of her husband's death was a mystery, because nobody ever admitted anything about Krechk, let alone sent out notices of accidents or deaths, yet Mrs Weiskopf knew everything in astonishing detail: the shooting, the bedlam, the burials behind the latrine. Maybe the ghosts told her.

Tired, General Wulf reached the foot of the hill. He looked for the path that would lead him back to the manor, but he couldn't find it. He had come down on the wrong side of the hill, he realized, and in order to get back to the manor he would have to cross the brook (in which the king had drowned on that fateful day of defeat and betrayal— though it was difficult to imagine how anyone could drown in such shallow water, unless, of course, poor chap, he was dead well before he was pushed from his horse), go past the arboretum, the vineyard, the tennis courts, the ruins of the old redoubt: a long walk.

General Wulf turned away from the mossy green of the giant oaks, towards the unfamiliar wilderness. Though the sky was still a cloudless blue and the sun shone with unabashed innocence, it was getting colder, an occasional icy gust hitting his perspiring forehead. A clearing lay ahead. General Wulf recognized its splintery, dead trees and the man-made mound in its middle instantly, and with some relief: now he knew where he was.

Here, during the last winter of the war, a stray two-ton bomb from a fatally wounded American Flying Fortress had gouged a deep crater in the soft, leafy soil. It had lain, a hidden trap, waiting for its victim, until that old beater fell into it and broke his neck. General Wulf remembered the crisp, cloudless day, the snow sparkling all over the forest, frozen, stone-hard branches swaying in the icy wind. Abruptly, the hunt had stopped; the beaters had hoisted the old peasant out of the pit, put him on a stretcher, made hastily of thick, snowy branches. The commander of the manor's Security Detachment, a young lieutenant the beaters seemed to know quite well, gave an angry bark and they lifted the makeshift stretcher obediently and set off at a slow trot into the woods.

At the edge of the clearing General Wulf had stopped them and looked at the body. Pale, his lips purple, his eyes closed, huge icicles already forming on his handlebar moustache, the old peasant was still alive. General Wulf had taken off his new greatcoat with its gold epaulettes and stars and, cautiously, so as not to hurt the bruised body, covered the man up to the chin. Then he ordered the lieutenant to take the man to the hospital, where he would receive immediate attention and a private room. Paler than the old peasant, the lieutenant saluted stiffly and was off, followed by the beaters with the stretcher.

After they had disappeared among the trees, a strong smell of tobacco and garlic lingered in the crisp, blue air. General Wulf walked up to the crater and looked into it. Full of snow, the impression of the old man's body was clearly visible in it. If it was a trap, it was cleverly arranged. He himself could have been killed there. He had been saved only by chance, as always. He fired his favourite old Winchester twice into the cold, grey cloud that seemed to be forming above the crater. Instantly, the hubbub of the hunt resumed.

That day General Wulf shot the old buck that for years
had eluded him and his hunters, appearing and disappearing behind ancient trees before anyone could get a
good look at him, his giant antlers raised contemptuously
high. Some said it was an apparition, the phantom-stag of
fable and, of course, of hunters' inflamed imaginations.
But there it lay on its white belly, still quivering, the snow
turning red around the long, graceful tines of its antlers.
Later, General Wulf was informed that the old beater had
died before the truck reached the hospital. The forester
responsible for enforcing the rules of the estate was arrested; the lieutenant was demoted to sergeant and transferred at once to defend the marshy minefields of the
western borders against renegades and infiltrators.

Now, General Wulf walked past the huge tumulus
where he suspected the old peasant had been clandes-
tinely buried by his fellow beaters. The air was sharp as a
blade now and the forest rumbled, dark, devoid of life.
Again, General Wulf felt the pressure over his heart. As
soon as he put the small nitroglycerine tablet under his
tongue the grip relented. Cautiously, he walked on.

In a matter of minutes he reached the edge of the forest,
exhilarated by the sudden thinning out of trees and undergrowth yet apprehensive in the face of the frigid hills and
bare meadows that billowed towards the bleak horizon.
Not far from where he emerged from the murkiness of the
woods he saw a small pond with a tree in the middle.
Stiffly circular, probably man-made, the pond was frozen
solid and dead, but the tree that arose from its icy centre
was gigantic and alive, its enormous trunk, covered with
grimy tufts, branching out into three immense heads at the
top, swaying, as if buffeted by winds General Wulf did not
feel. General Wulf had never seen the place before. Why

had nobody ever told him such a pond and tree existed on the estate?

He bent to touch the ice. Beneath the surface of its shiny mirror, he saw Copass, his moon-face elongated, as in his vitriolic moments of hatred, and next to him, Singer, his light-blue watery eyes full of dry cunning, inventing, no doubt, new traps for old friends. At the edge of the pond was a wooden bench and he sat down to take a brief respite.

'You see,' General Wulf said, shivering slightly, his jacket buttoned up to his throat, 'I never really had much time to ponder this so-called autumn ritual. I mean, the falling-of-the-leaves stuff, Professor Weiskopf, that repetitious spectacle of great lyrical significance. What was there to watch anyhow? Every year, more or less on time, the autumn arrived, the leaves fell, more or less predictably, and I didn't even look up. Why should I? I was a man of action, whose will was hardly affected—if at all—by the soft, melancholic moods of autumn. One doesn't, as a rule, wax poetic on battlefields or behind bars or in swampy concentration camps, though there are, one must admit, certain exceptions. But I wasn't among them. Until last autumn, that is.

'Let me explain this to you, Professor Weiskopf. That day, I was sitting in pious solitude in the middle of my garden, not too long after I'd been cast into outer darkness, as my old friend Anselm would say, deprived of everything I really cherished. An injustice of cosmic proportions, but let's, for the time being, not talk about that. I was sitting there among my tomatoes that had remained green and my green peppers that had turned flaming red, and I looked up—finally, I looked up—and saw the leaves fall. Truly, it doesn't sound like much of a revelation, but it was for me, for, suddenly, I realized that I was watching my life. The leaves had all been sentenced to death by autumn's martial law, yet which of them was to be executed first, and which next, was pure chance—incomprehensible, incongruous and meaningless. The leaves *had* to die. There was no escape. The law prevailed. Life was an illusion of freedom on a short leash.

'And wasn't *that* the mirror-image of *my* life? Haven't I always been buffeted around by forces beyond my control? Ordered about by people I didn't understand? Governed by rules I found disastrous? Executed plans I never comprehended? There, amidst the sad beauty of falling leaves, my heart stopped. At that moment, I realized what I've known all along, only never seen with such clarity: that everything I had done in my life was the manifestation of a deeper design. Sitting in my autumnal garden, alone and abandoned, full of misgivings about my future, my past gave me consolation. Nature, Professor Weiskopf, kindly offered me the help I needed. My life wasn't a waste: it reflected purpose, substance, history's solution to the puzzle. What a faint-hearted bastard I was! What a weakling! You might think whatever you like of its chances, accidents, detours, Professor Weiskopf, but my life, in the final analysis, *was* meaningful.'

'In other words,' Professor Weiskopf said, 'you're not responsible for anything you've ever done in your life.'

General Wulf sat on the bench in the cold for a while, then got up and walked back to the forest, looking for the spot where only a few minutes before he had emerged into the clearing. He couldn't find it, so, finally, he plunged into the high shrubbery. There, the woods appeared familiar, full of life. Partridges started from behind the thicket with a loud clapping of wings, rabbits loped through the undergrowth in fright, deer distrustfully lifted their heads in the air, then, with long, graceful leaps, vanished in the bracken. Beyond the treeline General Wulf saw the road leading to the village.

He jumped over a ditch, still muddy from last night's rain. Beside a culvert was a kilometre stone marked ONE. From the direction of the manor a gig approached, fast and light on its big-spoked wheels, drawn by a marvellous yellow gelding whose close-cropped mane and twitching ears glistened in the sunshine. Sitting erect on the form, letting the reins fall loose, Sybil Wald turned towards her companion, whose face was hidden by a cavernous cowl. Sensing freedom, the horse came around the bend at a high gallop. General Wulf waved to stop them, but they apparently didn't see him, so he decided to go and get somebody in the village to take him back to the manor.

He passed the abandoned mud-huts of the gypsies. Long ago they had been rounded up and relocated to help build the new iron-and-steel complex by the river, where they died or were killed or were moved to other labour camps, or the luckier ones escaped to join other wandering gypsy bands. The village lay before General Wulf, just as he remembered it. The long, meandering street was lined with old acacias and even older houses, all clean and white-washed, yet looking as if they had been built in that ancient spring when the first Széchy made his people settle here amidst the bounty of fish, fowl and game. He was then killed by a wild boar, whose vicious tusks became the family crest, visible everywhere on doors, gates, books, silver spoons and porcelain figurines of the manor.

General Wulf continued towards Main Square. In the centre, next to an ancient well, a statue of a conquering soldier raised his gun high, frozen in triumph. Behind the houses, ready for the winter, General Wulf could see the tender branches of the fruit trees and the straw-covered furrows of the little vegetable gardens that provided the manor's guests and the villagers with food. But no matter how much their small lots produced, they were forbidden to market any of the produce—in order to confirm the validity of Singer's sacred dialectical equilibrium between the production of cucumber and the re-production of capitalism. General Wulf had several times tried to talk to Singer about the astonishing profusion destined to wilt on the vines but Singer refused to discuss it with him, though he finally agreed that the surplus could be confiscated countrywide and used to feed the boys in General Wulf's army. Even if Singer didn't think much of him as a theoretician, he listened to his advice as a military man. General Wulf stopped in front of The Waldhorn.

The street was full of men in black felt hats, black suits, white shirts buttoned up but with no tie, and spit-shined boots. The women, black-scarfed, in soft, woollen wraps, and long black skirts that almost swept the ground, accompanied the children, miniature black-and-white replicas of the grown-ups. Silent and solemn, they all streamed down the street towards the small church, opposite The Waldhorn. As far as General Wulf could remember, it was Friday—not a holiday, religious or otherwise. If there was a funeral, he couldn't see the hearse. If they came for a baptism, which would have been unusual on a Friday, everything seemed much too solemn, almost despairing.

From under the leafless branches of an old acacia General Wulf watched the procession and was watched by it. He didn't know whether or not they recognized him, but they looked at him from the corner of their eyes, taking note of his presence, but never acknowledging it—Aunt Elsie, huge and dignified, passed him without a glance, as did Sybil Ward, head bent deeply—as if he did not exist, had never existed.

Suddenly the street was empty, dark except for the church glittering among the shadows, almost Protestant in its white simplicity. Motionless, absent-minded, General Wulf stood alone in the silence. Then he crossed the street and entered the church.

'Henryk!' Monsignor Anselm Beck said. 'Henryk, what are you doing here? You don't mean to say you've finally seen the light and come to confess your sins?'

TWO

AFTER a brief, dreamless sleep and a long, hot bath—he had never needed more than five hours sleep—Justice Krolthy came down, refreshed and relaxed, to have breakfast in the green room at precisely eight-thirty in the morning. Punctual and compliant—he saw no reason to disrupt Sybil's carefully constructed daily order—Justice Krolthy was in an excellent mood. Things were getting curiouser and curiouser. The table was set for three, as it had been yesterday evening, though there wasn't a soul about. Gerogen obviously hadn't arrived yet, for if he had he would be sitting there sipping unsweetened tea from an earthenware mug, as he'd learned to do in Moscow, or he would be out walking in the rose garden or the ruins of the old redoubt, tall and thin, his head lowered in deep thought, his face pained and melancholy, his back bent, as though carrying the weight of the world on his shoulders. And where were the others? Good old Henryk was probably still fast asleep in his room—not for him the politeness of kings, except when he reviewed his troops or had a new medal pinned on his already bemedalled chest—while the identity of the fourth player in this pedestrian thriller was still shrouded in mystery. A most promising prospect.

In the green room, the air was hot and stale, and Justice Krolthy quickly opened the big french windows that gave on to the rose garden. All the years he had been coming here for the hunt or for other important meetings Justice

Krolthy had admired that fabulous rose garden. It had
been started by the Countess Julia, one in a long line of
Széchy Anglophiles, soon after her return from England,
from a summer vacation at the estate of her great-uncle
Lord Agravain, around the turn of the century. Old Uncle
Karol, the gardener, nurtured and protected the roses as if
they were family. But old Karol himself was a miracle.
Already a gardener on the estate before the countess had
visited England, he had remained in his post ever since,
though the countess was long dead and buried in the
family plot beyond Crazy Hill. It seemed to him old Uncle
Karol must be a hundred, or older. Much older. Was he,
perhaps, immortal? Whenever Justice Krolthy saw him
pottering among the rose-beds, cutting shoots, inspecting
petals, with the thoughtful precision of a scientist and the
transcendent devotion of a saint, he couldn't help being
moved—and pleased with himself for being moved. Now,
old Uncle Karol was nowhere to be seen. Justice Krolthy
stood at the window inhaling the sweetly bitter emana-
tions of the garden.

'Your Honour,' a soft voice said behind his back. 'Your
tea's getting cold. Or would you prefer some fresh coffee
today?'

Caught unawares, though not altogether surprised—
ever since he entered the green room he had had the
distinct feeling of being watched, but then, in these years
of triumphant freedom, one always had the feeling of
being a slave—Justice Krolthy turned quickly and saw a
young woman at the table. She had a silver teapot in one
hand, a folded white napkin in the other, and an open,
innocent smile in her dark-blue, slanted eyes. She radiated
humility and obedience in the early morning sunshine.
She wore a simple, hand-woven linen dirndl, whose close-

fitting bodice and full skirt both concealed and exposed her small but mature breasts, inviting hips, strong yet shapely legs.

The apparition was strangely familiar, as if Justice Krolthy had seen her before, though he knew it was unlikely, for one could never forget a face like that. Used as he was to the sights and scents of exquisite women, Justice Krolthy felt a tremor in his body. Maybe he hadn't been dragged down here just to listen to Gerogen's bone-chilling exhortations about the new legal and moral system; maybe it *was* going to be a pleasant weekend after all . . .

'What a delightful idea, my dear! Perhaps I should have some coffee today for a change, yes.' The sylph was not only ravishing, but well-rehearsed, too: she knew that every now and again, instead of his daily Lapsang-souchong, Justice Krolthy would have coffee for breakfast. Whoever had trained her had done so with care and great circumspection.

'As you wish, sir,' she said and was gone, the swish of her skirt vibrating in the air. Cheered, Justice Krolthy lit his first cigar of the morning. He was willing to bet that the sylph knew exactly what mix of Brazilian and Colombian milds he bought in the government shop behind the majestic Corinthian colonnade of the Supreme Court, off-limits for ordinary mortals but open twenty-four hours a day for immortals with the proper identifications. Immortality, Justice Krolthy knew, was simply the correct mix of luck and protective colouration, a primitive formula.

The painting he admired whenever he was down here hung above the fireplace in a richly gilded baroque frame. The magnificent silver candelabra on either side held no candles, as if to inform the world that, while the altar of the goddess remained untouched, her worship was no longer tolerated by the management. Young and happy, the Countess Julia didn't seem to be bothered by such vulgar blasphemy. But it was easy for her: *her* immortality was secure. In a long, white summer dress made of the finest French cambric and old Belgian lace, which left her white swan-neck bare to set off an amulet on a gold chain, she stood in Lord Agravain's green garden in the midst of an explosion of flowers, more worshipper than worshipped, next to a small sundial which for ever showed half past ten. Her prominent cheekbones, slanted, dark-blue eyes and flaxen hair were lit by the health and happiness of youth. The artist, young Yoannis Philippus Augustus, must have been madly in love with her. In three days he created an apotheosis of innocence, a paean to the mystery of beauty.

Justice Krolthy wandered about the room, looking—in the commodes, in the chiffonier—for candles to light at her altar, but he couldn't find any.

'Your coffee, Your Honour.'

The same slanted eyes, the high Tartar cheekbones, narrow, slightly upturned nose, flaxen hair. The same sharpness of line, the same harmony of features. The same innocence. How could he miss such an obvious likeness, Justice Krolthy wondered as, discreetly but with growing interest, he watched her pour the coffee. For all he knew about the secrets of that ancient family (almost as ancient as his own), she might have been Countess Julia's granddaughter or niece.

'And what's your name, my dear?' Justice Krolthy asked, smiling.

'Julie.'

'Yes, of course.' Justice Krolthy sipped his coffee with delight. 'Excellent coffee, Julie.'

'Thank you, sir,' Julie said.

'My very own blend,' Krolthy said. 'Do you think, Julie, that you could answer a question or two?'

'I'll do my best, Your Honour.'

'Good girl,' Justice Krolthy said. 'It's about the others, my dear, for whom you set the table. Where are they? Do you know anything about them?'

'Yes, sir,' Julie said. 'General Wulf left the house early this morning. Uncle Karol saw him heading for Crazy Hill. And Father Anselm was called away to Krestur for some emergency. Aunt Sybil drove him to the village in the gig because the jeep wouldn't start. That's all I know, sir. Some more coffee?'

'Yes please, Julie dear,' Krolthy said quickly. 'Did Aunt Sybil tell you anything about the nature of the emergency by any chance?'

'No, sir.' Julie poured the coffee with graceful devotion. 'Aunt Sybil only said that since our Father Novak was away from Krestur, Father Anselm must go at once. He was needed urgently. And they went.'

'I see. And when did all that happen?'

'About an hour ago, Your Honour,' Julie said, smiling at Justice Krolthy. 'Will that be all, sir?'

'Thank you, Julie,' Krolthy said. For an instant, he thought he saw a flash of derision and contempt in her eyes, but when he looked again he saw only humility and obedience. Those were guileless eyes, innocent eyes, but he knew he had been amply warned: the sylph was dangerous.

Beyond the tennis courts and arboretum, the sun rose

above the eastern hills and, suddenly, the green room shimmered with the translucent greenness of the English countryside Countess Julia had fallen in love with. And, of course, Krolthy thought, puffing on his cigar, the paintings on that green silk-brocade wall, now slightly faded with age, yet still as green-glittering as dewy grass, must also have helped to make Julia think of paradise: a chartreuse Turner, a reseda Constable, an emerald Gainsborough, an aquamarine Grittin. It was the finest private collection of eighteenth-century English landscapes in the country and beyond, Professor Weiskopf had written in his last essay on Széchy Manor, which Gerogen, some years before, had sent over as part of Professor Weiskopf's dossier, together with the documents authorizing the professor's arrest on charges of treason, which by law Justice Krolthy was required to countersign. No wonder Julia loved sitting in her green room, meditating, engrossed in the richness and delicacy of its Chinese silk walls, Biedermeyer sofas, Oriental rugs, English landscapes: life on earth was brimming with joy, hope, love.

Justice Krolthy remembered the white, unadorned walls of his ancestral home, the narrow hallways, badly lit rooms, cold fireplaces of Krolthy House. No idols there, no icons, no ornaments, only the stark simplicity and uncompromising gravity of God's presence, declared by small wooden crosses above heavy oak doors. Here Adam Krolthy was born and grew up under the menacing shadow of his tall, thin father, with his twin sister Eve (another of his father's unintended jokes: Adam and Eve guilty before God, in Jan Krolthy's self-stoked inferno), among uncomfortable chairs, rock-hard beds and trembling servants who feared their master more than they

would ever fear *his* Master. And they were right to do so.
God commanded them only by a distant voice—a whisper
in the clouds, a word in the Book—but Jan Krolthy's
thunder rolled over them and they obeyed unhesitatingly,
as if they truly believed his tempestuous sermons about
the rewards of hard work and obedience. Young Adam
watched with wide-eyed mirth, Eve with boiling fury.

Every Saturday afternoon, in an empty barn fixed up
for the occasion, Jan Krolthy, retired captain of the Imperial Artillery, would stand on huge bales of hay, erect,
haggard, his face purpling with the wrath of God, and
teach his serfs—no matter that more than a hundred years
ago they had been liberated from serfdom, they remained
his serfs—the articles of faith, grace, and mainly, of course,
of sin and guilt. They were sinners—everybody was a
sinner—for having betrayed God from the moment He
created them, thus making betrayal man's first conscious
act, which even now was leading them into the fiery abyss.
Here, Jan Krolthy would stop for a moment or two to
savour his vision of the fiery abyss (one of Captain
Krolthy's favourite images: hell, like a city burning, with
Satan and his monstrous creatures stoking the fires) in
which bodies were ablaze and corruption was finally
reduced to ashes. He then went on to enumerate the
consequences of man's primordial *lèse-majesté:* if betrayal
was the sin, guilt was the most merciful and most divine
punishment, for suffering prepared the utterly unde-
serving sinner for God's gift of grace, for the armistice of
death and the peace of salvation. Even for the most hard-
headed recruit it wasn't difficult to understand that the
road to the summit of Mount Tabor—God's ultimate
fortress—led through obedience, humility, piety, submission: the weapons God had given *us* to fight *His* war. Yet

people continued to disobey His commands, to spend their time in pursuit of carnal delights. Was it any wonder that man's disobedience brought God's wrath upon humanity so that even on earth it was bound to suffer the tortures of hell?

Outside, God's guiltless hills bore the vineyards gracefully on their slopes, against the warm blue haze of distant skies; their very existence seemed to deny the validity of his sermons about sin. Down in the dry, cold cellars in the valley, the sweet yellow wines, favoured from time immemorial by popes and emperors, matured in silence and darkness, but because the 'war to end all wars' was being fought, the delivery wagons had all been impounded to aid the war effort. The loss of business or money did not particularly trouble Captain Krolthy. He was already very rich. He never saw any contradiction in selling his wine to the Roman Antichrist, or to his damned prelates, while blaming them for all the world's ills (more so than he blamed the Jews, whom he regarded with contempt but no particular animus); in fact, he was convinced that his success was God's way of rewarding his steadfastness against the Whore of Babylon.

And Captain Krolthy went on, he couldn't be stopped now: how vividly Justice Krolthy recalled his long, bony face and blazing eyes! They all prayed. Behind Adam's back, Eve made low, angry, threatening noises. This was a heaven-sent opportunity. For at least an hour, the house would be completely empty, the servants praying under the fiery eyes of their master. Without being seen or missed, she and Adam could sneak back to the house to pick the great padlock of the secret room.

In the oldest part of the old house was the room where, according to family tradition, Jan Hus had slept and

General Žiska had made his final preparations for the battle of Bystrica. There, it was whispered, the family secrets were hidden, secrets which might reveal the real reason for their father's abrupt resignation from the army ten years ago, when he was about to be promoted. Eve wanted to know everything. With her fine, inquisitive eyes, and soft, nervous fingers that touched things without ever leaving a trace, Eve was the questioner; she burned with curiosity and fury when she couldn't get the answers she wanted, while Adam only shrugged.

For a few years he had been a reluctant ally in her neverending schemes, but when they reached the age of ten, Adam, with his most enchanting smile, bowed out. He had no intention of breaking father's laws, not because he felt moral revulsion at doing so or feared the consequences, but simply because he had come to the conclusion that it was a stupid thing to do. By the time he had celebrated his eleventh birthday, he knew that the only way to outsmart the law was to obey it. Obedience was the wall behind which one was safe. He could do whatever he wanted: nobody suspected him of trespassing. So why pick the lock? The key to his father's secret—if there was one behind the door and the whole thing wasn't yet another of his father's witless jokes—was not pliers or screwdrivers but obedience. Eve thought it was just another of Adam's clever evasions, and of course, she was correct.

By eight, Adam had already established an unshakeable reputation as a God-fearing, obedient boy; by nine, he was the first among his peers in worship and study; and by the time he reached the age of eleven, he was regarded by teachers and pupils alike as one of the country's future leaders in whatever profession he cared to choose. By then, he had broken all the laws in his father's book and in society's invisible code. Meek Adam, modest Adam! And Eve? Lovely, angry Eve had finally succeeded in becoming the very image of disobedience, the rebellious angel whose acts of defiance, everyone said, were sure to cause her fall from heaven. She had hurriedly coaxed Yankó, the beekeeper's son, into helping her pick the lock (it wasn't difficult to entice him: a sixteen-year-old giant with blue eyes and firm, clever hands, he was head-over-heels in love with Eve). They sneaked out of the barn, but before they reached the lilacs around the inner garden they were caught by Jan Krolthy's henchmen who marched them, quick-step, to the white room, a huge, empty hall in the west wing of the house, always ice-cold even during summer's hottest days, with only a large, simple desk and a small, uncomfortable chair in front of the giant fireplace. Here their father used to sit and pronounce judgement on the living and the dead. From behind the barn-door Adam watched the procession—Eve held her head defiantly high, the beekeeper's son shuffled diffidently behind—with bemused indifference.

'Telephone, Your Honour,' Julie said. 'In the library, yes. This way, please.'

Justice Krolthy put down his cup and walked to the library. He was in no hurry and was sorely tempted to have Julie tell the caller that Justice Krolthy wasn't available—still in the bathroom; out for a morning stroll; dead and buried. Yes, dead and buried. But since nobody knew he was there—except for his charwoman, and his escort, Gerogen's gangsters following him in their coffee-brown Pobieda, deferentially, always at least two kilometres behind his black Skoda—the caller could only be Gerogen, and Krolthy had no intention of picking a quarrel with him. Since Copass had vanished through the trap-door of history (as he had been so fond of saying of others), Adymester had had a stroke after he was warned by *Pravda* that his latest book on twentieth-century revolutionary poets contained serious ideological errors, and old Henryk had been demoted to growing tomatoes on Lilac Hill, Gerogen was the only man in town worth watching.

'Yes, Ernest.' Justice Krolthy picked up the phone from the library's large polished mahogany desk at which evil Count Francis was supposed to have written his blasphemous *The History of God from the Beginning to the End*. 'What can a poor servant of the manor do for the master of the land?'

There weren't many people on a first-name basis with Gerogen, even fewer who could with impunity afford to crack a joke like that, but Krolthy could. Gerogen's inner circle was a strange bunch, Krolthy had often thought—poets of peasant stock, writers from the old *haute bourgeoisie*, high-ranking bureaucrats and army officers of the *ancien régime*, with a few world-famous scientists from the aristocracy, a group whose presence, Justice Krolthy had soon realized, betrayed Gerogen's innermost fears and desires. These were the people Gerogen longed to be accepted by, no matter how high he climbed—and he was now on the highest rung of the ladder of power, he, the son of a miserable tailor, the kid from the ghetto—for them he remained a parvenu, a usurper, a Jew. They obeyed him, declared their undying loyalty whenever they were asked to do so—after all, Gerogen had the keys to the elegant villas on Lilac Hill as well as to the hellish barracks of the camps—but never acknowledged him their equal, one of their own, a member of the club! Gerogen's power over their bodies was balanced by their hold over his soul: an effective equilibrium. Exactly what Gerogen deserved.

'Ernest,' Justice Krolthy said cheerfully, 'are you there?' The crackle stopped and suddenly Justice Krolthy felt cold, as if he realized that somebody had recorded his thoughts and was about to replay the tape before one of Gerogen's infamous boards of inquiry. The equilibrium was tilted.

'He's on the other line, Judge Krolthy,' Bellona Hagen said, charming and sprightly as always. 'He'll be with you in a second.'

'Ah, Bellona, darling,' Justice Krolthy said, strangely relieved. As if they hadn't talked for ages, he asked, 'How are things? Are you coming down for the weekend?' He was amused that she still called him 'judge', although, as president of the Supreme Judicial Council, he'd been a justice for more than five years now: another way of punishing him before her final grand act of vengeance— if it ever came.

'I'm afraid *we* won't be able to make it this weekend,' Bellona said, with a quick stress on the plural, intimating that she and her husband (that stupid blob whose testimony at the Jarek trial had to be rehearsed for almost a week) were now, despite rumours to the contrary, happily sharing a house and bed. 'Maybe next time, Judge Krolthy.'

Next time was as good a time as any, Krolthy pondered, while Bellona excused herself and went back to work. Unexpectedly Gerogen's voice came through, speaking to one of his underlings in quick, peremptory sentences, as the wires, in an apparent cross-talk, permitted Justice Krolthy to listen *in* without being listened *to*. It often happened. The equipment was obsolete and overused, running twenty-four hours a day seven days a week, and whenever one listened one could hear in the background the whoosh of tape-recorders spinning their lewd tales of last night's copulations for the early morning report-sheets to the Secretariat. 'I've had enough of your belly-aches, Vukovič,' Gerogen was saying loudly. 'We'll have the funeral next Friday as planned, rain or shine. Nothing's going to happen, Vukovič, *nothing*. In the mean-time, I want *everything* done *precisely* as directed by the Secretariat.' Vukovič made no reply.

Krolthy could imagine his face, whoever he was. Gerogen called everybody outside his inner circle by their last names—assistants, associates, even his old comrades-in-arms from the Spanish Civil War and the Moscow years. Krolthy often wondered why. It couldn't simply have been a tradition, though he knew that the emigrés in Moscow, whether they lived in the Lux or some godfor-saken rat-hole on the other side of the river, always called each other by their last names, as if trying to keep as great a distance between each other as possible, so that, when the time came, they could deny any close relationship. Maybe it was just a general sense of coldness, indifference and hatred among those desperadoes? But it was much more likely that it was a recognition and admission of complicity among those who had no secrets from each other, but couldn't look into each other's eyes without being reminded of their atrocities.

'Red flag for the coffin,' Gerogen continued impa-tiently, 'black drapes for the dais. Wreaths of red and white roses. A State Security detachment as guard of honour. I really don't know why I have to repeat all that for you. Do you hear me, Vukovič?'

Vukovič heard and promised prompt action.

'He's all yours now, Judge Krolthy.' Bellona Hagen's voice returned.

'Adam,' Gerogen said, 'I'm glad I caught you. Listen, I was supposed to be with you fellows by this morning, but something's come up. Sorry. Unforeseen business.' He sounded as mild and pleasant as he could ever manage to be, yet his voice carried an undertone of urgency and importance. But Gerogen's voice always carried undertones of urgency and importance, and Krolthy had long stopped paying attention, though now he thought he heard a rumble of genuine nervousness.

'In any case,' Gerogen went on, 'I'll be down there tomorrow afternoon, Sunday morning at the latest. Hold the fort for me, Adam, please. Keep an eye on those two, if you can. Have you met them yet?'

'No,' Krolthy said. 'I'm afraid, Ernest, I'm not one of your early risers. I hear that Henryk went walking in the forest, perhaps in search of another miraculous stag, and your favourite monsignor was dragged to the village on some mysterious mission by a pale beauty who calls herself Sybil. Not one of the Cumaean variety, one hopes.'

'I know about that,' Gerogen said, his voice already remote, as though he were about to hang up. 'A baptism, or something. The village priest, I'm told, is visiting his dying mother, and Anselm just came in handy. That idiot Wulf, by the way, is with him now in the church. How he got that far with his sclerotic arteries, heaven only knows! Immediately after that thing is over, they'll be taken back to the house. And they shouldn't stray away again, Adam; I don't need any more speculation and rumour in the village. I will want them to be there when I arrive. Will you do that for me, Adam?'

Krolthy wanted to say, 'Am I *your* brothers' keeper?'

but before he could utter a word, Gerogen hung up. Krolthy felt strangely stupid standing there, his mouth half open, listening to the empty static in the receiver.

He wondered what Gerogen's 'unforeseen business' could be. A new discovery of an old heresy between the seemingly innocent lines of a newly published poem? Another of his trusted lieutenants defecting to the camp of the critics who, since the death of the supreme *Vozhd* two years ago, were growing more arrogant, more vociferous within the Alliance, making absurd demands for more freedom, more justice, more truth, more democracy? Or, perhaps, another visitor from Moscow?

Visitors from Moscow had been in abundance this summer, especially after they had, with such consummate skill, spirited away Copass and his beloved little Uzbek wife, thus turning yesterday's *demiourgos* into today's *kakodaimon*. But why shouldn't those visitors come to the manor? They travelled with comfort and ease, all expenses paid, their entourage and their hosts intently watching their smiles and sneers to interpret their moods, anticipate their wishes and execute their commands. None the less these days they seemed to have lost their unshakeable certainty and unflappable deportment. They issued conflicting signals, advised restraint as well as force, attack as well as retreat, and Krolthy wondered if they really knew what they wanted or simply improvised on the stage of history (as they always called it), like so many bad actors who had forgotten their lines.

Justice Krolthy never asked and was never told what was happening—part of his compact with Gerogen. But what funeral was Gerogen talking about with Vukovič? As far as Krolthy could tell, nobody of importance had died lately; Gerogen's exhortations sounded ominous. In his office he could easily have found out everything through the grapevine, through Irene, his secretary, an absolute genius in tracking down rumours. For a second he was tempted to call her, but the moment he lifted the receiver he knew it was an idea unworthy of him. Besides, somebody had already made sure that he could not make such an ill-advised call: the line was dead, or half-dead, for the world could call *in* but he could not call *out* to the world. Justice Krolthy laughed. If his friends wanted him to stumble, he was saved by his enemies!

He put the receiver back in its cradle, and looked out of the library window at the rose garden, the orchards and the hills in the warm morning sunshine. Among the huge old rose trees, Uncle Karol with his little trowel and large garden shears was finishing his work before the onset of winter. Inexplicably, Justice Krolthy felt a sharp, intense longing for Julia.

'Sybil,' Monsignor Anselm Beck said, 'get some water, quick. And you two'—he pointed to two young men in black, sitting in the last row of the pews—'help him to the sacristy. But careful.'

'Yes, Father,' one of the young men said, springing soldier-like to attention.

The two burly, weather-beaten young peasants grabbed General Wulf under his arms, lifted him effortlessly, and led him carefully, as ordered, to the sacristy. Already in his cassock, with the alb secured at his waist by the white cord of the *cingulum*, Monsignor Beck followed them down the aisle amidst the silent crowd. He didn't remember Father Novak, who had been called away urgently to his mother's sick-bed. Novak was younger but must have looked very much like him—a tall, powerfully built peasant with wide shoulders and long arms—because the cassock fitted him perfectly. Monsignor Beck smiled. There were still young boys guarding the sanctity of old churches; in spite of everything, the Lord had not abandoned His flock; He was still watching over them, giving them young shepherds.

Slowly, without moving his head, Monsignor Beck looked around. The sunshine filtered red and yellow through the only stained-glass window between the third and the fourth stations of the Cross to survive the crossfire that had almost destroyed the church when the retreating Germans and the advancing Russians had fought for the bridgehead on the west bank of the river. The church was full, silent and alert. Whether they recognized General Wulf in his fancy hunting jacket and shiny boots Monsignor Beck had no way of knowing, but he knew that they recognized the menace of an intruder. Strangers meant trouble; they brought fear, hostility, disaster. From the corners of his eyes Monsignor Beck watched the people in the pews, black-clad, stiff, wary, prepared to meet yet another of history's spasmodic subterfuges with their age-old weapons of cunning and duplicity.

Monsignor Beck genuflected before the tabernacle, his forehead suddenly wet with cold perspiration. Behind him, the baby in the front row, for whose baptismal ceremony they had all come, had started crying in her mother's arms. The women and children began to sob, loudly, as though the baby were already dead and the ancient ritual wailing had begun. Without looking behind him Monsignor Beck entered the sacristy and closed the door.

'Henryk,' Monsignor Beck said, 'what has happened to you?' He hadn't seen General Wulf for more than a year

now, not since the General had retreated behind the walls
of his fortress on Lilac Hill, and he was astonished by what
he now saw. The glow of those famous deep-green eyes
had faded into dull yellow. His black hair, though still
without a streak of grey, was lustreless. Beneath a late-
summer tan, his complexion was waxen.

'You look terrible,' Monsignor Beck whispered. Then
he added haltingly, with a small smile, 'As if you had seen
a ghost.'

'As a matter of fact,' General Wulf answered with some
effort, yet with a flash of derision in his eyes, 'I've just seen
one.' He was sitting rather uncomfortably in the sacristy's
only chair, his elbow leaning on the oblong table on which
the vestments for the Mass had already been laid out.

'Oh, have you?' Monsignor Beck came closer to the
table. 'And it knocked you flat out, eh?'

'I must have tripped on the doorstep.' General Wulf
stood up, as if to prove that he was still in one piece, not a
bone broken, not a muscle sprained. 'And I certainly
didn't need the help of your altar boys, Anselm.' He
turned to the two young men who still lingered. 'Now,
scram, boys. And fast. Scram!'

Heads bowed, hats in hand, the two young men backed
out of the sacristy without a word. Again, Monsignor Beck
smiled. The spirit had not yet completely left Henryk's
body, no matter how ashen his face looked.

'Tell me *all* about your ghost, Henryk,' Monsignor Beck
said and started robing. He loved preparing for the Mass,
alone, if possible, in the solitude of the sacristy—a moment
of concentration and contemplation before his mortal
flesh would touch the immortal body of Christ. Now he
went to the table to inspect his maniple, and in the half-
open drawer saw Father Novak's old Bible and an even

older rosary. The much-fingered, tiny rosewood beads glistened wet—God's perspiration—in the morning light. 'What did it look like?'

'Later,' General Wulf said. 'First you tell me, why are you here?'

'I don't know, Henryk.' Monsignor Beck shrugged. 'I was simply told to come down and wait for further instructions. I haven't yet been made party to the secret.' He placed the white silk maniple with its three beautifully embroidered crosses carefully over his left arm. 'I'm only one of its smallest components. A miniature wheel. A negligible detail. A tiny screw.'

'Did Gerogen call you?' General Wulf asked angrily.

'Yes,' Monsignor Beck said, amused, as always, by General Wulf's quick temper. 'And no. Bellona did. She found me in the monastery on Mount Ephialt. I was on my regular autumn retreat before All Souls' Day. Naturally, I was reluctant to leave, but she said it was *imperative* that I be here. Imperative! She sounds more and more like Gerogen, even her voice creaks the same way. Have you noticed, Henryk? She sent a car with one of Gerogen's pug-nosed devils. And he was a taciturn bastard, too.' From among the white, red, green, violet and black stoles in the alcove where his Trappist habit hung on what appeared to be a giant fish-hook, he selected a white one and, with elaborate care, placed it around his neck, crossing the ends over the alb. Then, equally thoughtfully, he put on the chasuble.

'Krolthy is here, too,' General Wulf sat down slowly. 'Another of Gerogen's bastards.'

'So I heard,' Monsignor Beck said with a curt laugh. Among Gerogen's bastards, Krolthy was the biggest one, and General Wulf knew that better than anybody: he was not only Gerogen's best friend but also his victim. While re-adjusting the stole and the chasuble so that they would correspond perfectly to the supernatural perfection of the Mass, he watched General Wulf with growing amusement.

'Do you have any idea, Anselm, why Gerogen would want the three of us down here today?'

Before Monsignor Beck could answer that he had absolutely *no* idea, Sybil Wald entered the sacristy, carrying a big earthenware pitcher and two small glasses.

'There you are, Father,' Sybil said. 'Fresh from the well.' She put the pitcher cautiously on the table and filled the glasses with water.

'Bottoms up, Henryk,' Monsignor Beck said. 'It'll do you good.' After General Wulf had downed it thirstily and asked for another glass, he, too, wet his lips with the famous water from the well—sparkling, pleasantly acidulous and cold, as if it had been hidden for eons in the icy, underground caverns of the earth—but he didn't drink it, because he never touched food or drink for an hour before Offertory and Holy Communion.

It wasn't so long ago, Monsignor Beck remembered, that General Wulf had sat at the head of the dinner table in the big red hall, regaling his guests and underlings with stories about the well in Krestur's main square. 'One day just before the hunt was to begin,' General Wulf had said then, 'Count Francis Széchy fell ill. Now, we remember him best, of course, as the old fool who, shortly before his death, had that gazebo built on the hill we visited earlier today, but at the time of our story, our count—bless him— wasn't yet ready to die, not by a long shot, my friends, not at all! And why, one may ask, should he be? He was in the prime of life, healthy, powerful, with a lovely wife, beautiful children and as many peasant girls in his bed as he wished!' Laughing, General Wulf had lifted his narrow, pointed nose in the air, as if, Monsignor Beck thought at the other end of the table, to sniff the lingering musk of love-making almost two centuries before.

'A typical feudal lord, if ever there was one,' General Wulf had continued. 'He loved screwing around, giving orders, having enormous dinners, going hunting with a bunch of equally rich and powerful noblemen whom he invited to his *Oktoberfest* every year. They came gladly from far and wide; not to be invited to the Széchys' annual mayhem amounted to a humiliation, while not to come when invited meant suicide.

'In any case, according to the diaries of the tutor of Count Francis's children, who was present at the banquet the night before the hunt—an all-male affair—the count was in an exceptionally flamboyant mood, eating much and drinking even more, entertaining his guests with exciting stories about killer boars and phantom stags that lived in his forests when his ancestors had conquered the land and, at the command of the king, settled here to defend our southern borders from the infidel. The guests and the count enjoyed themselves tremendously. By the time the count reached his bedchamber, however, he experienced unpleasant rumblings in his stomach, which he attributed to excess gas, not an entirely unfamiliar phenomenon. That night, he filled his large porcelain chamberpot several times. Each time it was emptied by his faithful servant and most beautiful paramour, the gypsy Esmaralda.

'With morning came more pain,' continued General Wulf, with a twinkle in his eye, Monsignor Beck noticed. 'To restore harmony among the warring particles of the count's body, his personal physician Dr Theophrastus Bombastus prescribed plenty of fluids, massage, poultices, occasional tonics and a diet of rotting vegetables. But no matter how carefully they were administered, under the jealous supervision of Esmaralda, the count obtained no relief. The hunt went on as scheduled, at the request of Count Széchy, and ended, as planned, with the traditional roasting of an ox on Crazy Hill.

'His suffering continued relentlessly. The pain held his head in its vise, his body under pressure, as if he were being flattened by weights laid on him by an invisible master-torturer. He fired Dr Bombastus, had some of his servants flogged, his laboratory-assistants rewarded for their new concoctions, but nothing helped. As the days passed, and autumn turned into winter, his condition worsened.

'One night Esmaralda dreamed of a flood that came from under the earth, suddenly and unexpectedly, with such tremendous force that it spilled into the count's room, flooding everything but the count's bed. It surrounded the count's body gently, as if defending it from an invisible foe. Esmaralda understood the dream's meaning in a flash: water was the key to recovery! And so began the search for the miraculous spring.'

General Wulf always waxed charmingly poetic when he talked about his miraculous well, and that was probably the only miracle worked by the water, Monsignor Beck often reflected, for, according to the official analysis, it was ordinary mineral water, containing salt, bicarbonate of soda, lime, and some iron, sulphur and magnesia.

'From all over the country and from foreign lands,' General Wulf went on, 'diviners came by the dozens, lured, no doubt, by promises of money and fame, and, perhaps, by their own obsessions as well, to find the hidden spring, the source of the count's health and their wealth. And so the search went on, but, alas, with no result.'

'Father,' Sybil Wald touched gently Monsignor Beck's shoulder. 'It's time.'

'Not that there was any shortage of fresh little springs; on the contrary. The diviners knew their art well. Springs sprang up in the woods, in the valleys, on roadsides, in hillsides, hot springs, cold springs, lukewarm springs, springs with the taste of iron or salt, sweetish or bitter or without any special flavour; but no matter how often Count Francis drank the waters, they didn't seem to help his condition. Already a skeleton, his headaches split his brain like axes, and his abdomen, distended like an enormous ball, was pregnant with pain.'

'Yes,' Monsignor Beck said. 'Please, Sybil, take General Wulf over to The Waldhorn. Let him sit in the tavern. Give him some water or whatever he wants to drink. Or show him to a room if he wants to lie down. Take good care of him, Sybil.'

'Then, the stranger came.' General Wulf stood up in excitement, and Monsignor Beck knew that his tale was nearing its end. 'Regrettably, very little is known about his sudden appearance and curious disappearance, because the relevant parts of the tutor's diary have been unaccountably lost, or were, perhaps, still hidden in the library, as were so many other important papers and documents concerning the history of the Széchy family. One has to rely on legend. Some remembered him as a little man, almost a dwarf, dressed in a black waistcoat and knee-breeches with a black three-cornered hat on his jet-black hair; others described him as a tall, erect man with a beautiful smile, wearing a white toga and surrounded by an aura of golden light. Nobody had any idea who he was or where he came from, yet within half an hour of his arrival the servants were ordered to take him to Krestur in the count's private barouche. In the village he ordered the people inside their houses, while he went to the village green with a huge shovel. According to eyewitnesses, who watched from behind closed doors and windows, there was sudden darkness heralding a tremendous storm. He touched the earth at four points, emitted sounds that some interpreted as prayers, others as spells, and started digging. Scared, they could no longer watch him. By the time they pulled themselves together and looked again, the storm-clouds had disappeared without a drop of rain or hail, and they could see water spurting upwards. The stranger stood there, under a huge arc of spray, while the sun bathed the village in its rainbow of sparkling colours. Our miraculous spring had been found. Within days the count was cured: his headaches stopped, his swellings and distensions were gone, his strength returned, and, as suddenly and unexpectedly as he had arrived, the stranger disappeared.

'But therein lies the rub,' General Wulf had continued excitedly. 'The puzzle! The riddle! The mystery! For if it was the devil, as some said, who conjured up the water in order to rescue one of his most redoubtable disciples, how can it be that ever since that day the spring has never failed to bring relief to anybody who drank from it? But if he was the messenger of the Lord, as others insist he surely was, why would he create a miraculous spring to cure one of his Master's most bitter antagonists, an evil man, a cruel and heartless tyrant who after his recovery made the life of his family and his serfs more miserable than ever before, cursing the land so that their misery would last even after his death? Our legendary stranger: a well-intentioned devil—or a misguided angel?'

'Please, General Wulf,' Sybil Wald said. 'Come. It's just across the street.'

Monsignor Beck walked out of the sacristy into the church, now wrapped in silence. The baby had stopped crying, and the women and the children had stopped sobbing and wailing. With his back to the tabernacle, Monsignor Beck stood before the altar. It was a small church, and in the sunlight he could see the faces clearly sad, resigned, fearful, hostile, distinct but almost indistinguishable in a sea of black suits, black boots, black scarfs, black skirts—all unknown to him, yet all familiar. He felt the coldness of their resentment like an icy current and he shivered, though he understood them well enough: like General Wulf, he too was a stranger here. They couldn't possibly remember him from the couple of times, two or three years ago, that he had come down from the manor to say Mass, with the grudging consent of grumpy old Father Leo, Father Novak's predecessor. The people would have preferred young Father Novak here today to introduce Simon Wald's dying baby daughter into the community of saints. Father Novak was a gifted man, Monsignor Beck knew, for he had read his file (without Monsignor Beck's signature no priest could be sent anywhere in the country to take up a new post). But Father Novak wasn't here, so they had to make do with Monsignor Beck from the manor; the fact that he had been brought by Sybil Wald helped a little. Monsignor Beck managed to suppress a smile: though he was considered a stranger here, he felt completely at home, much as he would have in front of the altar in the church of his native village, where he himself had been baptized and where, in his early teens, had seen a vision of the Virgin and decided to become one of God's anointed servants. He saw General Wulf in the last row, sitting next to Sybil Wald, and, for reasons he couldn't quite fathom, he felt deeply pleased and surprisingly relieved.

Justice Krolthy hurried out of the green room, but by the time he reached the garden, old Uncle Karol was gone and only the memory of sweet fragrances filled the late-October air. Justice Krolthy knew that Julia was here somewhere, hiding among the bushes, in the ruins of the old redoubt, or in the arboretum. Here she had spent much of her time, composing letters to the cousin who had betrayed her. Justice Krolthy had once found one of those letters in the library. 'Oh, my dearest Cynthia, how could you do this to me? Why have you deceived me? Abandoned me? Betrayed me? Why? Why did you . . . ?'

The letter was unfinished and had never been sent, but the story of infamy and betrayal had quickly become common knowledge. Six months before his marriage to the Countess Julia Széchy, the Baron Adalbert von Alberich, tall, handsome, valiant captain of the emperor's own Hussar Regiment, was sent as a bearer of gifts and as a bringer of happy news to Gareth House. It was a joyous occasion, Julia introducing her beloved to her cousin Cynthia. But three months later Baron von Alberich broke his engagement to Julia and married Cynthia, who had, according to gossip, recently inherited a fortune from her maternal grandfather.

Much to the surprise of those who remembered Julia as a gentle, sentimental soul, she emerged from this betrayal a mature, resolute woman, as though in her soul and mind her famous soldier-ancestor had taken over from her renowned poet-laureate forefather. First, she returned her giant diamond engagement ring to Captain Alberich. When he gallantly insisted that the ring was rightfully hers, she climbed to the top of Crazy Hill and, standing next to the ruins of her great-great-grandfather's infamous gazebo, chucked the thing into the forest below, thereby creating the biggest treasure hunt in the country's history, which has continued ever since. Then Countess Julia closed the green room. Nobody was allowed to enter it. She herself never entered it again.

She never married, turning her considerable talents and devotion to her rose garden, with young Karol at her side. Soon new gossip blackened the blue skies of the estate. Justice Krolthy hoped that the gossip about their frequent meetings among the bushes was true, but nobody really knew. And Julia had never been bothered by gossip. When she got bored with the roses, she took up horse-riding, then driving, and finally flying—she flew for hours and hours a day, as if she had decided to spend as little time as possible on earth. Rumour had it that her small Fokker biplane was still preserved in one of the many ramshackle barns at the end of an overgrown airstrip beyond Crazy Hill. When she died of cancer, she looked more beautiful than ever. Justice Krolthy had seen the last photographs of her while browsing in one of the many family albums. Now he suddenly caught a glimpse of her again, flying—hovering, really—over the old clock tower, timeless, carefree, and his longing for her grew like a tumour, silently, in his body.

THREE

T HIS is my house,' Simon Wald said, 'and my family and I feel most honoured that Monsignor has decided to celebrate with us.' He turned off the engine of his jeep, and sat motionless, with his hands on the wheel, as if he wasn't quite certain that Monsignor Beck had actually accepted his invitation.

'The honour is mine, Simon.' Monsignor Beck smiled and bowed slightly. 'It's a lovely house.' The two-storey red-brick house with a red-tiled roof and two squat chimneys from which columns of translucent smoke rose high in the sparkling sunshine stood on a small mound a few kilometres south of the village, in the middle of unploughed brown fields, as if, Monsignor Beck wondered, Yahweh had already accepted the sacrificial offering of little Anna Julia Sybilla, though she hadn't died yet. Or rather, she was still alive after the Mass, when her mother, Anna Wald, picked her up from beside the baptismal font and without a word took her home. Monsignor Beck hoped, against all odds, against the well-documented diagnosis of the doctor, against Yahweh's inscrutable inconsistencies, that Anna Julia would live to become a tall, dark, silent, grey-eyed beauty, even lovelier than her mother. Still smiling, for if he no longer took the heavenly miracles of the ancients literally, he still believed, deeply and unreservedly, in the small, sublunary wonders of human life, Monsignor Beck put his left arm around Simon Wald. He at once felt those sinewy shoulders become rigid under the black serge of his Sunday suit. How much easier it was to deal with a mercurial God than with some of his recalcitrant creatures!

'Why don't we go in, Simon,' Monsignor Beck said. 'Anna Julia must be attended to.'

'Yes, Monsignor.' Simon Wald bowed exactly as Monsignor Beck had done, but whether out of obedience or insolence, Monsignor Beck had no wish to find out. 'Please, follow me.'

Simon Wald jumped off the jeep and walked round to the back of the house, where, fenced in by some chicken wire and wooden planks, a little vegetable garden shimmered in the sun. Monsignor Beck saw half-ripe tomatoes still on the plants, cabbages with giant, fleshy leaves rusted by the long, cold rains that had fallen before today's unexpected return of summer, rotting, green-streaked peppers, and a few huge yellow pumpkins—the grinning heads that frightened innocent kids among the mossy tombstones of the old cemeteries in Monsignor Beck's childhood.

Simon Wald, Monsignor Beck knew, wanted to use the back door, because to enter with a priest by the front door was supposed to bring misfortune into the house. It was an old superstition Monsignor Beck remembered from his youth, its origins anchored in a past beyond the grasp of the present. In his novice days, when everything reeked of heresy and everyone of apostasy, such superstitions had caused him to spew fire, but now they only made him shrug. The veneer of religion and civilization was as thin as ice on a pond on an early winter morning; underneath its glittering surface, spooks, ogres and iron-nosed witches of a sunken world continued their pranks with undiminished vitality.

The hill at the end of the vegetable garden, Monsignor Beck suspected, was an ancient burial mound. By its very presence it fused the living and the dead into a fragile yet resistant whole, much as his father's kiln used to blend clay, flint and feldspar into the lovely earthenware plates and mugs Monsignor Beck had loved as a boy. From here, he could marvel at the plains rolling down to the river, the forests spreading towards the mountains, the junction between God's breathtaking triumph and man's lamentable defeat. To the north, he saw the old tower with the clock that had stopped keeping time long ago; to the west the white spire of the church whose single bell, cracked by gunfire during the battle for the bridgehead, now sounded like the jangle of a broken, empty tea-kettle when it was rung at noon and midnight.

Monsignor Beck looked at his watch. It was twenty minutes to twelve, lunchtime already. He should have followed Simon Wald into the house, and, as he had promised in the sacristy, prepared little Anna Julia Sybilla for the long journey to heaven, but he didn't feel like confronting the crowd of mourners celebrating life at the gates of death, so he lingered among the cabbages and cucumbers, sweltering in his Trappist habit, but strangely at peace.

After the Mass, Simon Wald had stood, hat in hand, at the door of the sacristy. Under the expert guidance of Aunt Elsie, Monsignor Beck was putting away the vestments and other holy objects, though, judging by the critical severity in Aunt Elsie's eyes, Father Leo and Father Novak must have been far defter than he was or could ever be. Under the sway of the baptismal Mass, which he had not performed for years, with its rejection of Satan, its powerful denunciation of evil in human life, he was still meditating on the great doxology that was, he had insisted for a lifetime, the focal point of the Mass. More so than the *Gloria* or the *Offertorium*, or even that marvellous symbol of God's presence in the world, the *Agnus Dei*, the great doxology was a solid bridge between the human and the divine, a tangible proof of the possibility of interaction between man and his creator. *Through Him, with Him, in Him.* Wasn't that what Christianity was all about? A guide for the perplexed, a beacon on the road to the highest comprehension of Christ's partnership with humanity, the understanding of His reason by our reason, *intelligo ut credam.* Monsignor Beck had discussed all that in exacting detail in his much-maligned *Proslogion Two: Could God Not Exist?*, an essay which was both a continuation and expansion of the famous ontological argument of his saintly namesake, Anselm of Canterbury. That argument had first been expounded almost one thousand years ago, but it was still valid, *yes*, still very valid, whatever Monsignor Beck's Vatican detractors had tried to pin on him the last time they summoned him to Rome. Putting on his habit behind the white linen sheet of Father Novak's alcove, slightly annoyed by Simon Wald's intrusion into his meditations, Monsignor Beck looked at him, oddly interested.

Simon Wald wanted Anna Julia to be given extreme unction forthwith. Monsignor Beck, setting aside his vexation, explained to him with great patience and consideration that it would be utterly unnecessary, inappropriate and indeed impermissible by Church rules, since Anna Julia had just been baptized and, through her symbolic immersion, cleansed of all her sins (if any). But Simon Wald wouldn't budge. His wife had wanted the baby baptized immediately after the doctor in Sentelek had diagnosed the hole, or whatever it was that made her tiny heart miss its precious beat, and he, Simon, wanted her to receive the viaticum *now*. He wasn't bloody well going to let any goddamn priest cheat his little daughter out of her rightful niche in heaven because of some dogmatic blarney or theological hairsplitting, no sir!

Monsignor Beck had been warned about Simon Wald's sudden modulations in conduct and mood by Sybil Wald, his sister. While she drove Monsignor Beck from the manor to the village, she had told him a great deal about the changes in her brother's demeanour since he was released from the Krechk camp about a year ago. Even so, Monsignor Beck didn't expect such an insolent outburst. When he first met him before the Mass, Monsignor Beck had thought Simon Wald looked intelligent and steadfast, in every way a dedicated liegeman, who during the Mass behaved with dignity and piety.

Sybil Wald had told him that Simon was once a silent, self-confident soul, educated at the famous College of Forestry and Wildlife, founded almost a hundred years ago by Carolus Széchy. He was loved by his family, respected by the villagers, so much so that when it was his turn to take over as chief forester of the estate after his father's death, they soon acknowledged him as their undisputed leader, a cool-headed manager, a force to be reckoned with in the county. A loving father to his growing son, Simon was a true son of Holy Mother Church, just as all his ancestors had been who came here as vassals and serfs of the first Széchy, before he was made margrave and defender of the kingdom. Now Simon was a different man: moody, arrogant, capricious. Could Monsignor imagine such a change? Sometimes, Sybil said, Simon would be full of joy, telling long stories or cracking jokes, but more often than not these days he would fly into a bitter rage, be unreasonable with underlings and superiors alike. But, then, was it any wonder he behaved the way he did, Sybil Wald asked. They had arrested him for a crime he didn't commit, tortured him horribly to confess to something he knew nothing about, forced some of his closest relatives and friends to bear witness against him, and now, as a final insult to all these unutterable injuries, God had given him a sick daughter who was to die. No, it was no wonder at all, Sybil concluded, that Simon felt abandoned. Disowned by his family, betrayed by his country, forsaken by God, why shouldn't he feel that way?

His face pale in the waxen light of the sacristy, Simon Wald stepped closer to Monsignor Beck.

'Yes or no?'

'Yes, of course,' Monsignor Beck said. 'We must give Anna Julia the provisions she needs for her journey to Paradise.' With tears in his eyes, Simon Wald bent to kiss Monsignor Beck's ring and Monsignor Beck felt himself reddening with embarrassment.

The jeep, now repaired, was waiting behind the church, the old, long-banned Széchy pennant with the wild boar tusks fluttering from its bonnet, the Republic's red star on the left. Monsignor Beck was treated to a triumphal drive through the village, though the people, going about their business again, paid hardly any attention to him or his venerable jeep, and Monsignor Beck couldn't help but agree with their unconcern. The war memorial on the main square was an exact replica of the one on Citadel Hill in the capital, originally designed during the war to commemorate the Unknown Soldier's heroism in his fight against the tyranny of the godless East, but with a few deft strokes the sculptor had turned it into the Monument of the Liberator Hero. Monsignor Beck saw General Wulf standing in front of the blue basin of the well, his head immersed in the cold water as if performing an ancient pagan ritual.

Simon Wald turned south, driving slowly along a muddy road full of treacherous pot-holes. Beyond the acacias and poplars, in the middle of brown fields and meadows, the house appeared on top of a small hill, a distant, lonely outpost. 'It was the official residence of the estate's chief forester, built by order of Count Carolus Széchy, the son of Count Stephen Széchy, almost a century ago. Count Stephen was remembered as one of the nation's greatest reformer-patriots,' Simon Wald explained. He continued, suddenly excited and voluble, 'Though what was less well-known was that in his youth he led the dissolute life of a rich, spoilt aristocrat in Regency England. One day, realizing the emptiness of his life, the deceptions of his mistresses and the perfidies of his friends, he decided to mend his ways.' Simon Wald's face was red with excitement. 'Almost immediately, the count returned to his native country, determined to raise it from the poverty and darkness of the Middle Ages to the prosperity and progress of his own enlightened century.'

The rest was history. Count Stephen Széchy became the nation's greatest reformer, author of brilliant books expounding his vision of the future, founder of the Academy of Sciences, the National Museum, the National Theatre, and later, when the bugle-call to arms was sounded, commanding general in the Army of Independence. And, Simon Wald went on with great *élan*, Count Széchy was as successful amidst the thunder of war as in the quiet solitude of his library, winning one battle after another, threatening the core of the imperial forces until the emperor turned for help to the tsar. It didn't take long for the Autokrator of All Russians (and his advisers) to recognize the danger a rebel victory might mean to his empire, so, without delay, he sent his armies to fight that rebellious rabble. Much to the tsar's surprise, however, Field Marshal Prince Razumovsky's Cossacks, more accustomed to endless plains than to treacherous mountain passes and slippery river-beds, suffered defeat after defeat and were forced to ask the tsar for more and more reinforcements. The rebels, riding high on the wave of victory, waited for the right moment to administer the *coup de grâce:* at the battle of Vareges. Though General Széchy and his high command knew they were now faced with a most powerful enemy that vastly outnumbered them, they based their battle plans on a surprise attack by fresh troops under General Radak. What they didn't know, of course, was that General Radak had based his battle plan on betraying them to the Russians on the plains of Vareges.

As they drove on towards the big red house on the hill, Monsignor Beck discreetly studied Simon Wald. For one who had spent two years on the Eastern Front and almost four in the Krechk camp, Simon Wald at thirty-five looked healthy and vigorous. The shrapnel that had pierced his chest at Voronezh or the thumbscrew and strappado the thugs favoured in the camp appeared to have left no trace. A tall, sinewy man with a gaunt face, dark skin, slanting eyes, flaxen hair, and a strong, violent jaw, Simon Wald was a veritable cross, Monsignor Beck thought, between the dark warriors of King Coloman and the blonde maidens who, more than a thousand years ago, arrived as part of Princess Gisella's pious train, together with her Benedictine monks and Teutonic knights, but were unable to resist the musky advances of those savage little horsemen.

The yarn Simon Wald was spinning was so well known that every schoolchild could have recited it by heart, yet he told it as though Monsignor Beck were a foreign guest on a guided tour around the estate. He did so because, Monsignor Beck now realized, he loved to talk about his ancestors, his masters, his oppressors, his liberators, his judges, in order to reach back in time and touch them, much as you touch your executioner, the last human being who touches you with the warmth of the human body.

Suddenly Monsignor Beck saw Jarek, already on the scaffold—it was the only execution Monsignor Beck had seen—in the chill of the late October morning. He stood with such spectacular calm and superiority that it was impossible to watch him without admiration and horror, as though the atheist Jarek had finally understood about the abyss at his feet—something that, despite his long years as a priest, Father Beck had never come close to understanding. Jarek had whispered something into the hangman's ear, and the hangman's face turned crimson. Apologetically, head hunched between his narrow shoulders, he bowed to Jarek before he signalled to his assistants to begin.

'The battle of Vareges,' Simon Wald went on, his voice hardly audible over the jeep's loud engine, 'was, as everybody knows, fought and lost, as a result of General Radak's treachery, on 21 October. General Széchy's soldiers were disarmed; the general himself, together with twelve of his commanding officers, was captured by Prince Razumovsky's Cossack lancers, brought before a hastily assembled military tribunal, charged with high treason, and sentenced to death. They were hanged—

even the honour of the firing squad was denied to them—
five days later, under a steel-grey sky on a makeshift
scaffold in the middle of the battlefield, in full view of their
troops, exactly 106 years ago today. But we all remember
that, don't we, Monsignor?'

'Yes,' Monsignor Beck said, reddening again. 'We all
do, Simon.'

'Monsignor,' the boy said, 'would you please come inside?
Lunch is ready. They're waiting for you to say grace.'

Monsignor Beck looked up from the cucumbers and
cabbages and saw Simon Wald's son on the far side of the
chicken wire gazing at him intently. He was a good-
looking boy, tall and grey-eyed with sharp, angry cheekbones, as though his mother and father had conspired to
endow him with their most singular features. In church
the boy had behaved with the self-conscious dignity of his
father and the subtly controlled power of his mother.
Monsignor Beck had watched him with warm curiosity,
as if watching the son he could never have. Now, he was
delighted to see him again.

'Yes, Peter.' Monsignor Beck smiled. 'In a second. It's
such a nice day.'

'Do you like my vegetable garden?' Peter returned
Monsignor Beck's smile. 'My father gave it to me for the
summer so that I can learn how to grow things.'

'Are you going to be an agronomist, Peter?' Monsignor
Beck asked.

'No,' the boy answered. 'I'm going to be a forester,
like my father. And my grandfather. And my great-
grandfather.'

'My father was a potter, and I wanted to be potter, too.
I wanted nothing more than to be a potter and make the

kickwheel run and rotate the big wheel with the clay,'
Monsignor Beck said. 'You see, the clay was simply a
formless mass, a big, wet blob of nothing, before my father
picked it up and smashed it against the wheel. Then he
would turn the kickwheel with his leg, making the big
wheel rotate faster, while he touched the wet clay gently,
yet with great skill, with both hands, paying very close
attention to the ripples that seemed to quiver within it.
Suddenly I would see the clay move, really move, and,
ever so slowly, shapes, symmetries, harmonies rose to its
surface, then sank back to its depths, as though the clay
were coming to life. Although I could have been no more
than four years old at the time, I understood that it *was*
alive, and that it was my father who had created its form,
given it order and meaning. When he finally turned to me
and with a satisfied nod said, "Now look, son, here's a
fruitbowl. Isn't that something?" I knew he had made
something out of nothing, so I admired him and wanted to
follow in his footsteps. Just like you want to follow in your
father's, Peter.'

'Father Novak taught us that God created man out of
clay.' The boy's face was flushed with sunshine.

Monsignor Beck felt a wave of humiliation tremble
through his body, as though, after years of amnesia, he
suddenly remembered the simple source of his faith. 'Yes,
Peter, Father Novak was right.'

'I wish Anna Julia wouldn't die,' the boy said.

'Maybe she won't.'

'Do you believe in miracles?' The boy looked at Monsignor Beck inquisitively.

'I'm a priest, Peter,' Monsignor Beck said. 'Miracle is
the heart of my heart.'

'Nobody must believe in anything, my father says. He

says he doesn't believe in anything, because he was betrayed by God. He is very angry these days, Monsignor.
Sometimes, even when I haven't done anything wrong, he
beats me. And he shouts at my mother. Ever since he came
back from the camp, he shouts at everybody all the time.'

'Your father has suffered a lot.' Monsignor Beck
touched the boy's jet-black hair gently. 'But he'll be all
right soon. Give him time, and love, and patience. You
must be very patient with your father, Peter.' Slowly, he
steered the boy by his shoulders towards the back door.

'They've lost it,' the boy said unexpectedly. 'Why did
they lose it? Everybody said they were going to win it!'

'They've lost it?' Monsignor Beck repeated, confused.
'*They*'ve lost what?'

'Haven't you heard?' the boy asked, with slight contempt in his voice. 'The night before yesterday: the World
Soccer Championship in Lima! I wanted to listen to the
radio, but my father wouldn't let me, because he said it
was too late, and I had to get up early in the morning to go
to school. But we were leading two-nil until the West
Germans made a quick come-back and won three-two!
What a shame!'

Monsignor Beck now vaguely recalled something
about a much-heralded World Soccer Championship, to
have been played in Lima on Wednesday night, amidst
mounting tension and expectation of victory at home.
Everybody said that it was impossible for this team to lose
the final; only a few months earlier they had defeated the
British on their home-ground at Wembley (a humiliation
not witnessed since the last century) and had then gone on
to win one match after another. The smell of victory was
in the air, and even official instructions had been issued for
the triumphal return of the victorious eleven.

Monsignor Beck had been on retreat on Mount Ephialt. In the deserted gardens of the monastery the wind had already won its annual contest against the trees and bushes, and it blew triumphantly through the age-old arcades of the cloister, where a large community of contemplatives had once lived the life of sacred *anachoresis*. The Order of Strict Observance had been dissolved by government decree five years ago and its members sent to work as lorry-drivers, janitors or refuse-collectors—some had even been sent to jail. Now only a few old and infirm monks, like Brother Albert and Father Basil, were permitted to live and, with God's help, die here.

Monsignor Beck wandered alone, bundled up against the cold north winds, along the empty corridors and through abandoned dormitories, sang vigils and nones and compline in the sparkling light of the Divine Rose. He helped to cook for the sick and the aged—all five of them were sick and as old as Methuselah—just as he'd been doing for almost forty years during his long *peregrinatio* in the footsteps of Christ. In the afternoon, between tierce and vespers, he watched the leaves of venerable oaks fall in the cloister quadrangle, where year after year, Father Astrick's lovely garden had celebrated the changing seasons as manifestations of God's holy design, the order that was meaning and the meaning that was order. Now the leaves covered only a few spent dahlias and roses, and the narrow paths, overgrown with weeds, no longer led one to God's magnificent solitude, but to the unbearable loneliness of man.

There was no radio up there, no newspapers, no bulletins, and only one telephone for emergencies, so why should Monsignor Beck, high on the mountain, care about the soccer down in the valley? That was Copass's business, old Henryk's business—he used to lord it over goalies and gymnasts, sprinters and jumpers, regal in his glittering uniform, generously rewarding those who won with praise and medals, money, apartments and cars, and punishing those who failed with the loss of their privileges and perquisites. For years, they'd won everything, at the European championships and the Olympic games, but lately a series of defeats had plagued the jumpers, the swimmers, the gymnasts, even the fencers, undefeated for decades. Now they had lost the World Soccer Championship, too.

Monsignor Beck looked at the boy, who was still angrily complaining about the offside that the referee—a vengeful Englishman, of course!—had let the Germans get away with, presenting them the winning goal 'on a silver platter'—Peter was quoting one of the outraged commentators.

'Come on, Peter.' Monsignor Beck patted his flushed face consolingly and nudged him towards the house. 'Let's go. Mother's waiting. They'll win next time.'

'Perhaps,' the boy said, moving closer to Monsignor Beck. 'But my father says it's all done for money. The government's sold us down the river. My father says they need hard currency. That's what it's all about, hard currency, my father says. What is hard currency, Monsignor?'

'How old are you, Peter?' Monsignor Beck asked, still smiling.

'Ten,' the boy said. 'But I'll be eleven in December.'

'You have a fine boy here, Anna,' Monsignor Beck said at the door, suddenly uncomfortable in the glare of Anna Wald's steel-grey eyes. 'We had such an interesting conversation in his garden, and we still have all sorts of important things to discuss, haven't we, Peter? Do you think, dear Anna, that you could let him come with me to the manor later this afternoon? He'll be back by supper, I promise.'

But, without a word, Anna Wald turned and went into the house.

On the day of his arrest Simon Wald woke at dawn, as he had since he was a boy. He lit the kerosene lamp, pulled on his trousers, stepped into his boots and threw a few small logs on the embers glowing in the pot-bellied stove. He poured water from a pitcher into the tin wash-bowl that stood on a chair, tucked the corner of his towel into his belt, and washed. Outside, it was still dark, cold, the stars sparkling in the cloudless sky. It had stopped snowing and the snow-clad forest crackled drily. The kerosene lamp flickered while the embers in the stove suddenly burst into flames and the thin stove-pipe began to glow red. Simon Wald went to the other bunk where Peter was still fast asleep and shook him by the shoulder.

The previous night they had got stuck in this hut, trapped by an impenetrable wall of snow, after having searched the whole forest for signs of anything suspicious. There was nothing to be found, except rabbits in the frozen undergrowth. They were plentiful this year, the corporal had said cheerfully, there would be good hunting! Simon Wald had glanced at his son who had walked with them for two days without a word of complaint, though he was obviously exhausted, his eyes red, his forehead covered with sweat. Simon Wald knew that they must stop and spend the night in a nearby hut.

At the third cutting the corporal had to take his leave: it was time for him to return to his command post and report that he had found absolutely nothing suspicious.

He had arrived only the day before yesterday to join the Permanent Security Detachment, a hotchpotch of new recruits and veterans in the third year of their service, deployed to organize and maintain the security of the dignitaries taking part in the hunt. Simon Wald paid little attention to them. It had been like that ever since he could remember, and before that: five generations of Walds had been foresters on the Széchy estate, and whenever the count had had illustrious guests, their shadows—guards, policemen, aides-de-camp—had walked in front of them, not to protect them but as a token of their eminence and power. So Simon Wald listened to the corporal's excited mumbling with only half an ear.

It was perfectly understandable that the corporal should be excited. For the first time in his life he would see a prime minister, a minister or a judge. But the high and mighty no longer impressed Simon Wald; he had seen them all—prime ministers, generals, king's counsellors, high-court justices, even a few dukes from France or England. Sooner or later everyone came to hunt on his magnificent estate—it was his estate as much as the Széchys'—and he watched them all fiddling nervously with their guns. As far as he was concerned, that was part of the job he was paid for.

Quickly, he gave the corporal his directions, then put his hand on Peter's shoulder, and together they climbed the steep hill to the hut.

Simon Wald was proud of his son, proud of the speed with which the boy had jumped out of bed that morning, washed to the waist in the icy water, then, in a military fashion, reported that he was ready to go. Since he was going to be a forester, it was time he got used to waking at daybreak. Now they were descending the hill in the crackling snow, the boy rubbing his eyes sleepily, snatching his father's hand, as if he were afraid of being left behind in the white wilderness. Once or twice he yawned—loud, satisfied yawns.

They left the cutting behind, then the track. With loud clapping of wings the birds started up from the nearby trees and large cushions of snow fell off quivering branches. 'What were those birds?' Simon Wald asked, and without hesitation his son replied, 'Partridge.' A promising pupil. Soon, the woods began to thin out, and a few minutes later they reached the hill at whose foot the road forked, one branch leading to the village, the other to the main gate of the manor. Here Simon Wald stopped.

'You go to the manor,' he commanded his son, 'and ask your Aunt Elsie to make breakfast for you, then sit in the kitchen, keep your mouth shut and wait until I get there. Got it?'

The boy, used to orders, nodded and was off. Simon Wald followed him with his eyes until he disappeared around the bend, then he started uphill. In the waist-deep snow, it took him almost twenty minutes to reach the top, where the Crazy Tower guarded for all eternity the forests and meadows of Count Francis Széchy. Simon Wald leaned against one of the posts, panting for breath. He moved away from the rotting post, but all of a sudden turned and touched it again, slowly, wonderingly. The climb had tired him, and that was unusual and annoying. He didn't quite know why he had come up there. He had no business on the hilltop, but now that he was here, he looked around. Day was approaching, the stars growing dim, a blue-grey mist billowing above the snow-clad trees.

Simon Wald paid no heed to the legend that the old count put a curse on the hill so that whoever came up there would soon die. He was an enlightened man, a man of reason and science, with a degree from the famous College of Forestry and Wildlife, who had been up there many times before and hadn't died of it once. He had a good view of the manor. All the windows were lit, the chimneys belched smoke, and there was a line of black limousines in the driveway—many of the guests had arrived the night before. In the yard a huge camp-fire blazed, around which the beaters were already warming themselves. Simon Wald had ordered them to be there by six at the latest and that reminded him of his duty. On the distant highway, the headlights of big, black American limousines pierced the mist. The cars turned into the newly built service road and disappeared among the poplars. He had to go, but he walked around the Crazy Tower once more, touching its posts, then turned to stare out over the forest at the sun, rising slowly beyond the misty river.

By the time he reached the yard, the fire had been put out and around the edge the melted snow was already hardening into ice. There they were, as they had been every winter as far back as he could remember, the best beaters, the most experienced poachers, the sleepy resentment of early Sunday morning wine-red on their noses. Old Matthias was among them, his fur cap low over his eyes, chewing the long ends of his grey moustache. Simon Wald pretended not to notice him. He hadn't really expected the old scoundrel to show up, though he was badly needed, as usual.

Old Matthias knew the forest even better than Simon Wald did, knew every path, trail, short-cut and treacherous corner. Some said that his low whistling bewitched hares. When Simon Wald had visited him a few days ago to talk about the hunt, the old grouch had set his calf-sized wolfhound on the uninvited guest. He had been pretty difficult ever since the gendarmes had beaten his left kidney to pulp a good ten years ago, after he was accused of deliberately leading some of the Admiral's party into an uncharted swamp deep in a hidden valley so that they would freeze to death there. Nobody really knew whether that was true or not, but old Matthias had a reputation as a rabble-rouser, a malcontent, even before the war; Simon Wald's father had always talked of him with contempt mixed with admiration. A rebel and a cantankerous crab, old Matthias had grown even worse during the past few years, severing all ties with both friend and foe. What had made him come today? Simon Wald had no idea, but he shrugged, turned his back on the silent, resentful group, and entered the kitchen.

Hot steam hit him in the face, and the heavy smell of freshly gutted poultry. The women were peeling potatoes, plucking feathers, mixing dough for dumplings, stretching pastry for strudel. Aunt Elsie, the best cook in the village and prima donna of the hunting feasts, stood by the stove, pushing unruly strands of ash-coloured hair under her red kerchief, tasting dishes, giving orders. On the stove, water was boiling in enormous cauldrons. Cleaned chickens, ducks and geese lay side by side with chunks of bloody beef, pork chops, legs of lamb. The shelves were laden with fragrant loaves of fresh bread and, along the walls, in great, open baskets, apples, pears, oranges and bananas were lined up next to the wooden casks of wine and spirits. The fruit and the wine had arrived in a sealed truck guarded by the Permanent Security Detachment.

Simon Wald picked up an orange and a banana and threw them to his son, who sat there on a low stool in front of the shelves, expectant but silent, as he had ordered. The boy loved oranges and bananas, but he only ever saw such things during the hunt. Simon Wald kept a watchful eye on him while he ate the fruit. Last year the boy had smuggled two oranges and a banana out of the kitchen and was caught showing them to his schoolmates who stared at them, amazed and unbelieving, as if they were a mirage. The prank caused a veritable rebellion in the school, and in the village—kids and parents, even grandparents, were demanding oranges and bananas, until an official came down from Sentelek and started asking questions that nobody wanted to answer. A couple of days later the official returned to headquarters and the incident was forgotten, or at least Simon Wald hoped it was. In any case, he had forbidden his son to do such a thing again. He threw a glance at the soldier standing at the doorway. He was watching the women, the fruit, the wine, the meat and the fire, but he didn't appear to be watching them, so Simon Wald gave his son another banana, waited until he ate it all, then sent him home.

'Is there anything for breakfast, Aunt Elsie?' he asked.

From behind the clouds of steam, the old woman emerged, smiling contentedly.

'Here, Simon?' she laughed, looking back over her shoulder at the riches spread out on the tables and shelves, drying her damp palms on the hem of her blue apron, as though it all reminded her of the good old days in Chicago. 'Enough for the whole village. For the whole world! Do you want scrambled eggs?'

'Yes, please,' Simon Wald said.

'How many eggs?'

'Five,' Simon said.

'You certainly have an appetite,' Aunt Elsie said, laughing again.

'*That* I still have.' Simon Wald nodded amicably.

'And what else?' the old woman asked, suddenly serious. 'What else can I give you, Simon?'

Simon Wald made no reply, just watched the old woman as she fished out a basket of eggs from under the table, selected the largest ones, and went over to the stove. She spooned lard into a big frying pan and pushed it over the flames. After his mother died when he was four and his father refused to marry again, Aunt Elsie, his father's sister, had been his second mother.

'Would you like a glass of mulled wine?' she said. 'Why don't you sit down?'

Simon Wald said slowly, 'If there's enough,' but he didn't sit. He took the brown earthenware jug between his palms, felt it warm his cold fingers, but he didn't drink. He bent his head over the jug to catch the rising fragrance. He had loved the smell of mulled wine ever since he was a child—it had been his father's favourite drink on cold winter mornings before he left for his rounds in the forest. Now Simon Wald looked up and said almost inaudibly, 'Cloves.'

'That's right,' the old woman said in a low voice, and stepped close to him. She took a large mug from the shelf and filled it with steaming wine, cautiously, so as not to spill a single drop. 'Your father, rest his soul, wouldn't have touched mulled wine without cloves. Once he got so furious when there wasn't any in the house that he drove to Sentelek in the middle of the night in the sleigh. Or was it the buggy?' She paused for a moment, her face dreamy. 'And he came back with a bagful, he did. In the middle of the night! Anyway, you wouldn't remember that, you were in the army.'

'Cloves,' Simon Wald repeated. He remembered. It

was just before his regiment's train started towards the snowy plains of the Ukraine. He had been home on leave to say goodbye. In the middle of the night he had harnessed the horses, but his old man pushed him away, swearing, his angry growl lingering in the cold air. Two months later, he died of a stroke. Not since then had Simon Wald tasted mulled wine with cloves, as if the old man had taken its sweetish fragrance, as well as his anger, along with him. Simon Wald now lifted the mug and swallowed a mouthful. The wine cooled quickly; it was already lukewarm. He swilled it round and round in his mouth. He didn't like it. Carefully, he put the mug down on the table.

'There'll be some cloves left for us too, don't worry,' Aunt Elsie whispered and gave him a quick, conspiratorial wink. 'I stole a bagful. I'll take some to Anna tonight. You can tell her.'

'I'll tell her,' Simon Wald said.

'Here come your scrambled eggs,' the old woman said. She cut a thick slice of bread and put it on the table next to the plate. The eggs swam yellow in the fat, sprinkled generously with red paprika. But the forester was no longer in the kitchen.

The hunt had already begun, the yard was deserted, the hoarfrost on the windows of the big black limousines shone blindingly in the morning sun. For a while Simon Wald stood near the extinguished camp-fire, then he walked down the avenue of poplars, passed the army trucks in the clearing beyond the gate, jumped a little stream which was covered with an unusually thick layer of ice, and struck into the forest. His nose was still full of the fragrance of cloves. In the distance, he heard shots and quickened his pace.

On the other side of the snow-filled ditch the highway, lined with young acacias and old oaks, ran towards Krestur. Simon Wald lowered himself carefully into the ditch. With some difficulty, he advanced in the breast-high snow, raising his arms above his head. The side of the ditch by the road was high and icy. He laid hold of a kilometre stone, and pulled himself up by it.

'Stop or I fire!'

Simon Wald let go of the stone and dropped back into the ditch, his head between his shoulders. His lips touched the snow.

Behind him, on the edge of the woods, next to a great oak, the corporal stood shaking with laughter. He was holding the gunbarrel under his arm, aiming at Simon Wald with the butt.

'I'll bet you wet your pants,' he said, still laughing. He heaved the gun back on his shoulder. 'And what might you be looking for hereabouts where not even a bird would dare to wander?'

For a while, Simon Wald made no reply. 'For a bullet in my head,' he said as he climbed out of the ditch and slowly brushed the snow off his coat.

'*That* you get over there,' the corporal said, pointing in the direction of the gunfire. 'Were you going home?'

'I wasn't going anywhere,' Simon Wald said.

Side by side, they tramped along through the forest in the sun.

'If you have a fag, you can throw me one,' the corporal said.

'I don't smoke.'

'Lucky for you. I've left my pack in the truck. Let's go back and pick it up.'

'What about guard duty?' Simon Wald said.

The corporal laughed and shrugged. 'So someone steals a rabbit.' He turned in among the trees. Simon Wald touched his arm.

'The undergrowth is pretty thick that way. Let's go a bit further up, there's a track. It's shorter, too.'

The corporal stopped and looked at him, curious.

'You know this whole goddamn jungle?'

'It's my livelihood,' Simon Wald said.

They walked along the track, the corporal in front, the forester on his heels.

'Did you see the prime minister?' Simon Wald asked.

'I did,' replied the corporal.

'And General Wulf? Your boss?'

'Him too.'

'Good for you. And what did they look like?'

'Just like their photographs. General Wulf promised there'll be hare in paprika sauce with dumplings tonight. He shook hands with everybody.'

'That's what they always do.' Simon Wald nodded. 'Turn right now, follow the hawthorn bushes.'

'I can already feel my mouth watering,' the corporal said.

'You bet,' Simon Wald said, then suddenly stopped. 'Do you like mulled wine?'

'In any quantity.'

'With cloves?'

The corporal turned back, his ears red in the icy wind. 'Where do you live, friend?' he asked, laughing. '*That* plant doesn't grow in our part of the galaxy. I haven't even smelled cloves since I was a toddler.'

'You can smell it in the kitchen,' Simon Wald said. 'In any quantity.'

Beyond the bushes, on the clearing, the trucks stood empty. The corporal climbed into the old GMC, pulled a knapsack from under the driver's seat, and extracted a packet of cigarettes. He lit one. Simon Wald leaned against the bumper and watched the smoke, mixed with their breath, rising.

He heard snow crunching at the edge of the woods. Branches crackled. Carrying a stretcher, four panting beaters stepped out into the clearing. The emergency stretcher, made of thick branches, tied with trouser-belts and odd pieces of rope, landed with a thud beside the GMC. On it lay old Matthias, pale, his eyes closed, his body wrapped in an army greatcoat on whose epaulettes the stars of a colonel-general sparkled in the sunshine.

The corporal emitted a short, soft, whistling sound.

Simon Wald squatted down by the stretcher. The old man's face was surly and hard, just as he had always known it. 'What happened?' he asked.

'He fell into the crater,' one of the beaters answered.

'Christ,' the corporal said. 'Jesus Christ!'

'What crater?' Simon Wald whispered. He wiped his neck with his handkerchief: he was sweating heavily.

Lieutenant Magor approached running, followed by two of his security men. From afar, he shouted, 'Damn you, why did you put him down in the snow? You want him to get pneumonia so they can blame me for that, too?'

Without a word, the peasants picked up the stretcher and stood with it, motionless, at the rear of the GMC.

'Well, well,' Lieutenant Magor said, pulling his gloves from his belt, 'whom do we see here? I didn't even notice our *Mister* Chief Forester, silent as a mouse!' He stopped right in front of Simon Wald. 'Is your conscience bothering you, mister? Is *that* why you are keeping so quiet? Wouldn't it be better if you got it off your chest right now? Everything?'

Simon Wald watched the grey cloud behind Lieutenant Magor's head.

'He doesn't seem to be in a talkative mood, now does he?' Lieutenant Magor continued, slapping his high boot with his gloves. 'But we shall soon loosen that tongue of his, never fear. He will tell us what he was planning. Because he was planning *something*, with that snow-covered crater, with that invisible *trap*, wasn't he? Weren't you?' With his right hand he grabbed the lapel of Simon Wald's open coat.

'Don't you dare touch me,' Simon Wald said. The cloud had reached the sun, and abruptly it was very cold.

'Heaven forbid!' Lieutenant Magor said, mocking but surprised. 'We are deeply grateful that we don't have to search the woods for you.' He motioned to the corporal. 'You take this honourable gentleman to headquarters. Then, lock the door on him. Let's give him a little time to think. Perhaps he will remember *why* he forgot to warn us of that crater. Perhaps he will even remember *whom* he wanted to see in it with a broken neck. What do you think, Corporal? Shall we succeed in making him remember all that?'

Gently, the corporal touched Simon Wald's arm. 'Let's go,' he said. They walked back to the GMC slowly, the forester in front, the corporal on his heels. The truck's steps were icy; Simon Wald slipped. The corporal helped him up by his elbow.

'Wait,' Lieutenant Magor shouted. 'Are you crazy or what? You take this old man to the hospital in Sentelek first. Immediate examination, treatment, private room, the best of everything, that's General Wulf's order. Is that clear? I'll check everything personally, tell them that, when I come in tonight. Well, don't just stand there— *move!'*

Quickly, the peasants lifted up the stretcher and started towards the lorry.

'Idiots!' Lieutenant Magor roared. 'Not so fast. Take it easy!' He stood by the stretcher. 'Don't worry, old man. Everything will be all right. They'll straighten you out in no time, and that's final. You'll be as good as new. Better!' He laughed, a short, frightened laugh. 'Believe me!'

The old eyes remained closed, the face motionless.

'In a week you'll dance the barn dance,' Lieutenant Magor continued. 'Is there a wedding scheduled for next week?'

There was silence.

'Well, *is* there or *isn't* there?' the lieutenant yelled.

'There isn't, sir,' an old beater from the neighbouring village said, obediently, in a low voice. Strangely, Simon Wald couldn't remember his name, though he had known him since he was a child.

'Then you'll just have to find a bunch of gypsies to play for him,' the lieutenant said hoarsely, and turned away.

They lifted the makeshift stretcher into the truck, which started slowly down the narrow service road among the poplars, its exhaust expelling black, oily smoke, its snow-chains rattling. By the time it reached the highway, the sun had reappeared and absorbed the mist, though wisps of fog lingered among the trees. Simon Wald squatted next to an empty oil drum; the corporal sat beside him, legs crossed. Behind the truck a giant stag leaped out of the woods, its head lowered, its enormous antlers proudly readied for attack. The shooting sounded closer. The truck gathered speed. The stag disappeared among the trees.

'So that's your livelihood,' the corporal mumbled, as if to himself. 'That's your livelihood! You made me walk in that damn snow for two days with that poor little lad of yours, and you didn't say anything. Why the hell didn't you tell me about that goddamn crater so that we could have warned them?'

For a second or two Simon Wald felt a crushing weight on his shoulders, the weight of some unnameable anguish which was beyond hatred or revenge. 'I don't know,' he said at last. 'I really don't know. Maybe I don't like stolen cloves.'

The truck left the small acacia grove and reached the plain. The belfry of the Krestur church loomed in the distance, white and rigid, behind the huge red star of the town hall. The light was so strong on the snowy meadows that he had to close his eyes. The stray two-ton bomb of that wounded American Flying Fortress had landed in the forest a little over six years ago, on 16 December 1944, precisely two weeks before the big Russian T34s had first rumbled into the village. How could he have forgotten? It was the day his son was born. He smiled, opening his eyes, relieved, almost happy.

'Wald,' General Wulf said, sitting comfortably on the dry stump of what might once have been a giant oak or elm, a few steps from the kitchen door of Simon Wald's house. 'Come closer. I want to talk to you. Haven't we met before? You look familiar.'

The clear, crisp mid-afternoon sun, in its downward path, now reached the open windows at the back of the house. As he turned towards Simon Wald, who stood there in his olive-drab forester's uniform with the gold oak leaves on the lapel, in the middle of what appeared to be a little vegetable garden, General Wulf got a good glimpse of the women in the kitchen. Oblivious of his presence, in their old kitchen rags, they moved with practised swiftness and graceful dignity, silent, as circumstances demanded—no loud gossiping or singing here today—amidst pots and pans, copper kettles and heavy iron skillets, washing dishes, sweeping the floor, putting back into the ceiling-high cabinets the plates, knives, spoons, glasses from the lunch.

'But of course, General Wulf.' Simon Wald jumped over the chicken-wire fence. 'Don't you remember me? I was that young forester who escorted you when you came down to Krestur to speak to the election rally in '45. Or in '46?' Hat in hand, he stood to attention before General Wulf. 'Excuse me, General, but I'm apt these days to confuse dates and events. The doctor in Sentelek tells me it's only temporary. But I used to have a photographic memory! All the names and details! Sometimes, I still do. Even today, I can remember clearly the mess we found, General Wulf. Can't you? That crazy bunch of idiots! How fortunate that you came just in time and made them stop before they could destroy our lovely manor! How providential!'

'Yes, yes,' General Wulf said, pleased. 'At ease, soldier.' He smiled at Simon Wald with paternal tenderness. 'I remember you, Wald. You were slightly younger then, and had a big moustache, but once we were all younger and at one point or another in our lives we all had big moustaches. Ah, Wald, Wald. Something's happening to us. I can feel it in my bones. In my veins. A terrible thing. Don't try to contradict to the *nachalnik*, soldier. But you were absolutely right to report the vandalism of those barbarians before they did some irreparable harm. And now, our manor is lovelier than ever!'

'And they all got what they deserved,' Simon Wald added with sweet malice in his voice.

'Slow down, Wald,' General Wulf said, smiling. 'And sit here.' He pointed to a small bench near the trunk. General Wulf thought about that first generation of zealots who took over the manor and the village immediately after the war, only to disappear a few years later after they'd started grumbling about the tactics of Copass and the methods of General Gabriel and his minions in State Security. For years General Wulf couldn't have cared less about the fate of those zealots—he had much more important business to attend to—but now, somehow, he regretted their quick demise.

He remembered them well from the winter of his return from Moscow. He met them all over the country, walking tall and proud in the streets and towns and villages, their faces red from the cold northerly winds and the sudden excitement of power. Old supporters of the Alliance, they'd been hiding underground for years, suffered the torture of the old regime's Special Security Forces, and hoped and worked for a future promised by wise old books and clever new pamphlets hastily printed on primitive mimeograph machines or smuggled over the northern borders by courageous volunteers. But on that first winter of his return the past had been crushed by the hammer of the Red Army, the future became the present and they were free, they felt, to reap the harvest of suffering and oppression. No more hiding underground, no more torture, no more smuggled books. They had, of course, very little idea of the immense complexities of

building that promised future, but at least they were all for
building it enthusiastically, without reservations.

How different the masses had been—that great, oppressed multitude of humanity for whom General Wulf
had shed his blood on the barricades of Berlin, the streets
of Teruel, the endless steppes of the Ukraine. The crowds
lined the streets and squares of the wintry towns and
villages, waiting patiently for the rallies to begin and for
General Wulf to tell them about their happy future that lay
just around the corner. Yet, beneath their cheers and
applause, General Wulf sensed that the people were sullen, dejected; in response to his flowing words there came
only the mute, indifferent rumblings of the deep. Lost in
the thundering storms of history, the masses didn't
know—had they ever known?—what they wanted. The
zealots, however muddle-headed, at least had a sense of
what they were waiting for. But did they really get what
they *deserved?*

General Wulf closed his eyes. They were gone now,
almost all of them, vanished without a trace behind the
walls of General Gabriel's camps or prisons, or hanged,
like the agents of the cardinal or Jarek. They had been
replaced by a new generation of zealots, hand-picked by
Copass's cadre-commissars, spoon-fed by Adymester's
uproarious ideas in Singer's flagellatory schools. If General Wulf couldn't stand the first generation of zealots, he
simply loathed the second. Arrogant, conceited, cowardly, they adored him while he was the shining star of the
army but abandoned him the moment he was booted out
of his imposing office. Swine! Perhaps he had made a big
mistake when he voted with Copass and Singer in the
Secretariat for what Singer had glibly dubbed the 'delo-

calization' of those old zealots. Perhaps he should really
have voted against Copass and Singer, even at the risk of
finding himself a division commander in a parochial town
near the eastern borders, just as a couple of months after
that vote old Emerick had found himself in a provincial
university teaching a bunch of downcast undergraduates
the intricate problems of investiture in medieval agriculture.

For a moment General Wulf *had* been on the verge of
voting against Copass, if only for the fun of it! General
Wulf had hated Copass from the moment he met him in
Moscow, when, after sixteen years in the admiral's prisons, Copass had been ceremoniously exchanged for a few
old flags captured by Prince Razumovsky's Cossacks after
General Széchy's defeat at Vareges. Yes, he had been
about to vote against Copass, but Singer tossed him a
hastily scribbled note which at a glance convinced General
Wulf of the futility of such a lark. It was always prudent
and profitable to lend an ear to Singer, whose nose was
even more sensitive than the formidable private intelligence network he had constructed over the years inside
the labyrinth of the Central Apparat to satisfy his insa-
tiable need for quick and reliable information. How Singer
knew what was stirring in his brain at that precise moment, General Wulf had no idea, but after all those years
together, he accepted Singer's ability to read minds as
some kind of natural phenomenon, the best possible anti-
dote to his own outbursts of rage.

So General Wulf had sat silent in Copass's richly decorated office, with Polstitov's original oil-painting *The
Vozhd with Children among the Forget-me-nots* on the white
wall behind Copass's big swivel chair. Here, once upon a
time, the Baron von Goldstein's guests had been served

cocktails before dinner, but now every Wednesday morning at ten o'clock the Secretariat of the great Alliance
gathered to have their second and third *espressos* of the day
and to decide the fates of the living and the dead. From
behind his vast mahogany desk, where, if this were a just
world, General Wulf felt *he* should now be sitting, Copass
announced the unanimous decision to put an end, once
and for all, to the antics of those old zealots in the towns
and villages, farms and factories. General Wulf looked out
of the window.

In Simon Wald's abandoned vegetable garden on this
beautiful autumn afternoon the old trees were already
bare, but the sun was still strong. General Wulf felt an odd
yearning, an inexplicable envy, for those old idiots who
had wanted something else, even if they had no clear idea
what it was they had wanted—for wasn't he himself just
such an idiot once, a paragon of faith, a quintessence of
certitude? He would have liked to meet them once again,
liked to ask them one more question, a very important one,
though he wasn't quite certain he knew what that question
was. And he would have liked to shake hands with them,
something he had not done at the time—why? Out of
pride? Contempt? Fear? He would have gladly done so
now, not as apology but as a sign of sorrow, a gesture of
joy. But, of course, they were all dead.

'Wald,' General Wulf said. 'Listen. This morning I
walked up to Crazy Hill. To be absolutely frank with you,
Wald, I'm not quite sure why, but it was such a gorgeous
morning, and I haven't been up there for years, so on the
spur of the moment I decided to climb the hill and commis-
erate a little with wicked old Francis's ghost in the sunshine at his gazebo. But the old scoundrel wasn't there, as
if he wanted to deny me even that little pleasure, as he

always denied everything to everybody. So, I sat there for a while enchanted by the view, until suddenly the pangs of hunger hit my stomach. I walked down quickly and headed back towards the manor, but I came upon a place I've never seen before. Now, look at me, Wald. I know this forest almost as well as you do, but I swear I've never been *near* such a spot.

'Where was I, Wald? I couldn't have been further than a five minutes' walk from the fork—you know, where the paths turn towards Krestur or the manor—when I came to a clearing which had a small, circular pond with a giant tree in the middle. What's more, the pond was frozen solid, in this weather, Wald, yes! So, now you tell me, Wald, where was I? And why is it that nobody ever told me about the pond and the tree? I have given strict orders that I want to know everything that happens down here. Tell me, Wald, straight and quick, why were my orders disobeyed? Don't forget that I still have enough power to make you talk, *never* forget that!'

'But General Wulf,' Simon Wald said, 'I don't know what you're talking about. There's no such pond or tree on the estate.'

'Are you suggesting that I haven't seen the pond?' General Wulf roared. 'That I have invented the whole thing? Gone potty in the head?' General Wulf heard his voice explode over the little vegetable garden and empty flower beds, like a hand-grenade, exactly as it used to when, at the crack of dawn, he burst into the tents of his staff officers and caught them asleep, though they should long have been up directing *his* manoeuvres. He hadn't heard himself roar like that since his forced sequestration on Lilac Hill, but what a relief it was now, what a solace for his uneasy soul!

'Please, General Wulf,' Simon Wald said softly, 'please. Maybe you fell asleep at the gazebo and had a bad dream? The hill's known to have strange effects on travellers. Ask my sister Sybil. She could tell you stories you'd never believe. Yes, and who knows? Maybe old Count Francis's ghost *was* there and played one of his tricks on an unsuspecting visitor?'

'A dream.' General Wulf laughed contemptuously. 'A bad dream? Are you now saying, Wald, that I'm unable to distinguish between fantasy and fact? First, I'm disobeyed, then called a liar and a madman, and now I'm told I'm a child, too? I've no idea, Wald, what kind of game you're trying to play, but let me tell you two things. One, I'm most adept at solving puzzles. Two, if that place was a dream, then you, too, are a dream, in which case I'm a dream as well, and neither of us exists at all. But we both know that's nonsense. We *do* exist—wouldn't you agree?—but in case you still have some lingering doubts, I'll prove it to you tomorrow morning. At precisely six-thirty, come and wait for me in the green room, and the two of us will make a little trip to dream country. It'll be a most instructive expedition into the unknown, I assure you, Wald, so bring your shotgun, just in case.'

General Wulf walked around the stump, came close to Simon Wald, and grabbed the lapel of his jacket. 'Six-thirty sharp, Wald! Get it?'

'Yes, General Wulf,' Simon Wald said very softly. 'Just as you wish.'

'Good soldier,' General Wulf said, smiling at Simon Wald with paternal warmth and tenderness.

'Miss Wald,' Justice Krolthy said, 'I must have it, I must have them all.' He pointed to a little pile of books. They

looked old, frayed, brittle, but when Justice Krolthy
opened one of them cautiously, its paper felt soft, almost
new, as if time could not touch it. 'All nine of them, Miss
Wald. You can name your price, of course.' Slowly, he
picked up his cigar, inhaled and smiled his most convincing smile. 'If you want to discuss that with your brother,
or your family, by all means, dear Miss Wald, please feel
free to do so.'

After he had paced aimlessly up and down the manor's
creaking corridors, and dark, vacant stairs, their emptiness almost as ghastly as that of his father's secret room
when he and Eve finally entered it after his father's death,
Justice Krolthy decided to explore the clock tower. He
climbed the cobwebby stairs to the top where, according
to local lore, the ancient clock had stopped at precisely six
minutes past six on the sixth day of June 160 years ago, the
moment Count Francis gave up the ghost on Crazy Hill.
From behind the rusting, wrought-iron balustrade, Justice
Krolthy scanned the skies, hoping for the Countess Julia's
Fokker to dive down and pick him up. What a pleasant
surprise it would have been, what a priceless consolation
to fly with her carelessly through the skies! He ab-
sentmindedly watched the slow, indifferent river beyond
the lifeless trees and white steeple of the church. Around
two o'clock, after a quick, tasteless lunch of a piece of dry
ham on a slab of stone-dry rye bread, he took the Skoda
and drove over to Krestur.

At The Waldhorn two boys had given him directions,
and he drove slowly down the bumpy, muddy dirt road to
Simon Wald's house. He parked the Skoda and was heading for the front door when, from the back of the house, he
heard the unmistakable roar of dear old Henryk's famous
fury, and knew he'd come to the right place.

An old peasant woman in black led him through the house without a word but with awe-struck reverence, bowing deeply as she opened the doors. Her small black eyes in their withered sockets shone with curiosity, fear and suspicion. She showed him into a room and then vanished, leaving him alone with its ghosts. He waited until his eyes adjusted to the gloom, then, incredulous, looked around.

Here the servants had preserved what the masters had discarded or given them as rewards for their loyal services: a high Gothic sideboard stood next to a long baroque commode, gracefully ornamented by a rich variety of flowers. A Venetian chair, its cushioned, velvet upholstery still soft and bright red, linked arms, literally, with a heavy gilded Louis XV armchair, backed by an astonishingly ornate Italian *cassone* from the Renaissance. In a corner near the window was a mid-Victorian cabinet with several groups of old Meissen figurines behind its glass panel. He decided to take a closer look.

Leather-bound, slim, dusty, apparently untouched for a long while, the incunabula were tightly stacked on the top shelf between two porcelain figures: a young lady in a crinoline with a cat and a young gentleman in a tricorn with a dog, eyeing each other with undisguised curiosity. Justice Krolthy knew that he'd found something much more important than what he'd chanced upon in the Sorbonne Law Library while researching his doctoral dissertation on the laws of treason and treason trials in medieval Europe.

'But Justice Krolthy,' Sybil Wald said, her cheeks pale in the dying light, 'they're not for sale. These books have been in my family's possession ever since Count Francis Széchy, shortly before his death, entrusted my great-

great-grandfather, Eleazar Wald, with their safe-keeping, and made him swear that he'd never part with them—he or his descendants, needless to say. True, we have no idea what's written in those books, but we kept our word. And now, after almost two hundred years, you want us to break it, Justice Krolthy?'

'I greatly respect—no, I must say, admire!—your loyalty, Miss Wald,' Justice Krolthy said. 'It is a commodity we cannot easily come by these days when everything is for sale and nothing is sacred any more. But isn't that precisely the point, dear Miss Wald? What exactly *is* the meaning of loyalty, if we may be so bold as to ask? Would you rather be loyal to an age-old, meaningless promise or to a new, meaningful truth? *That* is our question. For the truth, dear Miss Wald, is not a giant, immovable piece of rock, forever unchangeable. The truth, the *human* truth, my dear Miss Wald, is our quick and lucid penetration of those perplexing circumstances that not only determine our lives, but have the truly magic power to turn yesterday's truth into today's lie, and vice versa. If the power of truth lies inescapably in its usefulness, however, it follows—don't you think?—that keeping a promise could mean breaking it, while breaking it could easily lead to its preservation. Thus, we may safely say that your fidelity, in fact, is a betrayal, though your betrayal could become fidelity. But just between you and me, dear Sybil, aren't you simply dying to know what *is* in those books?'

'Yes, of course I am curious,' Sybil Wald said. 'Ever since I was a child, even beyond my first conscious memories, I heard voices murmuring around me about those books—evil books, dictated by the devil after he had cured Count Francis of his illness. It is said that in those books the future is revealed, the terrible future of those who tamper with their secrets and try to solve their mysteries. I don't believe all that rubbish, but what if Count Francis was really in league with the devil, and if I should break my great-great-grandfather's word, I bring the curse down on my people?'

'My dear Sybil,' Justice Krolthy said, 'this is all tripe. We know you are a woman of reason and conscience. Surely you won't swallow that local concoction of the devil being at Count Széchy's court without some evidence?

'Count Széchy was an eccentric all right, and he dabbled in all sorts of practices. He lived extravagantly, but he also built a school for the village children, accumulated a superb library and a great deal of knowledge, while his experiments with plants and animals helped his people live better than anybody near or far. Yet the Church declared him a heretic, a satanist, and although they didn't dare excommunicate him because they feared his power, they forbade their priests to bury him in hallowed ground, started a smear-campaign against him that, as we can see, is still successful. He gave Krestur the best spring-water this side of the river, yet you still speak of him as if he had given you poison. Isn't it clear that his actions were not only misunderstood, but also deliberately misinterpreted, that he was accused of crimes—of sins!—he never committed?

'Don't you think the time has come to give justice where justice is due and to tell the whole truth about Count Francis Széchy? Rather than continuing to paint him black as the devil, shouldn't we start a campaign to clear his name, justify his cause, and ask the Church to bury him where he belongs, in the family vault in the company of his ancestors? These books might help us to do just that.'

Again, Justice Krolthy smiled and took Sybil Wald's small, delicate hands into his long, powerful ones. If he wanted to, he could have impounded those books by a stroke of his gold pen (a gift from Eve from New York for his fiftieth birthday last July). After all, they belonged to the State, not to any employee of the State. Or he could have simply set Gerogen's bloodhounds, always itching for a chase, upon the Walds, and confiscated them by force, but he didn't want to do that.

'Very well, Your Honour,' Sybil Wald said slowly. 'Take the books with you and see what you can find out. I don't know whether to wish you luck or to hope that you'll never solve the puzzle.'

'I need not tell you how grateful I am, dearest Sybil,' Justice Krolthy said. Just then the door opened and in came old Henryk, accompanied by Simon Wald and a young man in his twenties who, though slightly darker and taller, looked very much like a younger version of Simon Wald.

'Henryk,' Justice Krolthy said expansively. 'How good to see you again! You look enviably well, just as I'd been told. Not a single grey hair! Sorry you couldn't make it yesterday evening. Some sudden indisposition? Happens all the time. Appearances to the contrary, we aren't the old gang any more, are we, Henryk? Age takes its toll. What a pity! And I had so much hoped we could, the three of us, spend the evening together and chat about old times. But, alas, with you feeling low, and Anselm having one of his famous *moments mysticaux,* I was condemned to spend the whole evening alone in my little room. A waste of time.'

'It doesn't happen very often that you spend a whole evening alone in your little room, Adam, does it?' General

Wulf said, seating himself comfortably in the gilded Louis XV armchair as on a throne.

'I have always been blessed by the pleasant company of good friends,' Justice Krolthy said, smiling.

'And beautiful women?'

'You wouldn't object to that, Henryk, would you?' Justice Krolthy nodded, still smiling.

'But perhaps we can make up for all that tomorrow,' General Wulf said. 'Would you consider cooking dinner for us, Adam? Something exquisite only you can do?'

'Most flattering, of course,' Justice Krolthy said, taking another cigar from his soft calf-skin case (another of Eve's gifts, from Paris). 'But what's wrong with Aunt Elsie's cooking? And we'll still have plenty of time to sit around and talk.'

'Did you call Gerogen?' General Wulf asked.

'As a matter of fact,' Justice Krolthy said, with a glance at Simon Wald and his lookalike, both standing humbly in the darkest corner of the salon, present yet at the same time absent, 'as a matter of fact, Henryk, *he* called me this morning. He's been detained, he said. Something unforeseen's come up, as usual. Ah, the life of a leader! But you know all about that, Henryk, don't you? Sudden urgencies. Unexpected emergencies. In any case, he wanted us to know that he could be here tomorrow afternoon, or Sunday morning, at the latest. And he *will* be, Henryk, have no fear. *Ein Mann, ein Wort.* Remember Singer in Berlin? You talked about him so very often!'

General Wulf looked up from his Louis XV armchair, his eyes flashing under his long, black, curling eyelashes, which Justice Krolthy had always found so ridiculously feminine in such a masculine face. 'Is there anything to drink here, Wald,' General Wulf asked slowly, 'or are we supposed to go dry?'

'Of course not, General Wulf,' Simon Wald said with a grin. 'What would you like to have?'

'Scotch and soda, Wald, always Scotch and soda before dinner. Remember that.'

'I'm afraid, General, *that* we don't have. But, perhaps, you'd like a big mug of mulled wine from our best Furmint, with sugar and cloves? We have plenty of cloves, and Aunt Elsie has a way of making mulled wine like you've never tasted before.'

'I'm sure Aunt Elsie could do that,' Justice Krolthy said. 'Try it, Henryk. Riesling for me, pure and cold, Chief Wald. A treat as it is.' He looked around for Sybil Wald but she was no longer in the room.

'Mulled wine,' General Wulf said almost dreamily. 'Mulled wine with cloves? Very tempting, Wald. I haven't had a cup of mulled wine for ages. Now that you mention it, the last time I had mulled wine was the day I shot the stag and that old beater fell into the crater near Crazy Hill and broke his neck. A bitterly cold day, remember, Wald?'

'Vaguely,' Simon Wald said.

'Very well.' General Wulf smiled. 'Mulled wine it is. Very hot. Please, ask Aunt Elsie. With plenty of sugar and cloves.'

'Incidentally, General Wulf,' Simon Wald said, pouring the Riesling, pure and cold, for Justice Krolthy from an old, bluish-green bottle, 'this is my youngest nephew, Eleazar Wald. He's just returned from the city.'

'Good for you, Eleazar Wald,' General Wulf said cheerfully. 'And have you seen anything interesting in the city?'

Hesitantly, the young man first looked at Simon Wald, then at the floor, as if afraid to speak.

'Just tell General Wulf what you saw,' Simon Wald said.

'As you wish, Uncle Simon,' Eleazar Wald said respectfully and came closer to the throne. 'There was a big commotion in the city when I left this morning, General Wulf. All night long people were roaming the streets, and the police were everywhere, trying to make them go home. I even heard shots, though I didn't see anybody hurt.'

'People roaming the streets?' General Wulf said, suddenly sombre. 'Commotion? Shots? What happened, Eleazar? Come on, boy, speak up!'

'Well, sir, it all started yesterday morning,' Eleazar Wald said agitatedly, his young baritone tremulous, his long, large hands pressed against his sides, as if standing to attention, 'when the news came over the radio that we'd lost the World Soccer Championship. I was at a friend's down the island near the Southern Steel Factory, getting ready for a great victory celebration. Everything was prepared, block by block, in the doorways, or on the streets and squares, the flags, the handbills, the posters: *We greet wholeheartedly our victorious team! Congratulations to our golden-legged boys! Glory and gratitude to our great Alliance, leader and best friend of all sportsmen and women!*

'At first, people just came down from their apartments and talked about what went wrong and why and how, standing in little groups on the streets, but slowly, more and more people came and some started shouting obscenities and others tried to calm them down, but nobody listened to anybody. By mid-afternoon the streets were jammed with people, all very excited and angry. Then somebody said the police were coming. That did it! It was getting dark, the lights came on, and everywhere the crowd started knocking down the flag-poles, tearing the flags and posters to shreds. Somebody shouted, "Let's get Berg!" and suddenly everybody shouted—pardon me, General Wulf—"Let's go and get him! That shithead! That fucking traitor!" They all started marching towards the Sports Bureau, as if they could find Director Berg there, though they must have known that he was in Lima with the team, but nobody cared about that. They wanted him hanged, really.

'Then they started singing songs I haven't heard since I was at junior school during the war; somebody raised an old tricolour with the royal crown and the sceptre in the middle, and that made everybody even crazier. When the police came charging out of the dark streets behind the Bureau, with sticks and truncheons, the crowd fought back with broken poles or stones or whatever they could lay their hands on, some even with knives. That was when the police started firing. It was terrible.' He stopped, his face pale, his lips trembling.

'Go on,' General Wulf said. 'Go on, son.'

'There's nothing much more to tell, General Wulf,' Eleazar Wald said. 'Later, I saw police-vans crowded with people. Some people were standing with their hands in the air being frisked; others walked away down the streets littered with broken glass. I also saw small, excited groups start to gather again on the street corners or in dark alleyways, but the police were quick to break them up this time. I heard one lieutenant pleading with them, "Please, men, go home now and sleep it off, for God's sake." It was already dawn. And they went.'

'Yes,' General Wulf said, almost inaudibly. 'Yes.'

So that was it, Justice Krolthy thought, astonished. That was Gerogen's unforeseen business, his crisis. No more orderly, well-organized marches of closely controlled crowds on sunny May Day parades in front of the red-marble statue of the *Vozhd;* no more great, humble rivers of humanity, flowing obediently past Copass, Gerogen, Adymester and Wulf, who smiled and waved from behind the parapet, flanked by their assistants, associates and other dignitaries who, like Justice Krolthy, had been graciously invited to watch the parade from that exalted height. It was the real thing, the trial run on the Bastille, still perhaps somewhat hesitant and wavering, yet its battle-cry already loud and clear: *'Les aristocrats à la lanterne!'*

Suddenly Justice Krolthy saw the mob, a smouldering shadow milling around the badly lit streets behind the Sports Bureau and under the curtained windows of Director Berg's sumptuous office, demanding, louder and louder, an explanation. But Director Berg—a regular at Justice Krolthy's high-stakes *vingt-et-un* gatherings on Wednesday evenings—didn't come out on the balcony, as he usually did, to greet his old fans and new admirers (he had been a famous centre-forward in his salad days) after spectacular soccer victories and heart-rending Olympic triumphs. If somebody climbed the wall and entered the office through the shattered glass door of the balcony, they could easily find the old pot-bellied scoundrel's *chambre d'amour* hidden behind the showy façade of photos and trophies, with its soft, soft canapé, expensive perfumes and rare liqueurs he hauled back from his trips abroad to give to all those pretty little chicks who came to him for help and always left generously rewarded for their charms.

Fortunately for Director Berg—fortunately for all of us, Justice Krolthy reflected—nobody climbed the wall. The police arrived in the nick of time, and Director Berg's tedious secrets remained secret, for the time being, at any rate. But for how long? With a sudden chill, Justice Krolthy shivered. For how long? He didn't know.

'Here's your wine, General Wulf,' Sybil Wald said, a tray in her hands. 'Just as you ordered. Hot and spicy. Very hot. Please, be careful.'

'Yes,' General Wulf replied. 'Thank you, Sybil.'

Then they heard the cry from upstairs, a short, sharp burst of astonishment and pain. Anna Wald appeared on the landing, tall, white, her steel-grey eyes dry, her chestnut hair down to her waist, with Anselm Beck towering behind her, a mighty guardian angel, his large, strong hands clasped in prayer.

Anna Julia Sybilla was dead.

BOOK TWO
ENTRAPMENTS

BOOK TWO

ENTRAPMENTS

FOUR

ROM his large brass bed in the Walds' guest-room, whose windows stared like sleepless eyes towards the river, the eastern hills and the plains beyond, Monsignor Beck watched the moonlight's patterns on the white ceiling and walls. In the pale, powerful light the room became elusive, impermanent. Monsignor Beck closed his eyes.

He had been escorted up from the nursery well after midnight by Aunt Elsie, who gave him a mug of spicy mulled wine to help him sleep, leaving the room before he could thank her. The wine cooled quickly, turned bitter, so he put the mug down cautiously on the night-table and went to bed, but sleep didn't come. Wrapped in a long, cotton night-gown he'd found folded on a chair next to the bed, he lay motionless, propped up by feathery pillows and warm under a huge eiderdown. He still saw the nursery, so lovingly painted and decorated by Simon Wald, and the small wooden crib in which Anna Julia Sybilla lay dead. At her head stood Anna Wald, tall, silent, her chestnut hair covered with a black kerchief, her lovely face frozen, yet without a single tear in her steel-grey eyes. Later, old Henryk came up with Adam Krolthy, and they, too, stood in respectful silence next to Simon Wald, Aunt Elsie, Sybil, young Eleazar and a couple of elderly women Monsignor Beck didn't know.

Praying, Monsignor Beck watched Henryk and Adam Krolthy standing side by side, as if they had decided to put aside their old animosities in the presence of death. Small and stocky, his eyes wet with emotion, General Wulf made no attempt to hide his shock, while Adam Krolthy's nervous, intelligent face betrayed no emotion. Head bent, his elegant silver mane ashen in the candlelight, his sensuous lips trembling slightly in the chill that crept into the room through the window Aunt Elsie had opened to let Anna Julia's tiny soul, free now, slip away from among the living, Krolthy stood looking politely bored. Soon, they were escorted downstairs by Simon and in a minute or two, Monsignor Beck heard the Skoda's small engine rev up, then fade quickly. Relieved, Monsignor Beck continued praying for the safe arrival of Anna Julia's soul in Paradise.

Light already filtered through those lovely, hand-made curtains—the work of generations of Wald-women during long winter evenings—and fell on one of the old photos on the wall. There another Wald stood triumphantly next to a fallen tree, his handlebar moustache waxed, his axe raised high, his right leg on the giant trunk, as if he had just felled a dinosaur single-handed.

Monsignor Beck got out of bed, washed slowly, and then, just as slowly, he dressed and left the house without a word. It wasn't yet six o'clock. Monsignor Beck walked briskly towards the village among the bare poplars and acacias sparkling in the mirror of the morning. Above the eastern plains and the river, the sun pierced the mist over the brown meadows, heralding another unseasonably warm day.

Summer or winter, Monsignor Beck loved early morning walks. For more years than he cared to count, he had invariably started his day between vigil and lauds with a joyous, leisurely stroll in the gardens and fields of the monastery, welcoming, after the onerous reign of darkness, light's triumphal return, the beginning of another day of work and prayer *ad majorem Dei gloriam*. But after being appointed first deputy secretary five years ago, he had had to move to the city; he had abandoned his early morning strolls as he came to realize how much he abhorred the neighbourhood around the old convent in which he now lived—the pavement's rigid greyness, the dirty windows of fetid houses—and he understood that the day ahead would no longer bring him God's ethereal raptures, only the heavy sadness of man's inescapable miseries.

This morning he stopped under a young acacia and took a deep breath of the fresh air, waiting—hoping—for a sparkle of that old joy, but it did not come.

By the time he reached Krestur life in the village was already in full swing. People went about their business, unhurried but purposeful. He passed the well on the main square—old Henryk's favourite well!—and, suddenly thirsty, he stopped and drank a cupful of its crystal-clear water. In his dry mouth, the water was cold and tart, as if shot through with some light wine from the neighbouring vineyards. He sipped it slowly, wonderingly, as if measuring its miraculous effects on his body. Then he proceeded towards the church to say morning Mass.

Open and dark, the small church was empty except for an old peasant woman in black who knelt before the Virgin. The flames of two huge candles rose to illuminate the Madonna's face. When the old woman noticed Monsignor Beck approaching, she got up, genuflected, and, with a soft *Glory be*, kissed his ring before returning to her prayer. For a while Monsignor Beck stood behind her, looking at the Virgin's expressionless plaster face and eyes, which in the playful candlelight opened and closed, as if Our Lady were both watching and ignoring him.

In the sacristy, dressing, Monsignor Beck decided to offer the Mass to whomever the old woman was praying for, but when he returned to the altar with the bread and wine, she was no longer in the church. Only her huge candles flickered, then they, too, were snuffed out by a sudden gust. Monsignor Beck was left alone in the cool opalescence to utter the day's first *Kyrie.* And he needed Christ's mercy, *yes,* he needed it very much.

More than fifty years ago the Virgin had appeared to him over the tabernacle, surrounded by a glowing ring of candles, and had commanded him to watch over her Son's people. Now, a half century later, Monsignor Beck still wasn't certain whether he had fully obeyed her order, hard though he had tried, and would continue to try as long as he lived. How easy everything had seemed at the time—clear, simple, sweetly mysterious! After Mass he had slipped away from his parents. A big iron gate had been installed between the vestibule and the narrow, spiral staircase that led to the belfry after little blonde Marie had fallen to her death while playing hide-and-seek with her schoolmates. With his pocket-knife Anselm quickly forced the lock and climbed the stairs to the belfry, though he knew that since the accident it was strictly forbidden. Why, then, did he go up there in the pouring rain? He wasn't sure. Perhaps he secretly hoped to have another vision of the Virgin in the blue-golden light of her beauty. Maybe he simply wanted to take a look at his village below.

Anselm wasn't even five years old the first time his father brought him up to the belfry one sunny, late-October day. The village was commemorating the thirteen patriots executed after the defeat at Vareges, one of whom, General Dombinsky, was the son of the local squire. Standing in the sunshine, his grey hair gilded by the light, master-potter Beck pointed out to his son the little bell, whose gentle peal was Anselm's first memory, and told him about another, giant bell that had hung there for centuries to call the people to celebrate the birth or the resurrection of Christ, to warn of fire or water—the often raging river lay only two kilometres away—or of the approaching hordes of Tartars, Turks, Wallachians, Serbians. At the request of General Széchy the ancient bell had been taken down and melted into a gun so that the Army of Glory could continue the good fight against the legions of infamy. Ever since then, whenever Anselm climbed up to the belfry, he touched the little bell with pride in his heart, and his father's unforgettable tale in his memory.

In the pelting rain the day Our Lady had appeared to him, Anselm touched it again, as if expecting it to ring out and call her back, so that she might help him to understand her soft-spoken words. But the Virgin didn't appear, the bell remained silent, only the cold drum-roll of the rain and the echo of her enigmatic command reverberated in the air: 'These are my Son's people; look after them!'

Suddenly, under the lumbering shadows of grey clouds, Anselm saw the streets covered by mud, the houses reduced to shanties, shady gardens overgrown with weeds, the horses and cows mere skin and bones, while, silent in the rain, the people walked home from the Mass in threadbare coats and battered boots, as though they had long since given up all hope. Anselm shuddered. Where was childhood's idyllic playground, the cornets and carousels of happy boys and girls? This was no longer the village in which he was born and grew up; this was a godforsaken place of sadness and resignation, poverty and suffering. Anselm cried helplessly, not because he felt hurt, but because he had been betrayed and didn't know why or by whom. He understood that his playground had been turned into a battleground. Childhood was over. Manhood had begun. With a clarity and simplicity that touches one only rarely in a lifetime, Anselm knew he no longer wanted to be a potter: he wanted to be a priest.

In the silent, empty church, Monsignor Beck finished his morning Mass. *Ite, missa est.* He returned the bread to the tabernacle, the wine to the sacristy, neatly hung up his chasuble and maniple in the dark little alcove behind the white linen sheet, so that when Father Novak arrived he would find everything in perfect order. Then he snuffed out the candles on the altar and stood for a moment or two before the Virgin. In the liquid light he couldn't see whether her eyes were open or closed.

'Let's have some breakfast over at The Waldhorn, Father Anselm.' Sybil Wald was waiting for him outside the front door. 'Aunt Elsie is fixing something special for you. I'm sure you'll like it.'

'Of course,' Monsignor Beck said. But he wasn't hungry.

While Krolthy parked the Skoda in the old carriage-house now converted into a garage (the radio had forecast a night of heavy downpours, and already in the northern sky clouds were foaming ominously), General Wulf stopped in the stately entrance hall to take another look at his treasured portrait gallery.

It had been a long day, with his early morning climb up Crazy Hill; his aimless wanderings in the woods among the bare bushes, ponds, grim trees; Anselm's baptismal ceremony, and the death of the Wald baby early that evening. He felt exhausted, shocked. The pale beauty of the child as she lay there in her wooden crib, already dead yet so very much alive, her extraordinarily long chestnut hair, like her mother's, framing her peaceful face with a glow, had moved him so deeply he couldn't hold back his tears and wasn't sure that he wanted to.

On their way back to the manor Krolthy had talked endlessly, strangely agitated (the closest General Wulf had ever seen him come to excitement) about some old books he'd discovered at the Walds' which he felt would help him unravel the meaning of those monstrous ghouls and fiends of Hieronymus Bosch's *Garden of Earthly Delights* in a new book he was working on. General Wulf had listened with only half an ear, glad when Krolthy left to tuck in his beloved Skoda for the stormy night.

In the hall there was, at last, silence. On the slightly faded walls (he should have had them repainted while he was still in charge), in richly gilded old frames, hung the Széchy portraits: the despots and demagogues, lord chancellors, generals, poets, profligates and moralists, in their long ermine robes, tricorne hats, pink garters. Their swords, sceptres, croziers were extended for giving or taking, but mainly, General Wulf often mused, for grabbing whatever there was to be grabbed—money, land, women, power. From the door to the top of the stairs the masters of the Széchy tribe looked down at General Wulf with a disdainful yet curious twinkle in their eyes, as if prompting him to tell them everything that had happened since, by nature or by violence, they had been forced to leave the stage of history.

On horseback, with a glittering lance in his left hand, here was the founder of the tribe, Count Nicholas Széchy,

ready to kill the forest's legendary boar; reclining in his
tent on the eve of the battle of Sentelek, here was Count
Johannes Széchy, the traitor; in his red hat and cape before
the altar of the family chapel stood Petrus, Cardinal
Széchy, the first Catholic prelate in the country's history to
employ Jews in his court and treat them as human beings;
with his stylus in his right hand and his sky-blue eyes
turned towards the heavens, sat Alexander Széchy, the
poet, who told the story of the defeat at Sentelek in
magnificent heroic stanzas; there, behind his bubbling
alembics and gilded codices, Count Francis Széchy, the
alchemist, worked in his *laboratorium-cum-bibliotheka;*
with a compass and a map, here strode Julian Széchy who
travelled with Cabeza de Vaca from Florida to the Pacific
and lived to write about it; looking triumphant yet tense,
there was General Stephen Széchy, the martyr of Vareges;
his son, Carolus, founder of the College of Forestry and
Wildlife, with his charts and plans to improve life on the
estate; and here was Count Paul, the playboy, friend of Le
Corbusier and Gropius, himself a gifted architect and
supporter of abstract art, the last of the line.

Whenever he had time, or felt he needed different
company, or for no apparent reason, General Wulf would
come here; he felt bound to the Széchys by some invisible
bond stronger than blood, more fatal than the noose: he
liked them. But tonight, General Wulf stopped only to pay
homage to the memory of General Széchy, one of the truly
great men in that motley crew. Sybil had reminded him
that it was the anniversary of his execution on the way to
the Walds, when General Wulf asked her why the town
hall's flag was at half-mast. Slightly embarrassed, General
Wulf regretted his forgetfulness: he should have remembered the day, though officially it had long been dropped

from the roster of patriotic holidays, as if it could thereby also be excised from memory.

When General Wulf was at school 26 October had always been remembered as a day of glory and infamy. In crowded gymnasiums smelling of sweat and rubber, speeches and songs celebrated the courageous self-sacrifice of the thirteen of Vareges, exhorting the young to follow in their path by fulfilling their duties, even in time of peace, as true patriots, reminding them year after year of the barbaric cruelty of the Russian invaders. Even later, in the prison-camps and battlefields of exile, General Wulf had often thought of those famous sketches hastily drawn by Jean-Philippe August, a young Frenchman present at Vareges. They showed how the thirteen met their destiny on that makeshift scaffold, with their heads held high and their eyes open, refusing the executioner's black hood. In his full-dress uniform as commander-in-chief of the Army of Independence but without his sword (it had been removed, according to eyewitnesses, by a certain Colonel Bogaty, one of Prince Razumovsky's aides-de-camp) General Széchy stood on a little mound and watched them die, one by one. He himself was the last to be hanged, at his own request. A series of prints of those famous sketches had decorated the study of General Wulf's father. Henryk had often sneaked in to stare at the thirteen as they stepped up to the gallows, prayed and died. It had been his first encounter with death, and he could never forget it.

After the war, however, the autumnal ceremony commemorating the thirteen, with its echoes of Russian barbarism, didn't go down well with Singer's gloomy friends who sat in the splendid offices of the Allied Control Commission (all furnished by American largess). One night Marshal Shorovilov—one of the stupidest men

General Wulf had ever met—started ranting about it in his box at the opera. General Wulf realized only later that some of Shorovilov's high-ranking *politruks*—those gloomy bastards in their fancy offices—had complained to Moscow about chauvinistic, anti-Russian overtones in certain local patriotic celebrations; Moscow, always vigilant and sensitive, especially when it concerned old Mother Rus, even in her Tsarist guise, had immediately ordered Shorovilov to put an end to that outrage; Shorovilov, not noted for his resistance to Moscow's orders, acted without delay. So, at the next regular morning session of the Secretariat Copass suggested lamely that the anniversary commemorations of the October massacre be toned down, even phased out (the sooner the better, Copass added, visibly embarrassed, his bald pate glistening with perspiration). Singer at once seconded and applauded the motion, while Adymester undertook to work out its ideological justifications, with the assistance of Singer's sharp-witted acolytes. Remembering the sketches on the walls of his father's study, General Wulf had at first opposed the idea on emotional grounds, but Singer dismissed his argument as petty-bourgeois sentimentalism, and then, if only to preserve the unity of the Secretariat, General Wulf voted with the majority.

Now, standing before the portrait of General Széchy in the big hall, under the radiance of the giant crystal chandelier, General Wulf felt proud and ashamed. It was a magnificent portrait, the work of young Jean-Philippe August, who had risked his life by slipping through closely guarded borders and crossing fortified battle lines to reach General Széchy's headquarters, in order to paint him as the soldier of freedom, Europe's last ray of hope amid the rapidly spreading darkness of the Holy Alliance.

Jean-Philippe captured General Széchy at the peak of his powers, after a series of victories on the field, two months before the defeat of Vareges, determined and supremely confident. In front of his grass-green tent, in his tight hussar's regimental uniform, his pelisse lined with grey marten thrown dashingly over his shoulder, his right hand lightly touching his sword, engraved with the Széchy boar-tusks on its hilt, his slanted, dark-blue eyes shining in the soft, afternoon sunshine, General Széchy stood, tall, proud, daring the world to rise and take up his challenge for the ultimate confrontation between good and evil.

If the world did not pick up General Széchy's gauntlet, Jean-Philippe had accepted his call to arms: with the encouragement and tacit consent of the general, he joined the army as its unofficial artist-in-residence, and, for the short period that remained, went wherever the fortunes of war took it, so that his paintings, portraits, drawings and sketches could tell the world the true story of a nation's salvation and servitude.

In this gallery of fame and infamy, the portrait of General Széchy was General Wulf's favourite painting. But on one of his rare visits to the manor, Singer had called Jean-Philippe August a cold-blooded opportunist disguised as a starry-eyed romantic, whose work was a cheap imitation of David's neo-classicism without David's power of conviction and fury, evident in, for example, his *Marat*. Over the centuries the Széchys had entrusted the preservation of their faces to Dürer, Holbein, Titian, Rembrandt, Gainsborough, Delacroix; why, of all those fabulous portraits, Wulf should choose that pasty smile and fake glitter, Singer could never understand. The difference between Jacques-Louis David and Jean-Philippe

August, he maintained, was the difference between a romancer and a liar. The only thing they had in common, Singer had said, with a rare, wide, voluptuous grin, was that they were both perfidious bastards: both betrayed their youthful ideals. From being Robespierre's comrade, David became Napoleon's lackey; forty years later, as a member of the Academy, August was instrumental in blocking Manet's *Déjeuner* from the official exhibition, thus contributing to the birth of modern art—precisely what he wanted to prevent, and precisely what he deserved.

The following day Singer had sent General Wulf a copy of August's memoirs, *Candide et Constanter*, in which the grand (and rich) old man of French neo-classicism wrote disparagingly about his youthful revolutionary 'folly', describing General Széchy's war against the 'invincible glory' of the Russian empire as an 'abysmal adventure'. In glowing terms he expressed his admiration for General (later Governor) Radak and his charming wife, Judith, the former Countess von Hochleben, whose warm hospitality he had been fortunate enough to enjoy 'quite often' and whose selfless efforts had helped to rescue their beautiful country from the ultimate destruction wrought by General Széchy's 'reckless pride'. As for his own portrait of General Széchy (and, indeed, his other works during those fateful months), Jean-Philippe August dismissed them contemptuously as worthless juvenile fatuity. General Wulf was distressed for weeks after this.

'Ah, Henryk,' Justice Krolthy said at the door. 'Are you still communing with the general? Two military geniuses when they meet cannot, I suppose, refrain from exchanging ideas as to how the battle that was lost might have been won *if only* . . . But let's talk about something else now,

Henryk. It's too early to go to bed, and besides, despite my earnest efforts to amuse you with my wonderful story of how I found old Count Francis's notebooks by a supreme coincidence, you had such a pleasant nap in the car. But we *must* talk, Henryk; we must ask our questions today before Gerogen gets here tomorrow and starts asking his questions. There are so many puzzles only you can solve, you with your experience and wisdom, your unique insight into Gerogen's soul, assuming he still has one. So, would you join me in the library for a drink?'

'Adam,' General Wulf said amiably, with a flicker of unfamiliar pity in his heart. 'It's been a long day. I'm very tired. Maybe tomorrow? Breakfast at nine in the green room? I know you're not an early riser, and I've a six-thirty appointment with Simon Wald. We go to shoot rabbits. Good for the constitution. But when I come back, the two of us can have a chat and a cup of coffee together, why not? Perhaps we should ask Anselm to join us. I hope they have some of that fabulous mix of Brazilian and Colombian milds Inge and I so much enjoyed the last time we had dinner out on your balcony, remember? Such a lovely summer evening! Good night, Adam.'

General Wulf threw a quick glance towards the Széchy portrait, and once again, feeling his heart quickening, contracting, he put a small Nitromint tablet under his tongue and took a deep breath. Was there anything in this accursed world that bound two men together more inseparably than a deep sense of helplessness to control one's life? Astonished, he now realized that he had not eaten properly all day long, yet he was not hungry, he wasn't hungry at all, only dried-out, desiccated, parched. He climbed the stairs slowly, so as not to upset his heart further, locked the door behind him, and sat in his old armchair listening to the logs crackle in the fire somebody had thoughtfully lit to keep him warm during the long, wet, cold night.

'Can I offer you something to eat, Monsignor?' Aunt Elsie asked in the little breakfast-room adjoining The Waldhorn's main bar. Monsignor Beck's table was already neatly set with a long-stemmed rose in a graceful ceramic vase, brilliantly scarlet in the glittering morning sunshine. 'Coffee? Tea? With our freshly baked rolls *au beurre*? A glass of hot milk? Father Leo always drank hot milk, but Father Novak prefers a cup of coffee every morning. Very strong and very black, without sugar. It prepares him for the day, that's what he says.'

'Just a cup of tea.' Monsignor Beck smiled. 'Very weak, with plenty of sugar. It prepares *me* for the day.'

'But perhaps, Monsignor,' Aunt Elsie said, 'I should offer you the speciality of the house, strictly for our most honoured guests. A genuine American breakfast. *Un petit déjeuner américain*. I recommend it most heartily.' In her long white smock and white tennis shoes she looked smaller and more energetic than she did yesterday, all in black, at the Walds', though Monsignor Beck noticed that from under her grey kerchief her ashen hair fell in unruly waves on her pale forehead, and her tiny bright brown eyes looked tired.

'God doesn't want us to lie down and die, even after such a tragedy,' Aunt Elsie went on, pushing her hair back under her scarf with one hand, while with a quick, clever movement of the other she straightened the tablecloth under Monsignor Beck's setting. 'He wants us to go ahead and live. That was what He told me when my Timotheus died in Chicago only a few months after I'd arrived. There

I was alone in that big city, and what was I supposed to do? Monsignor *must* eat. Tell him, Sybil.'

'Yes, Monsignor,' Sybil Wald said. 'Aunt Elsie was very strong and she worked very hard in Chicago. And her American breakfast is most satisfying, if you're hungry.'

'Very well,' Monsignor Beck said, resigned yet still smiling. 'A genuine American breakfast it is, Aunt Elsie.'

The unusual warmth of the late-October morning drifted in through the open window, a few astonished finches and thrushes trilled in the bare tree-tops, and you could even hear in the withered grass an occasional chirr of an orphaned cricket which, by some miracle, had survived the cold rains and early frosts. The breakfast-room, with its pine wainscoting, clean trestle tables and neatly framed old photographs and drawings on its white walls, was lit up cheerfully by the sun.

Across the empty street the church stood cool and calm in the sunshine, its door still open, waiting for worshippers. Now Monsignor Beck noticed the rectory—a pleasant little house, newly whitewashed, its roof repaired, its grass-green shutters closed. It was separated from the church by a narrow path that led to a small plot. In old Father Leo's day, Monsignor Beck remembered, the garden had been overgrown, its rose bushes untended, the leaves of its old walnut tree shrivelling of some unknown disease; Father Leo, himself shrivelled, could no longer carry the burdens of man and nature on his bony shoulders. But now, under the forceful supervision of young Father Novak, the garden, like the church and the rectory, was emerging swiftly from its long years of neglect and decay. Monsignor Beck again felt a warm affection for Father Novak. It was not just that he had read his dossier, worn his vestments and prayed in his church—and in so doing had taken his place, assumed his personality, touched him; Father Novak unwittingly offered Monsignor Beck a vision of his own youth, long gone, when, tall, self-assured and angry (always angry), he used to assert himself among his Trappist brothers with such intensity of emotion that his abbot (dear old Balthasar) had had to call him to his office and, while praising him for his devotion, hauled him over the coals for his intemperate, unpriestly zeal.

Aunt Elsie appeared at the kitchen door with a tray in her strong hands, her brown eyes smiling, her face crimson from the heat.

'Here we are, Monsignor,' she said, 'a genuine American breakfast. *Pour commencer, des assiettes volantes.* Small entrées, little surprises, as our famous *chef-de-cuisine* used to say in his happier moments. From our choice of preserves, we offer a beautiful slice of cantaloupe. Then, we bring a medium-rare steak with a poached egg on top—*un oeuf poché sans pareil*—and potato, cooked, browned, salted or peppered according to personal taste. Following that, we recommend pancakes. There's no genuine American breakfast without pancakes and maple syrup, but, regrettably, maple syrup is unavailable here, so one must make do with our own strawberry or raspberry sauce, or that honey-and-butter cream which is our speciality and Sybil's favourite.'

The cantaloupe was exactly as Aunt Elsie had described it, truly delicious, ripe, firm, and nobody could tell that it wasn't freshly picked and cooled with ice from the ice-pit or in the small, deep well behind The Waldhorn. How Aunt Elsie preserved melon nobody knew.

'That is Aunt Elsie's secret, perhaps her last,' Sybil said pensively, while Monsignor Beck savoured every mouthful of the cantaloupe. After his sleepless night and the long walk from the Walds' house, he realized how empty and dry he had been; now the cantaloupe gave him juices his body needed for the coming day—likely to be a trying one. Now he felt better, less distraught, more alert, as always when he received the generous gifts of God's creation.

'There's a call for you, Monsignor,' Aunt Elsie said. 'In the kitchen. Please, make it quick. Your steak's done.'

'Anselm,' Justice Krolthy sounded impatient, 'what on earth are you doing at The Waldhorn? And where is Henryk? The three of us were supposed to meet at nine in the green room for breakfast, and now it's nearly ten. Have you seen Henryk since last night? He seems to have vanished. The gardener saw him going out to the woods with a shotgun, but that was almost three hours ago.'

So, old Henryk was gone, Monsignor Beck thought, as he picked his way back to his table among the benches and low chairs of the breakfast-room. He was suddenly hungry and slightly envious of old Henryk. At least for the moment Henryk was free. Nobody knew where he was; nobody could ask him questions he didn't want to answer, order him to do things he didn't want to do, make him hate people he wanted to love and love those he so much wanted to hate. He was a lucky rascal who had cleverly outsmarted the world. His Tirolean hat pulled rakishly over his deep-green eyes, his shotgun loaded, his finger on the trigger, his rabbit in the cross-hairs, he was probably having the time of his life.

Monsignor Beck saw Henryk as he had seen him for the first time, standing almost apologetically, with a cocked automatic in his hand, ready for all eventualities, in front of the monastery's main gate, the quick flares of the guns lighting up the dark summits of the mountains like an eerie *aurora borealis* as the battle raged down in the valley. The monks had been singing compline when the bell at the main gate rang. Abbot Gregorius had sent Father Anselm to investigate. It was pitch-dark in the garden, but Father Anselm moved swiftly among the roses, feeling resentful, but also helpless. It wasn't because he feared that the group of Jews they had hidden in the cellars since midsummer might be discovered (successive Gestapo searches had failed to find them, ending in badly concealed German displeasure and clipped Teutonic apologies); it was because he sensed that the monastery's brief isolation from the horrors and humiliations of history was about to end, and there was absolutely nothing he could do about it. For two full weeks the monastery had stood on neutral ground between the retreating German Tigers and the advancing Russian T34s, in the middle of history's no-man's land, free from the whims and vagaries of despots and dilettantes, owing allegiance only to God, and thus as close to heaven as any living human being was permitted to be.

The bell rang again, somewhat more impatiently, and Father Beck knew that whoever was standing before the gate possessed the weapons to blow their freedom to smithereens and start a new servitude. Reluctantly, he opened the heavy iron gate.

'Good evening,' a slim shadow said pleasantly, touching with two fingers his fur-lined cap upon which a little red star flashed in the dim light of Father Beck's depleted torch batteries. 'I am Commander Teruel. Where are we?'

The plural, Father Beck understood, referred to Commander Teruel's group of young soldiers, dressed, like him, in quilted parkas and fur-lined caps, their trousers stuffed into their heavy, black boots. They stood around their commander with an air of trust and expectation, as though willing to defend him to the end, but also like little orphaned children, hoping to be defended by him. Father Anselm invited them to step inside, asked the men to wait in the anteroom, then took Commander Teruel to Abbot Gregorius's office.

The day before yesterday Commander Teruel's group of scout-commandos had parachuted into the area between the wildly fluctuating lines of battle. Today, Commander Teruel admitted with a smile, they'd realized that they had got lost in the woods and had no idea where the enemy, or indeed a friend, might be. Abbot Gregorius, a gaunt, wiry mystic who, unlike dear old Abbot Balthasar of Father Beck's youth, seldom if ever smiled, was apparently taken by Commander Teruel's frank admission. He offered him some Benedictine, its amber dew glistening in the candlelight, and some bread and cheese, served on a white porcelain plate covered with a white damask napkin.

Commander Teruel kept talking about the bread—that miracle of fresh, home-made rye with a crunchy crust, the like of which he hadn't tasted since he had left the country twenty-five years ago, but had been dreaming about, on battlefields, in alien cities and prison-camps. After all those years, the first thing he had been given to eat on his return was fresh, home-made rye with a crunchy crust! It must be an omen, yes, a good omen, perhaps even a blessing, although—if Abbot Gregorius would forgive him saying so—he didn't really believe in such ancient superstitions. Still, he was profoundly moved, Father Beck could see. Suddenly Father Beck felt an unfamiliar intimacy, an odd affinity with Commander Teruel.

Later, Commander Teruel, like a good soldier, asked permission to withdraw for the night, first going down to the cowsheds to check on his little group of commandos, who were already fed, settled and fast asleep in the sweet-smelling hay amid the familiar warmth and exhalations of cows and horses. All peasant lads from faraway lands, Commander Teruel said they must be dreaming they were at home. Father Beck escorted him to the guest-room, on the other side of the quadrangle, where he wouldn't be disturbed by the monks descending the legionnaire's steps to the church for vigils before the crack of dawn.

In the morning, coming out of church after Mass, Father Beck had found Commander Teruel sitting on his favourite bench among the late-blooming rose bushes and bare lilacs in the small garden of the cloister. The guns in the valley were quiet. Commander Teruel looked well-rested and content. He had already visited his men in the cowsheds and found them in excellent shape: they had also had a restful night, had breakfasted on fresh milk, butter and bread, and were now awaiting marching orders. But Commander Teruel wasn't quite ready yet for the battles ahead; he just sat on the bench, looking at the great skies above, the brown mountain ranges and the misty valleys in the distance, the monks leaving the church one by one, their faces hidden in the shadows of their cowls.

'You must have a lovely garden here in the spring and summer, Father Beck,' Commander Teruel said. 'Full of lilacs and roses. I haven't seen flowers for such a long time now that I've almost forgotten what they look like. When I was a boy, we used to spend our summer holidays at the Western Lake, and I would often pick a bouquet of wild flowers for my mother, who'd put them in a vase on the dining table so that we could admire them. And when I was courting my future wife—a German girl—in Berlin in the early twenties, I once bought her a dozen flaming-red roses from an old *babushka* who sat at the corner of the Leipzigerstrasse and the Friedrichstrasse, her black blanket wrapped around her frail shoulders, her black kerchief on her withered head, day and night, summer or winter, with a basketful of fresh roses. But alas, when I appeared with the roses, my Inge, instead of giving me a passionate kiss of gratitude and delight, started to scold me, lecturing me—*hah!*—for my incorrigible petty-bourgeois sentimentalism and political unreliability. I should have known better—Inge said angrily—and given the money to the *Rote Hilfe*, which was setting up some legal defence fund for those arrested in that week's mêlée with Brownshirt thugs on the *Ringbahn*. I couldn't tell her that I got the roses practically free, how could I? It would have provoked another fiery outburst for having accepted them from an old proletarian woman who doubtless needed the money more than a young, healthy chap like me, whose only *real* need was a good lesson in class-consciousness on the barricades of the class war.

'I even noticed the flowers in Spain, Father Beck, if only as part of the landscape of war. I remember a giant magnolia tree, at least a hundred years old, in Valencia, red poppies on the meadows around Sagunto's Roman ruins, some purple oleanders in dried-out riverbeds, and an immense cluster of wisteria on the outer walls of the Dominican monastery in El Puig, which, from time immemorial, had guarded the hills, the villages and the approaches to Valencia from the enemy within and without.

'In Moscow Inge would have been glad of my roses, but there were no roses to be found, no carnations, no violets, no gardenias, not even lilies-of-the-valley. The only flower-shop I recall was a kind of Potemkin flower-shop, with colourful bouquets in its windows for every occasion, but inside you could only get a bunch of withered white or yellow chrysanthemums for funerals. But in Moscow you didn't really need chrysanthemums for funerals, because you never had any idea when your friends or relatives died or where they were buried.

'There must be something in the air of your cloister, Father Beck, that makes one talk about private things. So, before I tell you something I'd regret, I'd better say goodbye. Still, I want you to know, Father Beck, I loved your rye bread. And—take it as an unlikely confession from a Jew and an atheist—I must say it's good to be back in the land of flowers. Finally, I'm home.'

'Your steak and potato, Monsignor,' Aunt Elsie said, perspiring. 'Medium rare. Sybil, please take those dishes to the kitchen, and let Monsignor enjoy his breakfast alone. Come.'

'Anselm,' Cardinal Gaunilon had said slowly, 'Anselm, this is not going to work. We've been discussing your manuscript for three days and not getting anywhere, though we both know that God prefers short prayers. *Breve orazione penetra, caro Anselmo.*' A giant, mercurial man with a surprisingly young face and coal-black eyes that could burn a hole in your body, the cardinal was bending over a typewritten script on top of a pile of reports and comments he had elicited concerning Father Beck's treatise, *Proslogion Two: Could God Not Exist?*

Monsignor Beck saw Cardinal Gaunilon again, as he so often had in his dreams ever since his untimely death a

couple of years ago, when the cardinal was at the peak of
his political and intellectual powers: an astute administrator, a luminous thinker, a possible candidate for pope.

'Would you please stop staring out of the window and
listen to me?' He sounded like some Olympian deity ready
to unleash his vengeful thunderbolts. He certainly didn't
sound like a humble servant of the Church whom Christ
had taught to turn the other cheek. Still, he always controlled his displeasure superbly. He sat back and even
managed a quick smile.

'It is, as I have repeatedly said, an important work, in
many respects a brilliant one, the sort of work I had always
expected from you, my dear Anselm. And yet I am glad,
to say the least, that old Gregorius had the presence of
mind to send the manuscript to Cardinal Zenty, who
forwarded it immediately to me. Our Zenty may not be the
Church's greatest living theologian, but he certainly has a
fine nose for erroneous theories and fallacious ideas—
even, alas, when there aren't any. This time, however, he
was correct. Instead of grumbling about him, you should
be grateful that he has prevented you from making a fool
of yourself, and saved the Church from a divisive quarrel
about basic conceptions of faith and reason settled, one
would have thought, a thousand years ago. But you don't
seem to understand all that, do you, *caro Anselmo?*'

Monsignor Beck had understood *all that* all too well,
and would have answered His Eminence's quibble with
his usual *élan* had he been able to tear himself away from
the sights and sounds outside the window. He had neither
seen nor heard Rome for more than ten years, and he knew
that Cardinal Gaunilon, more than anyone, would
understand *all that* without a word of explanation.

When he had handed his manuscript—the result of a

lifetime's meditations and research—to Abbot Gregorius, he hadn't dreamed it would eventually lead him to Rome. Indeed, he had resigned himself to never seeing the Holy City again, but Gregorius, always on the safe side—'care-worn Gregorius', his monks called him behind his back—saw at once that he was neither competent nor powerful enough to deal with such a manuscript. He had sent it to Cardinal Zenty for advice and judgement, without consulting Monsignor Beck, who felt he had been betrayed. Within a week Monsignor Beck was summoned to the palace in Gesterom for an audience with the cardinal primate.

Monsignor Beck had only met the cardinal once and found him a slow, dull man with a dry, angular face and large, brown eyes that looked perpetually angry or dissatisfied. Now Monsignor Beck was curious. Had the cardinal really read his 567 heavily footnoted, typewritten pages? Or had he simply had it read by one of his court theologians (probably by Steve Kral, his secretary and confidant, the most dangerous, spineless worm Monsignor Beck had ever met), and was preparing to face him on the basis of Kral's one-page summary?

Much to his astonishment, in the first moments of the audience Monsignor Beck was compelled to admit that the cardinal had indeed found time to read his manuscript, despite being deeply embroiled in his crusade against the Alliance's foursome, whom he referred to in his pastoral letters as the Four Horsemen of the Apocalypse: Copass, Gerogen, Wulf and Adymester. He now discussed the manuscript freely, spiritedly, even with a sense of humour, which embarrassed Monsignor Beck more than he liked to admit. The cardinal politely did not mention Monsignor Beck's friendship with one of the 'horsemen', which was public knowledge—Henryk Wulf had visited him several times at the monastery on Mount Ephialt, and once or twice called Monsignor Beck to his office to talk to him. Like a meticulous and dutiful man, the cardinal lectured him at length on his distinctly gnostic, Pelagian heresies. Then, as befits a respected teacher and eminent theologian, he dismissed the disciple with a gracious blessing and a smile pleasanter than Monsignor Beck would have sworn he was capable of giving.

But the cardinal, too, had sensed that the material went beyond his competence, and had sent the manuscript straight to the Holy Office, to Cardinal Gaunilon. Before long Monsignor Beck found himself in a plush compartment of the Blue Adriatic Express, steaming through the mountains of Carinthia, the plains of Lombardy and the valleys of Umbria towards the hills of Rome.

'Before we close our most interesting discussions, *caro Anselmo*, at least for the time being,' Cardinal Gaunilon continued, 'I'd like to repeat once again that we regard your attempt at writing a definitive treatise on the meaning and role of reason in the theology of the Church, aimed specifically at unbelievers, agnostics and atheists, a very laudable and important undertaking indeed. We believe that in its present form the manuscript succeeds in accomplishing a great deal of that formidable task. Your substituting, or, should I say, paraphrasing the Cartesian *Cogito ergo sum* by a rather Augustinian *Cogito ergo credo*, is a debatable but witty opening gambit, if I may put it that way, which expresses the central thesis of the essay: existential doubt as opposed to scientific certainty.

'Doubt, in fact, is the very *core* of your argument, isn't it, *caro Anselmo*? The certainty of the fool who says there is no God can be challenged only by the doubt of the wise, who asks, "Is there a God?"—a doubt that can be dispelled, in turn, only by the certitude of reason. Very neat. Perhaps too neat? Too—*certain?* The problem is *not* that you say that God can be perceived by reason—that's old hat; the problem is your implication that God can be truly perceived *only* by reason. Well, so be it. But some have pointed out, and I tend to agree with them, that this is nothing if not the transformation of the *mysterium tremendum* into a kind of pedestrian *illuminatio rationis,* the dark night of the soul transformed into the bright morning of the body. Reasonable for some, unreasonable for others. Yet what should we expect in a relativistic world where the ascendant infinity of creation ends in the curvature of finite space?' He stopped for a moment, as if tired, his coal-black eyes fixed on the sunlit window.

'But let's not talk shop any more,' Cardinal Gaunilon went on. 'If we haven't been able to agree during the past few days, it's unlikely that we will now. We need time. We feel that you have a great deal to add to what you've already said in your excellent essay, and we know that it is precisely what you want to do. Therefore, it is the wish of the Holy Father—who, by the way, would like to see you tomorrow morning at ten—that you start working on it without delay and under circumstances conducive to creative efforts. For this reason, His Holiness has asked me to extend his invitation to you to stay in the Vatican as our guest for as long as you wish. I have already arranged for you to have an apartment near our completely up-to-date library and other facilities, such as the archives and the new radio station at Santa Maria di Galeria, which we know would be important for your research—as the Holy Father himself remarked, the references to certain distinguished contemporary works in your manuscript are quite conspicuously absent. Of course, we know that it isn't your fault; no doubt you didn't have access to books that had been published during or after the war.

'We have information—very reliable inside information—that the political situation in your country is going to deteriorate rapidly in the near future,' Cardinal Gaunilon continued, his mischievous face serious now, old. 'It is something we expected to happen, though it's happening faster than we had anticipated. We know, for instance, that Cardinal Zenty's arrest on charges of spying is imminent. A trial is being prepared which intends to prove that he had a leading role in an American plot against the leadership of the Alliance and the People's Republic. Naturally, we have informed Cardinal Zenty about all we know and we advised him to leave the country. He refused. Well, so be it. Perhaps he is right. Perhaps he should stay. It is sometimes inevitable and necessary that we should suffer and die for the Church, though often it is difficult to determine the precise moment when inevitability and necessity coincide to serve the cause of the Lord. As, for instance, in your case, Monsignor Beck. You are already here. We hope you'll elect to stay. Things might get so bad up there that not even your friend, Major-General Wulf, would be able to help, assuming that he'd want to, which is a moot point indeed.

'Why should you go back? Who would profit from such a move? Certainly not you, whose life and work would be in jeopardy; nor your people, whose oppression wouldn't be changed by your presence; nor the Church, whose very existence would be just as seriously threatened if you were in jail or in Rome. So, again—*why?* Unless, of course, you have a well-developed martyr complex, in which case, by all means, go and get yourself crucified. Otherwise, I wouldn't really advise you to take the train and travel north. But of course this must be entirely your own decision, a free man's decision with a free will. We could, as you know, order you to stay, but, let me assure you, we have no intention of doing so. We shall pray and hope that your decision is the correct one, regardless of your actual choice. Don't give me your answer now. No need to hurry.'

But Monsignor Beck had already made his decision. He wanted to return home.

It was very hot in The Waldhorn's small breakfast-room and Monsignor Beck took off his grey pullover. He realized that he had eaten a whole plateful of pancakes and suddenly felt nauseated and ashamed. He stood up to stretch his legs and calm his stomach. On the walls there were faded daguerreotypes and lustreless photographs of long-dead blacksmiths, foresters, shepherds, carpenters, together with sketches of birds and animals. The men in the photos stood looking straight into the lens, in rigid poses, holding the ancient symbols of their guilds—guns, sledgehammers, axes—their poverty and decency an open book. What ghouls, demons, devils had stoked the fires behind those gaunt faces and wrinkled foreheads Monsignor Beck couldn't guess. Some of the photos were of the heads of families, the rest of the clan gathered around them. There were no names on the photos and drawings, as if, born nameless, the subjects were all anonymous participants in somebody else's drama; even the photographer's name, usually printed in large, embossed letters in the lower-left corner, was absent, Monsignor Beck noted.

The pictures reminded him of his mother's cherished

photograph album containing perhaps a hundred pictures from all sides of the family. It had been burned in the fire that destroyed her house and the church where, as a child, Monsignor Beck had seen the vision of the Madonna. Monsignor Beck felt a longing for his village. Perhaps, after all these years, he should go back? Perhaps he should walk down Dombinsky Street under the shadows of old acacias; in his brother's workshop he would find the man who had inherited their father's talent, making jugs and jars and vases almost as beautiful as those their father had made. Perhaps he should climb the steeple of the new church, hoping that the Virgin might appear again and tell him, *at last,* how to look after her Son's people. Yes, perhaps, he should visit home.

Monsignor Beck saw Anna Wald crossing the street, heard the motor of the jeep rev up, then slow down, as it came into view, with young Eleazar clutching the wheel proudly, as though he had done some heroic deed. In the back sat Peter Wald and a young, tall, powerfully built man in black trousers and an open-necked white shirt, his left arm around Peter's shoulders. The jeep stopped in front of the rectory, and they got out. The young man shook hands with Anna Wald, who smiled and brushed her son's wind-tousled hair gently away from his eyes. Taking his well-worn travelling bag from the seat, the young man walked towards the rectory. Father Novak had arrived.

FIVE

JUSTICE Krolthy watched General Wulf trudge up the stairs, breathing with some difficulty, limping with his left leg, and disappear in the gloom of the long corridor that led to his old room in the west wing. There, in better times, Justice Krolthy had won many a small fortune in boisterous gin-rummy games. In the early hours of the morning, they would stop snaring aces and all go out to snare rabbits. What had happened to the man who, a year ago, had been, in his own clownish way, the driving force of the hunt, its boorish but generous host?

At first Justice Krolthy was annoyed by General Wulf's refusal to sit down with him for a sip of Courvoisier or Martell and to discuss the possibilities and puzzles of Gerogen's trap, for, the longer he thought about it, the more convinced Justice Krolthy became that it was a trap. They had been tricked into coming here, then they were to be kept in the gilded cage of the manor until the time came for them to watch the conjuring tricks of Gerogen the Great, the best magician in the circus. But old Henryk looked really very tired, so Justice Krolthy was willing to dismiss General Wulf's deceptively amiable rejection.

He took another look at General Széchy's portrait, then slowly walked back to the library, poured himself a Courvoisier, and lit a cigar. He couldn't stand those family portrait galleries, with their holier-than-thou ancestors, because he felt it was all posturing—they were as deceitful and murderous as anybody else, no matter how pious and valiant they looked in their pictures. Or perhaps it was because in one of his purifying rages his father had burned all the pictures of his ancestors, and without them Justice Krolthy felt strangely crippled.

He stood at the window that looked on to Countess Julia's rose garden and watched the ghosts of rose trees and bushes sway in the cold northerly winds that were blowing away the threatening clouds. Then he sat behind old Count Francis's huge mahogany desk. Because of the affinity he felt with Count Francis, he liked to sit in his chair, and he loved to linger among the ancient alembics, vials, and scales of Count Francis's laboratory, with its inexpungible vapours of camphor and camomile.

Justice Krolthy enjoyed the chair and the desk even more than usual tonight: by an incredible stroke of luck, the books he had borrowed from Sybil Wald might allow him to understand old Francis's secrets. He was almost certain he was about to make the greatest discovery of his life—something far more entertaining than his amusing revelations of the plover egg's aphrodisiac properties, incomparably more significant than the original *procès-verbal* of Olivier de Clisson's beheading on charges of high treason at Les Halles in Paris in the summer of 1342, which he had accidentally found between pages 75 and 76 of the *Chronique normande du XIV siècle* in the Sorbonne Law Library. Cautiously Justice Krolthy took the books out of his attaché case, placed them on the desk, but didn't open them. He wanted to postpone the moment of gratification, as he always did with a woman in bed or with the guests at his table: he wanted to savour the delights of his *trouvaille*. He turned off the lights and sat back in the big armchair.

It was amusing how all those Jews—Copass, Gerogen,

Adymester, Wulf and his confrères—loved their arch-
enemies, the aristocrats, dead or alive, in the dock or in the
portrait galleries. When they let them live, and sometimes
even hold high office, it was a symbolic gesture meant to
show the plebs the legitimacy of their own power, the
unbroken historical line ascending inevitably towards the
summit of the society they were both destroying and
creating; when they gave them perquisites and privileges,
they were privileges beyond the dreams of ordinary cad-
res; and when they executed them, they did it in style,
observing ritual and tradition, according them respect
and dignity. When Baron von Leyden and Count Eminescu, Cardinal Zenty's co-conspirators and fellow traitors, were led to the scaffold, to the sounds of trumpets
and drum-rolls, General Wulf, in full-dress uniform,
stood to attention by the gallows, saluting the *morituri*.
When poor Jarek was hanged (after they'd promised him
everything if he confessed: his life, his wife, his son, a villa
in the Crimea where they could live happily ever after), he
was hanged without fanfare or honours, with General
Wulf smoking his Gauloises in the background. But then,
Count Mircea Eminescu was a knight of the realm, whose
family roots, like those of the Krolthys, reached back to the
fifteenth century and beyond, while Jarek was the son of
an ordinary working-class stiff, without a present, let
alone a past, who had made his way to the top simply by
his own intelligence, courage, and capacity for self-sacrifice.

It was the past, Justice Krolthy mused, sipping his
cognac, that attracted Copass and his gang to the old
aristocracy which, though defeated, was by no means
forgotten. The counts and dukes possessed something
those bastards could never have: ancestry. Copass and his

fellow assassins had enough power to make any man's head swim in a glorified illusion of omnipotence, much more power than the barons had ever had, but they didn't have a family tree. History was their slogan, their god; as they declared day after day, they were fighting for the absolute fulfilment of human history, but they themselves were rootless upstarts, the *nouveaux riches* of historical inevitability, and *that* they simply couldn't take.

Justice Krolthy watched his cigar glow in the wavering darkness, while the cognac warmed his blood, his *blue* blood. Ever since Copass had returned from Moscow after the war, he had tried, according to rumour, to establish a link between his family and an old Protestant patrician clan that had owned virtually all the land and half the village where Copass was born; as far as Justice Krolthy knew, those attempts had never borne fruit, and Copass had remained what he was, the sixth son of the village grocer, a Jew without a family tree. History was a cruel god. And how often, Justice Krolthy remembered, would Henryk Wulf tell him about his great-great-great-uncle in Galicia, Chayim Zwii ben Jossif, who organized and led the armed resistance of the Jews against the murderous gangs of Bogdan Chmielniczky's Cossacks in the mid-seventeenth century. Captured and hanged, he had established his claim to history, not only as a fighter, but also as the founder of a family. It wasn't much to have a strung-up Galician Jew as an ancestor, Henryk would joke, but it was better than nobody at all. Although Justice Krolthy didn't care much about Copass and his search for a past, he would gladly have given old Henryk his own seven-pointed coronet. But alas, he had lost it long ago in the Tophet of history.

Justice Krolthy switched on the green-shaded reading

lamp on the desk and turned to his books. *The Book of Apollyon* had a brief introduction in classical Greek. The author, who described himself as a librarian in Alexandria, promised to tell the tale of a select group of men and women of high birth and education during the reign of the Emperor Septimius Severus, who understood that the only way to survive the vulgar turbulence of the world was publicly to obey its laws but privately defy them. If obedience was necessary, servitude was not: within the boundaries of walls one could stay unbound. Hence the moment they entered the secluded universe of their homes, they lived freely and happily, enjoying each other's company in bed, or in the bathhouse or at the table, never restraining their appetites, not being restrained by anything other than their own desires, least of all by the ridiculous precepts of self-sacrifice, love, peace, humility, which a new sect in their city had recently started preaching in the name of some god whose compassion and goodness, his disciples boasted, were surpassed only by his infinite love. Apollyon's select group had long been convinced that ours was an evil world created accidentally by an ignorant *daimon*. To throw dust into his eyes, to observe his laws *and* violate them simultaneously, was among the greatest gratifications they could experience. To be free meant to accept *chaos* as the essence of the *kosmos*.

Though it had faded over the centuries, the Greek wasn't too difficult to read, but then the hieroglyphs began—strange, indecipherable circles, squares, symbols, as though the ancient chronicler was trying to put his theory of chaos into practice. Here, Justice Krolthy had to stop. If he couldn't decipher them himself, he knew someone who could, and he was certain he would be able to get

him to do it. Young Stephanus Kral, an emerging star in
Gerogen's inner circle after leaving the priesthood and
joining the Alliance, was an amateur cryptographer (as
secretary to Cardinal Zenty before the latter's arrest, he
had been entrusted with the coded correspondence between the primate and the pope). Justice Krolthy didn't
know him well, but knew that all he needed was an
appropriate gift to secure Kral's time and effort. Pater
Kral, as Justice Krolthy called him, had a great interest in
his collection of erotica, and already held a few rare books
and etchings worthy of a better museum's shelf. It so
happened that Justice Krolthy had a copy in good condition of Urbain Grandier's well-known but rare *Osculum
Infame* (the only extant first edition was in the British
Museum, so it was a rarity indeed), a seventeenth-century
portfolio of woodcarvings by that notorious French en-
graver depicting the succubi engaged in the most lustfully
intimate act with their master. Justice Krolthy was certain
Pater Kral couldn't resist *that*. It was a valuable piece, but
a small price to pay, and if Kral managed to decipher the
codes, he would surely deserve it.

Young Kral deserved his price, no matter what. His
apartment on the southern slope of the Saxenberg, which
Justice Krolthy had once visited at Pater Kral's insistence,
offered a breathtaking view of the city, the river, the
plains, good German prints, exquisite Czech crystal,
French liqueurs, American records. Pater Kral's airy indifference Justice Krolthy immediately recognized as a
marauding inquisitiveness sufficiently pervasive and
dangerous as to warrant greatly increased circumspection. But Krolthy had to admit that living a scoundrel's life
among unsurpassable scoundrels, young Stephanus Kral
did extremely well. He was a small man with a big future,

provided Gerogen knew how to defend himself and his friends from the fury of that Bastille-wrecking mob. If he didn't . . . well, then God help us all.

So far as Justice Krolthy could tell, *The Book of Brethren* had no introduction, only 67 unbroken pages of symbols, letters, numbers, signs (perhaps of the Zodiac, or of the Sephiroth); he guessed it had something to do with the Brethren of the Free Spirit, those strange groups of remarkable men and women in the Low Countries and Germany during the late Middle Ages who pitted their determination to live as freely and independently as they wished against the tyrannical powers and murderous authority of the Church. In more than one sense, Count Francis was their spiritual heir. Count Francis must have picked the book up during one of his journeys, and now by an unparalleled coincidence it had fallen into Justice Krolthy's lap, allowing him to find the answer to the question that had haunted him for more than a quarter of a century.

No sooner had his father's funeral ended and the guests at the wake left than Eve had sent her brother word to join her in the white room for a family parley. Adam Krolthy was standing at the window of the huge hall. A light dusting of snow was on the ground, but the landscape was still dark—as black as the silhouette of the barn, where, only a week ago, Captain Krolthy had been preaching his weekly sermon to his people from the top of a ladder, his haggard face purpling with the wrath of God. Suddenly, in the middle of a thunderous sentence, he had lost his balance, fallen and broken his neck. Adam Krolthy went to the table and poured himself a glass of crystal-clear 1921 Blue Bond Riesling. He knew, of course, why Eve had asked him to come to the white room—the scene of so many of her humiliations—to participate in the ritual of revenge as she opened their father's secret room with the key she'd found among the old man's papers. This time she wouldn't be humiliated, thwarted or punished for trespassing; this time she'd get inside that room! But Adam Krolthy felt no inclination, nor, oddly, any urgency, to obey Eve's peremptory command. 'Please, Master Adam,' the messenger said, fretting at the door. 'Please, come. Mistress Eve is waiting for you.'

In the white room—the room of judgement and punishment—in the corners of the ceiling there still hung the cobwebs of his father's sacred arachnids, with God's indelible sign on their hard, glittering backs, though the giant creatures themselves had long since died or fled this airless room, whose windows were never opened, so no innocent fly could enter in search of food to become food. Behind Captain Krolthy's large, simple desk stood his small, uncomfortable chair, for in this house of uncompromising faith uncomfortable chairs were among Jan Krolthy's means of punishment.

Their father's secret room, Adam Krolthy had very little doubt, was a hoax. There was no secret, no mystery behind those thick, cold walls, only, perhaps, an unmade bed and a stinking chamber-pot; it was simply another of their father's insane tricks to frighten his people, to keep them guessing and trembling when, once in a while, he disappeared behind that heavy door and remained there for days. Eve ordered the boy and another servant out of the room, then turned the key. Creaking, the door opened.

It was a medium-sized room with a low ceiling and two small windows on both sides covered with heavy, grey material whose colour blended with the mouldering greyness of the walls, the ceiling, even the heavy oak door that, the moment they stepped over its high wooden threshold, closed slowly behind them. Trapped inside, they stood, silent and incredulous. The room was completely empty. Not even an unmade bed or a stinking chamber-pot there, no chairs, no table, no stove, no lights, nothing, absolutely nothing to remind them of their father who used to spend days here alone. After his pilgrimage to the other shore, as he called his excursions behind the door, he would emerge more obsessed than ever with preaching the gospel of punishment and sounding the trumpets of the apocalypse.

The room wasn't greatly different from the way Adam Krolthy had visualized it, yet its utter absence of life made it more overwhelming, more frightening. What it all meant, Adam Krolthy had no idea. If it was only a well-staged theatrical trick, it made very little sense, because no audience could ever watch the performance; if it was for their father a truly holy place, his *sanctum sanctorum*, an other-worldly sphere of worship and prayer where he wanted to be alone to commune with his God, it made even less sense, for it exuded not the fragrance of heaven, but the stench of hell. It was a dead room. And how did he live there? Where did he sleep? What did he eat? Or was he, perhaps, fed by God's poker-faced angels who surrounded him, consoled him, put new ideas into his stubborn head, or answered his questions—if he had ever asked one!

Shaking his head in disbelief, Adam Krolthy made for the door. Was his father sane pretending to be mad, or was he mad pretending to be sane? Either way, Jan Krolthy must have been deranged, and now there was nothing Adam could do for him, except to lock up the room again, this time for good. Gently, Adam touched Eve's shoulder, as if to ask her to come back with him to the world where, in the sunshine, they could discuss their father's aberrations. Much to his surprise, he felt Eve's body trembling and cold. Pale, her yellow, inquisitive cat's eyes wide with stupefaction and fear, she looked as if their father had touched her from beyond the grave. Suddenly furious, for never in his life had he seen Eve so helpless, Adam leaped to the windows and tore down the curtains. At once, sunshine flooded the shadows. Then they saw it.

It hung on the room's longest wall, between the windows, where a fireplace had been blocked with masonry. Although covered with a linen sheet which, very much like the curtains, blended with the colour of the walls, Adam Krolthy surmised that it was a large painting, but why it had been saved from his father's purifying rage, which, a few years ago, had destroyed all the 'painted images', as he called them, Adam had no idea. Perhaps it was one of his father's favourite pictures, one he couldn't simply smash or burn? Mother's portrait? That famous scene where Pavol Krolthy, their great-great-grandfather, whom father had idolized, knelt and prayed in front of the Taborite army before leading them into battle? Or perhaps that unforgettable landscape that hung in their nursery, which they so much loved? Adam looked at Eve. With a rare, soft smile in her cat's eyes, she stepped up to the wall and slowly, almost ceremoniously, uncovered the picture.

It was a huge painting indeed, though none of those he had hoped for. Adam Krolthy could see that it was a triptych, but nothing else. For minutes, it remained a chromatic blur. Slowly, as his eyes and his mind adjusted to the tumult of figures that populated the landscape, with its simmering cliffs and lagoons, Adam Krolthy began to sense the power that ruled the disorder of the triptych. Imperceptibly it commanded his eyes to follow its mighty inner sweep from left to right. He saw that the innocent, spring-like green of the left panel turned into a deep, sensuous, summery hue in the central panel, where, among the fruit-shaped pods and giant animals, a multitude of naked men and women were milling around—playing? making love? torturing each other?—surrounded by inexplicable shapes and indescribable monstrosities. As his eyes reached the right panel, he suddenly saw the darkness of winter descend on a terrifying land lit by the blazing fires of a city. Its flames cast an unearthly pall on a legion of strangely familiar monsters, which had taken over this world and, with uninhibited malevolence, were terrorizing it. It was the saturnalian orgy of a never-ending day of reckoning. Adam Krolthy stepped back a little in order to be able to take it all in, trying to come to grips with the triptych's unaccountable evil and inexplicable beauty.

Soon after his father's funeral, Adam Krolthy travelled to Madrid in great haste. He spent days in the Prado in front of *The Garden of Earthly Delights*, questioning its details in the hope that they might give him the answer to the whole, but to no avail. Old Hieronymus Bosch was, young Adam Krolthy realized, unlikely to betray his secrets to a miserable law student after successfully guarding them for more than four hundred years. Although he sympathized with the master's desire for privacy, over the years Adam Krolthy never ceased to feel an urge to search out the meaning of the *Garden*, or if that was impossible or forbidden by some unknown authority, at least to stand and marvel. It was a surprising impulse, for Adam Krolthy was not, by nature, a prying type. If in the course of his turbulent life he had occasionally eavesdropped at a door, collected gossip, or had stored some of his friends' and enemies' more interesting *faux pas* in the back of his mind, he had done so only to secure his own survival.

In the Prado his interest in the picture grew into a dangerous obsession, made more menacing and exciting by the silent threat of the painting's existence. In its shocking brilliance and teeming intensity, the original was, of course, much more powerful, terrifying and inscrutable than the copy at home, though anyone with any knowledge of art would have to admit that the copy was an exquisite forgery. Adam Krolthy couldn't free himself from the painting's hypnotic hold, even though he could hear the warnings of reason and common sense in his head. He should have taken the first train back to Paris, to resume his law studies at the Sorbonne, but he didn't. For the first and perhaps the last time in his life he wanted to understand something for the sheer pleasure of understanding.

A few months after his return to Paris he gave a lecture, or, as Adam Krolthy preferred to call it, some 'personal musings', entitled 'Bosch and his Garden' at the Tricolour Club—a group of compatriots, all students at the Sorbonne, who used to meet in the back-room of a bistro near St Germain-des-Prés. It turned out to be a fiasco. People had very little idea what he was talking about. Some yawned and read their books or made notes; others left, or looked at him curiously but forgivingly, as one might look at somebody slightly ga-ga.

A new chap, fresh from home on a government stipend to study French language and literature for his teacher's certificate, said, rather agitatedly, that instead of discuss-

ing the *cosmic* disorders of Bosch's *imagination* Krolthy
should discuss the *social* disorders of the *reality* of his own
time—and perhaps even try to do something about them
while it was still possible. Suddenly Bosch's ancient
apocalypse sank beneath the turbulent seas of contemporary misery. A lanky, bony man with a high, white forehead and dark-brown hair already thinning on the top of
his impressive head, Ladislas Jarek talked with subdued
passion and natural eloquence about the fate of the poor in
this rich world. His blue eyes flashed lightning at all those
capitalist ghouls and imperialist demons who oppressed
and robbed the people, but who, he promised, would soon
be swept away by a new flood, so that a 'new city' could
be built on the 'old hill' overlooking the Elysian fields—an
earthly paradise.

What all this had to do with Bosch and his demons,
Adam Krolthy couldn't quite figure out, yet he knew that
it was a rip-roaring soliloquy for which, back home, one
could easily be arrested. The admiral's secret police lurked
in run-down working-class districts, around taverns and
union halls, ready to nab anyone who talked louder than
they considered decent, or whose face they didn't like. In
Paris, of course, Jarek could say whatever he wanted.
Adam Krolthy couldn't care less *what* he said, so long as he
said it cleverly and wittily, but the other members of the
club didn't agree with the man: they booed and shouted
him down, then left in a huff. Exasperated, angry and
surprised, Jarek looked around. Wasn't it true, what he
said? Shouldn't they listen to him? Adam Krolthy liked
him—liked his decency, his defiance, his innocence—
from that first moment. And he knew that Jarek—no
sentimentalist, with that cool contempt for those who
were unlucky enough not to have been born into the

aristocracy of the working class—liked him too. When, many years later, he watched Jarek walk towards the gallows, erect, steady, as though he were strolling along the Seine or in the Bois, Justice Krolthy felt a weakness in his knees, a despair in his heart he had never before experienced.

One day Adam Krolthy took Jarek out to Neuilly-sur-Seine, where one of his aunts lived with her French husband (a general in the army). To his great surprise, Eve opened the door. She had come to visit him on impulse. As they stood at the door Adam Krolthy saw a familiar flash in Eve's eyes and a strange, unfamiliar sparkle in Jarek's. Childishly, Adam Krolthy hoped that those two would fall in love and that their love would give him something—he wasn't quite sure *what*—that he had been searching for for a long time.

That afternoon he had invited Jarek to come and live with him in the rue de Liège; he was willing to sacrifice his privacy and share the view from his balcony of the milk-trains, not to mention the blessings of the Pigalle and the Blanche and the lovely whores of the Chaussée d'Antin just around the corner, but Jarek refused. He felt it his moral obligation to remain with his old friends, also on government scholarships, in their small, cheap apartment in Saint-Denis, partly because he couldn't afford anything more expensive, and wouldn't hear of accepting anything from Adam Krolthy free, but mainly because the red-brick factories, belching chimneys and crowded tenements reminded him of the district where he was born and grew up. One always needed a reminder of one's roots, he said, and Adam Krolthy knew that he meant it.

Before Jarek could meet Eve again, she had left Paris because somebody was waiting for her in Rome, or was it

Athens, Weimar, Stockholm?—somebody, somewhere, was always waiting for Eve. Adam Krolthy and Jarek continued their walks, their disputations, their studies, until they finally received their diplomas *summa cum laude*. They had a big party, with girls and Cordon Rouge, at which Jarek was seen, for the first and last time, with a blonde on his lap and a bottle in his hand. Poor, *poor* Jarek! When, in the deadly silence of the big meeting hall of the Union of Metalworkers, Justice Krolthy had read Jarek's death sentence, he saw Jarek's thin lips widen into a grin, a terrifying, monstrous grin of vengeance and contempt that took hold over his sharp nose, pleasant blue eyes, high white forehead and thinning hair—by then, after months of interrogations, promises and threats, he had lost almost all his hair—and beyond him Justice Krolthy glimpsed the city aflame against the absurdity of total darkness.

Justice Krolthy got up, dutifully turned off the green-shaded lamp, but instead of going up to his room, he wandered out into the Countess Julia's rose garden for a whiff of fresh air. In the shadows, the garden lay cold, the trees, shrubs, leaves shimmering in the silver spray of the half-moon with breathtaking luminosity. Justice Krolthy's heart missed a beat, then almost stopped altogether. An evil world enveloped in unutterable beauty: *that* was the ugliest trick of the demon who had created it, his dirtiest joke, his most hideous fraud, his cruellest mockery, his most admirable achievement—his ultimate triumph.

Countess Julia's little Fokker rose so high above the fields and woods that not even the pitched whine of its noisy engine could be heard. Then, strangely transparent in the pale light, it hovered in front of the moon, before it glided westwards, as though about to land on her old, overgrown airstrip behind Crazy Hill, amid the fragrances of night and autumn.

Justice Krolthy undressed in darkness and went to bed. A warm, naked body lay next to him, asleep. Feeling her soft skin, soft hair, small, firm breasts, supple hands, Justice Krolthy whispered, 'Julia, Julia, my dear. You have come.'

'Want some breakfast?' Aunt Elsie said.

'No, thank you,' Simon Wald said. 'I'm not hungry.'

'You haven't had a bite since yesterday morning,' Aunt Elsie said. 'Do you know what the Lord told me when your Uncle Timotheus died in Chicago and I, in my great sorrow, refused to eat for days, just like you're doing now?'

'No, Aunt Elsie,' Simon Wald said slowly. 'You've never told me that one.' He knew—everybody knew— Aunt Elsie's cautionary tale by heart. A few days after the sudden and unexpected death of her husband in Chicago that left her, a young and inexperienced girl, alone in a foreign country, moaning and weeping and accusing the Lord of injustice, He appeared in her apartment and commanded her to stop her pig-headed defiance, to eat and live and let Him be the judge of right and wrong, of life and death!

Simon Wald did not remember his Uncle Timotheus— he was not yet four years old when Timotheus had emigrated to America, only to return in the large, ornate coffin Aunt Elsie had bought, to be buried in his native soil—but Simon's father had given strict orders never to interrupt Aunt Elsie in telling her story, and his word was law. So, Simon settled back comfortably in his chair, resigned to the inevitable, placing his shotgun gently against the leg of the oblong wooden kitchen table. His favourite double-barrelled Browning was a masterpiece of design and craftsmanship he had inherited from his father, who had received it as a gift for twenty-five years of loyal service from Count Carolus. The count had bought it directly from the manufacturer in Belgium while on his way to Ostend with his family for the early autumn hunt at Lord Agravain's. Simon Wald kept the gun in mint condition and was teaching his son—its future owner—its every little whim.

'There was a time when you could easily despatch five scrambled eggs with lots of bacon for breakfast, and still have a big lunch,' Aunt Elsie continued. 'Do you remember that?'

'Yes,' Simon Wald said, wonderingly, 'I remember that, Aunt Elsie.' Sometimes these days he could remember things—a lash, a knife, the glowing butt of a cigarette which bore into his belly—with such terrible distinctness that it forced him to close his eyes and suppress a scream, but then the next day, or often the next hour, everything suddenly blurred and went almost blessedly dark. One moment he recalled clearly the events of the day he was arrested—the snowy dawn on Crazy Hill; the black limousines on the new service road; the beaters around the fire; his son in the kitchen eating the banana; Aunt Elsie's mug of mulled wine with cloves; the improvised stretcher with old Matthias's stiff body covered by a general's greatcoat; the giant stag that leaped out of the woods, head lowered, its enormous antlers readied for the attack; the childlike, innocent face of the young, corpulent major at Police Headquarters in Sentelek, who received him with laboured politeness, offered him slivovitz and a comfortable armchair before taking him down to the cellars and whipping him half-dead. Then the next moment it was all gone, vanished, all except the stag.

He could not forget the stag. It had remained vivid in his memory all those years. When he returned from Krechk Labour Camp and learned that the stag had been shot the very day he was arrested, he couldn't believe it. His stag could not be killed! It was still there in the woods, contemptuously playing hide-and-seek with its pursuers. For weeks Simon Wald had criss-crossed the forest, looking for his stag, but it eluded him, and he knew that was the stag's way of telling him it was still alive.

Otherwise, everything was touch-and-go. He hadn't been feeling very well lately. His memory went blank more and more often and he remembered things less and less clearly. Sometimes, he was even unable to evoke the barracks, the latrines behind which Kopf—his camp-chum, his guardian angel—had got caught in the crossfire, the quarry, the barbed-wire fence, the guard-towers, the red-tiled villa of 'Captain Strappado', as Kopf had named him one evening when they were celebrating Garudy's more-or-less safe return from the 'Pleasure Palace', where for more than twelve hours, Garudy had been strung up and left dangling by his arms.

The other day, in the city, Simon Wald had bumped into Garudy—his friend with whom he had shared Bunk 66 for almost four years in Barrack Six. It was too bad he didn't remember, the poet had said. Too bad, *yes*, Garudy whispered for emphasis, grabbing Simon Wald's lapel with its golden oakleaf, because Krechk no longer existed. It had been demolished, burned down, ploughed under, and—get this, chum!—the site fumigated. A lovely green meadow now stretched there, between the mountains of

the north and the lake in the south, sprinkled with yellow
dandelions and white Queen Anne's lace, a meadow of
beauty, innocence and serenity, a tribute to nature's re-
generative powers under the wise guardianship of *our*
leaders! Even Captain Strappado's red tiles were turning
green, in harmony with the meadows, so that sheep may
safely graze, *hah!* Captain Strappado himself had been
transferred to a small provincial town where he reportedly tried, successfully, to seduce the withered, middle-
aged county secretary of the Alliance. It meant, Garudy
winked, that there was *some* justice in the universe.

Garudy was the most lovable idiot Simon Wald had
ever met in his life. He came back from America after the
war only to be arrested as an American spy, although his
anti-American fulminations were given wide publicity.
His poems were censored, partly because he used words
the authorities considered obscene, but mainly because he
nonchalantly equated the *Führer* with the *Vozhd* and that,
of course, was intolerable. But Kopf liked Garudy's
poems, with their stabbing rhymes, colourful descriptions
and historical allusions, so he often asked Garudy to recite
his latest for the assembled audience. Small, wiry, furious,
Garudy obliged with pleasure, shouting his poetic curses
at Captain Strappado and his minions, who stood, un-
blinking, at a distance. For reasons of their own, they never
interfered with those after-dinner congregations.

Those were wonderful evenings, Simon Wald remembered, between the watery soups of their dinner and the
rich, meaty feasts of their dreams. Then the Battle (as it
came to be known) broke out and Strappado banned their
gatherings forthwith. It was just as well. With Kopf dead,
as Garudy had said at a secret, midnight memorial service
in Barrack Six, nobody could take the place of the 'sage of

Krechk', and from now on, they would simply have to accept life's horrors without Kopf's wisdom, humour, consolation. Then, in a whisper, Garudy recited his poem in memory of Kopf. In the middle of it something happened, but Simon Wald could not remember what it was. He didn't want to forget, but he was forgetting. He didn't know what to do. If one day he forgot Krechk altogether—and he knew that could happen, it could happen any time!—what would be left of Simon Wald?

That morning he got up before dawn, as he had every day since he was a boy, and silently, so as not to disturb Anna in the large, old bed, went to the bathroom, shaved, washed, then came back and dressed in his best Sunday hunting outfit—though it was only Saturday, he didn't want to appear uncouth when he met General Wulf in the green room. Before leaving, he looked once more at Anna. Used to his early hours, she seemed to be asleep but he knew that she wasn't. She was lovelier than ever, her chestnut hair cascading around her white neck, her long, dark eyelashes fluttering in the dim light. Simon Wald loved her more now than he had when he asked her to marry him. Anna hadn't slept much since Anna Julia Sybilla was born, and he knew she hadn't slept a wink last night. The others had left them alone with their dead daughter in her beautiful cot to say a last prayer of farewell. But Anna didn't pray, she just put her long fingers on Anna Julia's head, as though trying once again to transmit the warmth of her soul to that cold little body. Then, without a word, she turned away and went to bed.

Bending over her now, Simon Wald wanted to ask if there was anything he could do, but he didn't ask; he wanted so much to touch her hair, her face, her hands, but he didn't do that either. He turned off the lamp and left the room, walking down the corridor towards his office where, in a locked closet, he kept his gun collection. He stopped before the guest-room, listening to see if Monsignor Beck was stirring or needed something, but there was silence behind the door.

Simon Wald's small but valuable collection of handguns was not comparable, of course, to the armoury of the Széchys, where you could find everything from original fourteenth-century German matchlocks to eighteenth-century French breechloaders and modern American semi-automatics with telescopic sights. Still, it was a selection he could proudly show to friends and guests when they came from neighbouring villages for weddings, funerals, christenings, Christmas celebrations, or for the Shrovetide ball in the ballroom of The Waldhorn. The Shrovetide ball was no longer held now that the gypsies had been rounded up and carted away, their instruments thrown into one of those abandoned grain silos in Sentelek, though a few of them, at the order of the new Alliance county secretary, had been put on display in the little high-school museum as 'interesting specimens of folk instruments from the eighteenth century'.

Without hesitation, Simon Wald picked out his favourite Browning. It had no telescopic sight, of course, but it was as accurate as a shotgun could be; if it missed the target, it was always the fault of the gunner, never of the gun. Simon Wald remembered the old tale his father told so often that, by the time Simon was six, he knew it by heart. Once, in the twilight of the woods on his way home from his daily inspection, the old man saw a rabbit snuggling among the broken twigs and hawthorn bushes. Even though his wife kept telling him not to bring home any more rabbits, for they had enough to last the whole winter, he aimed and shot, because he couldn't resist the lure of the target and the echo of the shot among the oaks and birches. The rabbit lay there motionless, although it should have leaped high and rolled over crazily when hit. Old Peter Wald couldn't believe he'd missed, but when he went closer, he realized that he'd mistaken a small tree-trunk for a rabbit: imagine that! Every time Simon Wald's father told the story, he laughed wholeheartedly. In this world of treachery even your very eyes betrayed you if you weren't careful!

At five past five it was still dark and cold under the glittering stars, but Simon Wald was dressed for the weather, and he knew the road to Krestur with his eyes closed. From the colour of the eastern sky he saw it was going to be another hot day, a bad omen Aunt Elsie had said yesterday as she opened the window to let Anna Julia Sybilla's soul, a white dove, soar to heaven, where she belonged. Simon Wald didn't believe in omens, good or bad, though Kopf had often speculated about a possible link between superstition and reality, as he put it, which led Garudy to write a piece of doggerel about a fatal accident which could be interpreted as coincidental or predetermined depending on your point of view. It was strange how the weather had changed the moment General Wulf and the others had arrived, but whether there was a connection between their arrival and the shift in temperature Simon Wald didn't know, and, frankly, didn't care. Why should he? There had always been things around him that he didn't quite understand, but life went on, and yesterday's riddle invariably became today's solution.

Simon Wald accepted what his father and his grandfather had told him about nature's obdurate and uncon-

querable will. Nature carried the seeds of survival. A freak
jump in temperature could not alter the seasons' invio-
lable sequence. He might be arrested, flogged, hanged and
buried, but spring would still follow winter as the harvest-
ing of wheat followed the sowing of seed. Was that too
simple, a platitude? Of course it was, yet he believed
unconditionally in the permanence of his meadows, forests, brooks, and that belief excluded any mumbo-jumbo
about signs and divinations. If, as Kopf had so often teased
him, he was 'a born pantheist thinly disguised as a Catholic' (exactly what that meant Simon Wald wasn't quite
sure, because Kopf died before he could keep his promise
to explain it), he must be a good one: he knew all about the
poisonous properties of mushrooms and the healing char-
acteristics of herbs, and if that didn't make him a pantheist, what did?

When he reached Krestur, the village was already
awakening. Simon Wald cherished those moments when
everything was about to begin, to change—the juncture of
sleeping and waking, of night and day, perhaps even of
life and death. He stopped at the well, as he had every
morning as far back as he could recall, and slowly drank
a cupful of water before he drove on. After a moment's
indecision in front of The Waldhorn, he went inside,
though he was neither hungry nor thirsty, nor did he have
any business with Aunt Elsie. Simon Wald stood there in
the spacious kitchen, realizing that since his return from
Krechk, he came here every morning before going out into
the woods, but he couldn't work out why. He was deeply
troubled by his recurring loss of memory, though he
mentioned it to no one, not even to Anna—least of all to
Anna.

'A cup of coffee, maybe?' Aunt Elsie asked, standing

barefoot, as she had just got out of bed. The powerful overhead light turned her long, ashen hair almost completely white. 'You're still asleep, Simon. I'll make you a pot of coffee and that'll wake you up.'

'No, thank you,' Simon Wald said slowly. 'I'd rather have some of your lime-blossom tea, if you've got a cup, Aunt Elsie.'

'With your usual slivovitz?' Aunt Elsie asked.

'With my usual slivovitz,' Simon Wald replied with a laugh.

In the dark dawn line-up for that dirty mess-can of slop Captain Strappado had had the temerity to call a cup of coffee, Kopf had often waxed lyrical about the fruit-brandies he loved. They were for everybody, prince or pauper, Kopf had said, and suddenly Simon Wald remembered why he had come to The Waldhorn this early in the morning. He laughed again and with one quick swill tossed down Aunt Elsie's exquisite, home-made plum-brandy, then left.

At the first kilometre stone outside the village—the spot where the stag leapt out of the woods, as the truck sped towards Sentelek with the ash-grey Matthias on the makeshift stretcher, the corporal beside him, wiping the cold sweat with a white handkerchief from the old man's forehead—Simon Wald stopped, as if waiting for the stag to shoot out from the woods, its head lowered, its antlers readied to attack all its enemies. In the deep, mellow silence that wrapped him in its soft, warm blanket and insulated him against the clamour of the world, Simon Wald stood there for a while. The sun was already high, and he took off his jacket and opened his shirt.

Staff-Sergeant Gottlieb and Sergeant Chortnik, Captain

Strappado's most trusted henchmen, had come for Simon Wald in the middle of the night. Though Garudy mumbled something, he probably didn't notice Simon Wald's disappearance until he woke up in the morning. Gottlieb and Chortnik—a tall, thin man and a small, fat man, as in the old slapstick movies—took Simon Wald to a huge, echoing room in the Pleasure Palace, where he had never been before, and let him stand by the wall decorated, he could see by the flickering flame of the candles, by meathooks of various sizes. Simon Wald surveyed them silently, with some interest. He suspected, of course, that he was going to hang from one of those hooks before the sun came up. With eyes closed, he prayed that, if hell was a matter of choice, as Kopf had once explained, he would make the right choice, escape from eternal bondage and become a free, dead man. There wasn't much time for meditation or prayer, however, because Simon Wald could already hear the laughter of Captain Strappado. When he arrived he stood in front of Simon Wald, looking at him with warmth and compassion, as if he was deeply interested in his fate and wanted to assure Simon Wald of his best intentions.

'Please,' Captain Strappado said, and touched Simon Wald's perspiring face with the miniature riding whip in his left hand, while handing him a handkerchief to wipe the sweat from his brow, 'please, Chief Forester, calm down. There's nothing to worry about! We asked you to come here only to have a little chat. Would you like a glass of water? Some soda? Or wine? A *spritzer* maybe? We want you to get out of here—and I don't simply mean the Pleasure Palace, as you and your pals have named it, but our whole establishment—as much as we ourselves want to be as far away from this godforsaken place as possible, because it is, as our Professor Weiskopf has so convincingly demonstrated, worse than hell. So, Chief Forester, sit down and have a drink with us.'

Dressed in his off-white summer uniform, with medals on his chest, and the insignia of the State Security Forces—hammer and fist crossed within a circle—glittering on his hat in the candlelight, Captain Strappado was smaller than Simon Wald, though about the same age: a good-looking man in his early thirties. His baby-blue eyes and pink, freshly shaven face revealed an almost childish petulance. Captain Strappado poured wine into beautiful crystal glasses then, slowly, removed his gloves, put his hat on the table next to the candelabra, and sat, legs crossed, waiting for Simon Wald to join the fun.

'All we hope to learn from you,' Captain Strappado said, holding up his glass with its clear, fragrant wine, as if he wanted to clink it with Simon Wald's glass, still untouched on the table, 'are some minor technicalities about the plan. We know, as I'm sure you realize by now, a great deal about your plan, for needless to say, we have our own means of finding out everything about the transactions our guests are involved in. But there are some—basically insignificant—details we would like to clarify. We could, of course, get them ourselves, but we felt that, if you were kind enough to provide us with the information, a great deal of pain and suffering might be avoided. For a man of compassion and charity, like yourself, this could not be a matter of indifference. Therefore, we assumed that such an idea of give-and-take between you and us could be worked out, provided, we kept reminding ourselves, that we could present it with decorum and clarity and give you time to think it over. So, please, Chief Forester, take your time. And have a sip of wine, for God's sake! You haven't even touched our excellent Bordeaux. We know, naturally, that you and your pals do not regard us exactly as your benefactors, and we can understand that, but in this particular case I dare say that we are closer to being allies than adversaries, for our cooperation is intended to prevent suffering, not to cause it. And that, I must add, is the essence of all I wanted to tell you, Chief Forester.'

Beyond the small, open window of the Pleasure Palace, Simon Wald imagined the camp still asleep in the darkness, though he hoped that those narrow streaks of light that he saw spreading across the eastern sky were not simply flashes of his imagination and fear: if dawn was really breaking over the hills, he might get away, at least for the time being, for Strappado and his henchmen worked only during the night. But, of course, Simon Wald knew that it was only dry lightning that, from time to time, raced across the eastern horizon above the dusty mountains and desiccated plains. For more than eighty days now, no rain had fallen and the dewy green mountains of the north and the moist, humid plains of the south had turned grey and arid. Everything disappeared under layers of dust: the watch-towers, barbed-wire fence, even the gravel-pit—beyond which they were planning to ambush Strappado and hold him hostage. Even Kopf's oak, as it was fondly called, became a heap of dust, though they still gathered under its gritty branches to listen to Kopf's tales.

Now, Simon Wald looked at Captain Strappado and his lick-spittles sipping their wine. He had no idea how long they were willing to sit or stand there staring out of the window into the dusty night, but with every passing moment he could sense that their patience was wearing thinner. If Gottlieb and Chortnik were famous for their inventiveness, Strappado was even better known for his mastery in balancing punishment and reward with such cunning that his victims laughed and cried, hated him and adored him at one and the same time, giving him, meanwhile, all the information he needed without even noticing what they had done. According to Kopf, Strappado was the arch-fiend himself, disguised skilfully as one of the State Security's lowly captains who, together with his henchmen, used pain for the purpose of pleasure. Strappado must know something about their plan, despite Kopf's meticulous safety measures to prevent unintentional leaks by the very few who had been closely involved in it from its inception. But *what* did he know?

Strappado was still sitting on his camp-chair next to the flickering candles, Gottlieb and Chortnik behind him, silent, watchful. Even if they knew something about the plan, Simon Wald was suddenly certain that they knew *nothing* about its details, and, most important, about its timing. Their informer, whoever he might have been, could only have reached the outer fringes of the organization; he might have guessed what was going on but could have no precise and concrete knowledge of Kopf's scheme. And yet, Simon Wald understood, no matter what happened to him there tonight, he had to get out *alive* so that he could warn Kopf and his friends about the danger. But what if it was too late already? Perhaps the plan never really had a chance. Perhaps from the very beginning it was a dream, or worse, a delusion. Was hope really the ultimate punishment of the damned? Simon Wald remembered the warm wave that flooded his body when Kopf first mentioned the plan to him on the latrine and asked him to become one of the founding members of what Kopf, with his conspiratorial wink, called the Committee of Public *Un*safety. What happiness Simon Wald had felt then! Now that they were so close, only a few weeks away from its culmination, were they to be defeated again—crushed by Strappado and his gangsters?

It was very hot in the meathook-bin. Simon Wald wiped his forehead with Strappado's handkerchief. His mouth was full of dust and grime and, despite the damp air, he felt utterly dried up. Slowly sipping their wine, Strappado, Gottlieb and Chortnik were sweating, wiping their brows, scratching their legs, staring out of the window at the darkness; for a moment, they looked almost touchingly human. On the dirty walls the candles played their ancient tricks, the hooks becoming swaying, elongated shadows of long-horned bulls, wing-flapping birds, sharp-nosed foxes. Simon Wald watched them dreamily, as in their childhood he and Sybil had watched their father conjuring up such images on the living-room wall opposite the fireplace on Christmas evenings, birthdays or those rare, happy moments when the mood hit the old man. He even used to imitate the sounds of the animals he so cleverly brought to life with his long, skilful fingers. Simon Wald smiled.

They bound his hands behind his back with a strong rope so tightly that he felt it cutting into his wrists, then threw the rope around a big iron hook. Now, he waited almost impatiently for Gottlieb and Chortnik to hoist him up. Anticipating the pain, he took a deep breath, but nothing happened. Pale in the flickering light, Gottlieb, with the rope in his hand, and Chortnik one step behind him, stood motionless. Simon Wald had no idea how long they waited there, immobilized by the damp heat; time had lost its meaning for him, as if he had been swept up by a cool current of eternity. Then, abruptly, Gottlieb yanked the rope, and Simon Wald felt himself slowly hoisted upwards so that he was forced to bend forwards, as though bowing humbly to Captain Strappado, who, still sitting in his chair, was sipping his wine, looking up at him with curious pity. At that moment time reasserted its reality: Gottlieb was pulling the rope with such deliberate, experienced slowness that the pain made Simon Wald remember one of Strappado's evening talks before the assembled multitude, on 'The Idea of Pain in the Service of Progress', which Kopf later called Strappado's 'Sermon of the Abyss'. The pain, Simon Wald sensed, was already there, but only in a distant, almost playful way, cavorting, as it were, through his bones and muscles and nerve-centres, foreshadowing all that was soon to happen, yet still giving him time—his sense of time now sharpened as never before—to think things over, to answer the questions, and so to end the suffering. But Simon Wald remained silent.

Now, they tugged the rope roughly and the pain with its lucid, terrible clarity took possession of him, excluding from his mind the possibility of misunderstanding, locking him firmly into the solitary confinement of his own being. Hauled higher and higher by his arms, bent forward by the weight of his body, he could, for a moment, see that he was already standing on his toes, but the next second, he felt himself leave the ground altogether. His arms, wrenched out of his shoulder sockets, dangled behind him like broken wings. And still, he was being hoisted upwards. His body became heavy, shot through with pain, a body totally *un*responsive to the commands of his mind. Simon Wald wanted to rid himself of this treacherous body so twisted by pain, but it was impossible to free himself of the fetters of his bones, muscles, nerves. They humiliated him. Betrayed him. The pain grew stronger and sharper, and as warm wetness trickled down his legs, he heard himself shouting. He could not understand what he was saying, but he knew he wanted to warn Kopf of the impending disaster. Louder and louder he shouted so Kopf would hear him, until, incomprehensibly, he was hit by the whiplash of laughter, and then he fainted.

At the kilometre stone Simon Wald jumped over the ditch, wading slowly into the shadows of the woods, his Browning on his shoulder. It was already very hot, though little wisps of mist still drifted among the birches and the oaks. Soon he reached the spot where old Uncle Matthias had been buried by his fellow beaters, in defiance of Colonel Vintner's orders. Much to his surprise, Simon Wald saw Captain Strappado standing there by the huge, slate-grey boulder—old Matthias's headstone—a Winchester in his hand, as if waiting for something or somebody. Behind a giant oak, Simon Wald took his Browning cautiously off his shoulder and took aim. With unmistakable clarity Captain Strappado's forehead loomed up in the sight, and Simon Wald knew he couldn't miss.

SIX

W ALD,' General Wulf shouted at the top of his lungs. 'Put that thing down at once! Have you gone stark raving mad? Start walking towards me slowly, very slowly!'

'General Wulf!' Simon said hoarsely from behind the oak. 'What are you doing here? Aren't you supposed to have breakfast with Justice Krolthy and Monsignor Beck in the manor?'

'Sit down, Wald.' General Wulf watched Simon Wald walk towards him, slowly, as ordered, his Browning in his hand. 'You look sick.' He felt his heart racing crazily, and, surreptitiously, he put a nitromint under his tongue. 'Green as a treefrog. Now, what the hell is happening here, Wald, would you kindly enlighten me? Never mind my breakfast. Tell me about yours. You were supposed to meet me in the green room, so that we could have a cup of coffee and take a trip to that tree and pond which, as you so convincingly argued yesterday, exist only in my deranged mind, but you didn't show up. At six-thirty sharp, Wald, remember?'

'No.' Simon Wald squatted down at the rock. 'I'm afraid I don't, General Wulf. Please, believe me. It happens to me often these days. I simply forget things. They just slip my mind. I haven't mentioned this to anybody yet, but I've always looked on you as my patron. I'm worried, General Wulf. And I'm very sorry.'

'Yes,' General Wulf said, touched by this outburst of

reverence. 'It's a good thing you mentioned it. You should have a check-up, Wald. I'll talk to the prime minister the moment he gets here. I'm sure he'll make arrangements for you up at Old Beggars' Hill in the city. It's an excellent hospital, take my word for it. Just a few months ago I was on the brink of death, but they brought me back to life in a jiffy, and, as you can see, here I am in mint condition. A miracle, don't you think so? I'll call my good friend, Dr Asklep. He'll take care of you better than any doctor I know of.'

In the sunshine a strange odour lingered in the air, hovering above Simon Wald, at once consoling and terrifying. General Wulf had learned to recognize it when, a few months after Kirov's assassination, he was arrested in Leningrad and taken to the Nizhegorodsky Prison, whose warden, Colonel OGPU Alexander Konstantinovich Zhestokov, had, over a period of weeks, explained in loving detail the peculiarities of the smell of dying and death.

Ensconced behind clouds of *makhorka* cigarettes, garlic and cucumber that filled his small, windowless office with the utterly irreverent tang of life, Colonel Zhestokov smiled. It had nothing to do with the vulgar, heavy odours of the body, like sweat or semen, urine or excrement, which, by their very nature, carry the fetor of decay and mortality. Contrary to expectation it was, Colonel Zhestokov maintained with supreme conviction, a light, pleasant, almost too sweet effluvium which issued not from the pores of the skin or orifices of the body, but from the immortal soul. It heralded the presence of the angel whom, in His mercy, God sent to lift up those who, while faithfully obeying His commands to their last breath, have

fallen by the wayside. Perhaps, Colonel Zhestokov speculated, inhaling his *makhorka*, rolled carefully in yesterday's
Pravda, perhaps that was God's way of rewarding those
who trusted Him without reservation. But why was it,
then, that even the unfaithful, the unbelievers, emitted the
same odour when, standing on tiptoe against the wall for
a couple of days or being hoisted by hands and feet tied
behind their backs for a couple of hours, they reached that
point of no return? Colonel Zhestokov considered that
perhaps it was an indication that God was indeed either a
bourgeois democrat or, as many of His *apparatchiki* had
often enunciated, an unshakeable egalitarian, and consequently, according to Colonel Zhestokov, unfit to rule the
unruly hordes of mankind.

Whatever the solution to Colonel Zhestokov's grand
metaphysical riddle—General Wulf had never been interested in its ramifications—General Wulf had had ample
time to reflect on Zhestokov's casual observations. Invariably, he found them precise and reliable. Wherever he
went, that sweet effluvium had followed him, in the
Nizhegorodsky in Leningrad, in the Lyubyanka in
Moscow, in the Arctic transit-camps of Ust-Usa, Pomoz-
dino, Shchelya-Yur on the Northern Dvina, until, finally,
Singer, already high in the hierarchy of the OGPU, managed to dig him out from under the permafrost and have
him brought back to Moscow, an act of courage and
friendship in the bloody sea of cowardice and betrayal
that had indebted General Wulf to Singer for a lifetime.
The odour pervaded his nostrils in Teruel, when Sébastien
LaCroix's antediluvian Nieuport was shot out of the
frozen-blue January skies, and Jarek, risking his own life,
brought Sébastien's broken body, still alive, back through

enemy lines to Brigade Headquarters. The room was suddenly filled with an aroma that lingered for days after Sébastien died and was tossed into the unmarked grave of the defeated. Later, when the Second Ukrainian Front under Malinovsky crushed the German defences, Colonel Zhestokov's fragrance enveloped the plains and hillocks from Voronezh to Warsaw.

General Wulf looked at Simon Wald lying beside him, silent. The forester appeared frail, his pale, gaunt face tired, his dark-blue eyes sleepy. With both hands he touched the huge, slate-grey boulder, as though expecting to renew his waning energies, and, almost involuntarily, General Wulf also touched it.

'This is the tombstone of one of our local heroes, General Wulf,' Simon Wald said. 'A cantankerous old rascal. My Uncle Matthias. Some people come here to worship him. Sometimes a long procession, men, women, children, the whole village. Do you see all those candle-stumps and burnt-out matches?'

'And what did he do to deserve such adoration?' General Wulf asked.

'He fell into a hole he wanted somebody else to fall into,' Simon Wald said.

'A most human endeavour, if I may say.' General Wulf laughed. 'It happens often enough.'

'Yes,' Simon Wald agreed. 'It does.'

'Then what happened?' General Wulf said.

'My cousins brought Uncle Matthias out of the woods on a makeshift stretcher,' Simon Wald continued. 'He was unconscious and covered with a brand-new army great-coat. It's all very vague in my memory. We were ordered to take him to the hospital in Sentelek at once. And we did.'

Now the sweet, light fragrance was unmistakable, and,

leaning against the cool rock, General Wulf took a deep breath. He felt very tired.

Despite the Morpholomin, or, perhaps, because of it, for he took three to make sure he'd sleep soundly, General Wulf had a bad night. The pills only caused him to sweat profusely and have stupid nightmares: he should have known better, but he had been slow to learn about the decay of his body. Before his heart attack, he had never needed much to send him to sleep, a stiff Scotch or a soft cunt would always do the trick, and he would sleep, inert, until someone shook him back to life: Inge, at home, Colonel Vintner on the field, or whomever he had been sleeping with elsewhere. Slightly dizzy, General Wulf sat on the edge of his bed trying, in vain, to remember something of his sickening nightmares.

Outside, it was still dark and cold. General Wulf walked to the window and threw it wide open. In the crystal-clear sky the stars still glittered, but the moon had already disappeared. The storm he had heard forecast yesterday evening on Krolthy's car radio had not materialized. General Wulf laughed: Copass himself couldn't have stage-managed it better! Copass had always maintained that a threatening forecast scared his beloved masses away from whatever entertainment he had devised for them, so eventually, despite Adymester's vehement protestations, he had phoned the night-editor of the *People's Truth* and instructed him to suppress *all* forecasts of rain before any important outdoor demonstration. That was Copass's theory and practice of power: if he couldn't control the weather, he could at least control the weather forecast!

Before going to the green room to meet Simon Wald for

breakfast, Wulf decided to fetch his old Winchester from the armoury. He had left it there after his so-called resignation, because they wouldn't let him take it home to Lilac Hill, as he used to do. As a matter of fact, they wouldn't let him keep *any* of his beloved guns; even his tiny German Kolibri, which he kept in his pocket, just in case, for every occasion, even for amorous ones, had been taken away from him. It was probably Singer's way of telling him that he was *really* finished, crushed, emasculated. And so he was, yes, he couldn't deny that. As always, Singer got what he wanted.

How like a charm Singer's cheap tricks had worked! Suddenly, everything Copass and Singer had contrived and been responsible for—the charges against Jarek, the execution of the generals, the organization of the camps, the attack on the peasantry—had come down on General Wulf's head. Copass and Singer had played it with their customary skill, using the Apparat to spread their concoction of slander and truth, circumstantial evidence and irrefutable fact. By the time General Wulf was finally given the floor at a secret meeting of the Central Committee, he was already blacker than the devil, and much more sinful. He said what he had to say quickly, humbly, with merciless yet passionate sincerity, cutting into his own flesh with the cold, sharp knife of self-criticism and letting it bleed freely before that bloodthirsty mob of zealots.

But a few months later, Copass, too, was gone, though that sweet moment of his departure was made sour by the arrival of Singer. Now Singer could sit at the head of the highest meeting without running the risk of being overruled by a higher authority—except, of course, by his grim-faced Moscow chums. But they, too, were busy dividing up the spoils after the *Vozhd*'s untimely death and had little interest or inclination to look into Singer's ever-boiling pots and pans. So finally, after all those years of being a preface, Singer had become the last word, the revealed utterance, gospel truth.

A few months ago Singer had visited General Wulf on Lilac Hill, for the first time since his retirement. With his customary soft-spoken polite cruelty, he had summed up his life as deficient, devoid of meaning, bereft of useful-ness. Red-faced, General Wulf was about to throw him out of the house, something he had never done to anyone, when Inge came in, as though on cue, and, in her soft voice, husky with grief and crying, said, 'Ah, Ernest, I hope you can stay for dinner.' At the table General Wulf had gone on proving furiously how wrong Singer was, how terribly in error! But now, General Wulf wasn't so certain. Maybe Singer was right. Maybe Professor Weiskopf was right, too. Maybe his life hadn't been worth a farthing. Maybe he should feel lucky enough merely to be alive. Maybe he was no longer the darling of the gods. In any case, what did Singer want from him now? Why had Singer dragged him down here, together with Anselm and Adam Krolthy?

Suddenly light-headed, General Wulf stopped at the top of the stairs. He had nothing more to give, no more lies, no more power, no more truth, no more passion. He was an old man exposed to the eyes of the world; wasn't it high time Singer left him alone, let him live out his remaining years in peace, in dignity?

Out of the corner of his eye General Wulf saw a quick flash—a white dirndl, a multi-coloured scarf on a blonde head—in the grey dawn of the eastern corridor. That scoundrel Krolthy had done it again! Here was General Wulf, having nightmares, wrestling with the important riddles of his life, and there was Krolthy merrily fucking the night away with the first scullery-maid he could find! General Wulf wasn't really surprised, and only slightly envious: if Krolthy was, as everybody knew, unbelievably successful with all those lewd and moist cunts around, he, General Wulf, couldn't complain about his conquests in and out of bed.

He hated Krolthy with a steely hatred—not because Krolthy had served Singer so loyally, but because Krolthy so carelessly accepted and so masterfully performed the role of presiding justice of the People's Tribunal at Jarek's trial. Why did he do that? Jarek was an old friend from his Sorbonne days, who had had a long, passionate love-affair with Eve Krolthy during the war and even used Krolthy's family house as a hideaway from the Gestapo. Krolthy didn't have to do it. He could have found countless pretexts not to: he could have left the country for an important conference organized by Jurists for World Peace in London, for a crucial panel-appearance in Paris, or simply have holed up in Old Beggars' Hill Hospital, pretending to be sick, as he had before Cardinal Zenty's trial. But Krolthy had conducted the trial with a strange, quite uncharacteristic zeal, and what's more, with tremendous success. For weeks, his name was on the front page of every newspaper in the country, on the radio from morning till night, the unconcealable contempt in the voice of the presiding justice exposing the villainy of the accused, until finally the jury brought in the verdict. The punishment, Adymester had proclaimed in one of his most passionate editorials in the *People's Truth,* was so well deserved and just that, if God existed, He Himself could not object.

Why did Krolthy do it? General Wulf had no idea, but he could never forgive him. He saw Krolthy standing by the gallows in the chilly, late-October morning, slowly, softly reading the sentence in the echoing silence of the cobblestoned courtyard, without the slightest sign of emotion, looking straight into Jarek's large, blue, blood-shot eyes. After they put the black hood on Jarek's head, he had looked up at the sun emerging from behind the threatening clouds, and General Wulf knew that, so long as he lived, he would hate Krolthy, and for that ultimate treachery he would do everything in his power to avenge Jarek.

Apart from the portrait gallery in the great hall, the armoury was General Wulf's favourite spot in the manor. Here was one of the world's richest, most extensive private collections of arms and armour. Dating from the neolithic period—glittering obsidian knives, beautifully carved blue basalt spearheads, clever, accurate blow-guns—to the present, the weapons served to show anybody who was interested, or so Anselm had once remarked, that time hadn't much changed man's nature and that the metaphor for original sin—Adam's rebellion against God and subsequent loss of divine grace—was today as emblematic of the human condition as it had been ten thousand years ago.

Anselm could never resist the temptation to preach of man's betrayal of God, though he always cleverly evaded questions about God's betrayal of man. General Wulf remembered the day he and Jarek were both invited to the consecration of the site of the new church in Anselm's native village, where the old one had gone up in flames. At lunch in the new House of Culture, Anselm had rattled on and on to Jarek, and such was the power of his words that, instead of brushing him off, Jarek listened intently, and at the next meeting of the Secretariat suggested that Monsignor Beck be considered for one of the leading jobs in the

new Office of Religious Affairs to be set up after Cardinal
Zenty's trial. Much to everybody's surprise, Copass and
Singer concurred. In no time, Monsignor Beck—a man of
peace and monastic tranquillity!—found himself in the
middle of a new religious war, and certainly seemed to
enjoy rolling with the punches.

General Wulf used to spend hours in the armoury, but
today he wasn't in the mood for lances, yatagans, matchlocks of bygone ages. He quickly picked up his old Winchester, which was waiting for him on the gunrack,
cleaned, loaded, exactly as he'd left it a year before.

In the green room, the little breakfast table in front of
the pale-green marble fireplace was set for two. Suddenly,
the first rays of the sun lit up the face of the beauty above
the fireplace. General Wulf could not stand that portrait.
Maybe the Countess Julia with her open smile was far too
happy for him, too innocent. Maybe her distinct cheekbones and Tartar eyes reminded him of Djenghizov, the
cruellest, most bloodthirsty of the guards who accompanied the long convoy of Stolypins to the Otdelny Lagerny
Punkt on the Northern Dvina. Maybe the lights and shadows of the background—green lawns, moss-covered
walls, the sundial's silence, the emerald spray of the
water-clock, the olive-dark azalea leaves, yellow daffo-
dils—made General Wulf remember something he had
lost, or had never actually possessed, and sadly, furiously,
knew he never would. Again, General Wulf experienced
a fleeting dizziness, and turned away from the Countess
Julia's happy smile.

Neatly folded, the morning edition of the *People's Truth*
lay on the white napkin beside his coffee cup. He hadn't
read the paper for months now, not only because it was
the world's dullest daily, but because he knew everything

that was printed in it before he read it. Now, furious that Simon Wald was late, and with nothing else to do, he opened it. On page three, in the column usually reserved for Singer's interminable statistics, he saw a black-framed press-release of the official Telegraphic and Telephonic News Agency. TTNA had been authorized to inform the populace of the commotion on the streets after the unfortunate defeat of our glorious soccer team in Lima. The commotion was caused by small groups of vandals and antisocial hooligans, incited by Western broadcasts. Assisted by hosts of outraged citizens, most of the vandals and hooligans had been rounded up by the police and taken into custody. After some spontaneous celebrations, hailing the Alliance and our leaders, the people had returned home and order was restored. The press-release emphasized the determination of the authorities to punish those responsible for the outrage with the merciless severity of the law.

More surprised than shocked, General Wulf re-read the press-release and found it even more revealing. *That* was the new Singer, the Singer of the post-Copass epoch. Under Copass's regime, no information whatsoever would have been published. Copass was the old guard defending the old methods to the bitter end; not for nothing did they call him the *Vozhd's* best disciple! What one didn't talk about didn't exist. It was the guiding principle Copass had learned from the *Vozhd*. General Wulf understood perfectly the idea of blacking out disagreeable news and agreed with its logic: there was no reason for the mob to be informed about everything, especially about events that would only make them more excited or furious, less controllable, so to isolate them from offensive realities was in their own best interest. But that

was theory. In the dirty reality of ordinary life, General
Wulf knew from experience, it was impossible to keep
things hidden from the mob for very long. Eventually,
everything seeped through even the most tightly controlled system—as the story of Jarek's life and death was
leaking through these days—and the best efforts to keep
the lid on would come to naught or, worse, would lead to
an explosion.

Singer must have learned from Copass's mistakes. He
couldn't do much while Copass still held the reins and,
besides, didn't want to, because it wasn't advisable to
cross swords with Copass so long as the *Vozhd* was backing him. Now, however, Singer was free to put his own
ideas into action. Singer had made an interesting move, as
simple as it was powerful. In all probability it was much
more effective than what General Wulf would have done
in a similar situation—he would have followed his impulses and used a show of force, with a clear warning of
even more Draconian measures. But Singer followed his
reason, never his impulses, believing in the well thought
out and gradual use of violence for the sake of power,
never, as his flunkies did, in manipulating power for the
sake of violence. Instead of sending Special Security
Forces to the city, as General Wulf would have done,
Singer had published a press-release which, without telling the whole story, bore *some* resemblance to the events
that had taken place last night, to what the 'man in the
street' might have seen with his own eyes.

Yes, Singer had handled yesterday's outrage extremely
well. The 'trial-run on the Bastille', Krolthy had quite
wittily called it, though with an odd apprehension in his
mocking voice, as they drove back to the manor from
Simon Wald's house. If Krolthy was worried about

whether Singer knew what he was doing, as he had implied in the car, here was proof, if proof were needed, that Singer knew exactly what he was up to. He had, in fact, killed at least three birds with one stone: informed the plebs of what they already knew and, with little or no risk, moved ahead of the fast-spreading speculation and rumour, thereby considerably reducing, if not eliminating, the damage done by the 'hooligans' and giving the crowd the impression that he was aware of their disillusionment—nay, grief!—at the unexpected loss of the World Soccer Championship, and, indeed, shared their distress. And finally, he had warned them in terms they could easily understand that no further outbreak would be tolerated. Singer, Singer, that blasted crook, that vile genius!

'Are you going to have breakfast now, General Wulf, or when you come back?' a sweet voice asked behind him. Immediately General Wulf knew whom it belonged to. Dressed in a cotton blouse and a modest, dark-blue skirt, with a white frontlet on her blonde head, Krolthy's hussy stood at the door, her eyes downcast in humble obedience and innocence. The resemblance to the Countess Julia's portrait above the fireplace was astonishing.

'No,' General Wulf said. 'Later.' But when he saw the girl prepare to leave, he added hurriedly, 'Wait. Give me a cup of coffee. And a schnapps, too.'

'We have some apricot-brandy, General Wulf, if you'd like that. We also have cherry, peach, walnut and, of course, plum. All home-made by Aunt Elsie from the best fruit.'

'A slivovitz. Get me a slivovitz,' General Wulf said. 'What's your name?'

'Esmaralda,' the girl replied.

'Esmaralda?' With a short laugh and one quick gulp General Wulf downed the slivovitz. 'Esmaralda? You couldn't be a gypsy, could you? Not with that hair of yours. Or skin.'

'Half-and-half,' the girl said, looking into General Wulf's eyes. 'My mother was.'

'And who was your father?'

'I don't know,' Esmaralda said, pouring a second slivovitz into General Wulf's green liqueur-glass. 'I've never met him, but my mother tells me he was a great man, and I believe her. She never lies to me. Never. Another slivovitz?'

'Why not?' General Wulf nodded, amiably. 'Always look for number *three*. Incidentally, you haven't seen Simon Wald around here by any chance, have you?'

'No, sir,' Esmaralda said. 'I haven't.'

At a brisk, steady pace that made him feel warmer and peppier, his Winchester dangling from his left shoulder, General Wulf passed the tennis courts, the arboretum, the ruins of the old redoubt, the vineyards. The sun was rising fast. At the base of Crazy Hill he reached the fork where one path would take him to Krestur, while the other, he was suddenly certain, would lead straight to the pond and tree, the existence of which Simon Wald had so arrogantly denied yesterday.

A light, almost too sweet fragrance in the air mingled deliciously with the acrid tang of the autumnal forest. Once or twice General Wulf stopped to take a deep breath. It was strange how quickly his anger against Simon Wald evaporated here. The path grew narrower, until, rounding a bend by a cutting, Crazy Hill appeared beyond the susurrating cables of the huge, concrete pylons that carried light to distant villages where for thousands of years only darkness had ruled. He felt proud for, as history was his witness, he had had his share in the glory of their illumination.

From where he stood General Wulf had a superb view of Crazy Hill. It was now quite hot and he was sweating profusely, so he took off his jacket and wiped his face with his forearm. Suddenly, he saw something move on the top of the hill. When he looked again he made out a tall woman all in black, standing, legs akimbo, on the edge of the rock, her long hair, long skirt, long black scarf fluttering in the warm breeze, her arms raised as if in prayer. She looked like Anna Wald, a towering figure silhouetted against the blue skies and distant hills. But what was she doing up there? Had she come in place of her husband? Was she following him through the woods? Haunting him, in the middle of a bright, sunny morning? From the moment he'd first seen her in the church, Anna Wald's serenity and beauty had attracted him, yet General Wulf was irritated by something, something present even when they came to express their sympathy in the nursery where the baby lay dead. Now General Wulf understood it was an unspoken hostility: that disdainful silence, that cold contempt at the corners of her fine mouth, that indifferent glare in her beautiful steel-grey eyes, which looked through him and Krolthy. General Wulf was startled by the realization. Had he offended her in church? Had he intruded at a moment when she wanted to be left alone with her dead child, just as Inge wanted to be left alone when, in Moscow, their three-month-old son had died of dysentery only a few weeks before General Wulf left for Spain? Not only was he annoyed by Anna Wald's spite, but also, most strangely, apprehensive. Almost alarmed. Maybe he should ask her the reason for her hostility and suggest she come with him to the pond?

He stepped out from under the big oak whose thick branches shielded him from the glare of the sun, turned towards the top of Crazy Hill, but Anna Wald, or whoever had stood there a minute ago, was no longer there.

The pond and tree were there, exactly as he remembered them, but in the water he saw not Copass's and Singer's cunning, vitriolic faces, but Professor Weiskopf's perceptive eyes looking back at him from under the duckweed and algae. General Wulf sat down on the wooden bench near the edge of the water.

'So one day,' he said, 'one warm, sunny day in April, Professor Weiskopf, my father came home from the bank to have his quick lunch and brief nap in our large bedroom on Acacia Street, before going back to his fortress of capitalist enterprise a block down the street. After almost twenty-five years of loyal service, he had risen to the high rank of assistant branch-manager in the bank. Between his favourite cream-of-cauliflower soup and chicken fricassée, he wanted an important word with me. At once, I knew I had reason to be apprehensive.

'My father explained that he and his brothers and brothers-in-law had arrived at a most important decision concerning the twenty-fifth wedding anniversary of our *beloved* Tante Goldie and Uncle Anthony, their oldest brother, and the undisputed leader of the Wulf-pack. At the forthcoming celebration, which was to be a splendid affair, it had been decided, my father said serenely, that on behalf of the children of the family I was to present the gift to Tante Goldie. All I had to do was to say a few words about Tante Goldie's love and care of children (she had lost her own child, little Georgia, many years ago in a flu epidemic), then give her the gift and kiss her hand, both as a show of respect and as a token of our love for her. I felt my face redden, my body stiffen, as a cold wave of rage rose from the depth of my belly. It would have been acceptable for me, at the age of fourteen, to reduce myself to an obedient marionette, to walk up to Tante Goldie's throne, recite a short verse, hug her, give her a peck on her slightly rouged cheeks, even to bow my head, in deference to her status as queen of the family, wife of the new *Hofrat*, perhaps soon-to-be *Baron* Anthony von Wulf. But kiss her hand? Lord, Professor Weiskopf, kiss her hand?

'Five weeks later, in Tante Goldie's magnificent dining-room, my uncles, aunts and cousins were sitting around the long table, waiting for me to step forward to do what I had promised to do.

'As I looked around and saw Tante Goldie and Uncle Anthony smile, the rest of the family smiling with a kind of reverence and envy mixed with *schadenfreude*—if I didn't deserve the honour, I surely deserved the humiliation!—I froze. Nobody had ever asked me, or any of us children, to kiss the hands of our other aunts, though they were just as loyal, hard-working and family-loving as Tante Goldie, even if they had less money, travelled only to the Western Lake or the Northern Mountains for summer holidays, never met famous celebrities at the opera or bigwigs at government receptions or royal balls. Why, I had asked myself several times over the last few days, were they never the subjects of special ceremonies of adoration? I stood there, motionless, waiting for an answer. Sweat trickled down my back, my chest, and my forehead was hot as a stove: I knew I had to make up my mind. I hoped for some miracle that would lift me up and spirit me away from this place, but it didn't come. I was still standing there, immobile, my whole family looking at me, somewhat uneasily. Suddenly I understood that I had to break out of there at once, I had to breathe fresh air, I had to be free. I turned, put the little present in the hand of my flabbergasted cousin behind me, and ran out of the room.

'Well, Professor Weiskopf, after the war, after twenty-five years in the wilderness of exile, when I returned home I visited the old villa on Lilac Hill as soon as I could. I knew, of course, that Tante Goldie, Uncle Anthony, and all my other aunts and uncles and cousins were dead, but I didn't know that the villa, too, was dead, bombed out and burned down during the siege of the city. It was a fine, sunny day in April, and I stood there among the charred ruins, under the yellow shower of forsythia, the sole survivor of history. Suddenly, the old puzzle occurred to me, the ancient riddle: *What would have happened if...?* What if I had obeyed my father? What if I had accepted the traditions and laws of my family? What if I had kissed Tante Goldie's hand?'

'Do you mean to tell me,' Professor Weiskopf said, 'that you wish you had?'

Slowly, in the cool, westerly breeze that had risen from behind Crazy Hill, General Wulf, his Winchester on his shoulder, walked towards the woods, Simon Wald, his Browning in his hand, following one step behind.

'And what happened to the coat?' General Wulf asked. 'That brand-new army greatcoat?'

'I don't know,' Simon Wald said. 'Uncle Matthias died before we got to the hospital, Corporal Hunor drove the truck to Special Security Forces Headquarters, and I can't...' His tired, gaunt face paler than before, Simon

Wald whispered, 'God Almighty! It was *your* coat, wasn't it?'

'How do you know that?' General Wulf said.

'You were the only colonel-general in the army,' Simon Wald said.

'Yes,' General Wulf nodded. 'It *was* my coat. I *am* the only colonel-general in the army.'

'And you're the one who shot my stag, too.'

'One of my lucky days,' General Wulf replied. 'So, tell me, where did they take you from there?'

'First to the city,' Simon Wald said, very softly. 'Then, later, up north. To the mountains.'

'Krechk?'

'Yes,' Simon Wald said. 'Have you ever been there?'

'No,' General Wulf said. 'Did you know Professor Weiskopf?'

'Kopf?' Simon Wald said. 'Kopf? Oh, yes, of course. Did you?'

'Yes,' General Wulf said. 'Not personally, though. I've read some of his stuff. What exactly happened to him?'

'He was killed by Strappado's gangsters,' Simon Wald said. 'Somebody must have spilled the beans. We were preparing to break out and take the camp commander— Kopf had christened him Strappado—hostage. But they knew the day, the hour, the plan, everything. Between Strappado's Pleasure Palace and the latrines they were waiting for us with machine guns. Kopf got caught in the crossfire.'

'I'll send you a copy of his last essay,' General Wulf said. 'A most beautiful piece. It's all about the manor and its evolution over the centuries.'

'I'd appreciate that,' Simon Wald said. 'I've always been interested in the manor. It's my livelihood.'

'I'm a bit of a history buff myself,' General Wulf said. 'The riddle of history and all that.'

They reached the edge of the forest.

'Kopf always told us that history was the sum total of human treachery,' Simon Wald said.

'Not to forget its celestial variety,' General Wulf said, 'as Monsignor Beck would willingly testify.' He stopped, looking for the narrow path that would lead them to his little pond and big tree, but he couldn't see it anywhere.

SEVEN

JUSTICE Krolthy sat at the head of the table, facing General Wulf in his dark-grey suit, Monsignor Beck in his black attire, with only a flash of Roman collar to remind the pious and the impious of his affiliation, and, above the pale-green marble fireplace, the Countess Julia, in her finest French cambric and Belgian lace.

'I am truly delighted that you both accepted my invitation to have dinner with Count Francis and his family,' he said. 'They are celebrating the marriage of their daughter, Anna Julia, to Erzherzog Karlhorst Adalbert Wilhelm, Ritter von Fressachgern, a rather corpulent young man and also the heir-apparent to the throne of Oberenzien-Bergengotz, a small principality somewhere between Prussia and Bavaria. Tonight, with the gracious assistance of our little Julie and Miss Sybil, we shall, in parts at least, recreate the feast of that espousal. What a feast it was! However, I must with sincere regret tell you that, owing to the brief time available to us, we shall only be able to serve a few items from the rich bill of fare that our Count Francis offered his guests at the wedding. No sliced boar with morel tidbits today, no plover eggs in aspic, alas, no tenderloin of roebuck in plum sauce, no braised wild goose with dumplings. Still, we might, if all goes well, have some roasted pheasant, smothered venison, braised quail, and, to begin with, the most delicious fisherman's broth you've ever tasted on this dark earth. That's all, I'm afraid. Can you ever forgive me?' His frozen smile turning

roguishly charming, Justice Krolthy poured some more
Furmint into General Wulf's glass, already half-empty.

'But first,' Justice Krolthy continued, 'before we taste
the dishes that distinguished company of friends and
relatives tasted on that joyful evening in late July 1789, you
may like to take a look at this.' Justice Krolthy picked up
a slim volume bound in gilt-edged calf's leather, and
showed it to General Wulf and Monsignor Beck. 'This is
The Book of Cooks, a marvellous essay of humour and
insight for those of us who interpret history not only as the
sum total of bloody wars and solemn statements about
bloody wars, but also as a compendium of witty dis-
courses about bloody beefsteaks, an honourable compromise between the feats of heroes and the feasts of hedon-
ists. In Count Francis's own old-Gothic hand, *The Book of
Cooks* reveals that formidable man in yet another of his
guises, as a *chef-de-cuisine*. The stern and taciturn alchemist is here transformed into a gregarious master of the
kitchen, who gives us an unparalleled treatise on the
organization and uses of a *fête champêtre* in the closing
years of the eighteenth century, only a few days after the
fall of the Bastille.'

'Cut it short, Adam,' General Wulf said, his voice
vibrant with impatience and asperity. 'We didn't come
here to listen to your crapulent stories. Just get down to
brass tacks. What's the reason we've been dragged here
and kept in such subtle solitary confinement we can't even
use the telephone? That's what we should be talking
about, not some old scoundrel's garden party two
hundred years ago. Well, Adam, what do you know about
that?'

'My dear Henryk,' Justice Krolthy said, his smile wid-
ening, 'I'm glad you now see the point I was trying to make

yesterday, but you mustn't harbour any suspicions about my inviting you both for dinner. After all, you suggested it, remember?' Justice Krolthy lit his cigar. 'Much as I'm interested in Count Francis's fancy garden party, I'm no party to Gerogen's schemes. I have no idea why he brought us together, although I'm reasonably certain the soccer riots must have forced him to rearrange his schedule, because otherwise he would have been here by now. Ah, Henryk, you know our Gerogen better and longer than we do: was there ever a moment in his life which wasn't determined by some plan, some purpose? Has he ever done anything simply because he felt like it? Did he ever play hide-and-seek? Blackjack? Stand in front of Rembrandt's *Saskia,* in the Hermitage in Leningrad, admiring its beauty without contemplating the rise of the bourgeoisie and its relationship to modern art? But I agree, let's concentrate on the business at hand. General Wulf is absolutely correct when he urges us to discuss Gerogen's intentions, if that's possible without penetrating that insidious mind of his.'

Still smiling, Justice Krolthy looked around. In the smoky flare of the candles and the glow of the small fire in the fireplace, General Wulf's face looked surprisingly puffy. Poor Henryk was ill. On the other hand, Anselm looked healthier than ever, defiant and convincing as only anchorites, for whom the impermanence of flesh is a mere inconvenience, could be.

'Therefore,' Justice Krolthy continued, 'I will not bore you with those magnificent recipes, nor will I tell you about Count Francis's astonishing confession concerning the conspiracy he led to depose the emperor and become king himself, though I can hardly resist the temptation to quote Francis—with whom I have always felt a kinship difficult to explain—as he teaches us how to organize a plot or to prepare the most divine fisherman's broth, a nectar of the gods, or, if Father Anselm wishes, of God. Unless, of course, He preferred fried chicken with cucumber salad on the dusty roads of Judea.'

'You're right, Adam, even if you don't know it,' Monsignor Beck said, a glass of transparent Furmint in his bony hand. 'Our Lord would no doubt have enjoyed Count Francis's broth, because while He appeared on earth, He was fond of eating and drinking in the company of His friends, and as delighted by a good meal as any man, for He *was* man. But the question is, would He have enjoyed the company of your spiritual brother?'

'Shut up, Anselm,' General Wulf whispered, and Justice Krolthy saw him glance towards Julie and Miss Sybil standing in the door with the steaming tureen of fish-broth on the trolley. 'Don't start that again. I warn you. And for once, couldn't you resist your goddamn sense of irony, Adam, and stop provoking him? I've had enough astrology, theology, history, gastronomy for one day. I can't believe you two are so stupid as to get involved in this nonsense about God's preference for fish or fowl when we might be in great trouble. Idiots!'

'As usual,' Justice Krolthy said, 'our Henryk is correct. With one blow of his famous directness and argumentative power, he has cut the Gordian knot. Thank you, Henryk. And *prosit!*'

'As for Gerogen's motives for inviting the three of us down here,' Monsignor Beck said, pensively, 'I can only offer a pedestrian explanation, gentlemen, which, I'm sure, you all know already. He needs us to do something that he could, perhaps, do without us, but that he could do a great deal better *with us*. I regret that I can't be more original. But I have a feeling that because he needs us more than he usually does, this time there's more to our sudden invitation than meets the eye.'

'Monsignor put his finger on a most sensitive point.' Justice Krolthy sipped his wine. 'We've been summoned here for whatever role we're to play in Gerogen's scheme—nothing novel in that. Yet, if Anselm smells a peculiar odour in the air, it's because it's there. I'm willing to stake my reputation as an experienced Gerogen-watcher, that we've been summoned not only to *help* him, but also to help him *out* in a situation that has become rather . . . ticklish? Difficult? Nasty? Perhaps even dangerous? So, while we are certainly in a fix, we have an unhoped-for and quite unique advantage: he, too, must be in some kind of a jam. Otherwise, he would have asked us, through dear Bellona, to come to his office, and given us our marching orders. Instead, he went to all this trouble to set up a meeting here, in seclusion—more like a retreat than a reunion, don't you think, Anselm? He has decided to travel to a place he doesn't particularly like, and to expose himself to questions he likes even less. Funny, isn't it? We may have an advantage we can't afford to let slip, and he cannot disregard. In an odd sense, we're on equal footing now: he needs *us*, but this time we may *not* need *him*. So, if this is a trap for us, why don't we rig it up for him?'

Little Julie and Miss Sybil pushed the trolley in with the second course, which, it seemed to Monsignor Beck in the candlelight, was braised quail. Moving noiselessly, they expertly changed the plates, silver, glasses and served up the birds, ringed with fragrant wreaths of fresh carrots, French beans, lettuce-leaves, huge red radishes.

'Get those wenches out of here, Krolthy,' General Wulf muttered under his breath. 'I can't discuss important

business with them looking into my mouth. Tell them to
get back to the kitchen and come only when called.'

'Yes, General.' Straight-faced, Justice Krolthy stood
and saluted. 'At your command, General.'

Monsignor Beck watched the women obey, without a
word, swiftly, indeed with a sigh of relief.

'If you think Gerogen will suddenly materialize before
you, surrounded by roly-poly angels of peace and harmony,' General Wulf said testily, after the echo of the
women's light footsteps had died, 'asking humbly for
your help in his hour of trial, or even bargaining with you
because of some imaginary pickle he's supposed to be in,
you don't know a thing about Gerogen.

'First, I'm sure his "troubles", which we can allegedly
take advantage of, exist more in Krolthy's inventive mind
than in the labyrinth of objective reality. We have no
concrete evidence of trouble. I don't mean that he has no
troubles at all, but that none of those constitute a threat to
his control. On the contrary. Ever since Copass departed,
things have been looking up for Gerogen. That a few poets
of meagre talent declared themselves to be the sole stan-
dard-bearers of truth and justice against the historical
truth and justice of the Alliance (whose praises, by the
way, they've been singing wholeheartedly for years, with
considerable financial help from the coffers of that self-
same Alliance), or that a few disappointed soccer maniacs
have gone on the rampage, proves little or nothing at all.
Besides, whether you like it or not, Gerogen handled both
the unruly poets and the rioting fans with consummate
skill. Our versifiers have been kicked out of their sine-
cures, so now they will have to work for their upkeep, like
the rest of us, instead of accepting money from us, then
with squeamish moral disgust on their angelic faces, scrib-

bling their couplets against us. Meanwhile, those crackpots on the streets have been swiftly herded home by our
police, and told in no uncertain terms—you must have
seen it in the paper—that no fresh outburst of soccer-
sorrow would be tolerated.

'Second,' General Wulf continued, 'I'm willing to bet
that, by tomorrow, nay, by tonight, poor old Berg's head—
not much of a head, anyhow, as Adam would probably be
willing to testify—will be placed ceremoniously on the
sacrificial altar of the Soccer God, and a new, energetic
head of the Sports Bureau named—perhaps that gifted
young rogue, Vukovič, from Gerogen's invidious little
group of apprentice taskmasters. That would take care of
the crackpots, wouldn't it? That was what they demanded
on the streets, wasn't it? Won't Gerogen again emerge as
the hero of the people, his popularity higher than it has
ever been since he rebuilt the bridges and put the trains
back on the track? And why not? He may not have been
able to give enough bread to the crackpots, but at least he
gave them lots of circuses. Hail Caesar! Hail Gerogen!
Defender of honour! Preserver of the soccer field!

'So, why should *he* be in trouble? We are in trouble, and
when he comes, he'll tell us, believe me, what *grave* trouble
we are in! Trapping him, Adam? Don't be ridiculous.
Gerogen's still the one who's calling the shots, and all you
can do is to duck, so that his bullets won't hit you.
Trapping him, indeed! Unless we can find out exactly
what he's up to, we can't do a thing. *We* are trapped. And
if you think you can outwit him today, when you haven't
been able to outwit him for years, Adam, you're really
worse than the guilty: you're an innocent! Bah!'

'Bravo.' Justice Krolthy laughed loudly and applauded. 'Bravo, Henryk! A most convincing perfor-

mance. You really *do* know your Gerogen. Either we
deduce what he wants from us, or we say goodbye for ever
to our braised quail. How true! But that's precisely what
I'm saying. Gerogen is no God—not yet, anyhow—but
he's almost as predictable: we know we shall be punished,
but we don't know *when* and *how* and *for what.*'

'Bullshit!' General Wulf shouted. 'Speculations! Sup-
positions! Is that all you can do? If you have *one* concrete
idea why Gerogen's brought us here, start talking.'

'I haven't the foggiest, Henryk.' Justice Krolthy
grinned and raised his hands, palms upwards, as though
capitulating before an overpowering force. 'But I know
that our Gerogen has a very legalistic mind.' Justice
Krolthy turned away from Monsignor Beck's glance, as if
he understood its meaning, but didn't want to face it. 'An
Orthodox mind, really. Strange—for a professional anarchist, I mean—but true. Everything Gerogen is doing and
has ever done must be *within* the framework of the law,
must be *sanctified* by law. Don't ask me the reasons. It is
probably because he is from the people of the Law. Or
perhaps because he thinks of himself as *being* the law. If
there were no law, he would, I assure you, invent one,
because for some compelling reason he must always stay
under the protective umbrella of legal justification. Have
you fellows been taught that way? *Always preserve a sem-
blance of legality:* one of the main commandments the *Vozhd*
handed down from his beloved Caucasian mountaintop.
One wonders. State Security could, without excuse or
apology, have shot the *kulak* right on the spot in his stable,
among those melancholy cows, but *no*, first they had to
find the automatic in the hayloft where they'd hidden it
the previous night. *Then* they could shoot him without
pangs of conscience. After all, the scoundrel had been

caught red-handed committing a crime punishable by death, and the law is the law.

'What is legal must, of necessity, be moral. Paradoxically, what is moral may not inevitably be legal, though it is always advisable to endow it with the hieratic symbolism of the law. I've been pondering this for years. Don't we have the handiest, most convenient system in all the world? At the wink of an eye, legality can be made moral and morality made legal: what an unsurpassable achievement! There's never been a regime so profoundly illegitimate and immoral which paid so much lip service to its legitimacy and morality.

'So, the answer to the question "Why are we here?" may lie in Gerogen's plans to legalize his next illegal move. It might, therefore, be interesting to analyse his schedule, say, for the next couple of weeks. Despite General Wulf's eloquent protestations, I maintain that Gerogen *is* in some kind of a jam. And, who knows, if we can pinpoint his moves, we might be able to chance upon his design. And trap him, *secundum legem*, as the saying goes. According to the law.'

'*Secundum veritatem*,' Monsignor Beck said. He picked up another sliver of radish from his plate, though he didn't touch the quail. 'According to the truth.'

'Oh, yes, of course,' Justice Krolthy replied, slowly nibbling at his quail. 'But to paraphrase the late and un-lamented Pilate who got into our *Credo* as innocently and inadvertently as the day before yesterday we entered here the gates of hell, what exactly *is* truth?'

In Justice Krolthy's bed, Julia's body was cool and smooth, stirring and sighing happily in her deep sleep, unaware of Justice Krolthy as he slipped under the blanket and quietly moved closer, trying not to wake her. Though he was famous among friends and enemies for anticipating and correctly predicting the reaction of women in certain situations, Justice Krolthy was astonished by her presence.

'Don't go away,' Julia whispered in her sleep, turning towards Justice Krolthy, 'don't leave me now.' Her body was pliant and soft, but strangely, Justice Krolthy felt only tenderness: no surge of desire, no shock of lust, only a quiet, limp contentment which, even more strangely, he didn't mind at all. With growing affection that was, incredibly, closer to repletion than to desire, he touched Julia again, her soft skin and soft hair, firm breasts, then, slowly, his hand moved towards her warm face, and, kissing her eyes, he whispered, 'I won't, my dear Julia, I won't.'

The apartment on the sixth floor with its spacious rooms and huge balcony overlooking the river and the Avar hills was truly magnificent. Justice Krolthy remembered clearly the moment when he opened the door, with Eve and McIlvey, her most recent conquest, behind him. He saw the apartment revealed in its dusty, cobwebby emptiness in the pale January sunshine, like a cunning woman whose unexpected nudity suggests more astonishing surprises. When McIlvey, a consular officer at the American Section of the Allied Military Control Commission, first mentioned something about an empty apartment on the sixth floor—the offices of the American Section occupied the first and second floors of the building—Judge Krolthy had thought it might make sense to take a look.

In the summer of 1944, after his old town-house on Castle Hill was bombed, Adam Krolthy decided to end his short-lived military career as a judge-advocate attached to

General Gylkosh's Fifth Army Corps (or to what little there was left of it by the time the warm, sunny autumn descended on the burnt-out plains and bombed cities). General Gylkosh, the most bloodthirsty Fascist major Krolthy had ever met, wanted him to sentence to death and hang everybody, Jew and Gentile, whom he perceived to stand in the way of his prophetic mission to create a nation of angelic docility and heavenly harmony under his generous, protective leadership. And so Major Krolthy walked down to General Gylkosh's dungeons and ordered the prisoners, Jews and Gentiles, out of their cells. Then, stiffly saluting the guards who knew him well, he led his little platoon of *moribundi* out of the prison in strict military formation, let them go, then watched until they disappeared into the crowd.

For a while, until the next air-raid siren sounded, Judge Krolthy contemplated the waves of humankind washing the shores of the world, then he swam with them in search of shelter. For the first and fortunately the last time in his life, he was one of the crowd, inconspicuous, invisible. Like other people, he had to scrounge for food and a place to live. Luckily, there was Eve in her latest role as right-hand to Jarek, leader of the Resistance, and it didn't take long for her to find Adam a modest room with a tiny bath on the western slopes of the Avar hills, far from the madding crowd (as she once said with angry sarcasm, when Adam flatly refused to do even the smallest favour for Jarek's Resistance groups).

Ever since he moved there, Adam Krolthy had been looking for a place of his own. Now, standing in the small, dimly lit hall of that apartment, he knew he had found what he wanted. He walked through the emptiness and light of the apartment, *his* apartment, while Eve and

McIlvey, sensing the inviolability of his private delight, remained at the door. He was glad it was empty, because it would have been unthinkable to live among other people's furniture, rugs, memories, odours. He wanted to furnish it his own way, or, rather, in the way the singular design of the apartment demanded. He thought of asking his new secretary, a young redhead who seemed to know all the ropes, to acquire the furniture he needed through the Bureau of Ownerless Properties. Set up after the war to deal with lost, abandoned or unclaimed belongings and paraphernalia, which were stored in huge warehouses, the Bureau used them to reward cronies for past deeds or to bribe them for future favours. But, Judge Krolthy realized, that, too, would involve him with other people's shadows, so he decided against it. In any case, he could get everything from Krolthy House. Since his father's death there were unused rooms full of old furniture, the stuff of his own ghosts and memories. All he had to do was ask Eve to open the rooms. After she broke up with Jarek, or, rather, Jarek ditched her with such callous indifference that two years *post factum* it still made Krolthy's face turn red, she had locked herself away in the house, and so she had the keys to everything.

Eve, still standing in the hall of the apartment, asked, 'Well, what do you think, Adam?' as if she didn't know. Then, slowly, affectionately, as she'd never done while she was Jarek's woman, she kissed him on the cheek, both cheeks. Two weeks later, Judge Krolthy moved in.

When he woke up in the morning, Julia was gone. It was half past nine. Justice Krolthy had a quick breakfast in the green room, served by a young, buxom maid, who disappeared before he could ask for more coffee. Slightly irritated, he went to the library to continue to study the notebooks. They lay there on Count Francis's desk, apparently untouched, *The Book of Apollyon, The Book of Brethren.* He picked up the third one, and to his great delight, saw it was entitled *The Book of Cooks.*

'Pinpoint his moves?' General Wulf said, with feigned incredulity. 'Pinpoint Gerogen's moves? A most intriguing idea! But may I ask just how you propose to do it, Adam? I mean, between now and eight o'clock in the morning, given that we can't even use the phone here? Could you possibly give us an idea of what you have in mind?'

'Yes,' Justice Krolthy said. 'I've been thinking about it all evening.' He stood up briskly and turned on the radio to frustrate the Archangel Gabriel's bugs from recording his secrets. Justice Krolthy had learned the trick from Gerogen, an old Chekist, who had learned everything he needed to survive in Moscow, that bizarre city of casual slaughters. Under ordinary circumstances, he would not have been bothered by the Archangel Gabriel's bad-quality tape-recordings of his love-life or of his savage political jokes. The Archangel was used to his humour; everybody was used to his humour—Gerogen, Adymester, Wulf, even Copass, before he was spirited away to his new cold home beyond the Urals. But now, he didn't want the Archangel and his gangsters to know that, suddenly, he felt apprehensive. Uneasy. Maybe it was just another misreading of the signs, but the more he pondered it, the less he liked the situation. He lit a cigar.

In the dim reflections of the candles, Wulf and Beck looked dispirited, old, as no doubt he too did. Of course Gerogen knew what he was doing! He was deliberately delaying his entrance on the stage, as he would have done, Justice Krolthy realized, even without the accident of the riots, so that his mummers would grow more jittery. Justice Krolthy was familiar with Gerogen's tactics—the tactics of every investigator and torturer since time immemorial—and he couldn't have cared less, had it not been for a growing sense of being the target of Gerogen's hackneyed exercise in intimidation. Were *they* under attack? Was *he* under attack? Suddenly, the image of the funeral whose description he'd overheard yesterday—'red flag for the coffin, black drapes for the dais'—surfaced in his mind. He sensed that, in some complex and intricate way, their being trapped down here was inseparably linked with that funeral. The only way to establish why Gerogen had decided to bring them here was to find out everything one could about that funeral. With a lucidity he hadn't experienced since his Sorbonne days, he perceived the truth—Pilate's goddamn truth—about his compact with Gerogen. Sealed on one magnificent summer night under a waxing moon on the balcony of his apartment only by a quick, cold, unfriendly handshake, that pact had kept him alive through those long, dangerous, volatile years, upheld by both sides through thick and thin with an almost chivalrous scrupulousness. Now, he realized, even if he could determine Gerogen's ultimate goal, their compact had at long last been violated.

'We're listening, Adam.' Loud, impatient, hostile, General Wulf's voice assailed him. 'Get on with it.'

'Look,' Justice Krolthy said. 'The only way to get a fix on Gerogen's plans is to get to a telephone. I can then call somebody who might be willing to give us the information we need. Of course he might refuse, but I think I can handle him. We must get to Sentelek, where, one hopes, the phones are still working in both directions. In order to get to Sentelek, we need two things: a car and an excuse. The car is Simon Wald's jeep. Anselm, would you go to the kitchen and ask Sybil to get Simon here with his jeep at once, because General Wulf seems to be having a heart attack? That's the excuse. I'm sorry, Henryk, there's no other way. You have chest pains. Heartburn. Your left arm is getting tingly. But you know the symptoms. Maybe it's only an upset stomach, the after-effect of our fisherman's broth, maybe it's nothing at all, but since General Wulf has already had a heart seizure, this is definitely not the time for guessing games. Since there's no resident doctor in Krestur, we insist that the general be taken to Sentelek hospital. I don't think we'll be stopped. If there's a Special Detachment around here, I haven't seen them yet, and even if they're hiding somewhere, they've probably been ordered to sit on their asses, for the time being, at any rate. Besides, Wald's jeep is a fixture around here, nobody would suspect a trick. That is one of the reasons I'd be reluctant to use the Skoda: much too conspicuous. Once we're in the hospital, and General Wulf is taken down for X-rays, I'll call my man. It should be past midnight, and, as you know, surveillance has generally slackened by then. If all goes well, we won't even be monitored, let alone taped. By the time they finish examining Henryk . . .'

'And how do you think you will be able to get to a phone?' General Wulf interrupted. Justice Krolthy noted with satisfaction that his voice had become softer, his hostility less sharp.

'Come now, Henryk,' Justice Krolthy said with a short laugh. 'I'm *still* the president of the Supreme Judicial Council.' He saw General Wulf's face become paprika-red, but for the moment, General Wulf's vanities were not his main concern. He had decided to call Pater Kral at his apartment after midnight, when Kral was likely to be at home and in bed, if not alone: for a deconsecrated priest, he had a pretty wild sex-life. Of Gerogen's bastards, he was the only one who'd know what Justice Krolthy was after, and, for a price, he should be willing to sell. Justice Krolthy knew Pater Kral's heart's desire. Ever since Justice Krolthy had brought it from Paris some years ago, the malevolent, dancing dwarf in its plain frame had been the object of Pater Kral's envy. He was determined, he swore, to possess it by hook or by crook, to add to his fast-expanding collection of erotica. And, indeed, one could understand Pater Kral's excitement. It was an original Picasso, given to him by the master himself, drawn quickly, casually, but, oh, with what absolute yet effortless control over idea and matter! Justice Krolthy knew he would be giving away a small fortune, but it was worth it: if he could buy his life and freedom with that damned Picasso-prick, well . . . Picasso be damned! Justice Krolthy needed to know whose funeral Gerogen was getting ready for, because it might be his own.

'Agreed?' Justice Krolthy said.

They both nodded.

'Very well, then,' Justice Krolthy said. 'Let's do it. It's now five past eleven. Anselm, please ask Sybil to send for her brother. He must be home by now, unless he's wandered away again. Simon Wald's acting rather strangely these days. Confused. Babbles a lot, too, for such a taciturn man. Maybe, it's because of his daughter's death. Have you noticed how he looked when we went to pay our condolences?' Slowly, Justice Krolthy put out the butt of his cigar on the edge of a lovely Gerend porcelain ashtray—a rarity, because Gerogen's unhinged planners had forced the factory to close down and sent all those master-potters, chisellers and pointillists to work in the potato-fields. He poured some more Furmint for himself. 'I hope Sybil can find him. He could be here in thirty *usque* thirty-five minutes. We could be in Sentelek by midnight. Just in time. And, yes, of course, Henryk, you too get ready.'

The rectory door was ajar in the warm sunshine. Monsi-gnor Beck entered cautiously, as if expecting somebody to stop him, but the room, small, freshly whitewashed, its green shutters open, was empty. Curious but slightly embarrassed, Monsignor Beck looked around. Both in his private and official capacity, as a priest and as a first deputy secretary, he certainly had the right to visit, but he came unannounced and uninvited and that made him feel uneasy. His stomach, stuffed and crampy from Aunt Elsie's heavy breakfast, had been bothering him, so he had decided to have a word with Father Novak before Sybil took him back to the manor.

Opposite the door, in the corner, was a low, round mahogany table with a white marble top and a brass rim and two old, high-backed chairs with cane seats, the Széchy-coronet in the centre of their rough-hewn frames. Here Monsignor Beck chose to sit and wait for Father Novak, who must be around somewhere, because Monsi-gnor Beck watched his arrival from the window of The Waldhorn.

'Good morning, Monsignor,' a raspy voice said behind his back. 'Welcome to the rectory. I am Papa Krauss. Thank you for a beautiful service yesterday. Father Novak's been called to the town hall. He'll be back in a jiffy.'

Monsignor Beck turned to see a small, elderly man with

a long, black beard and a threadbare black skullcap covering thinning grey that reminded Monsignor Beck of a tonsure. He remembered how, as a young monk, he had had to wear that vestige of the Middle Ages, and how difficult it had been to keep it round and well shaven.

'Papa Krauss,' Monsignor Beck said, startled. 'Thank you. Did you go to the Mass yesterday?'

'I often go to Mass, Monsignor,' Papa Krauss said pleasantly. He was carrying a small tray with a pitcher and two glasses, which he put down on the table. 'There's no synagogue in Krestur, and the one in Sentelek has been closed. No more Jews, I'm afraid. I like to pray, though I'm no longer a Jew. Neither am I a Christian. I'm only God's witness. A simple onlooker, really. So I go to Father Novak's service, as I went to Father Leo's, though, frankly, he wasn't very happy about that, the old anti-Semite. And maybe he was right. It's a rather unorthodox thing for a Jew, I admit. I'm sure my father and my grandfather would disapprove violently. But they're dead, whereas I'm alive, and I no longer need them to tell me what to do or how to do it. I'm an old man. Why shouldn't I go? Same God, different prayer.'

He poured water in one of the glasses and offered it to Monsignor Beck. 'Have some, Monsignor. Good for the digestion. I'm an old friend of the Walds. Also, young Peter's honorary godfather. So sorry that their little Anna Julia had to die. They're such very nice people.'

'You live here in Krestur, Papa Krauss?' Monsignor Beck asked, sipping the water from the miraculous well.

'Yes, I do, Monsignor,' Papa Krauss said. In the growing heat the pungent smell of manure from the barns wafted through the window. 'As a matter of fact, I was born here. So was my father, Jacob, my grandfather, Isaac, and my great-grandfather, Lazarus. Cardinal Petrus invited Lazarus to move down here from Gesterom to set up a grocery and provision shop, because the cardinal felt the village needed such a thing. And so they came, Lazarus and his family. Legend has it that they were good friends, the cardinal and Great-grandfather Lazarus; they played cards, even went hunting together, for the cardinal was a good hunter and a fierce falconer. One hopes it's true. However, we do have the original document signed by the cardinal, naming Lazarus Krauss as the only merchant of dry-goods and groceries permitted to open his shop in the village of Krestur.

'My grandfather, Isaac, fought beside General Széchy in the War of Independence. He was captured at Vareges and sentenced to fifteen years in Hufstein Prison for sedition, but when the general amnesty was proclaimed by Governor Radak in 1862, he was freed and came home to lead the quiet life of a family man and a shopkeeper. I can still remember how, once in a while, he would gather his grandchildren around him and tell us tall stories about a certain Lieutenant K., but most of the time he would be silent and prayerful, like a true Orthodox Jew preparing for his death.

'And so it happened, Monsignor. *Document yest?* as the Russkies would ask everybody when they first invaded the village in the winter of '44. "Let's see your papers." Yes, we have plenty of papers: thanks to the Walds who, after we'd been ordered to march by the Germans that summer, kept everything hidden—parchments, birth-certificates, books, letters, contracts, deeds, old bills, even, not to mention Great-grandfather Lazarus's *tallith*, Isaac's sword and my father's skullcap, the one I'm wearing now. Everything else got lost during the last months of the

war—our house was looted first by SS guards, then by Red
Army scouts, and, in between, by our friends and neighbours, though, I'm told, they were only after mementoes.
They did not think we would return, so they wanted to
remember us by our silver. And porcelain. And some
trinkets, of course. But I came back. They wanted to return
the stuff, but I told them to keep it.'

'Do you have a family, Papa Krauss?' Monsignor Beck
asked.

'I used to,' Papa Krauss said. 'But, I'm sorry to say,
they've all been killed. I survived a wife, three sons and a
daughter.'

Monsignor Beck touched Papa Krauss's arm and remained silent for a moment.

'Did other Jews live in Krestur?' he then asked. 'Apart
from your family, of course.'

'No,' Papa Krauss answered. 'We were the only ones.
It's a small village, Monsignor. They didn't need many
Jews. Who needs many Jews? There was a large community in Sentelek, though. A synagogue and a school. A
beautiful house for the *Chevra Kadisha* built from funds a
very rich local merchant had left for that purpose in his
will before the First World War. A good place to live a
good life.'

'Did you try to escape?' Monsignor Beck asked, very
softly. 'You *knew* what was coming, you *must* have known
it. Or did you hide? We had a group of Jews in the cellars
of the monastery, thirty or forty of them, young and old,
men, women and children, and they all survived, even
though the Gestapo had their suspicions.'

Monsignor Beck saw himself and the other monks,
sitting in smug conceit on top of Mount Ephialt, shielded
by the immutable permanence of their days ordered from

vigils to compline, cut off from the world below—though they had had their own Jews to protect, and they had done what, as good Christians, they were supposed to do. The way he and his Trappist brothers had so cleverly out-smarted evil always made Monsignor Beck proud, but now he only felt ashamed.

'Everybody knew you and your family. What did they do?' he asked.

'What *could* they do?' Papa Krauss looked at Monsignor Beck, as though astonished by the naïvety of the question. 'The Walds suggested that we hide in the forest in one of those putrid old shacks or coal-holes and offered to feed and take care of us as long as it was necessary, but I couldn't let them do that. How could I? With Simon at the front, Anna pregnant, Aunt Elsie, our dearest French chef, alone in The Waldhorn, and Sybil working in the big city, it would have been much too dangerous. Besides, my wife was sick with her stomach, and she needed medical attention. But even worse, we all had this lunatic sense of safety and security, Monsignor, the belief that the thing would blow over in no time, and, even if it lasted, it would never reach us in Krestur; we thought that Krestur was such a small, totally unimportant place, with such an absolutely insignificant population, that history would leave it in peace. Yes, we felt as though God Himself had directed His seraphim and cherubim with their flaming swords to keep us *inside* the garden.

'So, naturally, we were surprised when, one morning in June, a truck turned into our yard with two gendarmes and four other men wearing the armbands and visored caps of the Fascist militia, led by an old acquaintance from Sentelek. His mother was one of our more frequent customers, who used to buy a special knitting yarn for her pullovers. He was a well-known personality in his own right, a famous centre-forward, if my memory is correct, playing for the same team as Simon Wald in their high-school days. I wasn't a great fan of football, but my son Saul was, and he whispered to me, in a respectful voice, what a great centre-forward Andy Shvihak had once been and how gratified we should feel by his visit. Andy Shvihak seemed to remember my son, and they exchanged greetings and a few words which I didn't hear, but which made my son laugh a little and become quite relaxed.

'Indeed, Andy Shvihak was very nice, assured us of their best intentions and told us that we needn't be afraid. As the law of the land required, we'd simply be transferred to Sentelek for the duration, and we would live in a camp near the old grain-silos. Though it certainly wasn't going to be as comfortable as our own home, Andy said, with an almost embarrassed cough, it wasn't the end of the world, only a necessary precautionary measure, purely in our own interest. So, we smiled at each other, and Andy ordered his men to help us pack and carry the stuff—only what was absolutely indispensable for our daily existence—to the truck. Then, some of our old friends came—the Walds, the Flurs, the Felds—and hugged and kissed Nellie, my wife, and Esther, my daughter, and shook hands with me and George and Saul and David, my sons. We could see tears in their eyes and, no doubt, they saw tears in ours.

'I suddenly realized that the village was exceptionally quiet, the streets empty. Even the houses appeared to be deserted, which made me aware that something was different; it told me that we were abandoned, thrown to the wolves. I understood then that it was all over. Our friends, our neighbours, our customers, the children's playmates and schoolfriends, our drinking companions, whom we visited at Christmas bearing gifts, and who returned the compliment at Passover, had vanished. The weddings, the bar mitzvahs, the birthday parties, the funerals—it was all swept away by the New Flood, and there was no Old Ark to save us. Had God broken His promise?

'As the truck started moving down the main street, passing the well, which was supposedly bubbling louder and more cheerfully than ever before, as if the demon that created it was rejoicing in our demise, children appeared on the streets, shouting silly anti-Semitic slogans and sticking out their tongues at us. Though I knew they didn't know what they were doing, I couldn't help wondering from whom they had learned all that. Otherwise the village remained silent—no anti-Semitic outburst but no show of sympathy either, nor even a glance of curiosity or pity. Before we reached the road to Sentelek, between The Waldhorn and the church, Father Leo emerged from his sanctuary, his faded, food-stained cassock fluttering in the warm wind. He ran towards the accelerating truck, his lips moving and his hands raised high, but we couldn't hear what he said, so we didn't know if he wanted to damn us or bless us.

'Then, after two weeks in the Sentelek camp, freight-cars were shunted on to the disused sidings of the silos, and, together with the Jews of Sentelek and other villages and towns, we were ordered to get aboard.'

'Where did they take you?' Monsignor Beck asked.

'To the gas-chambers, Monsignor,' Papa Krauss said. 'Where else?'

* * *

What was surprising, at least for Monsignor Beck, was how few of the participants at the International Conference on Religion and Social Consciousness sponsored jointly by the Archbishop of Krakow and the Patriarch of Moscow—maybe ten out of more than sixty—decided to make the trip to Auschwitz, only an hour's bus ride from the Hotel Jagiello. Waiting for the bus in the lobby, Monsignor Beck recognized two East German ministers, a French rabbi, an Italian Jesuit, a Chinese Buddhist and some others, but the majority had left soon after the conference had closed with an ecumenical prayer, carrying their luggage and their gifts from the archbishop and the patriarch—a small, graceful porcelain bust of the Black Madonna of Czestochowa and a large, leather-bound edition of the *Vozhd*'s selected writings on religion and religious freedom. The hotel, which had buzzed with the excited chatter of several languages, fell silent, empty apart from sullen waiters and sleepy chambermaids moving through its halls and corridors on the old, moth-eaten carpets.

Silence followed Monsignor Beck on to the bus. In the weak early spring sunshine, the driver manoeuvred his age-old bus among the poplars and acacias, pot-holes and ditches, with experienced skill. Dirty patches of snow could still be seen on the roadsides, but in the pale light the soft, velvety nibs of pussywillow glistened with perfect innocence. In front of the famous gate they stopped.

Later, Monsignor Beck realized that what really moved him wasn't the old, red-brick barracks, built as a garrison for cavalry, artillery and infantry defending the eastern borders of the empire against the primitive Russian hordes. Nor was it the ignominious execution yard, where their guide, a young Polish girl, explained with bored indifference that the prisoners were executed without the benefit of 'spiritual consolation' (that was how she put it); or the row of torture chambers, where victims were forced to spend days and nights without food and water, standing or lying or hanging on huge meathooks until they died. Curiously, Monsignor Beck felt no emotional shock on seeing what their guide considered one of the most terrifying spectacles, the Museum of Remains, where huge glass receptacles contained heaps of toothbrushes, dentures, forks, spoons, luggage with names and addresses (as if they had been left at a railway station, to be returned without delay to their rightful owners). The walls were papered with the carefully documented records of every prisoner, ending with the final, irrevocable *'Vergasst'* stamped in thick letters across the file.

What moved Monsignor Beck to his very heart was Birkenau. He found himself alone among the vast, flat expanse of barracks, that unending monotony of order which, it seemed to Monsignor Beck, represented the most tormenting disorder man had been able to create, far from the ramp where, for millions, the tracks—and the world— had come to an end. He stood in mud and had the sensation of sinking deeper and deeper into it, between two barracks that were also sinking slowly, together with the ghosts that inhabited them, into the slippery slime. For the first time in his life, Monsignor Beck knew he stood face to face with evil. In the northerly wind that suddenly rose from among the barracks, Monsignor Beck shivered.

He knew a great deal about evil. In the seminary he'd read everything about it he could lay his hands on. By the time he was ordained, he knew, with a proud certitude, that evil was a transient unreality whose core was hollow, which could not exist for its own sake. Augustine was correct when he said that God was so powerful He could make good out of evil. Later, in the monastery, and during his travels and assignments, Monsignor Beck had had more time to contemplate the nature of evil, whose essence was basically *absence*, the absence of the reality of love. He agreed with Aquinas that there was no first principle of evil—whereas there was of good—for the original principle of the universe was essentially good and nothing could be essentially bad: every being as being *was* good, and evil did not exist except in a good subject. That was a redeeming knowledge. Good was instinctive in man as a rational being: to act rightly was to act rationally. Even as man piled sin upon sin, the instinct for reason and right action remained radically intact. Monsignor Beck had looked into the faces of the SS officers who came for the Jews hidden in the cellars of the abbey—dry, haggard, wary faces, full of hatred, distorted by evil—and yet, he was convinced, they were still the faces of human beings created in the likeness of God, so perhaps they still nourished some remote hope of redemption through penance and suffering. But here, amidst the relentless silence, under the empty eyes of the watch-towers, behind the fences that, even without the electric current, forever separated the inside world from the world beyond, Monsignor Beck saw that everything was different.

Cautiously, in order not to slip in the mud, Monsignor Beck moved away from the spot where he had stood for a long while. But soon, he realized he had wandered back to that point—he knew it wasn't the same, yet he also knew that it *was;* walking forwards, backwards, and round and round, he stood and did not stand where he had stood before, he moved yet remained motionless. The horror lay in the uninterrupted chaos, the unchangeable reality, of evil. From the ramps, where the trains stopped, to the gas-chambers, where life stopped, evil ruled, strong, unchallenged, irrefutable. It was a *presence*.

Aquinas was mistaken. He wrote that a ruling authority which sought evil for its own sake could not exist. Here, it existed. Aquinas wrote that there was no justification for the idea that there were two kingdoms—one good, one evil—but here, the Thomist argument was proved wrong. Here was the kingdom of evil. Loudly, Monsignor Beck wept.

'And you came back?' Monsignor Beck asked. 'In spite of everything?'

'Yes,' Papa Krauss replied. 'In spite of everything, I came back.'

'Apologies,' Father Novak said at the door. 'I didn't expect Monsignor to visit. We are honoured.' He came closer, bowed, and, with a brush of his lips, touched the abbot's ring on Monsignor Beck's finger. 'I was called away by Anna Wald. There's trouble with her uncle. He's chairman of our town council, Martin Flur. It seems . . .'

'What's the trouble with Martin?' Papa Krauss interrupted, his long black beard fluttering. 'Is he sick?'

'He's been arrested,' Father Novak said.

'I'm sorry, General Wulf,' Sybil Wald said, crumpling her white handkerchief in her hands, 'I hope you're feeling better. I can get the gig for you and have Eleazar take you to town, if you want me to. Simon left late this afternoon with the jeep to see Colonel Shvihak on some family matter. Our uncle was arrested this morning. We don't

know why. They just came and took him. Simon went to
Sentelek to find out why. He knows Colonel Shvihak well
from their soccer days. I'm so sorry, General Wulf.'

'Get him back here at once,' General Wulf shouted, his
hands on his chest. 'You'll be held fully responsible if I
die!'

'Leave it, Henryk,' Justice Krolthy said. 'It's too late for
the gig. We'll have to take the Skoda. We'll see what we can
do for your uncle, Sybil. Come, gentlemen.'

The Skoda was parked at the main entrance. Justice
Krolthy unlocked the door, slid behind the wheel, put the
key in the ignition and stepped on the starter, but the
engine refused to turn over.

Even as he emerged from the woods near the culvert at the
first kilometre stone and turned towards Krestur, Simon
Wald sensed that there was trouble in the village. It was
noon—he could hear the cracked old bell of the church
obediently fulfilling the first half of its daily service.
General Wulf, visibly exhausted by the long futile search
for his little pond and big tree, had expressed his wish to
go back to the manor and have a midday nap, so Simon
Wald had decided to head home for lunch. Now, he
stopped and listened intently. He had no idea what the
trouble in Krestur might be, nor could he see anything
unusual in the distance. The village looked as he had seen
it hundreds of times since he was a child, with its bare
trees, red rooftops, whitewashed walls and tall chimneys,
from which Anna's beloved storks had long departed for
the winter. Yet he felt a chill and quickened his stride.

As far back as he could remember, Simon Wald's body
had always reacted to danger by becoming cold. As a

young man, when he found himself alone in the middle of the forest at night, during a snowstorm, he would be filled with icy premonitions of disaster, but when the storm relented and the sun rose among the trees, he'd feel stupid and ashamed of having been so easily frightened—he, a well-read and educated man of science! If something happened afterwards, and something always did happen—a quarrel at home, altercations in the office, fistfights at the clearing sites—Simon Wald never wavered in his conviction that it was coincidence. But ever since the night of their 'homecoming' (Kopf's codeword for the breakout), when he lay sleepless and cold on his bunk—much colder than he should have been that fine, warm August night—amid the screams and whimpers of other people's nightmares, he had had his doubts. Again and again, he saw Kopf going down, a heap of flesh perforated by bullets, kicked into an unmarked pit by Strappado's thugs. If only he'd warned Kopf! How many times had he listened to Kopf's musings under the big oak behind the latrines about a possible link between premonition and future—how many times? It was one of Kopf's favourite subjects, one he wanted to investigate when, if, he got out of Krechk. There *must* exist, Kopf had said, a connection, something that transmuted forebodings into perceptions; after years of rumination, that was the only possible conclusion, Kopf said. Yet Simon Wald had rejected Kopf's ideas.

Now, as the months passed after his release from Krechk, Simon Wald felt more and more responsible for Kopf's death. If only he hadn't dismissed Kopf's musings with such smug superiority! If only he'd told him about his attacks of coldness! If only he'd understood them for what they really were! Again, Simon Wald shivered, and he started to run.

Beyond the crumbling mud-huts of the gypsies, Krestur's main street, lined with old acacias and even older houses, lay deserted. As he reached The Waldhorn, his son stepped down from the front porch and greeted him with a short cry of anxiety and relief. 'Father,' the boy shouted, running towards him, 'where have you been? We've been looking for you for hours.'

Unexpectedly, inexplicably, Simon Wald felt a cold rage tighten around his throat like a noose. A dense, black cloud enveloped him in its icy shroud. From a great distance, he heard a thin voice, 'Father, please, you're choking me, Father, please, let me go.' Then just as unexpectedly and inexplicably the cloud lifted, Simon Wald's eyes cleared, and, trembling, he saw his son standing next to him with tears in his eyes.

His hand on his son's shoulder, Simon Wald stopped in front of the old wooden gate outside the Flurs' house. The last time he'd visited had been on some errand from Anna, shortly before his arrest. He noticed that on the left a new room had been plastered to the wall, but otherwise, not much had changed since Simon Wald first came there to play with Lucas, their eldest son.

The gate was always locked, and the heavy iron bolt gave only if you knew the trick. There was a time when Lucas had permission from his father to show Simon Wald how it was worked, for the old man changed it every now and then, but that was long ago, and now Simon Wald didn't want to enter without the Flurs knowing he was coming. He thought of sending Peter around the house to the kitchen, to ask them to come out and open the gate, but the boy looked up at him, his pupils dilated, with such undisguised fear and suspicion that Simon Wald was taken aback. He quickly removed his hand from Peter's shoulders. What was the matter with the boy? Maybe he was too excited because he'd heard so many things about the Flurs but had never been permitted to visit them. Sara, the granddaughter of Martin and Gerania Flur, had invited him several times. Peter seemed to like her a great deal and whenever Sara was visiting her grandparents, they used to meet and go for long walks, in defiance of their fathers' admonitions, although always with the blessing of their mothers.

Simon Wald gave his son a wide, encouraging grin, to show that now he could enter the house with *his* blessing, and he slowly stroked the boy's jet-black hair. But still the boy didn't relax.

'Is your mother here?' Simon Wald asked, baffled that his son should spurn his show of affection.

'She said she'd be down,' the boy answered, 'when I went looking for you. I wouldn't know if she's here now, though.'

Simon Wald wondered why old Uncle Martin had been arrested. Of the small bunch of fanatics who had terrorized the village after the Russian T34s rolled in during the winter of '44, and who were later swallowed up one after another by the bottomless pit, as Father Leo used to gloat, Martin Flur had remained untouched. A member of the underground Alliance before and during the war, chairman of the town council since 1948, he had been awarded the Red and Gold Stars for Meritorious Service several times, and once, as a member of a delegation to study the methods and achievements of the world's most advanced agricultural system, had even visited the 'land of milk and honey'. But now, he too had been arrested, and Simon Wald wasn't surprised.

'Let's go inside,' he said, and Peter ran ahead and disappeared into the house.

Old Martin Flur—Simon Wald always thought of him as old, even when he was as young and active as Simon's own father—was Anna's uncle, who worked as a day-labourer in the Széchy forests. One of the poorest men in the village, he used to be the sharpest, most vocal adversary of Simon's father in Krestur. The chief forester was feared and respected by many, and resented, mutely, by a few, but popularity or power didn't seem to affect old Uncle Martin. On the contrary, it made his denunciations of the existing order even more provocative, arrogant, dangerous and—for such a bright man—surprisingly stupid. Simon Wald's father used to call his harangues the 'gospel of scum', and Father Leo, denouncing him from the pulpit, described them as the 'message of Satan'. All that, however, had very little impact on Martin Flur and Matthias Feld, his best friend and most loyal follower. Simon Wald laughed at the memory and entered the house.

'It's high time you came.' Father Novak sounded annoyed. 'Shouldn't you have been here sooner, Simon? Where are you when we need you?'

'What happened?' Simon Wald decided to ignore Father Novak's volley. He was a young, hot-tempered fellow. During his brief tenure in Krestur since Father Leo's death his flashes of anger mixed with his inexperience with country matters had often brought him into conflict with Simon Wald. Father Novak was Anna's priest, exactly the type she'd always dreamed of having in her

church: strict, humourless, resolute, uncompromising; he
knew his Latin texts, his catechism, fluently; and his litany
of the saints on Holy Saturday sounded as if it were sung
by angels. But what did he know about life's labyrinths,
perplexities, sufferings? Simon Wald hadn't really liked
Father Leo either, with his food-stained cassock, his nervous anti-Semitism, his docile submission to anyone a
rung higher up the social or ecclesiastical hierarchy, and
above all, his incessant nosiness and unabashed appeals to
the tear-glands. But at least Father Leo had many years'
experience of village life, and could occasionally provide
him with information, or remember events that had happened well before Simon Wald was born. And, most
important, he didn't jump down your throat if you did
something differently from the way he wanted.

'They took Martin at four-thirty in the morning, two
civilians in an open jeep from Sentelek who did not
identify themselves,' Father Novak said. 'They ordered
Gerania and the girls not to whisper a word to anyone
until noon. Something new, don't you think, Simon? Until
now they have wanted everybody to know everything as
soon as possible. What do they want to do now, Simon?'

'We'll know that soon enough, too, Father Novak.'

'A more relevant question,' Father Novak had sharp
edge in his voice, 'is what do *we* want to do, Simon?'

'I don't know,' Simon Wald said. 'Not yet, Father
Novak. Do you?' Simon Wald looked around, curious.
Anna wasn't there but Aunt Gerania and her daughters
were sitting, frightened and disbelieving, around the big
kitchen table. Their mother was silent, tearless, her expres-
sion vacant, her hands clasped in her lap, as if in her black
wrap and black headscarf she were already mourning the
loss of her husband. It was strange, Simon Wald thought,

to what extent she seemed to have forgotten (or simply didn't want to remember) the past. Uncle Martin used to be arrested frequently, disappearing for weeks or months into the belly of the admiral's prisons until, finally, the beast disgorged him. But that was a long time ago and people always managed to forget their bad dreams: why should Aunt Gerania be an exception? The girls probably didn't even remember those times. Simon Wald watched them with pleasure.

In the corner, Sara stood with Peter at her side. They looked handsome together, pleased at being able to appear openly in each other's company. Sara's strawberry blondness and Peter's intense blackness created a bright glow in the big, dark kitchen. Suddenly, Simon Wald felt good. Maybe Aunt Elsie was right. Maybe Sara and Peter were meant for each other. Maybe it was time to stop the stupid family feud and face the enemy united.

'I think,' Father Novak continued, 'you should try to talk to that scoundrel in Sentelek, don't you? He *is*, after all, your old soccer-chum.'

'I don't know yet what I'm going to do, Father Novak,' Simon Wald said, very slowly. 'I need time to think things over. Maybe Aunt Gerania should call Lucas and tell him what happened. Or her other son in the city? They could probably do a great deal more than I can, don't you think?'

'I have called them,' the oldest of the sisters, a tall, plump beauty whose name Simon Wald couldn't remember, spoke up unexpectedly in a clear, strong voice, 'from father's office, earlier this morning. But they both said we mustn't do anything hasty. It's important, they said, that we do not do anything hasty. We should wait. This must be some misunderstanding. Father will be back in no time.

calm and trust the authorities.'

The door from the kitchen to the clean bedroom was open and Simon Wald entered to be alone for a moment or two. He walked to the window and looked out. Here was the end of the village, where the reedy swamps of the wetlands began. The mallards and storks had gone, the bullfrogs were silent, the weeds turned a lifeless brown, the barren marshes soon to be frozen over by thin layers of ice. Simon Wald, too, felt a cold emptiness come over him. How right his father had proved to be! Over the years that big, incorrigible idiot had stopped at nothing to become an even bigger, more incorrigible idiot in his obsession to save the world against his friends' better judgement, and what was even worse, against the will of those he intended to save.

When he was at primary school, Simon Wald remembered noticing old Martin Flur wobbling along the streets of Krestur with his crony Matthias Feld—he couldn't help noticing them! When Martin and Matthias were pulled in by the gendarmes of the Sentelek Command (which happened fairly frequently), Simon Wald felt sorry for those two, and when they returned several weeks or months later, their faces blue and yellow and purple, he was outraged, despite his father's and Father Leo's gleeful approval of the punishment those ruffians had brought upon themselves.

Ruffians? Some in Krestur called them idiots; others declared them traitors, lackeys of the Jews, dupes of foreign powers; some sympathized with them, even helped them whenever they could, quietly, for fear of retribution. From the distance of the manor the Széchys looked at them with cool curiosity; Count Paul had once intervened on their behalf at the Sentelek Command and they were promptly released, even given a ride home. When Simon Wald was a boy, his father often sent him down to the Flurs with warnings of an impending search, so that Uncle Martin would have time to get rid of the incriminating evidence before the gendarmes arrived and turned everything upside down; but when his father invited Martin and Matthias to the wedding of Simon and Anna, they didn't show up. Obstinate scoundrels, real blackguards, weren't they, Simon's father had said, then never spoke to them again.

'I'll go to Sentelek and see what I can find out,' Simon Wald said and left.

It was a few minutes after five o'clock when he arrived at the new, drab grey headquarters of the State Security Forces. A large, rectangular building with a flat roof and a maze of antennae, it was situated near the old grain-silos at the edge of town. For a few minutes Simon Wald stood at a respectful distance from its main entrance. He knew he was late—the doors were open, and men and women in uniform or in civilian clothes streamed out and walked towards the nearby tram station or the bicycle-racks, some even towards the shiny, tan Pobiedas or sea-green, rusting Hudsons parked in the fields around the corner, where the town ended and the meadows began. None the less he hoped that he would still find Andy Shvihak in his office.

Simon Wald had meant to be there earlier, but after he'd driven home, washed and put on a fresh shirt, he was suddenly overcome with fatigue, with a profound, irresistible desire to lie down and sleep, and he did so, stretching out comfortably on their large, cool bed in the empty house. By the time he woke up, it was already past four. Simon Wald drove as fast as he could, without meeting any traffic, except two black-leather-clad motor-cyclists on their enormous Harley-Davidsons, who, Simon Wald observed in his mirror, did not turn down the access road towards Krestur, but continued towards the manor: probably the new recruits the Special Detachment people had been expecting for weeks now to replace some recently demobbed veterans. In front of the main gate of the SSF headquarters, Simon Wald spotted a GAZ—a cheap Russian imitation of his American jeep, a piece of junk that didn't even have a hydraulic brake-system, only a few wires which connected the pedal with the brake-shoes and which, of course, could snap at any moment and throw you, headlong, into the nearest ditch or against the unfriendliest tree-trunk. It was probably the one that had brought Uncle Martin to Sentelek, so Simon Wald knew that he had come to the right place.

'Simon!' Andy Shvihak bellowed, his cracked baritone resonant with familiar enthusiasm. 'Simon, old rascal! How good to see you again! It's been years! What a pleasant surprise to end an unpleasant day!' Agile despite his heavy frame and stout midriff, he rose from behind his big, cluttered desk, and, hands outstretched, came towards Simon Wald with an open smile on his large face. 'Let me take a look at you.' His handshake was strong, firm, but his fingers and palm were cold and clammy; Simon Wald had to make an effort not to show his revulsion. Andy Shvihak, of course, knew that he was coming, just as Simon Wald, from the moment he entered the building, had been aware that he was being watched.

'Sit down, old chap,' Andy Shvihak continued, at a slightly lower pitch, yet still with unexpectedly warm enthusiasm. 'What can I offer you? Tea? A good *espresso?*

I'd recommend that. We have a brand-new machine from Milan. Or some stronger stuff, maybe? A glass of wine? Beer? Vodka? Speak up, man! You haven't lost your voice wandering in the woods, have you?' He laughed boisterously, as he always used to laugh after a successful attack when he saw the ball dancing in the opponent's net and heard the fans explode with joy; behind the stoutness and wrinkles, Simon Wald suddenly recognized the young centre-forward he was once so very fond of.

'Tea, if I may,' Simon Wald said.

'Well, you may.' Andy Shvihak patted him on the back. He was two or three years older than Simon Wald, and on that pretext he had always loved to play the wise, experienced elder brother, not just to Simon Wald, but to the whole team—he was their guardian angel. Now, Andy Shvihak called in his secretary, a bespectacled young woman with a lieutenant's star on the golden epaulettes of her tight uniform, and ordered her to bring up some 'goodies' from the canteen, 'at the double'.

'I've been planning to visit you in Krestur, believe me, for months,' Andy Shvihak said, and lit a cigarette, 'but I've practically no time left for anything. Not even for my family!' He was busy with the cigarette which, like a flaming rose, opened up then went cold with an almost mocking fizzle. He threw it away. 'You've no idea what goes on here, Simon! From morning to midnight, every day, seven days a week. It's easy for you out in the woods among your hedgehogs and rabbits. How much I envy you sometimes! This here is a loony-bin. As the Republic grows stronger and more powerful, the enemy gets more and more cunning and daring. He's everywhere and would do everything to ruin us, yes! If only you knew, Simon! If you would only believe us!

'Ah, but let's not talk about that now. Tell me all about yourself. How's dearest Anna? Peter? I heard about little Anna Julia, too. What a tragedy! Please accept my sincerest condolences. Still, you look good, old buddy. Very good. But take a look at me! I'm fat, Simon, fat! Isn't that a god-awful shame? But what can I do? I don't even have time for a walk these days, and I can't remember when I was last out on the river with my boys. I have two boys, Simon, did you know that? Two very nice boys. We have a big old rowing-boat down on the river and once in a while on Sundays we used to paddle upstream to Chicken Island—you know, opposite the old Széchy marina—and have a picnic there. Just the three of us! But those times are gone, Simon, gone!'

After knocking politely at the door, the secretary-lieutenant came in with a huge tray of cheesecakes, tarts and éclairs. Amused, Simon Wald saw that Andy Shvihak could hardly wait till the girl had put the tray down on the least cluttered corner of his desk before he picked up a chocolate éclair and started devouring it.

Andy Shvihak wasn't really fat, Simon Wald thought, sipping his tea and taking small, cautious bites from a mammoth slice of cheesecake, but he was well on his way to becoming a fat man. Simon Wald remembered him from their triumphant soccer-years: a short, stocky chap, even then Andy appeared heavier than he actually was, yet he played the game with such skill, ease and speed, that he defied gravity, soaring above the field, while the ball, as if it understood his every command, obeyed him unconditionally. Without a doubt Andy Shvihak was the best centre-forward anybody could have wished for in Sentelek. But, alas, once he returned to the pastures of life, he became, Simon Wald remembered cheerfully, the dumbest ox, who never failed to entertain his peers with his endless gaffes, and then sulked because of the light-hearted banter they aroused.

As Simon Wald watched Andy Shvihak gobbling up his second éclair, happily licking his sticky fingers, he was intensely aware that he was looking at the man who, by some quirk of fate (or was it, as Kopf had so often argued, the selection process of the system, which always preferred the weak to the strong, the obedient to the defiant, the credulous to the doubter?) was now the commanding officer of the county's State Security Forces, with virtually unlimited power over the living and the dead. If Andy Shvihak had been once the butt of jokes, nobody was laughing anymore.

'Do you remember, old chap,' Andy Shvihak asked, deciding after some hesitation not to touch the strawberry tart, 'when we played the Bulls for the championship and they were leading three-two? We needed the equalizer in the second half, and Steinmetz passed the ball to me and I jumped over it so that Greko, behind me, could get it and give it to you, but Greko was a coward. Always staying on the safe side, he rolled it back to me and I knew that you must have it to score, so I passed it to you, though I saw you were just a *tiny* millimetre from offside. If the whistle blew my plan would collapse and we'd lose the championship, but I took the risk—remember?—I always took the risk and you . . .'

'Please,' Simon Wald said, 'Andy, please.'

Outside, the high squeal of the shoe-factory's whistle signalled the end of one shift and the beginning of the next. It was six o'clock.

'I give you my word of honour,' Andy Shvihak said, slowly, 'that I have nothing to do with this business. I

haven't the faintest idea what happened to the old man. I
heard about the whole thing only when I came to the office
this morning. It's the truth, I swear to you.'

'I see,' Simon Wald said. 'Can you ask?'

'I can try,' Andy Shvihak said. 'But don't expect too
much.'

'I won't.' Simon Wald started towards the door.

'By the way,' Andy Shvihak said, 'I almost forgot.
Colonel Eschara sends you his greetings. I met him the
other day at a conference. You don't remember Colonel
Eschara? You and your pals used to call him Captain
Strappado, even though he was already a major then. He
has fond memories of everybody, but especially of you,
Simon. He said you were a most reliable man. A model
inmate, he said. He even remembered how you once told
him the botanical names for all those trees. He said you
had an exceptional memory. He was delighted to hear that
you were back in your woods. That's where he belongs,
Colonel Eschara said, that's where that good man belongs.'

In his jeep Simon Wald passed the crumbling synagogue on the hillside, closed now except to the sparrows
who flitted in and out of its broken windows, where once
he'd witnessed the bar-mitzvah rites of young Saul
Krauss. He suddenly felt very thirsty. He drove slowly
along the cobblestoned streets under the dim lights, few
and far between, to Biberach's tavern, an old, damp cellar
further up the hill.

Whenever they came to town and for whatever reason,
the Wald men and occasionally even the Wald women
came to Biberach's for a beer, a glass of wine or a slivovitz.
Shortly before his death, Simon Wald's father, swearing
and cursing, had burst into Biberach's for a handful of

cloves in the middle of the night, in the middle of a war. Simon Wald himself had spent hours sitting at the sturdy hand-made tables retreating from the world. Now, he felt the world was retreating from him.

Biberach, the proprietor, an old fat Swabian with a grey beard, came over, sat down and talked loudly about the weather—this freak heatwave in late October!—and under his breath asked if Simon Wald could find out anything about the arrest of Martin Flur from Andy Shvihak. When Simon Wald said no, Biberach, grinning widely with satisfaction, went back behind the counter to serve his home-brew to the crowd of *stammgasts,* growing louder and livelier by the minute; he couldn't complain, his business was booming! For a while, Simon Wald sat alone and again saw Andy Shvihak's large, wrinkled face, with its triumphant grin. Andy Shvihak had scored again.

When Simon Wald came home from the war, on a muddy, sunny April afternoon in 1945, Anna told him about Uncle Martin, Matthias Feld and their cronies, who had crawled out of the woodwork, few but vociferous, the moment the T34s were firmly entrenched around Krestur and there was no longer any danger of the panzers returning. They ran Krestur as if they owned it, though anybody who ran their private property the way they were running Krestur, Anna said, would soon find themselves on the auction block or, quite deservedly, in jail. The Russkies wandered about the village, with one finger on the trigger, and one eye on the women, on anything they could eat, or, better still, pocket quickly—rings, watches, spoons, rockets, earrings, even rosaries. Those little slit-eyed boys from Uzbekistan or Mongolia or Kazakhstan, fresh on the front, had learned fast the possibilities and privileges of war—

just as Martin, Matthias and their cronies were learning fast the possibilities and privileges of power. They started carving up the lands of the Széchy estate, occupied the manor and, ignoring the angry growl of Simon Wald, began turning it into something 'useful', as Martin had said—a nursery, a school, offices for the newly established cooperative. They made a huge bonfire of the old papers and documents they'd found in the town hall, as if they were burning the past with all its ghosts. They danced around it in the eerie light of dusk, as though it were a pagan ritual, watched from a distance by indifferent Russians and flabbergasted villagers. Finally, they appointed Martin Flur chairman of the Krestur soviet and Matthias Feld his deputy, though at this point the Russian commander intervened, putting a stop to such nonsense, as he was ordered to do by his *politruk*, and sending everybody home. The old documents had burned through the night until a platoon of drunken Russians came by and pissed on the fire; with a faint hiss, accompanied by Uncle Matthias's loud bark of outrage, the fire went out. And so it had all begun.

The clear, cool moon, which a minute ago had lit up the whole landscape with its shimmering white glow, disappeared behind thick, menacing clouds rolling in from the east, and the night went dark and damp, smelling of rain. Simon Wald sat in his jeep, its engine silent, on the hard shoulder, almost half-way between Sentelek and Krestur. From here, to the north, he could see the oldest oaks of the forest marching towards the ancient hills; to the south, he saw Krestur on the plain, amidst the fruit trees, small, turned in on its white houses, its own confusions and sufferings. This was one of Simon Wald's favourite spots

on the estate. He came here often when he needed consolation and strength. Now, he didn't quite know how he
had got here, although he vaguely remembered having a
few beers 'on the house', at Biberach's insistence, then
driving around, the pressure in his head increasing at
every turn. But he was glad he was here. With his small
torch, he checked his watch: it was five minutes past two.
It had started to rain. He no longer felt the pressure in his
head, but he felt himself inside some strange sphere that
weighed his body down, flattened it against its invisible
walls, until he cried out in pain.

From Sentelek, he saw powerful headlights cut into the
darkness of the highway, the big car coming towards him
at great speed, then sweeping by and continuing towards
the manor. Simon Wald didn't know who was in the car,
and he didn't care.

BOOK THREE
VENERIES

EIGHT

S INGER looked exactly as he had looked a year
before, General Wulf thought, and shifted irritably
in Count Paul's celebrated cubist armchair. Indeed,
sitting behind Count Francis's huge mahogany desk in the
library, Krolthy's favourite place, Singer looked exactly as
he had thirty years before in Berlin, twenty years before in
Teruel, ten years before in Ceberden, when his rusty old
Ilyushin landed on a pot-holed, makeshift airstrip, and he
was whisked away in a big, black ZIM. General Wulf
hadn't seen him since Singer had visited him on Lilac Hill
after his heart attack—ostensibly to check on the progress
of a retired private citizen, but, in reality, to lecture him
about the meaninglessness of his life. Tall, thin, greying at
the temples, his back bent, his light-blue eyes bulging
slightly under his sombre eyebrows, Singer didn't age.
Inge had noticed that, too, when she invited him to stay for
dinner, and between the soup and the chicken she had
remarked wonderingly, 'Ernest, you haven't changed a
bit since Berlin.'

Inge didn't like Singer, had never liked him, from the
moment Wulf introduced him to her in the Botanischer
Garten. Singer had appeared, punctual, elegant in his
dove-grey flannel suit, and coolly paid for the ice-cream
they had in the Mielch-Casino. Having delivered the
Komintern instructions to Henryk—that naïve, young
idiot, still trembling with the honour of shaking such a
luminary's hand—he had taken his silver-handled walk-

ing stick with its Gothic monogram (someone else's initials, of course), and disappeared among the ferns without even giving them his address. Inge had been shaking too, but with rage. What an insolent petty-bourgeois phony! She never ceased to warn Wulf against Singer's schemes, but—how deeply he deplored his stupidity now!—General Wulf never listened to her arguments, threats, even, lately, tears, because he didn't think Singer a phony.

Who was Singer? Among many things, Singer was the man who had hooked General Wulf, saved him, elevated him, used him, dropped him, and General Wulf couldn't abandon Singer before he got his hot revenge.

Now, General Wulf listened with increasing interest as Singer continued his monologue, an uneasy tension beneath his dry, articulate analysis. Maybe Krolthy had hit on something, and Singer really was in some kind of jam? Maybe Singer was no longer in control? Maybe the time for revenge had arrived? It seemed unlikely but not impossible, though such a sudden turn of events might create its own dangers. For, if Singer was no longer in control, then who the hell was? Nervously, General Wulf sat back in his uncomfortable armchair. Whoever had cut the cables of Krolthy's ignition last night had also severed General Wulf's last, flimsy ties with the world: there was nothing he could do but wait and see.

'Already in early 1945,' Singer was saying, his eyes focusing on General Wulf, moving slowly to Adam Krolthy and Anselm Beck, then back again, 'when, after so many years of exile, we returned, we knew that the only way for us to establish and maintain power was to continue the war. This should come as no surprise to you. Our propensity for, and ideological commitment to, creating and fostering social tensions has been accepted by our

adversaries for quite a while, and, of course, like everything else, it has a grain of truth in it. At the moment,
however, we do not want to talk about the way others have
seen us over the years, only about the way we have
perceived ourselves. Therefore, before we proceed further
to examine the meaning of that reality in history we claim
to have seen first, we must stop and take a deep breath.
Reculer pour mieux sauter, our distinguished judge would
say, as he learned it at the Sorbonne, wouldn't you,
Adam?'

'*Mais bien sûr, mon maître des hautes œuvres,*' Krolthy
said, and stood, bowing, his right hand on his heart.
'Without a doubt, my Lord Garrotter, without the shadow
of a doubt.'

'The truth is, as you well know,' Gerogen continued,
'that we are neither power-mad megalomaniacs nor wide-
eyed chiliasts. There was a time in our distant past when
we were genuinely overwhelmed by visions of Utopia,
lion and lamb side by side in a new Eden, but that was only
a passing phase. We grew up fast. We learned that to use
power for its own sake, or to achieve an end, is to lose it
altogether. At that moment we knew that we were, finally,
free, no longer bound by old myths and dogmas. We
understood clearly that our true concern was power for
the sake of the present, without the dream of the future.
We were only interested in the *means,* without the ballast
of the *end.* Our historical mission was to devote all our
power and energy to shaping reality in our own image and
developing our tactics without the constraints of strategy.
For, if strategy is the future blown out of proportion,
tactics is the present freed from the yoke of the future. That
was our most important discovery, our unique contribution to history! We became explorers, analysts, philoso-

phers of the present, virtuosi of tactics, masters of im-
provisation. Of course, we continued to pay lip-service to
old visions of Eden, and that, too, proved an excellent
tactical move, for it fit in perfectly with those religious
traditions and sensibilities which longed for something
unfathomable, unattainable, unblemished.

'Besides, at the beginning, it was our best *raison d'être* to
develop our arsenal for warfare within the boundaries of
peace, to provoke and sustain tensions which, without our
tactical mastery, would easily have developed into peril-
ous predicaments. *That* was tactics at its finest, raised to
the level of high art! We rebuilt the bridges, put the trains
back on the track, had the ancient factory chimneys puff
black clouds into the skies and, under the banner of the
future, fought and won good battles against our enemies,
but always, always, for the sake of the present, a quintes-
sential reality which would remain for ever. And, for quite
a while, everything worked like clockwork.'

His famous half-smile flashed at nobody in particular,
yet with astonishing pleasantness. What was he driving
at, General Wulf wondered, and closed his eyes, partly
because he was still sleepy, but mainly because he always
preferred Singer imagined rather than seen.

'But recently,' Singer added, 'as I'm sure you all know,
certain problems have developed.'

After they'd come back into the manor from the sabotaged
Skoda, General Wulf went up to his room, took one
Morpholomin and slept remarkably well. He was deeply
grateful to Dr Asklep who, on the sly, had kept supplying
him with the drug imported exclusively for the distinguished clientele of the private ward at Old Beggars' Hill
Hospital. He woke at seven to the shrill ring of Inge's

portable alarm clock, and, for a while, lay motionless in the
bed, listening to the silence—that old, familiar void in
which everything seemed to have taken on a stronger,
sharper existence. Singer had arrived.

Singer took his silences with him wherever he went,
and they not only gave him away, but even in the middle
of the noisiest country fair or the loudest mass-meeting,
they separated him from the rest of the world. It wasn't
simply General Wulf's crazy *idée fixe!* Others had noticed
it too. Copass, who wasn't given to private confessions,
had once said that he never liked to be alone in a room with
Singer for fear of being suffocated by his silence. Adymester speculated whether Singer's ability to emanate
silence was an automatic function of his body or a conscious act of his will, something he could release and shut
off at his pleasure. For Inge—poor Inge!—it was Singer's
ectoplasm revealing his astral corpus, a rare, frightening
phenomenon indicating the presence of something malevolent, which she wanted to investigate if Ernest would
let her, but he wouldn't.

When little Sébastien was dying, Singer came down
from headquarters to see how long he had to wait before
he could make his final report on the death of Lieutenant
LaCroix. Singer and Sébastien had hated each other's guts
from the moment they'd met in Madrid when the Brigade
was first organized. As soon as Singer arrived his silence
took over the room and its dry emptiness drowned the
moans and groans of Sébastien's last moments on earth.
Nobody there could ever forget that silence!

Later that evening, while making notes for his novel,
Jarek wondered about the difference between a
snowstorm's silence and Singer's. The silence of a snowstorm, Jarek had said, his blue eyes flashing, implied a

sense of pure fulfilment, whose meaning Jarek couldn't interpret, though he could sense it. (Jarek often surprised his friends with such mystical outbursts, and once General Wulf had even caught him red-handed, so to speak, reading St John of the Cross; but then, in Spain, mysticism was part of the landscape.) In contrast, Singer's silence was intrusive, aggressive and, above all, overwhelming; it spelled confusion, an ulceration of the soul. Jarek was delighted to have made this observation, which he fully intended to use as a trait of one of his characters, when, and if—there was always that question—he ever got down to writing the novel; but General Wulf had been depressed by its implications and had remained so ever since.

He climbed out of bed and saw Singer, in the rose garden below, deep in conversation with Uncle Karol. Hatless, his long, grey coat around his shoulders, Singer was pointing to the bare twigs and bushes in the pink, early morning light with visible enthusiasm, and Uncle Karol responded with equal zeal, the two walking and talking among the rose bushes, old friends, experts in roses, members of the fraternal order of mankind. If Singer knew how to spread confusion and bewilderment, he also knew how to reverse their effects.

General Wulf closed the window. He very much hoped that Singer would come up to see him, whether to inform him, warn him, threaten him, or just sit and console him, as he always hoped Singer would do when he was despondent, down on his luck, and needed support. Lord, how often he needed support—a promise, at least, that there was nothing to be frightened of, that the world was solid, steady, on course, and that what had been true yesterday would be true today and might even be true tomorrow. But Singer never came.

'General Wulf,' Sybil said, standing at the door, 'would you prefer breakfast here, or would you rather come down to the green room? The prime minister asked me to tell you that he would like to see you in the library at eleven. At *precisely* eleven o'clock.'

Singer, of course, came when he wanted to. Every Wednesday he had come at *precisely* four o'clock in the afternoon to meet Wulf in the Botanischer Garten's huge, Victorian glass-house, whose transparent glitter let the sunshine in but kept out Berlin's cold, northerly winds. Under the giant doum-palms and lush acrocomias, they could discuss undisturbed the problems of the conspiracy that was destined to change the face of the earth. For weeks, Singer had listened attentively to what Wulf had to say about preparations for the uprisings in Neukölln, Wedding and Moabit, but recently he had become more and more interested in the activities of *Genosse* Herbert, owner of the basement apartment in Neukölln's shady Fünfgroschengasse. There, behind closed doors and shuttered windows, the revolutionary leadership met every Tuesday evening to plot the uprising scheduled for 25 October—to coincide with the sixth anniversary of the battleship *Aurora* firing the salvo that hit the Winter Palace in Petrograd and changed the course of history for ever. His back hunched, no doubt as a result of the weight he had had to carry as Zinoviev's man, Singer demanded to know what was going on in that basement.

What was going on? Quite a lot! The leadership discussed the attack-plan against the Polizeipraesidium on Alexanderplatz; then, at the request of Trotsky's people (quite numerous, Wulf had to admit), they talked about Trotsky's lectures to the Moscow Military Academy: *Can one set down the date of a revolution in advance?* Arrangements were made for receiving the next arms shipment from Czechoslovakia through clandestine links with the railway workers. A decision was reached to continue to buy arms from the *Reichswehr*, with American dollars no less, despite the recent fiasco: the morning after the last delivery, the truck, full of weapons and ammunition, was discovered and confiscated by the *Schutzpolizei*. Those goddamn bastards had known exactly what they were after and where to find it, but nobody suspected an inside job. They assumed it was the *Reichswehr*'s game to sell the arms to the Executive Committee and then report it to their *Schutzpol* pals. Nobody else could have done such a thing—not those undisciplined anarchists roaming the streets in their skeletal costumes, nor the hypocritical Trotskyites, nor those vacillating Social Democrats, and least of all *Genosse* Herbert, as Singer seemed to suggest, not so subtly either.

Frail and ageing, with varicose veins from a lifetime of standing at his lathe at Allgemeine Stahl, *Genosse* Herbert was by far the most trustworthy man Wulf had met during his short but intense career as a soldier of the revolution. Inge, who was no fool when it came to judging people's commitment to the cause, backed him a hundred per cent. Moreover *Genosse* Herbert was a long-time friend of Karl and Rosa, the martyrs murdered on the street in broad daylight by the *Freikorps* beasts. And last, but not least, quoting his favourite Goethe, *'geteilte Freud' ist doppelte Freude'*, a joy shared is a joy doubled, *Genosse* Herbert was the man who had introduced Henryk to Inge on that showery afternoon in May. *'Also, mein Bursch*, here's the girl I've talked to you about,' he had said. There, under the wet green glitter of the acacias, stood Inge, tall, strong, serious, yet radiating such irresistible gaiety and joy that

Henryk knew instantly that she was the woman he had been waiting for and there never would be another.

So, how could *Genosse* Herbert be an informer? Yet Singer was always wary of Social Democrats, especially old Social Democrats, those lapdogs of the bourgeoisie, who were ready to sell out the working class for a ministerial automobile with a chauffeur in tight-cut uniform. Singer insisted that *Genosse* Herbert be kept under strict surveillance and made Wulf responsible for executing his order. Wulf didn't like the assignment, but there was no appeal against the orders of Zinoviev's man. Besides, that he, Henryk Wulf—virtually a newcomer to Berlin, a drifter from Vienna, a survivor, wounded in the leg (not too seriously) during the battle of Dorovar-by-the-Tíza, where the tattered Red Army had suffered a crushing, final defeat—should be trusted by Singer and given an assignment so confidential and secret that not even Inge, a founding member of the Neukölln cell and secretary of the Executive Committee, was supposed to know about it, made his head spin, his long-healed leg-wound throb again. How could he say no? He was a footsoldier sworn to obedience.

In any case, ever since Singer had arrived from Moscow he'd been giving him confidential information about the meetings of the Executive Committee, about the attitudes and opinions of certain members who, Singer felt, deserved Komintern attention, since they might, albeit in some minor way, affect the transformation of the world. Yes, those were heady days for Henryk Wulf, spoiled child of the bourgeoisie, adrift on the stormy ocean of history. Paradise was about to be regained, and he was only twenty-two years old.

* * *

Standing in the small, dark entrance hall of their apartment on Acacia Street, telling his mother he'd be back for
dinner, Henryk Wulf had no idea that it was for the last
time, but his mother, with the sixth sense of mothers, knew
he would never come back. She embraced him, sobbing
softly, as if she knew all that awaited her foolish little boy
on what her husband had often called 'the testing ground
of character'. Though most of his life General Wulf had
hardly ever thought about his mother, that despairing
goodbye always came back to haunt him when he had to
say goodbye to people he liked—Sébastien, before he
died; Inge, before she was evacuated from Moscow to
Alma Ata and Lieutenant-Colonel Wulf was ordered to
report to Malinovsky's headquarters in the Ukraine; Jarek,
before his trial started.

The streets were quiet, the big market hall silent and
almost empty—after four years of war, the yahoos were
dead, the meadows lay fallow, production was low, re-
serves virtually nonexistent. On the steps of the Parliament building Adalbert Coon, chairman of the Council of
the People's Commissars, surrounded by his fidgety
bodyguard in long, heavy black-leather coats with shiny
epaulettes, was making a furious, desperate attack on
those imperialist-interventionists both within and without, he emphasized, whose machinations threatened the
rule of the people with ultimate disaster.

A little later, in front of the National Museum where,
hardly a century before, the poet Alexander Petrovich had
read his feverish poem that gave the signal for the War of
Independence, Henryk Wulf listened to Theodore Karuelly, chairman of the Committee of Public Safety. Standing
in an old, battered Austro-Daimler, he was demanding
that the enemies of the proletariat, both within and with-

out, be crushed mercilessly. He exhorted the best and bravest of the country's youth to join the Red Army and defend the future, if necessary with their lives. Small, bony, angular, his young, freshly shaven face crimson with the fever of that future, Karuelly looked transfigured, standing there against the dark-blue afternoon sky—an avenging demon of the past and guardian angel of the future, unshakeable in his determination. Suddenly Henryk Wulf knew that the moment of decision had arrived.

'Tea with rum,' General Wulf said. 'Dark Jamaican, preferably, please. Toast, lightly buttered. Some strawberry jam, maybe.'

'Yes, General,' Sybil Wald said.

'And Sybil,' General Wulf said, 'if you want to do me a favour, have this *prie-dieu* taken to Monsignor's headquarters. He'll probably make more use of it than I do. And one more thing. If you have any of that rye with the crunchy crust left, I'd appreciate that, too.'

'Tea with dark Jamaican. Strawberry jam,' Sybil Wald repeated. 'Very good, General Wulf. But I'm afraid we've run out of the rye.'

The night before the battle at Dorovar-by-the-Tíza, Corporal Wulf of the Fourth Regiment, under the command of young Lieutenant Saint-Imry, walked up and down the dark river-bank, listening to the silent running of the water and the occasional splash of a restless fish. On the other side of the river, around a small camp-fire, the heavily rouged, pomaded faggots of the Rumanian Auxiliary Forces sat in their brand-new uniforms, with visored caps and tight Sam Browne belts. The meandering river exuded its swampy summer smell, and Corporal Wulf heard the chirr of the crickets, and the long, wondering hoots of an owl that, according to old lore, announced the closeness of death. Tomorrow he might die.

Before dawn, a cool, moist breeze had risen from among the willows on the other side of the river. It was still dark but already getting lighter. Unable to sleep, Corporal Wulf stood by the muddy bank, watching the water, the shadows of trees, the sentries moving among men who were sleeping, turning and tossing, praying, or simply looking into the darkness above the battlefield. It might be his last day, and yet he'd never felt more fulfilled, happier. But then, around six, the guns of that wily old fox Clemenceau opened up and innocence ended for ever.

When the bullet hit Corporal Wulf, he stumbled, fell and lay—how long he had no idea—on the dewy grass near the river they had crossed earlier that morning, but now, in retreat, were being forced to re-cross. The battle raged, the air shook with explosions and the shrill sounds of volleys, like low-flying birds looking for prey. Was he going to die? Corporal Wulf saw blood seeping through his military breeches and, though he felt no real pain, only a slight throbbing in his left thigh, he was frightened. He *was* going to die!

In camp, he had heard innumerable stories about how pain would disappear before the onset of death, to reconcile the dying man with life just as he was about to be cut down by duplicitous Death. With growing trepidation, he listened to his turbulent heartbeat. He didn't *want* to die. But there he was, so young and so deserving of better things, dying on the battlefield. His eyelids grew heavier and heavier; he tried to stay awake, but couldn't. He drifted off . . .

In Vienna he had drifted, as though in a dream, through

hunger and loneliness, far removed from the security of his father's tobacco-brown study and his mother's spicy *Grenadiermarsch*. However, a couple of weeks after his arrival in Vienna with Lieutenant Saint-Imry, who soon vanished from sight, General Wulf had been lucky enough to find a reasonably cheap room, with a hard, narrow cot, a wash-basin with a clean towel, a mirror, a pail of cold water and a small window overlooking the Lichthof. His landlady was almost twice his age, but, oh, how ample, young and hot her breasts were, which she offered him with a sweet-tempered, motherly grace. Was he not lucky, already the darling of the gods?

Wandering in Vienna, young Henryk often stopped in front of the Café Apollo on Himmelpfortgasse. Behind that jaunty Biedermeier façade the exalted leaders of the cause that was defeated but not lost sat arguing and gesticulating—no doubt about the intricate historical dialectics of the disaster, and their obligations to the people they'd left behind at the mercy of the admiral's roving bands of cut-throats. Sometimes he was overcome by a desire to rush into the café and tell them how much he revered them and trusted their wisdom, how deeply he believed in their genius to rise once again, from the ashes of defeat, to crush the enemy, this time, for good. But for reasons he couldn't quite understand—too much reverence? fear?—he never did so.

He saw Adalbert Coon, former chairman of the Council of Commissars; Dr Lucas Gregory, the Jesuit, as his admirers and antagonists both fondly called him, the former commissar of culture; Julius von Halpary, scion of a historic family of country squires and public servants, former press chief to the former chairman; Rothman, the former deputy commissar of commerce, whose short, sharp, as-

tute remarks gave only the merest hint of the miraculous
intellectual powers and insights of his subsequent incar-
nation as Copass.

Singer wasn't among them, because Singer, as General
Wulf was later to learn, was already in Moscow, offering
the expertise he'd acquired as one of Karuelly's lieutenants to Felix Dzherzhinsky's Cheka; and alas, Corporal
Wulf's foremost idol, Theodore Karuelly, whose transfigured face and fiery words had made him join the Red
Army, wasn't here: before he could flee the country,
Karuelly was hunted down and summarily sentenced to
be hanged by the same group of White officers whom
Karuelly had been hunting down and hanging only a few
days before.

The *Neue Freie Presse* had run a front-page photograph
of Karuelly's hanging. Slightly blurred but quite dramatic,
the picture, taken by one of the merry participants,
showed the chairman of the Committee of Public Safety
('our Saint-Just', as later somebody acclaimed him) swing-
ing slowly in the dawn breeze, his contorted face covered
in long grey stubble, his tongue lolling from his swollen
lips. They hadn't even let him die under the black hood, as
any common criminal was entitled to do. (Perhaps that
was why, despite Jarek's protestations that he wanted to
see everything right up to the last moment, General Wulf
had insisted that he be hanged with a black hood over his
clever, clever head.) Standing at the corner of the Ring and
the Kärtnerstrasse, the *Neue Freie Presse* in his hands,
Henryk felt tears welling up in his eyes and swore revenge.

'Wulf?' Auschpitz said, as he stepped out from under
the blue, early morning shadows of the Opera. 'Wulf?
What are you doing here? Why are you here? How did you

get here? Shouldn't you be back on sweet Acacia, tugging at your mother's skirt? Tell me everything, Wulf. What happened to you?'

Auschpitz was an old friend from the gymnasium, a self-proclaimed anarchist and poet who, though only three years Henryk's senior, had already published a few poems in an obscure magazine called *oo-ZERO-oo*, committed to the idea of the total, merciless destruction of order. Although his pleasant, mocking baritone was the same, and his eyes flashed with familiar contempt, Auschpitz was now a different man. His long hair, filthy beard, shabby black shirt were gone, his hair was cut short, he wore a suit, his trousers were neatly pressed and his freshly polished black shoes sparkled like mirrors in the sunshine. The new Auschpitz, under his new name of Adymester, no longer wrote poems, only short, biting essays about the problems of violence and freedom, which he published in obscure but important little magazines in Paris, Rome and Berlin, though he had yet to publish one in Moscow. He was a disciple of Dr Gregory, the philosopher-historian and confidential secretary and political adviser to Chairman Coon.

'Come,' Auschpitz said, as they entered the Café Apollo. In the big mirrors, Henryk Wulf saw his own flustered, red face. 'Bertie,' Auschpitz said, 'this is Henryk Wulf. An old acquaintance. Also a veteran of the Red Army, wounded at Dorovar. Do you think we can give him some work around here? The man's been drifting in Vienna for weeks. Odd jobs, maybe? Like having him run up to Pressburg for the stuff? Anything.' Lighting a cigarette, Auschpitz ordered a *Kapuziner* with a *Kaisersemmel* for Henryk, and Henryk knew he'd found home.

* * *

'We feel,' Singer continued under the lush, sunlit palms of the glass-house, 'that *Genosse* Herbert, merely by his presence on our Executive Committee, damages our work. We also think we can no longer tolerate his being privy to all our confidential plans, actions, ideas. Therefore he must be removed without further delay. Here's a letter to the *Freikorps* that'll take care of it. It identifies him as a Soviet agent. It's the truth. Even if it's a lie, it's the truth—a higher, more meaningful truth, which only a few people can comprehend and act upon. *Genosse* Herbert is a lie. *We* are the truth. Sign it here, Wulf.'

In Count Francis's armchair behind the large mahogany desk, Gerogen paused for a second, and Justice Krolthy followed the gaze of his watery blue eyes, fixed briefly on each of the participants at that ludicrous meeting, as though their reaction would betray priceless information.

'There are many problems inherent in our perception of the present,' Gerogen went on, 'but the first, most important, indeed stupefying problem is its virtual intangibility. You see, it's easy to deal with the past, for it's not only tangible, but also alterable: it is what you make of it. It's even easier to deal with the future, because it's not only shapeable but penetrable: it is how you invent it. But the present is an entirely different dilemma. The present simply exists, it is what it *is*, much like the Old Testament God, an unpredictable, vengeful, jealous spirit, who thrives amid the lawlessness of his own laws, because he's not only the giver but also the violator of the law, and nothing pleases him more than to punish those against whom *he* has transgressed. *Bah!* That, exactly, was what the present was all about, a mêlée of randomness mixed with instability, the coincidental, the casual, the haphaz-ard—until we discovered its secret.

'No wonder human history was such a disaster! We soon realized that we could reinterpret the past, even change it if necessary; we could also invent the future, as fancifully and as often as we needed, but what could we do with the present? It took some time for us to understand that, in order to master the present, as we had mastered the past and the future, we had to define its boundaries and neutralize its randomness. We had to perpetuate it.

'When the prophets of the Old Testament whipped their people for their sinfulness, it was always to remind them of the sublimity of the ancients, whose transcen-dence had been imbued by the spirit of God and was therefore perfect. If the prophets wanted to conquer the future, they wanted to do so in order to restore the holiness of the *past*. When the Jacobins talked about those pure, sensitive souls who understood the passion of their hatred of tyranny, they invoked the vision of a *future* Republic of Virtue, which would fulfil the public good. For millennia, peoples and prophets turned to the past for perfection. Since the destruction of the Bastille, people have turned towards the future for consummation. Who has ever paid attention to the present?

'The Old Man himself had neither the patience nor the time to deal with the ramifications of the present as a historical phenomenon. It was only the *Vozhd* who, for the first time in history, had the courage to face the vacuum that is the past, the void that is the future, and set out to define, stabilize and extend the boundaries of the present. We, his modest, second-rate disciples, only tried to follow in his footsteps and apply his methods. Consequently, we claim no originality, although we *do* claim results! We've managed to free ourselves from metaphysical constraints, left behind the shackles of traditional ethics, and so become the world's first genuine controllers and practitioners of a de-historicized history. And we did quite a good job, wouldn't you agree?'

He looked towards the rose garden. Outside the open windows the loud quarrelling of crows and blackbirds filled the sunny air until a few bursts of buckshot made them scatter in the direction of the arboretum and the tennis courts.

'Nobody could deny,' Gerogen continued with an unusual glint in his watery blue eyes, 'nobody could possibly deny that the early tensions we created laid the groundwork for the present. The masses recognized that something extraordinary was going to happen, was already happening, that *our* way was the *only* way to achieve the harmony and peace they'd been striving for. In a fundamentally secular epoch, we became mythical heroes—re-creators of the Garden of Eden!—and the enthusiasm of the masses reached such heights as to surprise even ourselves! But you remember all that, for you were not idle observers but active participants in our triumphs, which led to a union between leaders and people hitherto unparalleled in history. After decades in the wilderness, what vistas opened up before us!

'Remember our annual parades in front of the *Vozhd*'s statue? Those picnics in the Avar hills where the new rituals of our new epoch expressed the hopes and wishes of the people who could never before articulate them so freely and with such fluency and power? Remember how parents and children wept and laughed with joy and gratitude? Ah, the outpouring reverence and kindness of those simple people towards us! What an unforgettable experience! Didn't we hand them their rightful inheritance on a silver platter, free? The land, the factories, the . mines, the banks, the big monopolies and merchant houses? Drove the old masters from their palaces and castles? Taught the people how to organize, how to play, how to win? Yes, yes, we were their parents, teachers, leaders, prophets. And they trusted us, respected us, feared us and loved us.' A pale, almost ethereal smile wreathed Gerogen's bloodless lips, as he sipped his weak, sugarless tea from an earthenware mug. 'That was our present!'

Justice Krolthy listened with incredulity. He was unwilling to believe his ears. Never since he and Gerogen had sealed their compact on the balcony of his apartment had he suspected that Gerogen really believed the gibberish he was obliged to deliver. That intelligent, urbane, sophisticated cynic? That cold-blooded murderer? How could he fall for his own rhetoric? The creator, in one of his less guarded moments, of the equation of power: $S = lt^2$, *success equals lie* × *square of improbability of truth!* Gerogen recited it because there was nothing else to say; because he had wasted his lifetime repeating those fetid words, *exploitation, oppression, revolution, freedom, people, imperialism, sacrifice,* always for the ultimate truth of *la lutte finale,* until they became a meaningless blur. But by then, it was too late for Gerogen to change course; by then, he was committed to the lie. And he must have *known* it was a lie. Everybody knew—Henryk, Anselm, Copass, Adymester, Pater Kral, even the man in the street, *especially* the man in the street. But now, Justice Krolthy realized that he was wrong. Gerogen believed! Deep beneath the shimmering surface of polished platitudes, Gerogen believed his lie was actually the truth.

For years, Justice Krolthy had been convinced that Gerogen was the man he appeared to be, a man of power and will, not particularly troubled by pangs of conscience, with whom, therefore, other people equally unbothered by pangs of conscience could safely do business. But now Justice Krolthy understood that beneath all that coldness and cruelty fluttered a heart full of zealous love for mankind. It was more than frightening: it was dangerous; it was funny. Oh, God, how irresistibly funny it was! The leader of the unbelievers caught in the act of high belief, the Eternal Jew enunciating his unflagging faith in the coming of the Messiah! Instinctively, Justice Krolthy reached for his cigar-case, but then remembered that smoking was discreetly discouraged in Gerogen's presence, so he took his handkerchief from his breast-pocket instead, wiped his brow, and tried to conceal his merriment before Gerogen noticed. Justice Krolthy knew he was in mortal peril, but he no longer felt threatened; he was intrigued.

'Then,' Gerogen said, 'the *Vozhd* died.'

At two-fifteen in the morning, Justice Krolthy had awoken with a start to hear a car drive up to the main portico, then, a minute or two later, drive off again. He knew that Gerogen had arrived. He went back to sleep straight away and woke at seven, his regular hour. Now, luxuriating in a hot tub, he pondered yesterday's fiasco. The rage he had felt when they'd discovered the Skoda, the dismay that followed, seemed to have diminished during the night and, among the fragrances of the bathroom, completely evaporated. He understood clearly that what was happening was inescapable, and that he would have to face it without the protection of his compact with Gerogen. On the other hand, he thought, his assumption that Gerogen was in serious trouble was no longer a hypothesis: it was unquestionably true, a fact that he was quite prepared to take advantage of.

The crippled Skoda was exactly where they'd left it last night, in front of the main portico. Justice Krolthy turned the key in the ignition, put his foot on the accelerator and the engine came alive. Then he walked to the green room where on the sideboard breakfast awaited in abundance. The coffee was the correct mix of Brazilian and Colombian mild. The scrambled eggs, kept warm in the silver chafing dish, had just the right consistency. With delight, Justice Krolthy took a large portion.

In the pale glimmer of the morning which spread pleasantly through the half-open french windows, the Countess Julia, in white dress and tennis shoes, appeared more beautiful, and more innocent, than Justice Krolthy had ever seen her. On the mantelpiece two candles were waiting to be lit in homage. Yesterday or the day before, Justice Krolthy had turned the place upside down for a candle (a stump would have done), but had found none. Now, here were two white, slim, elegant candies with the sign of the rose, Countess Julia's favourite flower. Since Gerogen had arrived everything had changed. Justice Krolthy lit the candles and watched the flames' nimble flight.

He could never fully understand his attraction to the Countess Julia. What was the nature of her charm? Why did he invariably feel that sharp, intense longing for her the moment he entered the green room, that irresistible pull which wasn't lust but some quiet wave of jubilation, a sense of triumph in the middle of defeat? Surely it wasn't her beauty, her life? Nor was it her legendary innocence, because Justice Krolthy wouldn't have fallen for that. All his life he had steered clear of innocents, men and women alike, shunned them, scorned them, flouted them. The world was a dangerous enough place without innocents, but with them it was a quagmire. Innocents were worse than sinners. You could talk sense to sinners. You could, if you wanted, even talk them into repenting of their sin, but what could you do with innocents? They never listened, never heard what you said; with the ascetic peremptoriness and absolute certainty of the chaste, they demanded that *you* listen to their endless sermonizings about unity and brotherhood, beauty and harmony, understanding and love.

Love! Surely it couldn't be love that attracted him to Countess Julia, because you couldn't love a painting, and, with the possible exception of a certain Judith Gaya, whom he had once come dangerously close to loving, Adam Krolthy had been lucky enough to avoid its complications and coruscations. So what was this fascination all about? It was something Justice Krolthy couldn't fathom, no matter how hard he tried. Might it be something that was inherent not in the Countess Julia's strength but in his own weakness? He wasn't sure. He tasted his eggs, but they were now cold, so he walked over to the french windows to look out on the Countess Julia's rose garden. His good mood had vanished.

'Have you ever been out to that old redoubt behind the tennis courts, Adam?' Gerogen asked, his long grey coat over his left arm, sweat beading his forehead. 'I've just come across it, accidentally. Never seen it before. Quite something, isn't it? Probably late thirteenth century, early fourteenth, maybe. Or the Tartars might have built it even earlier. They understood the importance of such defences.'

He carefully put his coat on the back of a chair and, with a hint of a smile in his melancholy eyes, poured himself a cup of tea and sat opposite Justice Krolthy. 'That's what the whole thing's all about, Adam, defence. Caesar knew it all too well. Vercingetorix must have thought himself invincible inside his impenetrable Alesia. That's how Caesar wanted him to feel, that impertinent Gaul who dared rebel against the empire! Then, suddenly, Caesar surrounded the barbarians and let them stew in their own juices. Precisely how it should be done, Adam. You know that. Make your enemies come together in what appears to them a protected citadel, then, as quickly as you can, surround them, cut them off from the world, and wait until they turn against each other before you turn against them. *Ce monde est plein de fous,* my esteemed judge. They'll never learn.'

'Apparently not, my esteemed prime minister,' Justice Krolthy said. 'But you can take comfort in the fact that your very own idiots have fully learned your wisdom.'

'Meaning?' Gerogen asked.

'Meaning simply that, as late as yesterday, they surrounded and isolated your leading village idiot—an old fool called Martin Flur—who has been chairman of the town council and has served you and your other high-ranking lunatics better than anybody else around here. None the less your thugs came yesterday and took Flur, just like in the good old days, although I'd been labouring under the impression that those good old days were over, as you yourself so graciously told me some months ago. But I had absolutely no idea what was happening.'

Gerogen sipped the bitter tea from his earthenware mug. 'Couldn't you have called the command and found it out for yourself? So why didn't you?'

'I don't really know,' Justice Krolthy said. 'Maybe I thought, being chief *nachalnik* and all that, you might like to be informed about what was going on around here. Or maybe it was because since we've been gathered here—surrounded, isolated, cut off from the world—our phones have been working only in one distinctly pre-engineered direction.'

His face expressionless, Gerogen picked up the phone from the table in front of him. It worked perfectly. He dialled a number.

'Yes,' Gerogen said. 'Get me Vukovič. At once. Yes.'

Vukovič came on the line instantly.

'Vukovič,' Gerogen said, 'I'm told your morons have done it again. Do you have any idea what's happening here and why? I want an answer in fifteen minutes. Yes, Vukovič, in fifteen minutes. I'm waiting. On this number.'

He hung up the phone and walked over to the french windows. Justice Krolthy followed his glance towards the old redoubt beyond the arboretum. There was silence in the green room. Gerogen closed his eyes. He often boasted how he'd learned to sleep standing up, or even marching, in Spain, and how profitably he had used this skill later in the Ukraine and on the Polish plains. Now he again went to sleep, and Justice Krolthy wondered what he was dreaming.

Justice Krolthy quickly tossed off a glass of schnapps from Aunt Elsie's famous collection and watched Gerogen. He looked exactly as he had almost ten years ago, standing in the moonlight on the balcony of Justice Krolthy's apartment overlooking the river and the Avar hills. Gerogen hadn't aged, and Justice Krolthy couldn't help being envious. Maybe Gerogen was immortal? Like Uncle Karol, Aunt Elsie, the Countess Julia, Sybil Wald, little Julie—all those strangers around him here who never showed the ravages of time. What was their secret? Looking at Gerogen, standing at the window asleep—to refresh himself so that he could face whatever was to be faced while waiting for the call from Vukovič—Justice Krolthy suddenly felt old.

When he came home a few minutes after midnight and put the key in the lock, Judge Krolthy sensed something was amiss. He listened intently, but could hear nothing suspicious, so he slowly opened the door. There was a sharp, vivid silence, but, with a shrug, he took off his dinner-jacket and went to the kitchen to prepare his favourite bedtime drink—a glass of milk with a shot of Martell laced with a dash of cinnamon. He decided to drink it on the balcony, to enjoy the warm, clear night for a few more moments before going to bed (alone, though with the tingling promise of a new tryst). He hoped to have a brief, dreamless but invigorating sleep to prepare him for the beginning of tomorrow's trial, his first one as a full member of the Curia. His recent elevation from assistant judge to full membership of the Curia added to his feelings of pride and contentment: at forty-two he was not only the youngest of the fifteen full justices, but in every respect, the most successful.

He was in excellent humour. It had been a splendid garden party. Given by Major-General Jefferson-Smith, the American representative of the Allied Control Commission, to celebrate the Fourth of July, the party was held among the miniature ponds, cascading brooks and small waterfalls of the late Godolphus Goldstein's world-famous Japanese garden, or what was left of it after the war. The prime minister (a huge peasant), the cardinal (a lean monk) and the chief justice of the Curia (a portly grandfather) all came. There was plenty of champagne and caviar, the best Beluga one could have, old Marshal Shorovilov's generous gift for this celebration of America's independence from British colonialism. And Judge Krolthy had been pleased, excited even, when Mrs Lavinia Jefferson-Smith, a tall blonde who was a former beauty queen, had finally consented to take a look at the view from his balcony.

Judge Krolthy took a glass of champagne and some caviar from the waiter's silver tray. Moving among the guests with a frozen smile, for all anybody knew, the waiter might be one of Jarek's agents, with a photographic memory and a small tape-recorder under his white tunic, but Judge Krolthy didn't really care. For the moment, even his hatred for Jarek diminished. It might not be the best world possible, but it was an acceptable one, at least, and one would be well advised to accept it. It would be hard for him to leave, as Eve and McIlvey wanted him to do— before it was too late, they kept arguing—to go with them to Paris, and, later, perhaps, to America. Even the idea of leaving made him feel homesick for his town, for those lights coming on down in the valley and on the plains beyond the river; for his sixth-floor apartment; for his new office in the Curia (had he been a superstitious man, the fact that the office overlooked a quiet cul-de-sac might have filled him with foreboding, but he wasn't, so its spurious symbolism left him untouched). Though Eve and McIlvey were pressing him hard to make a decision, his mind wasn't made up.

He watched Lavinia gliding nimbly from one group to another, from one table to the next, the perfect hostess with the perfect poise, and Judge Krolthy knew that, however little hope the future might hold, his present was promising, amusing, satisfying. In her pink muslin dress, with her long blonde hair swept up into a chignon held in place by a large, black, diamond-studded conch-comb, and a string of pink pearls around her lovely neck, Lavinia passed him several times without once glancing at him, yet Judge Krolthy sensed the message of her body.

He took another glass of champagne from Jarek's agent and became aware of the laughter that rolled towards him from the next table, which stood under a huge, multi-coloured beach-umbrella. Judge Krolthy saw that, as far as entertainment was concerned, he couldn't have chosen a better spot. In the middle of his regular coterie of friends and enemies sat Gideon Weiskopf, giving one of his usual lectures. Being an old Social Democrat, it was probably about the social and psychological complexities of educating the ordinary man so that, eventually, he might become master of his own destiny. How many times Judge Krolthy had heard all that from Gideon Weiskopf—the depravity of totalitarian autocracy, the impotence of capitalist technocracy, the self-governing ethics of a populist democracy—during the early summer of '44.

He had taken Eve and Jarek down to Krolthy House to hide them from the Gestapo. They had hoped to return to the city within a few days, but had had to stay for almost two months. It wasn't too bad a time, Eve had later confessed to Adam, even though Jarek turned restless and wanted to go back to the 'battlefield', as he called it affectionately. In fact, Eve said, it was a wonderful time for love among the vineyards and mulberry bushes. Jarek had never been more passionate, more loving, more selfless. (It wasn't easy for Adam to imagine Jarek in the role of passionate lover, but Eve sounded convincing and convinced.)

He drove up from the city to visit them whenever he could, and one day he had found Gideon Weiskopf on the porch. He was an old acquaintance of Jarek's and was now their next-door neighbour, having gone into hiding in Bethulia House, his brother's abandoned home. Since the Germans had occupied the country in March, he and his Social Democrat brothers had been forced to go underground.

Major Krolthy used to listen to Gideon Weiskopf's lectures whenever he could. Even Jarek listened to the professor with a respect akin to admiration. Though they often locked horns about the method of creating that ideal society—Weiskopf scorned Jarek's radical theories of destruction as the idiotic wish-fulfilments of an infantile ego, while Jarek castigated the theory of the slow building-process of the architect in the face of a bourgeoisie armed to the teeth with weapons of oppression and exploitation—they laughed a lot. But, of course, they were both innocents. Also, Major Krolthy realized with astonishment as he drove back to General Gylkosh's headquarters in the city, they were oddly and unaccountably free.

At the garden party Judge Krolthy watched Gideon Weiskopf with great interest. He hadn't met him for three years, since Gideon Weiskopf, representing the Social Democrats in the new coalition government formed after the war, was named minister of education and culture. Judge Krolthy had sent him a note of congratulations, wishing him well in realizing his ideas about the common man and his self-governing destiny, but, alas, destiny did not grant Gideon Weiskopf enough time to turn his ideas into realities. A few short months after he took office, Copass and his gang demanded that the Ministry of Education and Culture be added to their territory of control. Their control of the Ministry of the Interior, the Ministry of Reconstruction and the Ministry of Agriculture had already given them full command over the police, industry and land redistribution. With the Red Army backing them and Jarek organizing the new State Security Forces, Copass and his cohorts threatened to withdraw from the fragile coalition if all their demands weren't met immediately. So, Gideon Weiskopf resigned. As a consolation prize he was given the presidency of the Academy of Sciences, which he accepted with grace and humility, and vanished from the public eye into the rarified air of scholarly research. A strange man.

Judge Krolthy stood up and walked closer to the magic circle; Gideon Weiskopf acknowledged his presence with a sly wink of his dark-hooded eyes. An extraordinary man!

'They are on the march again,' Professor Weiskopf was saying, indicating with an almost imperceptible movement Copass and his entourage, who, on a lower terrace of the garden, were proceeding towards the major-general and his wife. Jefferson-Smith greeted the first deputy prime minister, the minister of education and culture, and the head of the army's Political Department with a firm military salute and a wan smile. Copass reciprocated with the broadest, friendliest grin he could muster. Adymester's eyes remained cold, and he stood motionless, as if facing the firing squad, not the sunlit countenance of a beautiful woman. Major-General Wulf appeared to be more interested in the display of bottles on a table covered with an exquisitely embroidered damask cloth than in the polite words of a fellow general.

'Yes, they *are* on the march again,' Gideon Weiskopf repeated, bemused by the show being played out on the second terrace, 'the medieval *prophetae* of the *pauperes* with the chiliastic fantasies of an imminent *Parousia*. See for yourselves how familiar they are! Descendants of the spiritualists and the enthusiasts, progenies of the Waldensian *perfecti*, successors of the Taborites of Prague, the Anabaptists of Münster, the Jacobins of Paris, the nihilists of Moscow, the Bolsheviks of St Petersburg, knights of the apocalypse, the vanguard of history! It has all happened before and now it is going to happen again, and we can do nothing about it.

'Unique representatives and sole interpreters of the divine will, the general will, the will of the people, the law of historical inevitability, *they* will do everything for *us*, in our name, since that is the object of their mission! For, of course, they know precisely what needs to be done, have always known it, and there's nothing more frightening about them than the fearless certitude of their own sense of infallibility. Like their forerunners, they are convinced that they have attained a perfection so absolute that it makes them immune to error, so they can do whatever pleases them, uncontrolled by law, unshackled by tradition, accountable only to themselves. Observe them, friends, before it's too late.'

When Eve arrived with McIlvey the sun was falling slowly behind the Saxenberg, and the shadows of dusk surrounded them. In her silk blouse, light-grey worsted suit and jaunty, dark-blue beret, Eve looked more like a traveller than reveller. Judge Krolthy knew that it was Eve's way of telling him and all concerned that they had come not only to celebrate but also to say goodbye, though they didn't want to leave without Major-General Jefferson-Smith's blessing. He shook hands with his chief political adviser, kissed Eve's cheeks lightly, then turned them over to Lavinia, who flagged down one of Jarek's agents with the champagne trays, and they raised their glasses, drank and laughed joyfully, relaxed. Even in her travelling outfit Eve looked ravishing, happier and more in love than Adam could remember seeing her, certainly during her years with Jarek, when she complied with Jarek's ideals of a revolutionary feminist—no make-up, no fancy clothes. Eve had done everything she could to please Jarek not only because she loved him, but also because, at that point at any rate, she believed, wanted to believe, Jarek's tales of *liberté, égalité, fraternité*.

One day, in the first, lazy months of the 'phony war', Eve had come back from Paris and just appeared on the doorstep of Jarek's house in the shadows of the blackened chimneys and rotting warehouses of the Sixteenth District. She went inside—without being asked, as Jarek used to say with a satisfied laugh when he recounted the story—and, in no time, that experienced, intelligent girl emerged as a starry-eyed enthusiast. What really *did* happen, Justice Krolthy often wondered, in that sooty shanty? Eve had never said a word about it, but Adam could make a guess or two. Maybe Jarek was irresistible as a man. Judge Krolthy remembered him, lean and angry, in the little bistro in Paris behind the Deux Magôts; his tirade against the world had sounded entertaining, some might say convincing, but Jarek's way with women didn't seem an unmitigated success . . . Maybe Eve just wanted to love

Jarek and give him her greatest gift—her faith in his nonsense, her devotion to his cause? Or maybe it was something he'd never understand.

Judge Krolthy had resigned himself to having Jarek as his brother-in-law. He didn't really mind; he'd liked Jarek in a curious, bemused way the first moment they met in Paris at the Tricolour Club, and hadn't he offered Jarek his apartment, complete with Mme Escande's famous vegetable soup, the milk-trains of Saint-Lazare, the whores of the Chaussée d'Antin? Then, one morning, before leaving for the ministry he then headed, Jarek told Eve, casually, as if informing her about his daily schedule, that their relationship was finished, and he wasn't going to return home that evening or, for that matter, any other evening. Jarek didn't say why, didn't explain or elaborate; he simply said, 'Sorry'. Then, his shabby old attaché case under his arm, he left unhurriedly, as if going for a walk.

Eve took the next train to Krolthy House and locked herself up in her father's secret room with the Bosch (which was still hanging there, exactly as they'd found it so many years before, for Eve wouldn't hear of removing it from its original spot). She had stayed there, as though immured. What did she eat? Where did she sleep? After a week, Eve had emerged, her old self again, cheerful, capricious, challenging. Six months later she'd met McIlvey.

'Judge Krolthy,' Gerogen said, rising from a folding chair on the balcony, 'I took the liberty of letting myself in. I hoped you would understand. My apologies. We must talk, but it wouldn't have been advisable for us to be seen together in public.'

'Minister,' Judge Krolthy said, caught off-guard, with

his brandy-milk in his hand. 'By all means. Please, take a seat. I'm honoured. Can I get you something? A Scotch? Some beer, maybe?'

'Thank you, Judge,' Gerogen said. 'I'm not allowed to drink. I've had an ulcerous stomach ever since I can remember. Maybe a little tea later. What a beautiful place you have here, Judge Krolthy. I especially admired your Polish things. Do they come from Krolthy House? That magnificent cupboard with the marquetry of elm, black oak and green-dyed walnut looks like a Kolbuszowa piece. Or is it from the Poniatowski collection? But please, please, have your brandy-milk even if I can't join you in drinking a toast to what I hope will be a most profitable collaboration between us.'

From the table he lifted a crystal glass full of what in the scintillating moonlight seemed to be pure water, and raised it. 'To our past, Judge Krolthy. *And* to our present!'

'I'll drink to that,' Adam Krolthy said. He took a sip from his brandy-milk, and seated himself in the other folding chair facing the river and the Avar hills. 'The cupboard is from Krolthy House, and so is the chair. According to family legend, it was Jan Hus's favourite when he stayed with us; after heavy meals he loved to have a little nap in it on the west porch, where there was always a breeze from the mountains to cool bodies and tempers. You must come in the daylight to see it for yourself, Minister. The Krolthys go back to the fourteenth century, so there's quite a lot to see.'

In the moonlight he studied Gerogen's face, familiar from posters, cartoons and photos. Judge Krolthy had met him in person only once or twice, and then only for a few seconds, at crowded government receptions or other public functions to which Judge Krolthy was now invited.

The minister of reconstruction was popularly known as the 'Bridge-builder', for it was under his captaincy that the bridges blown to smithereens by the Germans had been rebuilt, quickly and efficiently. He looked more or less like the photographs, a strong, silent, honest servant of the people. But the 'Bridge-builder' bit was a failed piece of agitprop to counteract Gerogen's reputation as an old Chekist, a shrewd tactician and ruthless executioner. People seemed to know, or at least to sense, what Gerogen really was, although, as McIlvey once told Judge Krolthy, they didn't know that Gerogen was the *real* boss of the country.

He was even higher than Copass in the hierarchy, by virtue of his rank, his past connections in the Cheka, and his odd relationship with the *Vozhd*, who seemed to favour this withdrawn, taciturn man who kept his own council among the noisy, ever-quarrelling, hate-filled émigré dignitaries. Once or twice, the *Vozhd* had even invited Gerogen to his small Kremlin apartment to join the frolics of his inner circle. They needed Copass, McIlvey had said, for his legendary sixteen years in the enemy's prisons, his round, pleasant, ordinary face—the face of a kindly old Jewish village grocer who'd give credit to his customers and free rock candy to their kids—but it was Gerogen who actually held the reins of the present in his gnarled fingers. So, McIlvey advised, if you wanted to keep your head on your neck, you'd better keep your eye on Gerogen.

'Another glass of water, Minister?' Judge Krolthy said. 'An excellent vintage.'

'You are a man of many ironies, Judge Krolthy,' Gerogen said, and Judge Krolthy saw a faint smile slither over his melancholy face. 'And also, as your reputation clearly suggests, a man of great foresight and deep perception. So, permit me to be frank. Our offer, as you'll see presently, is simple and self-explanatory. The brief comments I'm about to make serve only as a background sketch, but one we believe you must consider in order to make a well-reasoned decision, tough enough to withstand the erosions of time, yet subtle enough to accord with a complex situation. We want our relationship to be based on an understanding of mutual interests.

'As we see it,' Gerogen went on, 'the country is at the crossroads, and I'm sure you wouldn't be surprised if I told you that we already know which direction it is going to take. Disorder is rampant, Judge Krolthy, and we must introduce order and discipline. Therefore, let me simply say that together with our political and economic structure, we also require the general reorganization of our judicial system. For that reason, we have decided to abolish the Curia. We know, of course, that the Curia is an institution deeply rooted in the past, but, as such, it has long been tainted by barbaric acts of class-vengeance—tortures, life-imprisonments, summary hangings of those who dared to disagree with its actions. Its elimination from the stage, so to speak, could be seen as an act of historical justice rather than some perverse mutilation of tradition.

'We don't think we should pay much attention to voices from the past. It is, after all, the present we are most interested in. So, in place of the Curia, we plan to erect a new edifice of justice—metaphorically speaking, of course, for we propose to keep the old shell and fill it with new life, though we might, in time, replace the gilded Roman motto above its portico, *Fiat justitia*, with an epigraph more appropriate for our purposes. The new judicial system will be headed by a presiding judge. The post

represents a historical undertaking, a challenge for anyone whose devotion to the law takes precedence over his
personal concerns. We have decided to offer it to you,
Judge Krolthy, because we believe that our cooperation
will be based on a clear understanding of our respective
interests, and that we will each fulfil our respective commitments with honour and without suspicion. So, Judge
Krolthy, the job is yours for the taking. But don't answer:
I haven't finished yet. Hear me out fully.'

Gerogen took another sip of the water and wiped his
white forehead and black eyebrows with a crisp linen
handkerchief which he then folded carefully and put back
in the inside pocket of his grey jacket.

Judge Krolthy thought of the prime minister, the chief
justice of the Curia, the cardinal, Prince Primate of Gesterom, whom he had seen less than a couple of hours ago
in that lovely garden of serenity and harmony under the
pale lights of the lanterns; now he saw them all dead and
buried, some literally, some figuratively, under the grey,
burnt-out fields of the future, while Copass and his prae-
torian guard roamed over their graves waving official
death-certificates signed and sealed by Presiding Judge
Krolthy. Was he ready for all that, Judge Krolthy wondered. Perhaps he should leave with Eve tomorrow morning, sneak out of the back door, as it were, in the boot of
McIlvey's big Ford? Perhaps he should simply say no, and
accept the consequences? He had never been interested in
power—he had been born into it, used it successfully, but
didn't really care for its responsibilities and dangers,
though he didn't mind its perks. So why should he accept
now, just when he was about to settle down to live the
good life?

'We know, of course,' Gerogen continued, 'that Miss

Krolthy is going to leave us for good tomorrow morning—
she has hardly made a great secret of her intentions—with
Commander Fontanelle, alias McIlvey, of the American
Naval Intelligence. During his tenure as chief political
adviser to Major-General Jefferson-Smith, Commander
Fontanelle has been somewhat secretive about his real
work and identity, but we want you to understand that we
bear no ill-will towards him and have no objection to their
departure. We realize how deeply Miss Krolthy cares for
the commander. Besides, we remember her loyalty and
devotion during the war. Despite rumours to the contrary,
we have, Judge Krolthy, an excellent memory as well as a
good sense of appreciation. Therefore they can depart
with our blessings. We also know how very much Miss
Krolthy would like you to join them, and we might as well
tell you that, if you so decide, you, too, are free to leave. We
won't stop you, though we would regret your decision.

'If you choose to stay, this is our proposition: we offer
you freedom,' Gerogen said. 'We recognize how greatly
you treasure your personal freedom, and, we believe, we
understand it well. We are, therefore, offering you personal freedom, without restrictions or restraints, in exchange not for your loyalty and devotion—we cannot
expect that, perhaps nobody can—but for your signature.
Your stamp on *our* documents: that is all we want. A
reasonable offer, wouldn't you say? We hope you'll be
able to accept it.'

The telephone rang.

'Yes,' Gerogen said. 'Yes, Vukovič, I see. Well, tell them
to let the old geezer go at once.' He made an impatient
gesture with his left hand. 'Now, wait a minute, Vukovič.
First, get those nitwits to apologize to Flur. Then, have

them drive him home to the bosom of his family. And Vukovič, report back to me the moment you've heard from your man.'

He put down the receiver and turned to Justice Krolthy.

'They've arrested old Flur because of the flag.'

'What flag?' Justice Krolthy asked.

'Flur had the flag in front of the town hall at half-mast.'

'At the risk of sounding more inane than your very own nitwits, Ernest, may I ask you to be just a little more specific?'

'To commemorate 26 October. Have you forgotten, Adam? The day of the martyrs of Vareges. The day you went to lay a wreath at the Cenotaph with a black armband on your left arm in Ceberden. The day we dropped from our national holidays a long time ago.'

'And the day he still remembers?'

'Apparently,' Gerogen said. 'An old-fashioned patriot? A senile simpleton, more likely!'

'Probably both,' Justice Krolthy said. 'And three cheers for him!'

'The death of the *Vozhd*,' Gerogen continued from behind Count Francis's huge mahogany desk, 'created a number of problems for us, most of them foreseen, but some baffling, I'm afraid.' He paused, his voice cracking, his face ashen, as though he were still in shock, more than two years after that fateful day, when, as Copass said in his celebrated oration at the catafalque, the world was orphaned.

Monsignor Beck always found it revealing to observe how uncomfortably ambivalent Gerogen and his colleagues became in the face of death. It was not just the death of the *Vozhd*—because of the *Vozhd*'s growing paranoia, they must have hoped he would die, though his death found them unprepared—but the very existence of death in the world that troubled them. In public, they viewed death, as Adymester had written in one of his little pamphlets, *Notes of an Optimist*, as nature's way of creating a balance between its two opposite but equally important parts, thereby fusing them into one inseparable whole, in which the survival of the individual was secured by the survival of the race. When Monsignor Beck had pointed out that his formula was an ancient cliché, Adymester had boasted that, cliché or not, it had achieved what he had always wanted to achieve: the translation of a reactionary metaphysical concept into a simple, earthy proposition, tailor-made for simple people unequipped to deal with theological subtleties. If death was a necessity, so was history. An argument could be made about biological and historical necessities whose basic function was to lead man towards perfection, which was not Father Beck's solipsist heaven, but humanity's well-deserved haven of freedom. Freedom was the recognition of necessity; by definition, we were all immortals, like the gods—*nay*, we were gods ourselves!

'Not that we didn't anticipate the death of the *Vozhd*.' Gerogen got up from the desk and started pacing the room. 'We did. Unfortunately, he, too, was mortal, like the rest of us, although secretly, deep in our hearts, we hoped that God or nature or history would make an exception and let him live for ever, thereby absolving us from having to face the void we knew he would leave as his legacy. But our silent supplications were left unanswered, as is, Monsignor Beck would no doubt be delighted to tell you, usually the case. So, here we are.'

The shadow of a distant smile fell across his eyes and

mouth, and his voice again became even: the man was fully in control again. As Henryk had so often mumbled, in fury or in admiration, Gerogen was control personified. If Monsignor Beck couldn't admire him as a spiritual being, as a monk, trained in exercising self-control and composure, he could at least appreciate Gerogen's physical powers of recovery, of self-discipline.

'As you well know, we had to cope with his passing.' Gerogen walked back to his chair behind the desk, and Monsignor Beck felt a wave of sadness in his heart, such as he had not experienced since the death of good old Abbot Balthasar, his mentor and protector in his novice days. For Monsignor Beck knew how deeply Gerogen and his fellow unbelievers dreaded death, despite Adymester's slick optimism and blundering agitprop attempts to explain the horror of extinction as the happiest, richest sacrifice the individual can offer his fellow human beings.

'But,' Gerogen continued, 'we faced it well. Not for nothing did they call us the *Vozhd's* best disciples. We knew what we had to do. We fortified the bases of our power and strengthened our defences, yet, there was one thing we didn't expect. In the middle of our mourning, we didn't expect the swift, forceful re-emergence of the past. When we least expected it, the past came back to haunt us, is at this very moment haunting us. We must talk about the past. More precisely, we must talk about the dead. For it is not the living that bother us these days. I'm sure you understand that I'm talking about Ladislas Jarek.'

Soon after he had finished morning Mass for the souls of the martyrs Saint Simon and Saint Jude—*Gloriam, Domine, sanctorum Apostolorum*—Monsignor Beck heard a knock on the door. He opened it and saw a young boy with the old countess's *prie-dieu.*

'Where should I put this, Father?' the boy asked with a respectful smile. 'I was told you need it urgently.'

'And who might you be?' Monsignor Beck said, opening the door wide for the boy. 'You can put it over there.' He indicated the wall under the window.

'Just a visitor.' Swiftly, effortlessly, the boy lowered the *prie-dieu* into place, then made for the door. 'My mother's in the hospital, and my father had to fly.'

'Is he some kind of a bird?' Monsignor Beck asked. 'A new species I should know?'

'Yes.' The boy laughed. 'He's a pilot in the Air Force. Everybody knows that, Father.' His hand was on the doorknob.

'Now wait a minute, visitor,' Monsignor Beck said with mock seriousness, 'you can't just charge into my room and charge out without even introducing yourself.'

'I'm Berti Lucas Flur,' the boy said standing at attention. 'My father is Colonel Lucas Flur and my grandfather is chairman of the Krestur town council. Can I go now, Father? My grandma said I'd better be home by nine, and Aunt Sybil said I still have lots of things to do here.'

'Well, run, Berti Lucas Flur.' With a quick, practised movement Monsignor Beck made a cross on the boy's forehead. 'By the way, do you happen to know somebody called Peter Wald?'

'He's my best *secret* friend!' The boy's large black eyes lit up. 'That's why I have to hurry back to Krestur, Father. I promised to help him with the funeral and the wake tomorrow. But, please, Father, don't tell on us. I'm not supposed to be friends with Peter. My grandfather says the Walds are all scum and traitors, and we must never talk to them.'

'I see,' Monsignor Beck said. 'So, go and help your friend, Berti Lucas Flur. You can trust me. I won't tell on you.'

The *prie-dieu* was old, but as solid as it was when it was made almost two hundred years before. Why Henryk Wulf had had it sent up to him, Monsignor Beck couldn't imagine. He knew Henryk had loved the old thing so much that he wanted to take it with him to Lilac Hill, but taking anything from the manor was against the rules he himself had issued. Monsignor Beck rose, put the Eucharist back in the little silver box he always kept with him— his *mini-ciborium* as he liked to call it—and finished the wine he had consecrated the evening before, after they'd found the sabotaged Skoda in front of the main portico. For a while, they'd stood around the little car without a word, then, speechless, went back to their rooms. Monsignor Beck slept quietly until two-fifteen, waking as he had done every day for almost forty years in the monastery, for vigils. As he softly chanted the brief office of Psalms—'For the Lord knows the way of the righteous, but the way of the wicked shall perish'—he heard Gerogen's car pull up to the main entrance.

Now it was Sunday morning, and he thought he should go to Krestur to help Father Novak say *Missa Defunctorum* for little Anna Julia Sybilla, but from the moment he met him Monsignor Beck had sensed the young priest's hostility. He wasn't surprised. He knew well what, these days, exercised the hearts and minds of those young men who, despite the immense pressure exerted by the State and the Alliance, decided to enter the service of God and endure the consequences.

Over the years Monsignor Beck had had trouble enough with those hotheaded youngsters. Angry, impulsive, condescending, contemptuous of anyone except members of their own generation, they saw themselves as saviours of the Church, divinely elected to face oppression, uphold tradition and fight moral decay. As much as he admired their courage and faith, he resented their posturing. He understood their anger and impatience, even their hatred of their tormentors; but they were not the only ones who fought in the Church's defence, and if they thought they were, they were living in a fool's paradise. For if they still had churches where they could say Sunday Mass and rectories where they could read the Gospel to the people or secretly teach the catechism to the young, if they could go out to the fields to celebrate the harvest in one of the most moving and ancient rituals of the Church (already widely imitated by Gerogen's clever agitprop tacticians), if they were still alive, it was because others were willing to compromise, to make concessions, to use the entire arsenal of subterfuge and subtlety where necessary.

Few as they were and innocent as they remained after leaving the only remaining seminary in the capital (Monsignor Beck had fought in vain for another in the heart of the country), those youngsters could live and work and pray in relative safety only because others, more humble and more experienced, were willing 'to fraternize with the murderers'. How many times Monsignor Beck had warned them not to say such things among themselves! They knew that their offices were bugged and their churches wired. But the truth was that they didn't care if they were arrested, beaten until their bodies were bruised purple and their bones cracked; on the contrary, they rejoiced in the pain, found glory in their wounds—*in imitatio Christi,* of course!—because what they really wanted was not hard work and life-long service, but quick and easy martyrdom. They demanded to be understood, but they themselves understood nothing. Redemption was their catchword, but what did they know of being saved?

In the rose garden, soggy with last night's heavy rain, Monsignor Beck stopped to marvel at Uncle Karol's magnificent order, through which, in loving memory of Countess Julia, the old gardener celebrated the changing seasons. From behind a long row of tall pines that sheltered the manor against the storms from the east, Monsignor Beck heard the high-pitched cawing of crows, and his stomach's low rumble: he hadn't touched the breakfast Sybil Wald had left on the table while he was saying Mass—as always before All Souls' Day, he was on his one-meal-a-day fast. However he had opened the envelope addressed to him on the silver tray.

In his characteristic, nearly Gothic script, Gerogen invited him to an important meeting in the library at eleven, and signed it, uncharacteristically, 'cordially, Ernest'. As usual, Krolthy was right: Gerogen must be in trouble. Touching one of the rose bushes bordering the path, Monsignor Beck could see the raw green buds of next summer's flowers, that small, mundane miracle. If there was still something in the world that could make his heavy heart leap with joy and awe, it was that tiny bud, capable of surviving the deadliest winters, which would blossom next summer into the most magnificent rose: a minute spear of life piercing the impenetrable armour of death!

Monsignor Beck loved roses. In front of the house where he was born and grew up, his mother's rose garden

bloomed from late spring to early winter. In the quadrangle of the cloister, Father Astrick's exotic roses radiated
happiness, their perfume penetrating the incense-filled
interior of the big church. Watching the mystical rose at
the western end of the nave sparkling during lauds, sexts
or nones, but especially at compline, when it was lit by the
setting sun, Monsignor Beck felt closer to the Virgin than
at any other time. And perhaps he felt closer to Henryk
Wulf than he should have felt because of that bouquet of
roses Henryk had bought from the old *babushka* at the
corner of the Leipzigerstrasse and Friedrichstrasse, which
made Inge so mad and so happy. And last but not least,
Monsignor Beck cherished roses because twice in his life
he had given roses to women he loved.

When Julishka Dombinsky (a great-granddaughter of
General Dombinsky, one of the martyrs of Vareges) asked
Anselm to go for a swim in the river, he should have said
no at once. He knew it was improper for him to go alone
with a girl who belonged to a family of nobility and
wealth. Yet, before she could have second thoughts,
Anselm answered, 'Yes, of course, Julishka, let's go.' And
so off they went, hand in hand, whistling and singing,
down the dusty path among the mulberry and elder
bushes in the hazy heat of mid-summer, avoiding the
shorter but much-travelled highroad, both fully aware of
their transgressions. Anselm had sneaked into his
mother's rose garden, cut the most beautiful red rose he
could find and, blushing, offered it to Julishka.

It had been one of those rare, menacing hot days when
sky and mountains completely disappeared behind the
grey haze on the horizon, when the water, generally fast-
flowing and cold here, turned tepid and stale, like the

rainwater Anselm's mother collected in her big old barrels under the leaky gutters to use for washing hair and fine linen. Julishka and Anselm swam and played in the river, then in the hot sand among the pebbles and marsh grass, happy, yet scared, as the first couple must have been after they ate the forbidden fruit and saw each other's bodies revealed naked. Anselm waited for something frightening to happen. Then, Julishka kissed Anselm on the cheek, and Anselm kissed her back, her cheek soft and warm, her skin tight as a drum's. She kissed him on the mouth, and her lips were dry and hot, as if she were feverish. Scared, Anselm wanted to run, but Julishka held him in her powerful embrace, and he knew he didn't have the strength or the will to break away. There they lay in each other's arms until the sun was low and they had to go home.

In the distance, beyond the tennis courts, Monsignor Beck saw a tall, thin figure walking among the remains of the old redoubt. He knew it was Gerogen. Monsignor Beck withdrew to the safety of the woods, then resumed his walk towards the ruins. It was getting very hot again, so he took off his black cardigan and loosened his collar. For a while, he stood on the northern edge of the redoubt; from there he could see Gerogen, but thought he couldn't be seen by him, though with Gerogen one never knew. Leaning listlessly against the crumbling revetments of the ancient fortress, his pale face turned to the sun, Gerogen stood there just as Monsignor Beck remembered him that morning eight years ago when they first met in the quadrangle of the monastery. Gerogen was then still a relatively young man (nobody knew exactly how old he was; the dates in official biographies were contradictory, and during the war the town hall of his native village had been destroyed). He was a man more or less of Monsignor Beck's own age, very much the stubborn child of the presumptuous nineteenth century. But now Gerogen looked old: his expressive face was lined with deep furrows, his hair had receded and turned grey. Even from a distance, Monsignor Beck sensed the weariness that prompted Gerogen to sit down on the withered grass.

Before tierce, Father Beck had been called to Father Pascal's office in the tower. On Cardinal Zenty's orders, Father Pascal was acting as abbot pro tem, since Abbot Gregorius had been transferred to the south to defend the country's largest, richest diocese from the attacks of the Alliance. The Special Security Forces, one had to admit, chose their targets with remarkable tactical insight and precision, arresting, one by one, the most prominent and influential teachers, lawyers, landowners, civil servants of the diocese, thereby leaving the Church almost completely defenceless. Cardinal Zenty had ordered his clergy to mobilize for massive civil resistance, clearly spelled out in his latest pastoral letter:

> We fear that the government is waging a war against the Church. We believe the government is following a systematic plan to abolish the Christian religion in the country. We have been called to our office by God Himself, hence it is our duty to speak out on behalf of our Church. We must refuse to be driven into forsaking our faith!

The ideas were the cardinal's, Father Beck had thought, as he read it out at last Sunday's Mass, but the words were Kral's: stagey, unctuous. Everybody knew that there was a great deal of truth in the cardinal's assessment of the situation, which grew worse day by day; but few accepted Father Beck's argument (often discussed in the monastery) that, as well as being the most spectacular way to go down in history as a martyr, the cardinal's tactics were also the most stupid, inept means of fighting an enemy so well equipped with historical experience and modern machine guns. Instead of trying to reach some compromise with Copass and his henchmen, the cardinal was sharpening his sword: his stroke might be his last, but at least he had struck!

It wasn't too difficult to understand or to sympathize with his motives; but what was at stake was not the cardinal's glory and place in history, but the survival of the Church. Monsignor Beck even tried to use what little influence he still had at the palace in Gesterom, but he could achieve nothing. Blocked by Father Kral with marvellous aplomb and villainous cleverness—there were moments when Monsignor Beck couldn't help admiring Kral's extraordinary perfidy and duplicity—he couldn't get close to the cardinal's office, let alone his ear.

Whatever the cardinal thought or felt about him, Monsignor Beck had been out of favour ever since the news about his *Proslogion Two* had reached the palace in Gesterom. After his unforgettable but disastrous visit to the Holy City, publication of his essay had been forbidden, at least until Monsignor Beck made the emendations Cardinal Gaunilon and the Holy Father himself had suggested; Monsignor Beck had solemnly promised to consider them, but knew he could never make them. *Proslogion Two* was dead before it was born, locked up in the papal archives. Monsignor Beck was crushed by an orthodoxy whose main preoccupation was comfort not commotion. Sitting back in their plush theological *fauteuils,* their feet resting cosily on their philosophical ottomans, they were content to leave matters as they were.

For months after his return from Rome, and especially since his inglorious expulsion from the palace in Gesterom, Monsignor Beck suffered. He prayed that the pain which stabbed his heart every time he thought of the fate of his book would diminish, even disappear with time, but instead it grew stronger, sharper. He knew with unshakeable certainty that *Proslogion Two* was the work for which he had been created by God. If a man's life was a complex of purposes, the sole and simple purpose of Monsignor Beck's life was to prove God's existence in ordinary human terms, God as friend and participant in Redemption, not as a distant, alien being, the incomprehensible and ambiguous Other, as some contemporary theologians sought to portray Him. But the experience of a lifetime had come to naught. Monsignor Beck remembered his vision as a boy, when the Virgin appeared to him behind the altar of his village church and ordered him to look after her Son's people; now it seemed to him that the Virgin herself had had second thoughts. His mission was annulled; he felt old, used, wasted. Trained to obey, to discipline himself rigorously, he could not forget his manuscript, lying on a shelf in some dusty archive, generating dust, turning to dust itself, as Monsignor Beck now longed and prayed to become himself. But that too was denied him.

'You have a visitor waiting in the quadrangle,' Father Pascal said, with heavy sarcasm, pointing to a little window in the thick wall of the tower. 'Would you care to look? Do you have any idea who he might be? Perhaps he has come to tell you something important. Please, Father

Anselm, do not feel detained. Shouldn't you offer him some tea or coffee? This morning Father Basil baked some exquisite *Kaisersemmeln,* our General Wulf's favourite, and your guest might also like to have some. It's almost lunchtime.'

'Monsignor Beck,' Gerogen said, hat in hand, his face bisected by the sunshine and the shadows cast by the arches of the quadrangle. 'It's kind of you to see me. I am Ernest Gerogen. I've heard so much of you from our mutual friend. I hope I'm not intruding. I'd like to have a word or two with you, in private, if I may.'

Father Beck still had hours to waste before he was expected for dinner at Claire D'Azzizi's apartment on the corner of the Avenue Émile Zola and the rue du Commerce. It was very easy to find from the métro LaMotte-Picquet, she had whispered to him yesterday in the office when, after weeks of her subtle, soft persuasion, he had finally agreed to come. She had smiled her stunning smile, which made Archbishop Gaunilon's dark Nunziatura, overlooking the Seine and the Grand Palace on the other bank, light up with the brightness of the sun. '*Ah, cher Anselm, cést le premier pas qui coûte,*' she had said and then went back to her typewriter.

Finishing his usual cup of strong Ceylonese camellia tea on the terrace of his favourite café, Father Beck watched the traffic on the Champs Elysées. Last December a telephone call from Archbishop Gaunilon to Abbot Gregorius had broken the monastic silence and Father Beck had been ordered to report to the papal nuncio's new office on the Quai d'Orsay on 15 January 1936 (a Monday, of course) at nine o'clock. Father Beck had decided to contest the order, though he knew from experience that

resisting the archbishop's decisions was almost as impossible as resisting God's will. Still, Father Beck protested,
because he believed that the promise his superiors, including Archbishop Gaunilon, had given him two years ago
had been broken.

After his return from the odious lecture tour in Germany (where the reverberations of the Reichstag fire had
made him tremble to think what the consequences would
be for Germany and the world), they had promised he
could spend the rest of his life in the monastery, surrounded by the silence of his beloved wilderness, and
finish his monograph on St Evagarion, the cranky, fourth-
century Greek cenobite who was banished from his community in the Syrian desert because he insisted that
Christ's humanity had equal significance with His divin-
ity. St Evagarion's only surviving words—'The monk
fulfils his duty only when he is separated from all, so that
he may be united with all'—had helped Father Beck to
understand his vocation when, after the slaughter at
Przemysl, he had decided to enter the Order of Strict
Observance.

Now his superiors wanted him to leave home again, to
be united with the ugliness of the world and divorced
from the beauty of his daily *horarium*, the cloister's sacred
balance of work and prayer. 'The vocation of the monk,' he
had written in a hastily composed letter to the archbishop,
'obliges him to live separated from the world, but in his
solitude he finds the very heart of that most intimate of
reasons which simultaneously isolates and unites him
with the world outside the monastery; that is, simply, the
reason to understand God's design for man and communicate it to mankind. I hope Your Eminence would not
want to deny the satisfaction of such service for one of

God's servants.' But it was all in vain, as from the beginning he had known it would be. They coldly reminded him of his vow of obedience, and that was the end of the matter.

Much to his surprise, Father Beck adjusted to Paris more easily than he'd ever expected. Under the giant cupola of the grey, wet winter, he soon saw emerging the green meadows of an eternal spring: Apollo and Aphrodite in the Louvre; Monet's poplars in the Orangerie; the wild chestnuts in the Parc Monceau. There was a mischievous spirit in the air, an intelligence at once outrageous and penetrating, which made him curious, angry, impatient, as he sensed the city's powerful spell. He liked Paris more and more every day, yet he knew with increasing clarity that he was walking in a minefield.

The trouble was that he had developed an attachment which he had not wanted nor, as a Trappist contemplative, was he supposed to have. Trappists belonged to the Word, not to the world; by being slaves, Trappists were free, and by being free, slaves. Naked before God, free from the burden of the world's appurtenances, Father Beck was ordained to stand in the cold wind of the universe, unattached though not indifferent, loving yet not possessing, always in debt, but never delinquent: those were, Father Beck remembered clearly, the very words of his erstwhile novice-master, the venerable Father Rancé. And here he was, collecting souvenirs! Two magnificent etchings: a grove of aspens in the Bois de Boulogne, and an old beggar with a huge beard and a shifty look, standing in the Père-Lachaise at the grave of Professor Abelard!

One afternoon in May Father Beck found the nuncio in deep conversation with an unknown young woman who, elegant and relaxed, sat behind the secretarial desk where,

until a couple of weeks ago, blessed little Thérèse Luseaux
had used to sit, her consumptive chest concave, her light-
blue eyes closed, as if she were already dead.

'Ah, *caro Anselmo*,' the nuncio said, 'just in time. This is
Claire D'Azzizi. Our new factotum, if I may put it that
way. I'm afraid our Thérèse will no longer be able to serve.
She was taken to hospital last night. Claire, this is the
barbarian I mentioned to you the other day. A Hun but
tamed.'

'Are you really?' Claire D'Azzizi said. It wasn't quite
clear whether she meant was he really a *barbarian* or really
tamed, but Father Beck felt her dark gaze slither up his
body until, for one breathtaking second, it connected with
his eyes. That was enough for Father Beck to know that he
had been probed, winnowed, and found intriguing.

It wasn't for the first time. Soon after Julishka had left—
her father was named a high government official and they
moved to the capital—other girls came in quick succes-
sion, first from the village, then from the nearby town,
later from the city beyond the river: blondes, brunettes,
and once, during the siege of Przemysl, an astonishing
redhead, whose face he could only vaguely see under her
veils, but whose sultry passions kept him out on the banks
of the San all night long, despite the most vicious Russian
bombardment. He now knew that, for reasons he couldn't
quite fathom, women found him intriguing, and he
couldn't resist their attractions. He was sinking deeper
and deeper into the abyss. He prayed, fasted, offered
sacrifices, but to no avail: women kept tempting him and
he kept giving in to their lubricity. How well he understood Augustine's desperate cry in the wilderness, '*Da
mihi castitatem et continentiam, sed noli modo*'—'Give me
chastity, give me continence, but not yet, oh Lord!'

Even before he became a novice in the Seminary of St
John the Baptist, Anselm Beck had wanted to be a celibate
and couldn't. Then, one night, among the corpses in the
streets and trenches, after the slaughter of Przemysl, he
had finally understood that man could be saved from his
own madness only through God's will, but that His will
can work only through man's will. He decided to enter the
Order of Trappists, and he knew he must put an end to the
frolics of his salad days. It wasn't easy, for the smells and
sights of limbs and loins continued to haunt him even
among the sacred walls of the monastery, but in the
seminary in Rome Father Rancé took him by the hand and
led him through the most dangerous and most difficult
passage of his life.

Father Rancé was a celibate not of intention, but of
conviction. It was the Virgin's demand from those who
consecrated their lives to her. So simple. Father Rancé saw
women as sweet yet inexplicable creatures of God, whom
He must have created with some purpose other than
procreation, but, Father Rancé told his novices with a
wink, invariably eliciting a big laugh, He must either have
forgotten that purpose, or, more likely, changed His mind
at an important juncture during Creation. As a priest,
Father Rancé often had to deal with women, participate in
their sufferings, share their chimeric joys, wander through
the labyrinth of their minds, listen to their sins, console
them in their grief. He always managed to keep them at
arm's length, but when he was alone in his cell, Father
Rancé confessed to his students, his small, wrinkled face
turning scarlet, they returned with a vengeance, revealing
shamelessly their naked breasts, thighs, mouths, buttocks,
eyes, their long, bony fingers whose light touch could drag
you into the abyss. It was the price you paid for being the

descendant of Adam. But what about the price for being the son of Christ? Father Rancé knew what he was lecturing about. *Apage Satanas!*

When Father Rancé died, Father Beck remained at his grave after the burial for a last confession, a final absolution. They had never been close to each other, but now, at their last meeting on earth, Father Beck admitted to himself (and to Father Rancé, whom he used to consider an oddball) that he had learned from him everything he needed to know for his monastic life: the power of faith and the force of will. He learned to be a true celibate, whose desire first became commitment, then turned into conviction, just as Father Rancé had predicted. Father Beck now knew how to deal with those sparks before they turned his body into the bonfire of the Devil. St Francis extinguished his flames by fastening the cord of his habit so tightly around his penis that it almost killed him; Father Beck doused his own incandescence with will-power. If he could live without the love of *one* woman, as he had elected to, surely he could live with the love of *all* women, and that was, he felt, as unblemished a love as one could wish. He was content, proud of his strength, confident in the righteousness of self-mortification. Redemption wasn't about what you gained by losing, as Father Rancé had argued in the seminary, but about what you lost by gaining.

Then came Claire D'Azzizi.

She took him for long walks in the old quarters of the city, travelled with him along the Oise, where ancient kings had established their seats, and where Pissarro and Van Gogh invented the countryside with that unbelievable blue sky above the wheat-fields and churches. She strolled through parks with him, floated down canals, ate in country inns, stood under the arches of old churches, always with that almost surprised look in her incredible dark eyes, as if she was seeing all that for the first time, as if it existed only for the two of them. She was the warmest, dearest friend Father Beck had ever known. Tall, slim, vital, the symmetry of her angular face perfect, her black hair streaked with grey, which somehow made it shine even blacker, she moved his soul with concern, surprised him with insight. 'If you think the Sacré Coeur is nothing but a syrupy sprite of the heart,' she said one day after Father Beck had expressed his distaste for that pretentious mélange of Romanesque-Byzantinism in no uncertain terms, 'don't you think Nôtre Dame is a dark miracle of the soul?'

At the corner of the Boulevard de Grenelle and the rue du Commerce, Father Beck saw a big flower stand. On impulse, he bought a dozen red roses for Claire. He knew he would regret it, but even so, as he walked towards the Avenue Émile Zola, amid the hubbub of the street-market, he was so delighted with his roses that he stopped to inhale their aroma. He shouldn't have come, yet there he was.

The lift he took to the fifth floor of the old, elegant building was adorned with fading Victorian décor. It moved slowly, as if offering its passengers ample time to marvel at its arabesques, parquetry, panelling. Father Beck saw himself, pale and uncomfortable in his grey jacket and old-fashioned trousers, in the opposite mirrors, multiplied *ad infinitum*. It was one thing to have steak *tartare* (as befits a barbarian) with Claire in a bistro in Pontoise; it was quite another to have dinner with her *à deux* in her apartment. Finally, the lift stopped and as he stepped out into the long, empty hallway, Father Beck felt distressed.

'Roses, roses, sweet Anselm,' Claire said. 'Come.' She closed the door behind him, took the bouquet and buried her head among the roses. In the office or at their outings she always wore a long, grey skirt with a lacy blouse and an amber-and-ivory cameo, her hair smoothed into a huge chignon at the back of her head, but now she was dressed in a tight, wine-red Chinese silk robe on which two dragons lay submissively at their mistress's feet. Father Beck remembered having read somewhere that Chinese dragons were essentially friendly beasts, mediators, in fact, between heaven and earth, the divine and the human. He was just about to tell Claire that when she disappeared with the roses.

The room was sparsely furnished with a few old chairs, a table, somewhat threadbare rugs and on the walls four unframed Cubist canvasses in the manner of Léger and Braque. Father Beck was amazed by the affinity between the shapes and colours of the paintings and the room's careless simplicity. The blinds were drawn, but the door to the balcony, overlooking the river, the sunlit gardens of the Trocadéro, the gentle inclines of Passy and the grey skeleton of the Eiffel Tower, was open. He stepped into the brightness of the late afternoon with a turbulence in his heart he had never before experienced.

'Sweet Anselm,' Claire said. 'It's hot out there. Have a cold drink with me.'

Father Beck saw his roses blossoming in a grass-green lead-crystal vase on the table, covered with a white damask cloth and set for two. Claire offered him a glass of some pink liquid, then, with a swift movement, withdrew a step or two, and shook her head, as if saying no. The tight, wine-red Chinese robe fell on the floor, and in the hot semi-darkness she stood before Father Beck, naked.

'Anselm,' she said and smiled, her splendid breasts and
small nipples hard, the muscles of her arms and legs tense,
her black hair tumbling to her buttocks. 'My sweet
Anselm. *Mon enfant trouvé.* Didn't you know? I love you.
Don't you love me?'

Yes, he knew now that he loved her. He knew that by
losing his will-power he could gain his happiness; but he
also knew, as he had known ever since he became a priest,
that by gaining that happiness he would lose the sanctifi-
cation of the Spirit. Among the trials of his life, it was
perhaps the cruellest ordeal God had devised for him. He
put the glass on the table, careful not to spill a drop on the
white damask, then turned and left.

'Yes,' Gerogen said, sitting on a cold stone bench, sipping
his tea under the Romanesque arches of the quadrangle.
'I've studied your manuscript with great avidity, Monsignor Beck. I'm sure you can see our reasons.' An ambiguous but not malicious smile appeared on Gerogen's thin
lips. He put the empty tea-cup down on the ancient stone
floor and stared absent-mindedly into the air, as if en-
thralled by Mt Ephialt, rising behind the northern wall of
the monastery like its invincible guardian.

'I am, of course, no expert,' Gerogen went on, still
smiling, though with more irony now, 'but I can say that
Proslogion Two is a splendid work of such convincing
power that even those who, like myself, reject its conclusion must pay attention to its intriguing syllogism. For me,
Monsignor Beck, it was so absorbing to read that I decided
to go back to the origins of your so-called ontological
argument and read St Anselm's explication of his rational
proof of God's existence in his memorable *Proslogion,* a
superb example of medieval rationalism, more effective

and certainly more convincing than I'd ever imagined. And I'm not surprised.'

'You don't surprise me either, Mr Gerogen,' Monsignor Beck said. 'But you make me curious. You may not know this, but in a monastery curiosity is looked upon as a sin, pardonable but not excusable. Still, what exactly is your point?'

'Monsignor Beck,' Gerogen said, 'let me just tell you first how greatly interested I was in your essay on the rational foundations of faith, which so elegantly and convincingly developed the Anselmic thesis about the proof of God's existence by simply adding one more "way"—that's what you call it, isn't it?—to the five Thomistic ways of approaching and rationally understanding the Deity. What struck me really was the seemingly simple proposition you made that our perception of God is rooted in our existence—in nature, as you so poetically put it— which is essentially pre-existent to ideas. This, I think, is a most important proposition. For if I understand your argument correctly, and you are suggesting that existence is the basis of all, the material *core* of everything that follows, I believe we have common ground upon which we can build our future. I may be using a different terminology, even a different value-system, but so long as we can agree that our perception of essence is based on our recognition of existence, everything else is secondary. Unimportant, I'd say. Wouldn't you agree, Monsignor Beck?'

'When I talk about the primacy of existence, Mr Gerogen,' Monsignor Beck said, suddenly interested, 'I do not intend to talk about the economic substructure as it affects the historical or social superstructure of class-societies, but only about existence in God's mind. My certitude is not rooted in the absurd capability of inert matter to turn, by some unexplained and inexplicable evolution, into marvellously sentient beings, but in scientific evidence integrated with metaphysical speculation. If we cannot prove that we exist in God's mind, we can at least prove that we *cannot* exist outside it. *Esse*, therefore, in my context, is the existence of an intellect above and beyond time—*intellectus supra tempus* — which is God. How about that as common ground, Mr Gerogen?'

'I never had much illusion, Monsignor Beck,' Gerogen said, with a short, unexpectedly pleasant laugh, 'that I could emerge victorious from a theological boxing match with you, so in the absence of a referee, I must declare myself the loser. However, I still regret that your superiors have forbidden the publication of your manuscript, which, in my lay opinion, is one of the most profound and potentially influential statements on the subject. I say that, though I hold diametrically opposite views on the matter in question, and, as a scientific atheist, have very little interest in having your religious views widely aired or even published. But that hardly matters. What matters, for me, at least, is the attempt to prove God's existence rationally and scientifically—something that has fascinated me since childhood. I grew up the rebellious son of an Orthodox Jew, under the scourge of the Talmud, which posited the existence of the Almighty as self-evident, un-questionable, an integral, though baneful, presence in our miserable lives, who brought only destruction and sorrow, yet demanded undying loyalty and faith. And, personal reminiscences apart, what matters even more is that the publication of *Proslogion Two* would be beneficial to *our* nation—please note my emphasis on the possessive plural—it would be beneficial for our people, but mainly our intellectuals, to read your ideas, listen to your argument and compare it with *our* ideas, *our* arguments.' He stopped, watching an old monk with sunken cheeks, hooked nose and mouse-grey beard approaching with a cast-iron tea-pot, who filled their cups with fresh, steaming tea, then disappeared behind the refectory door.

'I could, of course,' Gerogen went on, 'surprise you with an offer to publish the manuscript *in toto*, without changing one word, within three months, but I know you'd never consider such an offer, for you'd never break the rules of your order and the final dictum of the Church. I respect you for that, Monsignor Beck. Still, I feel that to 'rescue' your ideas, not for posterity, but for the present, would be an act of historical and theological importance, and I'm sure you know that. You also know—and it would be foolish to deny it—that I have an axe to grind; the publication of *Proslogion Two*, for reasons I do not want to discuss here and now, would be an event of some significance for the Alliance. But I'd like to add that it would also be an event of tremendous significance for the national Church, whose leadership, with Cardinal Zenty at the helm, does not seem to be showing the necessary qualities of firmness and imagination one would think are required in these stormy times. But, of course, you know that better than we do. So, taking into consideration a situation in which both sides have potential gains and losses, here's what I'd like to suggest.

'Since you wouldn't want the manuscript published without ecclesiastical approval, and we have no intention of embarrassing you by publishing it without your consent (although we could do so, if we chose), we are asking you to write a pamphlet or a small book for publication, a brief of the work, aimed especially for intellectual audiences. Here, we believe, is the solution to your dilemma. We know how close *Proslogion Two* is to your heart. We know how deeply you care about its ideas. We know how greatly the ban depressed you. Now, we offer you a chance to cut the Gordian knot. It is a truly Solomonic decision, for it would involve no disobedience to the Church, nor obedience to the government; and it would put you fully in control of *what* you say and *how* you want to say it, without an editorial red pencil or a censorial black stamp.

'But, please, Monsignor Beck, do not give an answer now. I'm here only because I've heard so much about you from our mutual friend, and I wanted to tell you how deeply impressed I was by your manuscript. And, of course, to talk about an idea that might be beneficial to our people, to all of us, regardless of religion and politics. I hope to hear from you, Monsignor Beck. Call me at any time. You'll get through directly. Whenever you feel ready. I'll be there.'

'Lately, over a period of some months, we have seen a resurgence of the past against the present,' Gerogen continued, 'or, to be more concrete, the crystallization of a rebelliousness unheard of during the past years, among intellectuals, mainly writers, and even among the *hoi polloi*, as the march on Director Berg's office demonstrated just the other day after we lost, rather unfortunately, the World Soccer Championship. There can be little doubt— and there is no doubt in *our* mind—that what we are witnessing is part of a wider, deeper conspiracy, which uses, as its fuel, real problems within the system, magnifying them out of all proportion, to make them portents of an imminent collapse. It is an old trick, which we ourselves have used many times against hostile regimes, so we know a great deal about it. The most important thing is that we mustn't let the disease spread and take hold among the lower and middle classes, which are our shakiest and most unreliable allies. We must be ever-vigilant so that the poison doesn't get into the tap-water of the proletariat, either, for they, too, can be fickle and treacherous. Petty complaints by intellectuals make little difference. But to establish an efficient tactic, to deal with the conspiracy, we must face certain facts.

'First, we must recognize that the conspiracy's ideological focus is the trial and execution of Ladislas Jarek. It now seems clear to us that he, or rather his memory, is being manipulated quite cleverly to make him the symbolic victim of a terrorist regime which has completely lost its moral and ethical claim to rule, and which, therefore, must be overthrown, and its leaders, responsible for those crimes, brought to justice. I need not talk here about the slanderous fallacy of this charge, only about its political ramifications and our tactical response. I would like to remind you that, at the time of Jarek's arrest and trial, we all agreed that by accepting the role he'd been asked to play, Jarek was serving the purposes of both the Alliance and the people; Jarek himself agreed, as his tape-recorded conversations with General Wulf, Justice Krolthy, Monsignor Beck and others prove beyond the shadow of a doubt, that we were acting in good faith and in the best interest of the nation. As for Jarek's swift execution after the trial, we can only say that our course was determined by objective conditions over which we had no control.

'Still, the second fact we must recognize,' Gerogen continued, 'is the assertion that the charges against Jarek were fabrications used by us in order to remove him from the leadership for two reasons. First, because he represented a different type of *national* leader—a home-grown cabbage, if I may put it this way—as opposed to us, Moscovite weeds (or so the invective goes), trained and educated abroad to serve *other* interests. Second, because our aim, according to this interpretation, was to create and maintain an atmosphere of terror as the mainstay of power. Those are charges unworthy of reply. However, it is true that we could have been more vigilant in supervising the administration of the case, even though the reins were exclusively in Copass's hands, and there was very little we could have done to prevent his and General Gabriel's behind-the-scenes machinations.

'Yes, it was Copass, and he alone, with the help of General Gabriel, who finalized the details of the case. We need no better proof of that than Copass's own admission at the time at a mass rally, fortunately widely reported in the press, that he himself had spent "sleepless nights" trying to unravel and understand the villainy of Jarek's plot to overthrow the regime and kill its leaders. Knowing Copass, we know it was only his usual bombast, which the enemy today tries to exploit as proof of *our* complicity in Jarek's death. But we can safely point out that, if it proves anything, it proves that Copass himself was responsible for the whole charade, knew everything that was going on, and with General Gabriel's fabricated case-histories, misled everybody else. Copass is gone now, and we cannot do much about him, but yesterday morning we arrested General Gabriel on charges of high treason, and that should be proof enough that we are moving full speed ahead to clear the Augean stable.

'The third fact we ought to examine is, of course, that the enemy, getting noisier by the day, can boast some success in the factories, in working-class districts, and especially among younger people, many of whom are still at school or were educated in our own colleges and universities in the proper ideological disciplines. This is a new phenomenon. Up to now, all we had to face was a small group of disillusioned writers, politically and, alas, mentally unbalanced, who suddenly discovered corruption they should have known about long ago, and were therefore wallowing in an ocean of guilt about their mythical yarns and Pindaric odes to Copass, which had reinvented that provincial Jewish grocer as some kind of Apollo. We have already cut off the funds to which they're accustomed, and we've scattered them all over the country on various assignments, which has deprived them of each other's company and the possibility of prattling ceaselessly about a situation they do not understand. We could also, if it becomes necessary, demonstrate the high morality of those new-born moralists by exposing their little liaisons at home and their one-night stands abroad. And, of course, if the worst comes to the worst, we might throw one or two of the loudest into jail, but we don't want to do that because we don't like to see poets behind bars.

'However, the spreading agitation in the factories, and even on the farms, must be stopped at once. To achieve that, we have made two important moves. One, we have doubled the strength of our State Security Forces in and around the cities and towns; and, two, we have decided to grant ceremonial burial of Ladislas Jarek's remains, requested by his widow, in the National Cemetery Park beside the graves and monuments of the nation's heroes. He will be a hero himself, victim of an international conspiracy, martyr of the working-class movement, like Luxemburg, Liebknecht, Kirov and countless others who offered up their lives, consciously and courageously, on the altar of the people. The press release, written by Kral and Vukovič, will run on the front page of the *People's Truth.*

'Draped in red on a black catafalque, Jarek's coffin will be surrounded by candles, wreaths of red and white roses, and a guard of honour from the State Security Forces, a company of fighters Jarek himself created from young men and women of the working class. In front of the catafalque, Jarek's widow, Susanna, will stand with her eight-year-old son, together with the representatives of the Alliance, the government, and other social and political organizations. Much as I'd like to, I'm afraid I myself won't be able to be present because of previous commitments in Moscow, but I assure you that my absence will not in any way detract from the significance and solemnity of the burial, which is going to take place next Friday—All Souls' Day, whose symbolic meaning must not be underestimated.

'We think that the reburial of Jarek is one of our better ideas and, under the circumstances, the best tactical move we could make. First, it steals the enemy's thunder, takes the wind out of their sails; second, by making it possible to create the event, instead of just letting it happen, it leaves us fully in control of the situation. You must realize, of course, that the pressure for such an event has been growing lately. Jarek's widow and her friends have gone as far as trying to blackmail us if we do not comply with their demands, threatening to publish in literary magazines the sob-stories of the widow's sufferings in the camps where she was kept after Jarek's execution; and, in particular, the sad tale of what she insists on calling the "kidnapping" of her son, who was put in a foster home after the death of his father and the disappearance of his mother. When his mother was released, however, I'm embarrassed to say that we couldn't find him. Nobody knew where he was or under what name, so we had to mount an operation to search out and identify the boy. Now, of course, since we have agreed to clear Jarek officially of all charges brought against him, threats and blackmail are no longer a trump card; whether or not the widow keeps her mouth shut, Jarek is no longer *theirs:* he is *ours.*

'All that remains to be done, therefore, is to carry out our plans. At noon on Friday—the time and place will be announced in the press and on the radio on Wednesday morning—the band of the First Infantry Regiment will play the national anthem and then Chopin's Funeral March. We assume that a sizeable crowd will have gathered in the park and around the catafalque, large enough to be called a multitude of friends and loyalists, small enough to be controllable (we may be willing to understand their sorrow, for it is our sorrow, too, but we are certainly not willing to risk or tolerate another mob scene). After a minute of silence, Secretary Arpó will speak on behalf of the Alliance, followed by Minister Zhantó on behalf of the government. Then, it will be your turn.

'And this,' Gerogen said, 'is the reason we asked you to come down to the estate for the weekend, so we could discuss this problem undisturbed. It is, after all, our common problem, for the success or failure of our tactics will affect every one of us profoundly. What we want you to do is simply to say a few words of farewell at the catafalque to an old friend, and to admit your personal responsibility, and deep feeling of guilt, for his untimely and unnecessary death.

'All three of you were involved in Jarek's life as well as his death; it is, therefore, just that you also be involved in his rebirth. General Wulf fought with him at Teruel, and, as an old friend, was instrumental in convincing him of the rightness and importance of accepting the charges against him and playing the role assigned to him by history. Chief Justice Krolthy knew Jarek from their Sorbonne years, tried him in public, and pronounced sentence on him. Monsignor Beck befriended him only late in life, but nevertheless spent some time with him, including the night before his execution. All three of you saw him die. Now, the day of admitting errors and asking for forgiveness has arrived. We believe that your eulogies—brief but moving—will have a lasting impact on the nation's present; and for that, we shall always be infinitely grateful.

'This, then, is what the Alliance is asking you to do, what the Alliance hopes you will not refuse to do. It is not asked lightly, nor is it an easy request to comply with, but we also know that eventually it will have a wonderfully liberating effect on you, on us, on our society. Will you agree to do it for the sake of all?'

NINE

AS he slowly regained consciousness after a long night's sleep, Simon Wald followed the contours of the bedroom where he'd slept ever since he and Anna were married almost fifteen years before. He had built it himself with the help of Papa Krauss and Lucas Flur, then a young mechanic at old Shvihak's grimy garage and repair shop in Sentelek. (Despite their fathers' enmity, Simon and Lucas remained friends until after the war, when Lucas joined the Air Force and was sent to fly those new MIGs, so rumour had it, somewhere near the Caspian Sea.) They began the bedroom soon after Simon Wald's engagement and finished it four months later, one week before the wedding. Attached to the official chief forester's residence, it was a marvellously modern bedroom, with special heating, double windows, Esslingen roller-blinds, and a bathroom whose ceramic tub, powerful shower and large wash-basin with fancy copper taps were Anna's pride and soon became the envy of the village. Since then, Simon Wald thought, it had lost its shine but at least it had retained its memories. His eyes still closed, he sensed that somebody was standing at the foot of the bed. Listening to his visitor's soft, quick breathing he knew it was his son. The sun was already high and hot, and from the dining room below, he heard the old Westminster chime ten o'clock. Today was Monday, the day of the burial and refection of his little Anna Julia, and if he didn't want to miss Father Novak's ceremonies, he had to get up.

Around five o'clock on Sunday morning, he'd been found by one of the Special Detachment patrols at Buck's Bend, collapsed over the steering-wheel of his jeep, unconscious, soaking wet in the driving rain. The soldiers recognized him and took him home as quickly as they could. Anna had called her cousin, Dr Kiron Feld, at the Freedom Hospital in Sentelek. Kiron diagnosed him tentatively as suffering from either pneumonia or complete nervous exhaustion. Just in case, he gave Simon a jab in the rump and left. But, as Aunt Elsie said, the doctor must have known what he was doing, for within a couple of hours Simon Wald was showing signs of improvement. By the time Anna, her son and the others came home from the Requiem Mass, Simon Wald was lying quietly in bed, his fever down, his eyes opening now and again, trying to listen to Aunt Elsie's endless tale of what had befallen him since he left the Flurs and went to Sentelek to see Andy Shvihak about the arrest of that old idiot Martin. He remembered none of it.

'Father,' Peter said from the foot of the bed, 'are you feeling better?'

'Yes, son,' Simon Wald answered. The room hadn't changed overnight, it was the same as it had always been, but somehow everything felt different. He had no idea what it was, but he was overwhelmed by a nauseatingly powerful sense of difference.

'Shouldn't you be getting ready for the burial?' he said. 'I'll get up at once. In the meantime, could you ask your mother to get me my black suit? It's late already.'

'Yes, Father,' Peter replied. 'You mustn't get up, though. Mother said you must stay in bed and rest.'

'I feel fine,' Simon Wald said. He rose, but a wave of dizziness made him fall back on to the pillow. 'Christ!' he whispered, astonished by his weakness, his throat suddenly dry.

'See?' Peter said.

'My apologies, dear Dr Wald,' Simon Wald said.

'May I ask you something, Father?'

'Ask away,' Simon Wald said. He remembered Kopf's lectures about the joys of early morning fruit distillates and decided to get some apricot-brandy from Aunt Elsie when she came back.

'Berti Lucas is here, Father,' Peter said. 'He's in my room. He promised to help me with the chores today. Would you mind if he stayed? I wish you'd let him stay. He'll be going back to the city in a few days, and we haven't met for ages. He's a friend. He tells me his grandfather is back. They drove him home yesterday afternoon in an old Hudson. Berti says his grandfather is very angry with you and wants to see you at once in the town hall, but Berti told him you had an accident. Can he stay?'

'If he's a friend,' Simon Wald said, 'tell your mother you have my permission.'

'Thank you, Dad!' the boy shouted triumphantly and was gone.

Alone again, Simon Wald wondered about Uncle Martin's return to the town hall, from where he had lorded it over the village for almost ten long years. If he wanted to understand the meaning of Uncle Martin's return, he had first to find out the reasons for his disappearance. Why did Uncle Martin leave and where did he go? Why was it so important, even for Berti Flur, that they drove his grandfather back in an old Hudson? As a minor functionary, he had no car at his disposal, so he was always driven to and from discussions, meetings, conferences; nowadays nobody batted an eyelid when the big, curtained government limousines, leaving a swirl of dust and a cloud of foul-smelling ethylene behind them, sped through the main street, stopped in front of the town hall and disgorged the old codger, who, without even nodding to his flunkies, spies and bootlickers, disappeared into his office. Why was it different this time? Simon Wald didn't have a clue, but he knew now that there was an almost forty-eight-hour gap in his memory, a loss he might never understand, nor recover. He felt as though he had fallen into a deep pit, just like Uncle Matthias on that fateful day when General Wulf shot the stag, and he himself was arrested. All Simon Wald could do was rely on Aunt Elsie's interminable account of what had happened—for Anna remained silent: his visit to the Flurs after Uncle Martin's arrest, his trip to Sentelek to see Andy Shvihak, then drinking at Biberach's before collapsing in the jeep at Buck's Bend.

Though he felt scared and angry, Simon Wald also couldn't help being amused. So that was what it all came down to in his enterprising middle years—Aunt Elsie, his only link with reality, his bridge to the past and the future! He laughed out loud and sat up. This time, to his surprise and relief, he managed to remain sitting without becoming dizzy or weak. He inched slowly towards the edge of the bed and sat there trying to remember. Slowly, vaguely, it was all beginning to come back to him.

He saw Aunt Gerania with her girls in their kitchen, old Martin's bedroom with the books neatly lined up on his bedside table between the ceramic book-ends. He saw, more distinctly now, Andy Shvihak's large, cluttered office with those small windows, then, very clearly, an enormous, fleshy mouth devouring a chocolate éclair, its yellow custard squirting over a bulbous nose. Simon Wald cried out with joy: he remembered everything, from Aunt Elsie's whispered gossip to Andy Shvihak's loud soccer anecdotes and old Biberach's sly pleasure at Uncle Martin's unexpected arrest. However, Simon Wald still had no inkling as to why the old fool had been hauled in or why he had so quickly been released.

'Anna,' he shouted, still sitting on the edge of the bed, but suddenly stung by a desire to get out of the room, the house, the village, 'Anna, please! Could you come and help me?'

Instead of Anna's quick, light footsteps which he knew so well and loved so much, Simon Wald heard Aunt Elsie's loud clumping. Her small brown eyes reproachful, her large, angular face red from the heat, she was already dressed for the funeral. 'For God's sake, Simon, go back to bed. Don't you remember what Kiron told you? You're not supposed to get up today. Please, Simon. Besides, you have a guest here. And get yourself covered, will you?'

'Wald,' General Wulf said, standing at the door in full-dress uniform. 'What the hell happened to you? I hear you had some kind of accident. You look fine to me, Wald.' With one impatient gesture of his right hand, General Wulf waved Aunt Elsie aside, then pulled up a chair near the bed. Simon Wald managed to ask her to bring them some fruit-brandy before she left the room.

'So, what's the big fuss all about? You're not going to die. Are you listening to me, Wald? I came to ask a few questions about Captain Strappado. Remember? The man who knew all the answers? Your wife wants you to stay in bed all day, so we have plenty of time. I can go back to the manor any time I want to. I've got my own jeep in the driveway, borrowed it from those Special Detachment boys. See what those stars on my epaulettes can still do? By

the way, I mentioned your problem to Prime Minister
Gerogen, and he said to check with the Beggars' Hill
people as soon as you can. They'll know all about you,
guaranteed. So, let's get on with the Strappado story,
Wald.'

'Of course. What could be more interesting?' Simon
replied. 'Captain Strappado. Actually, he was a major.
Funny you should ask right now: I've just heard from him.
A remarkable character. But why the sudden interest?
Why now? Why didn't you ask about him when he was
giving us the whip? And what is it you want to know,
General Wulf? He was always dressed impeccably and
used an after-shave lotion whose sweetness reminded me
of women. He liked colourful candles and worked only at
night. He's just been made a full colonel. Apparently, he's
doing fine. But all right. Help me to get out of here. Once
my family's gone, I want to go to the town hall to see my
Uncle Martin. Then, we go to the funeral, after that to the
refection at The Waldhorn, and I'll tell you everything you
want to know about Strappado. Even what you *don't* want
to know. How about that?'

'A deal,' General Wulf agreed. 'Some apricot? Or
plum?'

'Both,' Simon Wald said. 'A pleasure doing business
with you, General. I'll do my best to deserve your trust.
According to Strappado himself, I'm a most reliable man
with an exceptional memory. So, you see, you can count
on me.'

'Soldier,' General Wulf nodded, 'you've said it.'

Around four o'clock in the afternoon, Singer walked in to
General Wulf's room. Without knocking, he just nudged

the door open and caught General Wulf catnapping on his bed.

'Wulf, I want your final draft on my desk Thursday morning at the latest,' he said. 'I've made arrangements for the three of you to stay here until Wednesday evening, so that you can all work on your orations undisturbed. It's imperative that you get the correct tone and style. You must be self-critical, repentant, humble, dignified and, above all, optimistic. But you know all about that, don't you, Wulf? So I want you to stay close to those two, and help them. And watch them, of course. I don't need any unnecessary mess before the funeral, I have enough as it is. I'll leave you in charge here, Wulf. You have my permission to use the Special Detachment should anything suspicious occur. The lieutenant has been given orders. He's under your command now, Wulf. Be alert. We're counting on you.'

They shook hands firmly and Singer left, though, yet again, General Wulf would have liked support, relief, solace. But most of all he needed a promise from Singer that, when all this was over, when Jarek was reburied with full military honours, General Wulf would be permitted to retire to his villa on Lilac Hill to live out his remaining years in peace and quiet. But, as usual, Singer hadn't said a word.

Now, General Wulf stood at the open window of his bedroom and watched the dusk descend over the rose garden, the arboretum, the tennis courts, the old redoubt. While they were in the library, discussing the problems of the past and the present, his legendary drinks cabinet had been filled with the best collection of spirits from all over the world, restoring it to its former glory. General Wulf poured himself a glass of Black and White with soda, and sipped it in the silence Singer had left behind as a memento.

At least Singer had put him in charge, a sign of confidence that almost moved him to tears. Maybe Singer hadn't forgotten their youth. Maybe he remembered that, in moments of confusion and danger, Wulf had always been at his side? General Wulf was in command once more, if only over a platoon of raw recruits. He could give orders, countermand them, charge and discharge, reward or punish. Though it seemed highly unlikely that anything of significance would happen while they were confined to barracks, General Wulf was excited. As Singer's car reached the end of the service road and turned on to the main road to Sentelek, its engine revved up, but its echo quickly faded into the woods. General Wulf closed the window, walked back to his bed and stretched out comfortably once again. Singer be damned.

And what was he going to say? 'Honourable guests, fellow mourners, kindred spirits, before you lie the remains of a man who in his younger years had every reason to believe that, like his father and grandfather, he would grow up to become a leader of the oppressed against tyranny and injustice, but. . . Ladies and gentlemen of the jury of history, you must understand that the man who was accused of treason is *innocent* of all the charges levelled against him, though you must also understand that those who falsely accused and executed him are not guilty either, because . . . Ladies and gentlemen of the jury of humanity, we must all be grateful, from the depth of our hearts, for this glorious day of compassion and justice, which offers us, the victims of historical necessity, an opportunity to forgive all those against whom we have

sinned, therefore . . . Friends, Romans, countrymen: we
come to praise Jarek, not to bury him, because we have
already buried him once without praise . . .'

When Copass called an emergency meeting of the Secretariat that Monday, General Wulf didn't even notice
Jarek's absence. It was a strange morning in late February
that couldn't quite make up its mind between winter and
spring. While waiting for the others to gather in Copass's
office, General Wulf watched the snowflakes through the
iron bars of the window, freezing and melting on the
narrow, empty streets where nobody was allowed to live
any more. Only Jarek's security patrols paced up and
down, protecting the headquarters from intruders. The
Secretariat was still in the old, grey, five-storey building
with minuscule rooms and musty staircases that Copass
had chosen when they returned from Moscow after the
war. Genuine working-class people used to live here side
by side with members of the petty-bourgeoisie and the
lumpen-proletariat in this district, which was why Copass
had chosen it. But now they were about to move into the
new headquarters, the sumptuous Goldstein palace on the
river—Gerogen's *trouvaille*—only a stone's throw from
Parliament, which was in the process of being remodelled
to fit the growing needs of the Alliance. General Wulf was
looking forward to working in its spacious offices, sitting
on the balconies overlooking the river and the pastel Avar
hills, walking along its wide corridors among its ghosts.
They were dead; he was very much alive.

General Wulf became aware of Jarek's absence only
when Copass, in an unusually voluble way, started telling
anecdotes about Jarek's preparations for his trip to Milan,
where he was to attend an international conference on the

historical and political implications of Gramsci's philoso-
phy as embodied in his letters from Mussolini's jail. With
a doctorate in literature from the Sorbonne, Jarek was
eminently qualified to go to Milan, but Copass was on to
something else. His bald pate, gleaming in the dim light,
his huge pumpkin face, almost liquescent, as always when
he had mischief in mind but didn't know how to hide it, he
babbled on. Outside in the empty street, the snow
sparkled. Copass played with a green folder on the table
before him. Adymester snickered, Singer blew his nose.
Suddenly, General Wulf knew without a shadow of doubt
that something was wrong with Jarek. He didn't know
what it was—he was always the last one to know—but
Jarek was definitely in trouble. Perhaps they had engi-
neered his trip to Milan, so that, in his absence, they could
pull the rug from under him. From the moment they had
arrived from Moscow, Copass and Singer had disliked
Jarek, and Adymester, though on more or less friendly
terms with him, always appeared to be jealous of Jarek's
Sorbonne doctorate, his considerable knowledge of
French literature, and, most of all, his clear, concise style
and concrete, straightforward delivery. General Wulf had
become Jarek's friend the day they'd met in Madrid, when
the Brigade was first organized and Jarek was made
deputy political commissar, but the rest couldn't stand
him. He was a local 'cabbage', as Singer had once described him, home-grown and nurtured by a particular
kind of rain, a lapsed Catholic among lapsed Jews; and
with lapsed Catholics, he argued, you never knew what
might make them lapse back into the Church, and, with a
casual reference to the Holy Spirit, blow the whole goddamn edifice they'd so carefully built on the direct instruc-

tions of the *Vozhd* to smithereens. Yes, General Wulf thought, poor Jarek was in trouble.

'Let me now turn to the reason I've called today's meeting. A few weeks ago,' Copass said, his eyes on the green dossier in front of him, 'the *Vozhd* called me personally to inform us about the intelligence his people have gathered concerning the imminence of a strong attack against the people's democracies.' He looked around triumphantly, for his direct line to the *Vozhd* had always been his greatest boast. General Wulf knew, though, that Copass never dared to call him; he just watched the shiny red phone on his desk, dreading the moment when it would ring and he would hear the *Vozhd*'s raspy, Georgian-accented Russian, which could only mean trouble.

'It is the *Vozhd*'s opinion that the period of coexistence and cooperation of the war years is now definitely over. The spirit of Yalta is dead. A new offensive is in the offing. The infiltration of our ranks by their agents has now, as in the twenties and thirties, become the enemy's main tactic, as we already suspected. Our task, the *Vozhd* told me, is, on one hand, to prepare the necessary steps to halt their advance, and, on the other, to expose their treachery before the court of world opinion—the *Vozhd* repeated that very emphatically, several times—so that it should be, and I quote, "crystal clear to the masses who is their enemy and who is their friend". Therefore we . . .'

'A trial?' Adymester cut in quickly.

'Yes,' Copass said. 'Unless you have something better in mind.'

'As in Moscow?' Adymester asked.

'More or less,' Singer said.

'Admissions and confessions?' Adymester said.

'That's the general idea,' Singer replied.

'As a matter of fact,' hastily Copass took over, 'we have already made some tentative arrangements for such an eventuality. I'd like to ask Gerogen to tell us about the outcome of his preliminary inquiries. Needless to say, all this is top secret. Not a word to anyone outside the Secretariat, especially not to Jarek, for reasons that will become obvious presently.'

General Wulf saw Adymester's face turn red then pale, his piercing black eyes flashing with the fury for which he was so well-known among his associates. General Wulf knew that Adymester understood the implications of Copass's quick introduction to the mysteries of the netherworld, and he felt sweat running down his back. Ever since General Wulf had returned from Moscow after the war, and, much to his regret, had been ordered to shed the image and uniform of Commander Teruel, he had hoped and prayed that the horrors of the Moscow years would not be repeated.

And why should they? Everything proceeded smoothly, calmly, according to plan. Copass reorganized the system; Singer rebuilt the bridges; Adymester revamped the schools; Jarek restructured State Security; and he, General Wulf, revived the army's officer corps by injecting new blood from the worker and peasant lads eager to join the adventure, which, apart from its glamour, paid a good deal better than standing for eight hours a day at a lathe, or ploughing the land from dawn to dusk with two decrepit horses. There was a chance—maybe only a slight one, but still a chance—that after a victorious war the terror of the thirties could be avoided, might even be necessary to avoid. There were, of course, minor incidents like the prime minister's flight to the West, under cover of darkness, the trial and imprisonment of Cardinal Zenty, which sent shockwaves through the country, but those were inescapable interruptions in an otherwise orderly transition of power, and once they were over, life quickly returned to normal. Why should anyone want to remember a prime minister who fled to Switzerland and sent messages to his abandoned people from behind the steel doors of a Lausanne bank vault?

But now, in the sudden sunshine that flooded Copass's grey office with its presage of spring, General Wulf realized how wrong he was. It was going to be repeated all over again: the arrests, the tortures, the admissions, the confessions, the trials, the executions. He understood that Jarek had been singled out to become the next sacrificial lamb on the altar of the *Vozhd*. And there was nothing he could do about it, even if he wanted to.

Lately, he had had problems with Jarek. There was, for instance, Jarek's totally unexpected marriage to Susanna Amnos, hardly a month after he had, equally unexpectedly, left Eve Krolthy. A student at the People's College who was working part-time in Copass's office, Susanna was a large, thick-set, blonde young peasant girl from the eastern plains. She was already famous among her fellow-students and co-workers for her noisy enthusiasm for Copass and his plans—one of those unbearable female zealots who made life, never exactly smooth, extremely difficult.

Then there was that incredible business of Colonel Yuri Andreevich Negodyan (the bald worm, as he was fondly known among his officers), Jarek's chief Secret Police adviser. Jarek had once caught him lying to him and thereupon kicked him out of his office. The affair made such a stink that Copass had to explain it personally to

Marshal Shorovilov, who demanded a written apology, which Jarek refused to give. Finally Shorovilov backed down and accepted a letter of explanation.

And just the other day, General Wulf's secretary had reported, somewhat flabbergasted, that an old lady, dressed in the style of the early twenties, was waiting— and weeping—in the lobby. Her name was Agatha Saint-Imry, and she demanded to see the general at once. At first, General Wulf told his secretary to get rid of the old hag quickly and undramatically, but because her name sounded vaguely familiar, he finally asked her to show her in. She was a tiny, frail lady with a withered white face so distorted by layers of wrinkles as to be completely indistinct. Still, General Wulf found something in her smile intriguingly familiar. He asked her to have a seat, and then he remembered: that was the smile of his erstwhile commander, Lieutenant Saint-Imry, who almost thirty years ago had saved his life in the battle of Dorovar-by-the-Tíza. Saint-Imry had vanished without a trace in Vienna, but had become a major-general and had fled the country before the Red Army could capture him with the remnants of the admiral's seedy legions. He was now dying of cancer in Frankfurt-am-Main, and Miss Agatha, his sister, wanted a passport to travel to Germany to be at her brother's bedside, but she couldn't get one. Would General Wulf help her, for old times' sake? Her brother had always talked about him with respect and esteem. She was an old lady, and she couldn't possibly cross the marshes and minefields of the western border on foot, now could she? She had a snapshot of her brother, in a colonel's uniform, taken just before he left for the Russian front, but General Wulf couldn't recognize him. The storms had turned Lieutenant Saint-Imry's warm, youthful smile into a frozen, threatening jeer, but those deep-brown, curious eyes still shone with irrepressible humour and contempt for those who took life too seriously. For a second, General Wulf wondered whether Lieutenant Saint-Imry would recognize him as he looked now, if they passed each other on the street. He thought it unlikely. They were changed, not by time or age or experience, but by the malignancies of the world. What a pity! They might have been friends. He picked up the phone and called Jarek on the direct line which connected the members of the Secretariat. But Jarek had refused, on the grounds that Saint-Imry had been the most cold-blooded, merciless killer on the admiral's *Generalstaab*, who had ordered the Second Army to certain death in the Ukraine just to please Field-Marshal Hölle and so secure his own promotion to general. If Saint-Imry had the guts to send thousands of young worker and peasant lads to their death at Voronezh, he deserved to die alone on his comfortable bed in Frankfurt. General Wulf was furious. At Voronezh everybody had behaved like a monster! Jarek was adamant. Wulf had to go over Jarek's head (and behind his back) to make a deal with the Archangel, who ultimately controlled the passport-office, so that the old lady could catch the train to Germany.

Although General Wulf had problems with Jarek, those were, he now realized, truly insignificant altercations that arose from the daily exercise of power. The real trouble was that, unexpectedly, Jarek was changing: he was becoming arrogant, sometimes even stupid, dizzy with success. What had happened to that young, no-nonsense commissar who fought like a lion in Spain and emerged triumphant even from under the wreckage of defeat; who had risked his life, to bring the broken body of little Sébastien back through enemy lines, so that Sébastien could die among friends? Jarek still dressed in frayed shirts, shabby jacket, rumpled trousers, but he wore them like a tailor-made dinner suit. It wasn't enough for him to be surrounded by the emblems and levers of power, he had to be surrounded by adulation. The students at the People's College, which he had created to educate the sons and daughters of the peasantry and the proletariat, had become his power-base, his most reliable cadre, his private little army. He spent most of his free time with them, gave them money, sent them to the country, ostensibly to do sociological and statistical research, but actually to get first-hand information he could not obtain through official channels about the situation in the towns and villages. For the students, young and innocent, he became both the symbol of power and the promise of the future, the legendary hero of the Spanish Civil War, the leader of the anti-Fascist Resistance, the man who led them towards the Promised Land. They loved him. For, if Jarek was an innocent, they were his mirror image. They were also, General Wulf often thought, his undoing. He did try to warn Jarek, but Jarek wouldn't listen. He did everything he shouldn't have done, became what Copass had always wanted to be, but could never be: a hero, a sage. Jarek was digging his own grave.

'We all remember quite well,' Singer was saying, looking at General Wulf with a flash in his watery-blue eyes that brooked no disagreement, 'Jarek's antics at Teruel as the Brigade's deputy political commissar: how he tried to build himself up as the most popular leader in the Brigade by fraternizing with the volunteers—especially with the Americans, who were his constant companions, and the most vocal supporters of his cultural activities, such as his much-touted weekly poetry-readings. We haven't forgotten his attempts to shape the Brigade's ideological attitudes to fit his temperament, rather than the other way round. We recollect his arguments in Barcelona with Ambassador Antonov-Ovseenko, who brought us the *Vozhd*'s analysis of our problems and his orders for their solution. We know all about Jarek's friendship with El Campesino, his sympathies for the Trotskyites and Anarchists of the POUM, already engaged in the conspiracy to destroy the Republic from within. But there's no need, at this particular juncture, to enumerate Jarek's infractions. We have recently asked General Gabriel to investigate and prepare a detailed report for further discussion, keeping in mind Jarek's activities at Teruel before the Fascist counteroffensive in January 1938. We have also instructed Friedrich Hagen, who was then a liaison officer with General Heredia, and who knew Jarek closely, to assist Gabriel in his investigations.'

Teruel was perhaps the bleakest, greyest town General Wulf had ever seen, with its ancient walls, crumbling fortifications, narrow streets and decaying medieval houses. According to Jarek, who always knew everything about a place even before they arrived, the famous lovers of Teruel—Diego Juan Martínez de Marcilla and Isabel de Segura—lived and died there in the thirteenth century. Jarek solemnly recited some old Spanish poem and said that you could see their remains in the Cloister of San Pedro, if you were interested in such morbid sights—'providing we take the town by surprise and send Colonel D'Harcourt's garrison to hell,' he added. They were standing on the low banks of the Guadalaviar, frozen solid in the numbing cold. Little Sébastien was cursing the snow-

storm, which made flying impossible, while shouting his
doggerel with the usual poetic flourishes of his Provençal
ancestors:

Let those who love their country take up arms,
let the women bake bread and bring food without alarms,
tralala, tralala, tralala, let the warriors sing, *ça ira!*

'You can fly tomorrow,' Jarek said, pointing to where,
as if by a miracle, a blue patch of sky had appeared in the
middle of the snowstorm. Sébastien stopped humming
and did not say a word all evening—a rare phenomenon
indeed. They listened to Singer's briefing for the next
day's surprise attack on the west ridge of La Muela de
Teruel, and when they all went their separate ways to
prepare for the offensive, under his breath Sébastien
whispered, *'On commence par être dupe, on finit par être
fripon.'* At the time, General Wulf had no idea what he
meant; now he knew.

'However,' Singer continued, while Copass kept nodding in agreement, his chubby fingers spread, as though
for a blessing, 'we must take a few preliminary tactical
steps. First, we must remove Jarek from the ministry,
so that he cannot, either by coincidence or through
somebody's sloppiness or stupidity, get a glance at what
we are planning to do. Second, in order to isolate him completely from our evolving stratagem, we propose to trans-
fer him to the Ministry of Foreign Affairs, as its head, of
course. He must not, I repeat, *must not,* get a whiff of
suspicion. Being foreign minister should appeal to his
vanity and suggest the Secretariat has confidence in him.
After all, he has achieved some measure of success as
minister of the interior by organizing our new security
forces, and keeping law and order as we told him to. It

would put him in a relaxed frame of mind, which is exactly what we want. Third, we suggest that we do not give him too much time in the Foreign Ministry, because there's always the danger that he might get wind of the international conspiracy General Bukov's people are setting up, even come across certain facts that might lead him to conclusions we definitely do *not* want him to reach. Since we would need four to six months to complete our investigations and organize the details of the case, we propose that we should aim to arrest Jarek and his co-conspirators, who are now being carefully selected, around mid-May and begin the trial some time in September. Barring unforeseen developments, Gabriel and I agree that two, or at the most three, months will be sufficient for Jarek to get himself adjusted to the general idea of the trial and, subjectively, to understand his predicament. For that to happen, we must have an excellent, convincing scenario, which we thought perhaps Adymester would be willing to write for us.'

'Get me the facts, Gerogen, your precious *facts*, as soon as possible,' Adymester said. 'If you want me to write an eloquent text with all the intricate complications and a dramatic climax, you must give me the details.'

'Perhaps I should say,' Copass interjected, looking at Adymester with warm complicity, 'that, though we fully understand Adymester's desire for an *eloquent* script—in the best sense of the word: a revealing and instructive fusion of fantasy and fact—we feel that we must warn him against an intellectual exercise in high dialectical logic interspersed with theological references to the meaning of heresy versus orthodox faith. No, all we need is a straightforward, hard-hitting, emotionally charged accusation, powerful enough to shake up the audience—readers of the press and listeners to the radio, for we will probably broadcast the proceedings from start to finish. It must make them believe their hero was a bad apple, rotten to the core; and convince them that he must be removed forth-with from the body of the nation. So, think of the simple man, Adymester. Keep a snapshot in front of you on your desk—a miner, a peasant, a steel-worker. Be mindful of his primitive fantasies. Appeal to his impulse to violence, release his vengeful energies. But you know all that, my dear Adymester, without my giving you advice. After all, you're familiar with our common man, our simple, artless, natural devotee, *our* constituent, whom we represent in the councils of state, and for whom you have unselfishly fought all your life with such great distinction!' He smiled good-naturedly, then picked up the green dossier. 'I'll have a copy of this sent to you, Adymester. It'll tell you exactly what I have in mind.'

'I'll read it with great interest,' Adymester said, yellow with rage. 'You really *are* a great help, Copass. Without you, we would be nothing but a bunch of helpless found-lings in a malevolent orphanage.'

'And, by the way, one more thing,' Copass went on, ignoring Adymester, 'before we adjourn. We must make contingency plans in case Jarek refuses to accept our offer. Knowing him, that is possible, if not probable. I wouldn't be at all surprised if he threatens to die in silence rather than play the role we've assigned to him. We cannot let him do that, we simply cannot afford to let him withdraw into his private nirvana. So, I suggest we ask Wulf to prepare himself to see Jarek when and if such an eventu-ality occurs. Wulf knows Jarek well. They've been friends since Spain, and Jarek would listen to him more atten-tively than to the rest of us. It's not an easy task, I know, but it must be done. You'd better get ready, Wulf, while there's time. You have a couple of months, roughly speaking. If you wish, Adymester will compile a list of arguments, logical, ideological, personal, that you can use if Jarek gets too intractable or simply mad. But I assume such crutches won't be necessary: you'll be able to handle it, Wulf, on your own. Any questions?'

General Wulf had Staff-Sergeant Kell drive him in his old, black Hillman through the inner city, then around the outer districts, and, making a wide loop, back to the city again. Usually boisterous, full of old jokes and anecdotes about life in the admiral's army, all of which General Wulf had heard a million times, Staff-Sergeant Kell now remained silent, for which General Wulf was grateful. He looked out of the window. At a corner that appeared familiar to him, he ordered Sergeant Kell to pull up, got out of the car, told Kell to come back and pick him up at this exact spot at two o'clock in the afternoon. Then, having cautioned him not to tell anybody—not a soul—where he might be found, General Wulf waved him into the slow trickle of traffic and watched his Hillman vanish.

According to the bells of a nearby church, it was midday. General Wulf walked down the empty street, which became more familiar, as did the houses—solid, old mansions built to last for ever by solid, old merchants during the boom at the turn of the century, when General Wulf was born. Despite wars and revolutions, the houses, however run-down and decayed, retained a sense of pride and importance reminiscent of General Wulf's youth. They reminded him of his family, which, despite its caprices and bickerings, understood the meaning of stability.

It astonished him to realize that he hadn't seen these

streets since he'd left the country almost thirty years before—after his return, he had always found some excuse to justify his reluctance to revisit them. Yet, he knew these streets from one end to the other. With a strange, undeserved happiness in his heart, he even recognized an old door-frame or a little French balcony or the slanted chimney that he and his schoolfriends would watch for hours, waiting for it to topple in the keen winds from the river. The streets hadn't changed much, if at all, since his youth. Their names were different, but street-names were the flotsam and jetsam of history. They changed whenever power changed hands and old heroes became new villains and vice versa. General Wulf didn't much care about street-names, old or new. Still, he now felt that he preferred the old names to the new ones.

The moment General Wulf glimpsed the park at the bottom of Ship Street, he recognized it, though it was now called Rosa Luxemburg Park instead of Queen Elizabeth Park, as it was when he came here with his mother and his friends to play. The bare trees, shivering lilac bushes, well-tended rose-beds looked the same; in the centre was the little Milk Kiosk (now closed) where you could buy milk or yoghurt or lemonade, or dark, sweet, ice-cold chocolate, his favourite, to sip through a long straw, in the shadow of the statue commemorating the 1848–9 War of Freedom and Independence. The bronze soldier's cap was covered in a patina of pigeon shit: the just reward of all soldiers of every war for freedom and independence.

General Wulf felt a small tremor in his heart. With Jarek soon out of the way, he could make it to the top. It wasn't going to be easy, but nothing had ever been easy, and yet he had survived. He hoped Jarek would accept his role in that sordid melodrama of history with the humility, courage and discipline he had displayed in Spain. But with Jarek you never knew. He was a capricious man, a man of principle and will-power. Worse, he hadn't graduated from the Moscow school of confessions (as Adymester had so succinctly put it), and therefore he had no idea how one was expected to act in such a situation, no idea of the consequences. He could, conceivably, do anything. Yet he might be clever enough to understand his predicament and steer clear of unnecessary aggravations—a few agonizing weeks in solitary confinement, a few excruciating hours in a torture chamber—which would make no difference to his situation, only further corrode the body and soul he would need more or less intact for the final confrontation in Krolthy's court.

General Wulf hoped, and prayed, that he would be able to avoid a personal, savage collision with Jarek in his cell, as he tried to persuade him to let himself be enmeshed in that web of lies and deceptions Singer and Copass had woven for him, in which, though General Wulf couldn't tell him that, he would be both spider and fly. General Wulf would hate to go to Jarek and ask him to back up a lie that was actually a higher and more meaningful truth— wasn't that the bullshit Singer had taught him under the lush doum-palms of the Botanischer Garten aeons ago?— but, if Copass and Singer wanted him to do it, General Wulf knew he would do it. If the road to the top was precipitous, strewn with heavy boulders, the landscape from the summit looked green and sunny, filled with the promise of the good life. From one of Singer's chance remarks earlier that morning, which, of course, had nothing to do with chance—Singer always worked that way, testing the waters before he put his toe in—General Wulf inferred that he would be next in line to become minister of defence. And Copass had let drop—another chance remark?—that General Wulf might be elected secretary of the Alliance, provided he handled the Jarek case as effectively as they fully expected him to handle it.

Then, General Wulf would finally be able to make his move to acquire the Széchy manor, and this time there wouldn't be anybody to block him. What a day that would be! He'd restore the manor to its former grandeur; he'd put the illuminated codices back on the shelves in the library; the old, carved tables and chairs in the red room, the green room. From the damp crypts and empty wine-cellars, where they'd been rotting since the end of the war, he would return the family portraits to their rightful place on the walls of the great hall and the staircase. Yes, he'd turn that dilapidated old manor, which he'd visited several times to prevent those zealots of the People's Cooperative from ruining it completely, into his private *château*, his hunting-lodge, his very own *pavillon d'amour*. He'd organize hunts, parties, picnics among the trees in mid-summer, and dances in the winter under the big crystal chandeliers. Everyone would vie for an invitation, because not being invited to General Wulf's picnics or soirées would mean being consigned to limbo. He would have fabulous feasts, sit at the head of the table and regale his guests with fantastic tales, drink from Count Széchy's magic well and stay healthy for ever. And one day, he'd shoot the miraculous stag.

Dressed in black for Anna Julia's funeral, Simon Wald sat next to General Wulf in the jeep—a brand-new model he coveted greatly—and watched him drive along the narrow dirt road to Krestur like someone who hadn't sat behind the wheel of a jeep for a long time. Occasionally, General Wulf would forget to depress the clutch when he shifted gears, and the engine would harrumph and stall; or he would accelerate too much when he wanted to avoid a pot-hole and the jeep would buck high then settle back with an almost human whine of complaint from its springs. Simon Wald wanted to talk about Strappado. Ever since General Wulf had mentioned the name, the vision of Strappado hadn't left him. He heard his mocking voice, saw his baby-blue eyes, his pink, freshly shaven face, his immaculately pressed uniform with medals on his chest, his guards Gottlieb and Chortnik, whose jealousy was unmistakable. But General Wulf was preoccupied with the road and the jeep, so Simon Wald kept silent.

They found Martin Flur in his small, airless office in the town hall. On the whitewashed walls, next to the famous picture of the *Vozhd* lighting his pipe, hung Uncle Martin's awards and citations, neatly framed. Uncle Martin was sitting behind his small, cluttered desk reading the morning edition of the *People's Truth*. When he saw the general enter, his wrinkled face turned pale, almost yellow, under its healthy tan. He sprang to his feet, stood to attention and saluted. Uncle Martin might have been expecting him, Simon Wald thought, amused, but he definitely wasn't expecting General Wulf.

'Carry on,' General Wulf said amicably, then shook Uncle Martin's hand. 'No inspection today, Chairman. Just a friendly visit. How are you, Flur?'

'I'm fine, General, thank you,' Uncle Martin said and bowed. 'I'm greatly honoured. If I'd known you were coming, I'd have brought in some drinks for us. We have the best Furmint in the valley. But I wasn't expecting you, only this nephew of mine. Excuse me, General. I have a few things to discuss with this idiot.' He bowed again, then turned to Simon Wald.

'So, tell me, Simon, why on earth did you go to Sentelek, when nobody asked you to do anything? Why? Who told you to speak to Colonel Shvihak on my behalf? And then to go to Biberach's and spread the good news that I'm in trouble so that those bandits there could drink Biberach's home-made snake-juice all night long to celebrate my downfall? Do you want to know why, Simon? Because you're nothing but a goddamn busybody, like your father was and your grandfather and your whole family—always so good, always so quick to rush to the help of others, whether or not the others wanted or asked for it! Well, I didn't ask for it. And as you can see, I can take care of myself without your help. And my brothers can take care of me without your help. I don't need your goodwill, charity and sympathy, so don't you *ever* do it again. That's an order.'

'Yes sir,' Simon Wald said.

'What happened, Flur?' General Wulf asked.

'They got a phone call from headquarters,' Uncle Martin said. With deliberate ceremoniousness, he seated himself behind his small desk and put on his glasses.

'Who called?' General Wulf asked.

'I don't know that,' Uncle Martin said, sheepishly. Suddenly, he looked tired, slumped in his old chair, the high back carved with the Széchys' wild-boar tusks, which reminded Simon Wald of the frivolities of power. 'But they let me out without delay. Just a little misunderstanding, they said. They were very sorry for the inconvenience, they said. Then they sent me home with an escort in one of their big American cars. I have no doubt it *was* a misunderstanding.'

'What was?' General Wulf said.

'I don't know that either, General. They didn't tell me. But my brothers know me, even in the highest places, see? They know my life, my work. Why would they arrest a man who has spent his entire life in the service of our Alliance? For isn't that true, that I have, General Wulf?'

'Indeed,' General Wulf said. 'True as hell. You're an honest warrior, Flur. Take a good look at your uncle, Wald, you won't see many like him around these days. He's a vanishing breed, believe me. You have lots of medals and citations, Flur, I can see that, but I'll put in a word or two for you at headquarters so they'll give you another one for devotion beyond the call of duty. How old are you, Flur?'

'Seventy-one,' Uncle Martin said, proudly. 'On 10 December.'

'Then it will be my birthday present,' General Wulf said. 'You may invite me for the celebrations.'

'You're most kind, General Wulf.'

'Think nothing of it. I wish they'd give me one for the very same reason. But listen, Flur, I have another question. Do you remember the chap who fell into that crater a few years back and broke his neck? An old beater, I think he was.'

'Matthias?' Uncle Martin rose from behind his desk quickly, stung. 'Matthias Feld? But, of course, General. He was my oldest brother in the village and my most trusted . . .'

'I know that,' General Wulf said. 'I know all about your buddies. But that's precisely the point, Flur. An old underground warrior. Why would he want to kill *me*? Another old underground warrior? His *brother*, you might say. Why, Flur?'

In the brief, sharp silence that filled the small office, Simon Wald saw old Matthias as he had seen him when he went to ask him to help out with the hunt that time, standing behind the high earth walls he'd built around his house. Nobody really knew why he'd isolated himself from the world like that, not letting anybody in, never visiting anyone. That dreadful accident, according to Anna at any rate, was the fulfilment of some crazy death-wish; he died just as he lived: taciturn, mouth sealed with hostility. How clearly Simon Wald remembered that grim deaf-mute on that emergency-stretcher hastily assembled by his fellow beaters! Yet Simon Wald's father always talked about him as the most garrulous scoundrel in the county, a shameless driveller!

'I'll tell you,' Uncle Martin suddenly said, his face ashen under the tan and wrinkles, his voice quavering. 'I'll tell you why, General Wulf. I've never talked about that before, but I'll tell you now. Because he was mad. For years, after the war, I tried to save him and make him see the light, but he wouldn't listen. Not to me, not to anybody, that stubborn old bastard. He just cursed and hated us, because, he said, we'd betrayed everything he'd fought and suffered for in his life. We gave our word that we'd build a new Promised Land, he'd say, and look at what we built: we built a prison. The whole thing was a fake. It wasn't the dictatorship of the people, as we promised it would be, but—forgive me for saying this, General Wulf—a dictatorship of gangsters. He no longer wanted anything to do with it. He went to Sentelek and threw his Alliance card in the county secretary's face and told him he could wipe his ass with it. That's just what he said, the secretary told me later. Then, he built his fortress and withdrew behind its walls with his bloodhounds. He came out only during the night, when he went trapping and poaching in the woods. And he never talked to me, or anybody else, again.

'When Simon went to ask him to help out with the hunt, because he had only a few beaters, he must have reckoned his time for revenge had come. We know that because Andy Shvihak and his people found a whole arsenal of weapons in his house, and plans worked out in minute detail to blow up the manor with the guests in it, or to trap and shoot them. All crazy stuff, but very cleverly put together, very dangerously too. All he dreamed about was revenge. My faithful old pal, General, that brave, strong fighter. He went bonkers, that's what he did, poor old bugger.'

'Ladislas,' General Wulf said slowly, after the warden's steps had faded into the high, dry stonework of the old eighteenth-century building, and he had made sure that the guard was out of earshot. 'Ladislas, listen. I came here on behalf of Copass. He wanted you to know that he's very sorry about what happened, but it *had* to happen. He feels certain that once you see the full scope of the enemy's conspiracy, you'll understand his move. Until then, Copass said, you must be patient and trust your friends. The situation—and now I'm quoting Copass—isn't as bad as it may seem to you at the moment. We have a great deal to discuss, and the sooner we get things tied up, the better it'll be for both of us. So, would you please stop staring at me as if I were some monster out of a bestiary? Sit down and hear me out.'

His eyes bloodshot, his light-brown, thinning hair dishevelled and dirty, his face twisted by contempt and rage, Jarek, wearing a faded blue shirt and loose slacks without a belt, was standing at the other end of the long, narrow cell on the fifth floor of the old *kaserne*, below the window set high up in the wall. From there Jarek—poor Jarek—could see only a blue patch of sky or a grey swell of clouds. General Wulf had seen the insides of so many jails in his time that he considered himself an expert on the comforts and discomforts of such abodes; Jarek's cell, to his satisfaction, appeared to be among the more acceptable ones. It was clean, dry, light and virtually bare, which allowed Jarek to move around. It had only a rickety table and chair and a wooden bunk with a flimsy mattress covered by a grey horsehair blanket that was heavy and prickly but warm. General Wulf saw no paper or pencil on the table, no book on the bed or chair, which meant that Jarek was not allowed the privileges of reading or writing, not yet, at least. General Wulf knew how important they were to Jarek, and fully intended to grant them once their 'understanding' (as Copass in one of his inimitable overstatements had called their deal) had been reached.

Jarek came closer to General Wulf, but before he sat down on the edge of the bunk, and politely invited General Wulf to sit, too, he urinated, long and powerful, in the bucket in the far corner of the cell. The strong, acidic odour of the urine hit General Wulf and made him unaccountably angry, but he quickly checked himself.

'You still have a good rattle and hiss, chum,' General Wulf said.

'Very good, pal,' Jarek said. 'Excellent. But I'm still a young man. Just passed forty. How about you?'

'I can't complain,' General Wulf said. 'Although I'm

fast approaching fifty, and who knows what comes after that?'

'You look perfectly all right to me,' Jarek said. 'And I haven't seen you for quite some time, so I can tell.'

'Not since the May Day reception,' General Wulf said. 'Wasn't that something?'

'Quite a set-up,' Jarek said. 'In both the literal and metaphorical sense, I'd say. Champagne flowed like piss. And, of course, you already knew what was in the offing, didn't you?'

'I'm afraid I did,' General Wulf said. 'But it was part and parcel of the concept, as you must know.'

From the porch of an old, beautiful inn on the Mount of St John, they had looked down at the river and the city beyond. From there, a hundred years before, General Dombinsky had led his ragged regiments of volunteers to victory against the emperor's well-drilled artillery occupying the high ground of the Citadel and the Royal Castle, before ending up on the gallows at Vareges. After the long, exhausting May Day parade, where they had to stand, waving and smiling, on the parapet, the relentless ocean of faces, slogans and flags swimming before their eyes, they could now afford a little celebration at a historical spot. From there, they could see not only the city—*their* city now—bathed in the golden light of the afternoon, but also symbolically, as Adymester put it eloquently in his toast, the future and its boundless horizon. That was an unforgettable afternoon. Copass was magnificent, at once passionate and warm, shy and outgoing, philosophical and homespun, an old gentleman with old country manners, almost rococo with his elaborate gallantries and *Handküsse* for the ladies. Everyone knew that it was just one of his many tricks, but he did it with such charm and feeling that everybody applauded and laughed and they all felt themselves to be in the presence of an extraordinary human being. When Copass was about to leave, Jarek caught up with him at the door, embraced him and gave him a kiss on both cheeks; Copass responded with a smile that transformed him—a short, fat, bald, ugly man—into an almost angelic creature.

'Then, you came up to me as the representative of the army,' Jarek said, 'with a glass of champagne and congratulated me on my first successful international agreement as foreign minister.'

'You always had a knack for negotiations.' General Wulf smiled.

'Now, you come as Copass's emissary.'

'True, but untrue.'

'To prepare me for the trial.'

'Yes,' General Wulf said. 'Did they torture you?'

'No,' Jarek said. 'But they asked some very funny questions.'

'We are under siege, Ladislas. As we were at Teruel. Surely, you must know that.'

'To all of which I must possess all the answers.'

'Copass is convinced that, if anybody can, you can pull it off without a hitch.'

'And confess everything publicly,' Jarek said.

'Yes.' It was very hot in the cell, and General Wulf had to unbutton his tunic.

'Confess that already in my mother's womb I was an enemy agent.'

'Ladislas, please.'

'Upon which a sentence of death will be pronounced.'

'Yes, but . . .'

'. . . but it will not be carried out. With Susanna and Ladi,

I will be taken to a far-away place, reminiscent of the Garden of Eden, where we shall live happily ever after. In the Crimea, for instance. In Livadia, where bloody little Alexei used to play tennis with bloody little Nikolasha under the watchful eyes of that giant bloody monk or conjurer or sorcerer or whatever he was. And once in a while, Copass will visit, and we'll drink to the good old times, and when the storm subsides, a few years hence, we'll be brought back in jubilation. And why not? Haven't more bizarre things happened before? Executions? Resurrections? Redemptions? Intriguing analogies spring to mind, Henryk, don't they?'

'Where the hell did you get all that?' General Wulf asked, startled.

'Some of it I dreamed up myself,' Jarek said. 'Parts of it I surmised from Captain Eschara's hints, which sound so fraudulent as to be taken for genuine. He's my chief-investigator, Henryk, I'm ashamed to say. A duplicitous beast. A pansy, too. He made me offers in his own insidious way. More coffee, more meat, more books, paper, that sort of thing. In exchange for a quick bugger on the desk between two confessions. As you can imagine, I wasn't quite in the proper mood for such sport. Although, frankly, he made me ponder the mistakes I must have made when I organized State Security and recruited my officers. I wanted to have the best, most loyal, most intelligent and devoted young workers and peasants become the first line of defence against a cunning and well-trained enemy. And look, Henryk, look what happened! Have we lost our sense of direction? Our common sense? Did we overestimate our powers of perception? Our moral superiority? Our understanding of history?' He fell silent for a moment, his eyes on the ceiling.

'Or do the roots of our failure go even deeper? What if our theory is in error? A misjudgement of human nature? A misinterpretation of social phenomena? But maybe we are on the right track, only we didn't think this experiment through when we embarked upon it; it is hardly two years after we took power, and already we are offering a pack of lies as truth, justice as . . .' Abruptly, he stopped, walked to the window and touched it with both hands, as if he wanted to reach out and grasp the fading rays of the sun. 'I hate to talk about these things, Henryk, but I can't escape them. They're in my mind day and night. I must understand them. And, if I must hang, I want to hang with my eyes open. No hood on my head, Henryk.'

'Ladislas,' General Wulf said, 'calm down, for God's sake. Even if what you say were true—and I'm not saying it is—we have to live with it. We can't change it.'

'That,' Jarek said softly, his voice now steady, his eyes flashing like blue lightning with contempt and shame, '*that* is what is so utterly difficult to accept. We can't change it? We? But *we* are history's grand-masters of change, the only strategists who promised not only to explain the mysteries of the universe but vowed to change them. What's more, we had an airtight theory to do exactly that, remember? It should have been a cinch! If anyone could do it, we could; and we never had a shadow of a doubt that we *would* do it. Change is our buzzword, our prayer, our first and last commandment. To us, history revealed its meaning. And that meaning *was* change. Not simply tinkering with the fabric of the world, but cutting it up and sewing it back together so that not even God would recognize His own handiwork! *We* were the gods of a new Creation! And now you come and tell me that *we* cannot change our condition?

'Remember our first meeting with Copass, soon after he came back from Moscow, when he talked about our plans, and strategies? Later, he asked me about the situation in the Sixteenth District. Very bad, I said. He smiled, and almost nonchalantly, with just the right amalgam of certainty and pride, as if he knew something nobody else knew, he said, "*We'll change it!*" And I knew he was right, he was telling the truth, the absolute truth, the *objective* truth, as Gerogen is so fond of explicating. How much I respected Copass for that! How much I admired him— loved him, Henryk! I was willing to do anything for him, yes.

'And one day, he asked me to his office and said, "Listen, Jarek, I don't know what your intentions are, but I want to be frank with you, and I must tell you that I don't think much of your relationship with that Krolthy girl, I don't think she's good for you, so why don't you consider a clean break with her and marry somebody else. It's high time for you to marry, anyhow. We don't like bachelors fooling around with secretaries and assistants. Find a nice working-class girl from the Fourteenth District or a comely peasant lass from the plains who'll understand what you're doing and won't be a millstone around your neck. That Krolthy slut—forgive me—will never be interested in your work; even though she ran errands for you in the Resistance, all she wants is to be entertained and fucked and given expensive presents. I know it's not easy, but I'm sure you can do it." I was astonished, furious as hell, I tell you, because I loved Eve, yes, I loved her as I've never loved anybody before, but I walked back to my office and started thinking about what the old fox had told me. The longer I thought, the clearer I saw his experience and wisdom and truth. Within a week, I broke with Eve, and soon afterwards Copass introduced me to Susanna.'

'Ladislas,' General Wulf said softly. 'Why didn't you tell me that before?'

'I never told that to anybody,' Jarek said. 'It was *our* sweet secret, Copass's and mine.' For a moment, he fell silent, then, whistling his favourite old song—*Ich came nach Spain in Januar, Yo hablar seulement English*—he stretched out on his bunk and relaxed, as if he had suddenly come to a conclusion.

'I just wanted you to know about my deep commitment to Copass, my willingness to serve him, my readiness to sacrifice everything that was dear to me for him. Whenever he shook my hand, or patted my back in his own, inimitable fatherly way—he is so small that he has to stand on tiptoe to reach my shoulder—I trembled and remembered my sacred oath, saw him as its symbolic manifestation. In other words, Henryk, I was an idiot.'

'In other words,' General Wulf said, 'you want me to tell Copass that you refuse to play the game? You reject his offer?'

'Not at all,' Jarek said, cheerfully, with a big smile on his haggard face, 'not at all, Henryk. On the contrary! I want you to tell Copass that I'll do whatever he wants me to do. I'll play. I *am* game. I'll give him a performance he's never seen before. I'll be more villainous than Iago, more treacherous than Richard the Third, more bloodthirsty than Dracula. Do you have any idea, Henryk, what they want me to confess? I'm not going to bore you with the details, but it's pretty dirty stuff. Still, I'll surprise Copass with some of my own inventions. I'll add some flavour, *couleur locale*, authenticity to the story. Tell Copass that I'll be a perfect hero of his imperfect script. In exchange for the life of my wife and son. Tell him.'

'I'll tell him,' General Wulf said and stood up. 'There's one more thing you should know, Ladislas.'

'I should know everything,' Jarek said, very serious now. 'I'm the key to the door, Henryk, remember?'

'At Gerogen's suggestion, Adam Krolthy's going to be your judge.'

'Yes. Somehow I suspected that. But don't worry. He'll survive it.'

'Whom did you talk to?' Simon Wald asked General Wulf. After leaving Uncle Martin's airless office Simon Wald had stopped the jeep by the well in Krestur and General Wulf had got out to have a long, thirsty gulp. They still had an hour until the burial in the Cemetery of the Assumption, at the other end of the village, near the marshes and the Flurs' house.

'There was an old man in a black robe,' General Wulf said. 'He asked me who I was, then disappeared behind the statue. A very tiny old man, Wald.'

'Did you see him?' Simon Wald said.

'Of course I saw him, Wald. Didn't you?'

'No, I didn't. Only a few people can. You're one of them. Lucky for you.'

'What the hell are you talking about?' General Wulf asked.

'Some say that he's the ghost of Count Francis,' Simon Wald said. 'Others say that he's the demon who created the well. Others insist they're one and the same: a good angel and an evil spirit in one person. Take your pick.'

'Bullshit!' General Wulf grunted, but Simon Wald saw that he went pale, took a small, white pill from a vial in his pocket and put it carefully under his tongue.

TEN

EVER since he was a boy, Justice Krolthy had liked Mondays, as much as he had hated Sundays, for Mondays freed him from the unbearable piety and excruciating boredom that reigned while the grim shadow of God fell on Krolthy House. Justice Krolthy remembered all those hushed, petrified Sundays when, at his father's command, time came to a standstill and the house was filled with silence. They all had to sit in their rooms and, on Captain Krolthy's orders, write down the sins they had committed during the previous week. When his father first invented that inane game of sin and contrition, Adam simply refused to submit, provoking the old man's ire and the inevitable twenty-five strokes on Adam's bare ass; later, when he understood the possibilities of obedience and the fun behind Sunday's grim façade, Adam became Sunday's most celebrated confessor. He revelled in inventing his weekly catalogue of errors and sins, colouring and adjusting them to match his father's moods, because Adam knew that the longer and more lurid his confessions became, the better they were appreciated—a repentant sinner, after all! To the utter fury and amazement of Eve and the rest of the household, who sat in their rooms chewing their nails, denying ever having committed any sin, Adam emerged the winner, an obedient son, a good boy, in Captain Krolthy's mind, a promising future *paterfamilias*. Yet, despite his little victories (and minor defeats), Sundays were still a pain in the ass. On Mondays everything was possible. Or was it?

It was now Monday again and Justice Krolthy had been invited to the refection of Anna Julia Sybilla, to be held that afternoon in The Waldhorn, by Sybil Wald. As he dressed for the occasion he realized that his fondness for Mondays had diminished considerably overnight. It was not as if Sunday had reeked of boredom or piety, not with Anselm saying a private Mass in his room, Henryk endlessly cursing those fucking doctors because of his recurring chest-pains, and with Gerogen's clever revelations of his plans for the present. But now that Sunday was over, Justice Krolthy could start laying the foundations for his future, if such a thing still existed. In the morning silence, he walked down the stairs, past the bemused indifference of those pale Széchy forebears to the green room for breakfast.

Before Gerogen had left yesterday afternoon, he had sent for Justice Krolthy. On the table in the green room there was coffee and a large cake, iced with dark chocolate cream, but Gerogen only sipped his bitter tea. He had interrupted Justice Krolthy's siesta, he explained, simply in order to ask him to keep an eye on Wulf and Beck, to help them in any way he saw fit if they needed help in dealing with the situation, or, Gerogen suggested, they might need help in composing their eulogies for the burial, because he, Gerogen, was fully aware of the difficulty of their task. Besides, Gerogen felt Krolthy was the only one who had a clear conception of both the implications and the consequences of the Jarek funeral. So, beneath the smiling portrait of Countess Julia, the president of the Supreme Judicial Council had been singled out to be wet nurse to those innocent babes who were finally having to walk through difficult terrain on their own feet.

'Adam,' Gerogen said, 'do your best. I'm counting on you.' And he shook Justice Krolthy's hand. Unlike the quick, cold, unfriendly handshake on Krolthy's balcony that had created a bond between them which had lasted for almost a decade, this handshake was long, warm and friendly. Gerogen had even patted Justice Krolthy's shoulder with his left hand, an impressive and surprising show of confidence and trust. Then, hastily, Gerogen left. From the window of the first-floor landing, Justice Krolthy watched Gerogen's big ZIM turn clumsily into the service road, then disappear in the oncoming dusk among the poplars.

'You're not having any breakfast, Your Honour,' Julie remarked, her slanted eyes and full red lips reflecting her displeasure. She came closer to Justice Krolthy, although she maintained the proper distance between servant and master. 'Perhaps, you prefer something else?'

'No, thank you, my dear,' Justice Krolthy said. 'I'm not really hungry today.' She was even more beautiful than yesterday, or the day before. Justice Krolthy knew he had only to say a word, to put his hand around her waist, or simply smile, and she'd come to his bed tonight. But Justice Krolthy didn't say a word, nor did he touch her waist. And Julie understood him; a small, contemptuous flash of her dark-blue eyes told him that, and astonishingly Justice Krolthy felt grateful. He didn't want anybody in his bed, not for the time being, perhaps not for a long time.

He decided to go to the library to jot down the outlines of the eulogy already taking shape in his mind: a brief, powerful, emotionally charged colloquy on the mistakes, sufferings, self-delusions and final, if belated, apperceptions of a man misled by circumstances he could not quite grasp, or was perhaps unwilling to face, mainly due to an overarching desire to serve (*that* must be fully emphasized, given an entire paragraph and a most convincing delivery). Instead, he found himself wandering around the empty corridors, confronted at every turn by his own reflection. Those were the old quarters of the famous seventeenth-century beauty, Countess Calpurnia, who surrounded herself with mirrors and every morning bathed in the blood of freshly slaughtered ewes.

Justice Krolthy had determined to take up Gerogen's challenge to speak at the funeral *and* to make a huge success of it. He decided not to talk about the Jarek case in legal, judicial or even political terms, only in emotional ones. It would have been impossible to explain to anybody, least of all to that bloodthirsty crowd of Jarek's relatives and friends, how a judge, renowned for his rational judgements and sharp opinions, could have fallen prey to a gang of second-rate illusionists and nonchalantly tried a man with such total disregard for due process. How could he have accepted Jarek's confession of guilt as evidence of criminality; admitted inventions as facts; allowed four frightened, contemptible human wrecks, the jurors, hand-picked by Gerogen for the job, to sit through seven days of accusations and self-abasement without once interrupting the procedure to ask questions and then vote for a sentence without discussing the case? To those questions, and to others, there were no palatable answers; therefore, Justice Krolthy decided that those questions should not be asked. On the other hand, if he talked simply and eloquently only about himself (almost as if Jarek had never existed), about his own misjudgements, he could evoke the interest, even the sympathy, of his audience. He would get away with flying colours, much to his own amusement and, no doubt, to Gerogen's displeasure, though from now on, whether or not Gerogen was satisfied with his performance was no longer his concern.

Besides, it was his private joke. Wasn't it the most hilarious irony of his life, that now, after all these years, he was once more compiling a catalogue of sins as the only way to save his neck from the noose of a piety which differed from his old man's in form but hardly in essence? Looking into another big mirror in a gilded baroque frame, he saw himself grinning. If that was the end of his public life, which to all intents and purposes it was, he might as well start his private life on a high note of merriment and abandon.

Immediately after the funeral Justice Krolthy would submit his letter of resignation as president of the Supreme Judicial Council to the prime minister (which would be accepted with 'sincere regrets'), and he would be free as air. What should he do, footloose and *dégagé*? He could ask for his passport and fly to Massachusetts to visit Eve and her husband in their new Greek-revivalist house, but he doubted whether Gerogen would let him go. Perhaps he'd just clear his desk, kiss Irene twice on the cheek, close down his apartment by the river, fill up the Skoda at the petrol station behind his office (where they called him 'excellency' to his face, and 'Jack Ketch' behind his back) and head north to Krolthy House.

A curious twinge troubled Justice Krolthy's heart. It had been years—three? four?—since he'd last visited the old house. He used to get occasional reports on its condition from his steward, Yankó, until Yankó suddenly disappeared, and then from various other servants or tenants. It seemed ludicrous, but it was true, that all his blue-blood neighbours were dead or gone—the Weiskopfs had emigrated to America; the Count and Countess Nida had committed suicide; the Barats had been arrested on charges of conspiracy—but old Václáv and Prunella, Aranka, Ludmilla and Milena, and the rest, whom he had grown up with, played ball and hooky, had survived. And he was going to see them all!

He'd enjoy tremendously being a country squire, the last one, perhaps. Gerogen had driven all of them away, but he would probably see to it that his old associate, however much he had outlived his usefulness, would not be disturbed in his solitude and contemplation. The monk of Krolthy House! Not that he had any intention of denying himself everything life could still offer to a middle-aged wayfarer finally come home to rest. On the contrary, Justice Krolthy thought, he'd lead a pleasant and sportive life. He'd enjoy long sleeps and leisurely breakfasts on the west porch. He'd go for long walks in the woods or ride his horse—he must find an old sumpter and learn the tricks of the saddle late in life—or help old Václáv in the vineyard or in the pressing shed. During their simple lunch, the old vintner would tell him stories about his father and mother, from an age that would emerge from the ocean of time like an island, after the volcanic eruptions of history. He'd become drowsy and would have a nap in the haystack with bees and yellowjackets buzzing around his head, offering him the sweetness of midday dreams. Later, back in the house, he wouldn't listen to the radio, nor read the papers—certainly not the *People's Truth*—but would put *Don Giovanni* on the record-player, read *Oblomov* and *Dead Souls*, which he hadn't read, and re-read *Madame Bovary* and *Le Rouge et le Noir*, neither of which he'd read since his Sorbonne years. But he'd spend most of his time in his father's secret room with the Bosch, if only to find out whether he, too, could live for days without food, drink or sleep, and how exactly those roly-poly angels and skinny little devils did the trick. And, of course, he was going to finish his essay, *The Garden of Earthly Delights*, his *chef d'œuvre*, his legacy, his unique interpretation of hell. What an idyllic life it would be! What a consolation for everything he had lost, for everything he had won!

Justice Krolthy stood in the middle of the armoury. He had never been interested in weapons, but now, curiously fascinated, he walked among the swords and guns. He stopped in front of a small glass box which, according to its caption—fine cursive letters engraved on a polished copper plate—contained the pistol General Stephen Széchy had been carrying when he was captured by Prince Razumovsky's agents after the defeat at Vareges. It was an early American Colt pepperbox pistol with six revolving barrels, fully loaded, exactly as it had been when General Széchy handed it over to Colonel Bogaty under the ancient oak near the battlefield. Legend had it that the night before the execution, Colonel Bogaty offered to give it back to General Széchy, so that he could commit suicide and be spared the shame of the gallows. Not only did General Széchy reject the suggestion but he demanded to be the last hanged, so that he could take leave of his fellow officers as their commander. And so it was done: General Széchy saluted them, one by one, shook their hands and watched them die with eyes open—all refused the hood and looked death bravely in the eye—then, with brisk steps, he himself walked up to the gallows and died without a word. The last of the honourable men. Justice Krolthy opened the glass box, in which General Széchy's pistol lay on a faded, dark-blue velvet cushion. The metal felt cold under his fingers. He picked it up, held it against the sun, then suddenly, much to his surprise, put it in his pocket.

In the library the warm morning air was streaming through the open windows and the remnants of yesterday's lunch had been cleared away. On Count Francis's old mahogany desk Justice Krolthy found Sybil Wald's books, *The Book of Apollyon, The Book of Brethren, The Book of Cooks,* but now he noticed that there were six others. Justice Krolthy smiled. Were those the Sibylline Books, containing prophecies for his future? It was high time he knew something about his future, instead of guessing at it. He opened the fourth book—a slim, yellowing volume bound in calf's leather—and saw, in Count Francis's unmistakably sharp hand, *The Book of Despair.*

Justice Krolthy lit a cigar, settled comfortably in Count Francis's rocking chair by the french windows, from where he could see the heat shimmering above the shrubbery, but he didn't open the book. The smoke swirled around his head, and he realized that he hadn't smoked a cigar since before his meeting with Gerogen. He took a deep breath and let the aroma fill his lungs. In his pocket he felt General Széchy's pistol, its metal still cool. Justice Krolthy had never carried a pistol. When he served in the army, he did not take his revolver out of its holster until he deserted; then he dropped it into a sewer. It occurred to him now that he had actually, if unintentionally, stolen the pistol from the armoury. He toyed with the idea of taking it home as a memento of a place he knew he would never visit again, but decided to take it back to its glass box. He still didn't open the book on his lap. It was strange, but he was no longer irresistibly curious, as he had been when he first saw those dusty scripts in Simon Wald's house. In fact, he wasn't curious at all. He put *The Book of Despair* back on the desk next to the rest of Sybil Wald's incunabula, went to the green room, had a cup of hot, strong coffee while taking a long look at Countess Julia's portrait above the fireplace, then walked out to the Skoda and drove to The Waldhorn.

'When your grandfather dies,' Father Novak boomed over Anna Julia's tiny grave—he had a powerful baritone he modulated skilfully, in a theatrical, self-conscious way Simon Wald didn't like—'you look at him in the bed where he lies, washed and dressed for his last journey. Perhaps you sob a little and remember with a smile the days when the old curmudgeon used to sit on the bench in front of the house on long, hot summer evenings, whittling a whistle from a willow-twig, a real whistle that sounded like the conductor's at a train station, which you loved. Now, gratefully, you touch the old man's cold hand, perhaps even whisper a prayer for the salvation of his soul, but truly, even if you feel sad and confused—for death with its incomprehensible rigidity always confuses the living—you also feel that his death is part of life, part of the order that includes birth and death. You feel that this is the way things must inevitably be, the old leave this world and the young enter it. You are standing on the spot the ancients called the intersection of opposites—life and death, love and hate, salvation and damnation; even if you don't understand the Divine Will, and we never really do, you have an inkling of its meaning, as if you were standing in the middle of a snowy meadow in February and suddenly a warm breeze from nowhere touches your cheeks, and you know that spring is just around the corner.

'And when your father or your mother dies and you cry

inconsolably, because it is always difficult to imagine a
loss that is irreplaceable, irrevocable, yet you know that
that too is part and parcel of the order, and your refusal to
accept it is simply the first step towards reconciliation
with God's will. It is natural for the children to bury their
grandparents and parents, to remember them with sadness and joy, because even if you grumbled, quarrelled
with them—and is there one among us who didn't?—it
was the only bond in your life that endured through a love,
a singular generosity of heart and mind, you never find
afterwards.

'But what do you say, what do you do, when your child
dies? When your baby who has just been born dies without having time to open her eyes and look around at the
world into which she was sent by laws over which she had
no control and against which she could not protest? Why
was she born if she was to die instantly? You know that it
is *unnatural* for parents to bury their children, and if there
is a reason for it, it is shrouded in mystery. So, how do you
understand the Divine Will when it seems to make no
sense, when, in fact, it appears hostile, an ironic grin on a
malevolent face? What do you do when you see sinners
live long, rich, powerful lives, while innocence is visited
with misery and hopelessness? If you say you accept the
verdict of death without bitterness—*"Thy will be done"*—
you are lying. Nobody, no human being created in the
image of God, can accept such injustice without questioning its meaning, by virtue of the fact that we were created
in the image of a God who would not inflict an injustice of
such magnitude on us unless it had a purpose and a
meaning. So, then, what do you do? Curse God? Snarl at
fate? Utter threats? Turn your head away from the heart of
Christ? To fight against the cruelty and injustice of the

rulers of the world is not only our historical legacy, but our moral imperative, our civic duty. But how do you fight against the ruler of the universe, when you have absolutely no inkling as to what His intentions are, what His purposes signify, what His design means?'

Behind the latrines, under the big oak and the suspicious eyes of Strappado's gangsters, Simon Wald recalled, Kopf had often talked about God's mysterious design. What an argument it was, Kopf had said, to justify the most unbearable miseries of human life—wars, poverty, hunger—as part of a deeper, invisible meaning by which good would ultimately win out over evil! There had never in history been any organized force other than the Church that had exploited the mysteries of heaven so cleverly and with such formidable skill, to further the acceptance of its own influence and power here on earth. Though this was a vale of tears, as the Church had rightly taught us for centuries (with less than original insight, Kopf added, making a quick gesture of scorn with his right hand, while, with his left, he embraced the trunk of the big oak with grateful tenderness), don't despair! Everything has a meaning and a purpose, but if you cannot find those elusive things, all you have to do is to consult regularly with God's friendly, local representatives. They know what you don't! Trust them! Weren't they the ones who'd invented the world's most effective slogan and used it for millennia: *Credo quia absurdum*—I believe because it's impossible? Instead of feeding their hungry clients with thin barley gruel on earth tonight, they fed them with the promises of a rich banquet in heaven tomorrow. Was it any wonder people remained hungry? In his heart, still aching for Kopf, Simon Wald felt a wave of tenderness. Grumbling against the historical misdeeds and 'canonical malefactions' (as he called them) of the clergy, Kopf had always been at his entertaining best: he didn't mind the mystery, just hated to be cheated by its avatars.

Yet, watching Father Novak, Simon Wald felt sympathetic to everything he was saying, closer to him than ever before. Maybe Father Novak really knew something Simon Wald didn't, and wanted to share it with him, with everybody. At the very least, he had the courage, in the presence of his boss, to talk freely and eloquently about the doubts and questions that arose in moments of sorrow and grief; Father Leo would have rattled on endlessly about the mercy of God, who, sitting on a puffy cloud—'right above us, my brothers and sisters, right above us!'— would take innocent little Anna Julia's hand and deliver her straight to heaven. Simon Wald looked at Father Novak and, standing behind him in his black garb and narrow Roman collar, Monsignor Beck. For the first time he noticed how much those two resembled each other, both tall, muscular and strong, God's mules pulling the wagon of faith.

Earlier in the day General Wulf had stopped at The Waldhorn to pick up a flask of slivovitz from Aunt Elsie. Waiting for him in the jeep, Simon Wald couldn't help but overhear rising voices coming from the rectory opposite. From what he could make out, Father Novak and Monsignor Beck were having a tremendous argument. Outraged, his strong baritone hoarse, Father Novak was blurting out words Simon Wald couldn't hear clearly, though he sensed that they were words of accusation and condemnation. Monsignor Beck was answering softly, with considerable dignity and discipline; Simon Wald couldn't catch his words either, though he guessed by their cadence

that they were words of bitterness and denial. When
General Wulf emerged from The Waldhorn with a small,
flat metal flask in his hand, the battle in the rectory was still
raging. Simon Wald was sure General Wulf wouldn't
want to miss it, but he didn't seem to pay attention. He got
into the jeep and drove off. Simon Wald laughed. 'What's
so funny, Wald?' General Wulf asked, but Simon Wald
knew he wouldn't be interested in his answer either, only
in his new toy. Or in his old ghost?

Now, Simon Wald looked at General Wulf in his re-
splendent uniform standing on the far side of the grave,
restless, his black hair ruffled by the breeze, slightly tipsy,
although still bolt upright, as though inspecting his
troops. All morning Simon Wald had wanted to tell him
Strappado's story—after all, wasn't that why General
Wulf came to see him in the first place? For months after
his release from Krechk he wouldn't mention Strappado's
name, couldn't think of his name, but now, all of a sudden,
he was ready to tell the tale—oh Lord, what a tale!—but
General Wulf wouldn't listen. Simon Wald regretted it
very much. He saw Strappado standing between General
Wulf and Justice Krolthy, his baby-blue eyes half-closed,
his pinkish face radiant, but the apparition vanished, and
Simon Wald was left with a high, dry fury in his chest.

Next to General Wulf stood Justice Krolthy, tall and
elegant in his dark-grey suit and white shirt, his expres-
sion proper yet so indifferent. He had come in the gig with
Sybil and Aunt Elsie, though he looked as if he'd just
arrived from another world. Still, Simon Wald was grateful to him for having come at all. He was grateful to all
those who had come to accompany his little Anna Julia on
her first and last journey. And everybody had come, the
Walds, the Felds, the Flurs, relatives and friends—if you

weren't a friend, as Papa Krauss had once jokingly said, then you must be a relative—just as they had come to Mass on Friday morning, and to the house at the weekend, bringing flowers for Anna and homemade cakes for the wake. There was Papa Krauss, his beard long and greying, his thinning hair carefully groomed, his skullcap respectfully removed. There was Aunt Gerania and her children and grandchildren, Sara and Berti, Lucas's kids. Even Andy Shvihak was there, in an old, frayed dark-blue suit, uncomfortable without his uniform and decorations, yet properly solemn and mournful, as the occasion warranted. Only Uncle Martin wasn't there. Despite his grief, Simon Wald couldn't help being amused. No matter what happened yesterday or was going to happen tomorrow, Uncle Martin would remain a hopeless imbecile.

From the corner of his eye, without moving his head, Simon Wald looked at Anna's profile; the shadow of the large, black scarf only heightened the beauty of her grey eyes, her determined mouth, white neck. Hesitantly, Simon Wald touched her hand, held it for a second or two, then squeezed it strongly, as if he wanted to communicate everything he couldn't put into words. To his surprise and relief, she reciprocated with so much tenderness and affection that he felt himself blushing with joy, with love, with that unnameable rapture he had experienced when first he took Anna's strong hand into his own and she had clutched it tightly, as for months he had hoped she would. The next week they became engaged. Now, Simon Wald knew she loved him still, and, despite his sorrow, he felt immensely happy.

After the last echoes of Father Novak's dirge—*Libera me, Domine, de morte aeterna*—had faded, and the mourners had left, Simon Wald stayed behind to spend a few more moments with his daughter, whom he had seen only for seconds. The pressure he felt inside and outside his head on Saturday night at Buck's Bend had returned and was growing fast, brutal and fierce. His head, his heart, his limbs, his whole body throbbed with pain and, in panic, he cried out, but nobody was there to help him. Then, unexpectedly, the pressure vanished, the pain stopped, and, dazed, he wandered away. He wasn't quite sure what he wanted to do; he knew that he was looking for something, or somebody, though he had no inkling as to what or who it might be.

He found himself following the rust-covered tracks of the narrow-gauge railway that once had carried a miniature locomotive up to the sawmill where, as a child, he had loved to watch the buzz-saw cutting the giant treetrunks into sweet-smelling planks. After walking for more than forty minutes—it used to be a ten-minute ride on the train—Simon Wald reached the sawmill and walked slowly around it. It was a shambles, its walls collapsed, its roof leaking, its steam-engine rusted, its blades broken. He hadn't been there for years, certainly not since he'd come back from Krechk. Why had he come here now? Beyond the creek, where the meadows ended and the treeline began he saw a house shimmering in the heat like a mirage. But he was not imagining it: it was real; it was Uncle Matthias's house.

'Your name?' Justice Krolthy asked.
    'Dr Ladislas Jarek.'
    'Born?'
    '8 May, 1909.'
    'Occupation?'
    'Former minister of the interior and foreign affairs.'

That cool, pleasant mid-September morning Justice Krolthy had driven through unfamiliar streets to the old, ornate building of the Union of Metalworkers, in the middle of the city's tough working-class district, where the trial of Ladislas Jarek was about to begin. Justice Krolthy had listened attentively to the ticking of what he fondly called his 'endogenous hardware', but noticed no irregularity that would indicate a heightened state of anxiety or even simple nervousness: his pulse was calm, his respiration regular, his mind clear. He felt a slight tremor of tension in his temples, as he usually did at moments like this, but it didn't bother him.

He'd arrived earlier than he'd intended, but the place was already swarming with people holding tickets to the circus, ready to enjoy the legal acrobats, moral contortionists and simple-hearted clowns who'd been assembled to provide an unforgettable show. For a minute or two, Justice Krolthy watched the crowd jostling and elbowing at the door—the sooner you got in, the closer you could sit to the 'monster' and observe him stripped of his powers, lies, pretensions, a traitor and a murderer. Then he took the lift to the fourth floor, where a private office for the presiding judge, together with smaller makeshift cubicles for the public prosecutor and his assistants, as well as the four members of the jury, had been secured. In the corridor, Justice Krolthy exchanged a few early morning pleasantries with the public prosecutor, that young legal genius who was his most persistent enemy. He chatted briefly with the jurors, pale, nervous, dressed simply and solemnly for the occasion—a journalist, a farmer, a lathe-operator and a housewife: Gerogen's idea of a cross-section of the population. They listened to the few last-minute instructions he gave them about their duties and responsibilities with melancholy gravity, as if they were listening to a funeral oration, which it in fact was. In his temporary office he sat at his desk, his papers still in his pigskin attaché case (Eve's latest present from Paris), and stared into space, as if waiting for something to happen that could save him from having to perform his absurd role as straight man in this stupid farce.

'Do you understand the charges brought against you?'

'I do.'

'Is your counsel present?'

'I waive my right to a defence counsel.'

'It is your privilege.' Justice Krolthy shrugged without looking up from his papers. He had been advised weeks before of Jarek's refusal to have a defence lawyer. 'How do you plead?'

'Guilty.'

'On all counts?'

'On all counts.'

'Very well, then,' Justice Krolthy said in the silence of the great hall of the Union of Metalworkers. He could see the audience clearly—553 carefully selected administrators and functionaries from all over the country, perspiring heavily in the heat. 'Perhaps we should begin at the beginning. I believe it would be easier for all concerned to follow the tortuous road the accused has travelled over the years if we asked him to tell us how and when he became an agent of the admiral's Secret Police. Dr Jarek?'

'Yes, of course.' Jarek was standing in the dock. 'However, I'd like to go back a little further in time, if I may, Your Honour, and give a broader view of the situation which eventually landed me in the service of the Secret Police.'

'Briefly,' Justice Krolthy said. 'Very briefly, Dr Jarek.'

'As is known,' Jarek said, 'I was born into an intensely political family. Before the turn of the century, my father, a metal-worker, was already a union organizer, and, in her younger years, my mother had also participated in strikes and demonstrations. In the Fourteenth District where I was born and grew up, our family was regarded as one of the leaders in the fight for a better future. Early in life, my father taught me the political realities of our country and the theory of socialism. He imbued me with a violent hatred of the enemies of the working class. I learned my lessons quickly and well. I was arrested when I was thirteen for taking part in a street demonstration for higher wages and better working conditions in the Stahlberg-Zerelemy Metal Works in our district. Because I was a juvenile, I was soon released, though not before I was forced to listen to the strictures of the local police captain, who warned me not to get involved in such activities again, or else, juvenile or not, I would have to take the consequences. I did not heed his warning. I was arrested several times more and spent weeks and months in the Central Prison, where I became acquainted with many of the leading underground revolutionaries of our country, some of whom faced summary trials before the Curia's Special Courts, which, as we knew all too well, meant no appeal and instant execution. On one occasion . . .'

'Dr Jarek.' Justice Krolthy spoke loudly into the microphone before him, so that everybody in the hall could hear clearly, and the tape-recorders could faithfully preserve his forceful and authoritative handling of the trial, in case of future scrutiny. 'Please refrain from telling us your

family history. Your family is not on trial here. *You* are. So,
just answer the question, please. *How* and *when* did you
become a police agent?'

Justice Krolthy looked at Jarek with sudden interest,
and Jarek returned his inquisitive stare with a mischievous, almost triumphant smile at the corners of his mouth.
The last time Justice Krolthy had seen Jarek was three
weeks ago, when he had gone to his cell to check the
preparations for the trial but also to ask questions he
hadn't asked before. Jarek had seemed like a shadow of his
former self. Always lean and sinewy, he was feeble,
wasted, his ribs showing through his dirty, sweat-stained
shirt, his high, pale forehead mottled with deep, dark
furrows, his skin sallow, his eyes—those intense, vivid
blue eyes Eve had loved so much—colourless and opaque.
Now, he looked a different man. The Archangel's thugs
had not only dressed him up in a tolerably good suit but
also appeared to have fattened him up for the kill. His skin
was tight again, healthy, well-shaven; even the colour,
clarity and intensity of his blue eyes had returned. What's
more, Justice Krolthy thought, they had unwittingly given
him back his originality, his wit.

Jarek's opening gambit was a stroke of genius. Without
straying from Adymester's script—or, at least, not from its
general tenor—in less than two minutes Jarek had almost
demolished an argument that had not yet been presented.
He had managed to inform his audience—and the trial
was being broadcast to the whole country, on the air from
morning to midnight, on Copass's orders—that he came
from an impeccable working-class family, whose credentials as leaders of their tribe were as convincing as they
were indisputable. He had also established that he himself
was a tried-and-proven captain of the proletarian army,

who'd learned both from experience and from the mar-
tyred leaders of the movement, whom he'd met in the
enemy's jails and supported when they suffered the
utmost sacrifice.

Jarek's was an enviable performance indeed: you could
almost feel the tension tighten among the members of the
Western press, all herded together in the gallery, who fully
understood the implications of such a daring move!
Anything that might come later had already been denied
and refuted, the lie of the trial turned into Jarek's truth.
Quickly, Justice Krolthy made a few notes on the pad
before him. No doubt Gerogen had noticed the trick and
would call as soon as the day's proceedings were over. He
would be furious. The irony that Jarek's father, a union
organizer around the turn of the century and, as such,
surely one of the founder-contributors to the union headquarters where his son was now being tried as a traitor to
the working class, exposed the trial as travesty; Jarek's
passing reference to the summary trials of the Curia only
added to the power of his mockery.

Justice Krolthy sensed the excitement of a contest.
What he had expected to be a boring regurgitation of a
well-rehearsed script seemed to be developing into a
vivid, unpredictable *rencontre*. He suspected—no, he
knew—that Gerogen would hold him responsible for the
muddle Jarek's sudden recovery might have created, yet
Justice Krolthy felt invigorated: anything but the unbur-
dening of a bone-dry conscience! As much as he hated
Jarek for what he'd done to Eve, Justice Krolthy was now
looking forward to their duel.

'On one occasion,' Jarek continued, without paying
attention to Krolthy's admonition, 'I was taken to the
office of Colonel Kronenberg-Freinitzer, then head of the

Third Department—the counter-intelligence section of
the Secret Police—for further investigation. There was
another officer in the room whom I knew, because he was
a distant relative of my mother's. Captain Drazhek explained to me that my situation was indeed very serious,
and, if it came to trial, I could get a severe sentence and
spend years in jail. However, there was a solution to my
problem, Captain Drazhek said, which would not only
allow me to go free but also help me to get the scholarship
to the Sorbonne for which I'd applied a few months earlier
in order to finish my studies and receive my teacher's
certificate. All I had to do, Captain Drazhek said, was to
report, once in a while, on the internal situation in the
directorate of the Youth Movement, of which I was a
member. I agreed to do that. Captain Drazhek then typed
up a statement to that effect, which I signed. That was how
I became a police agent.'

'And did you fulfil your obligations as stipulated in
your agreement with the Third Department?' Justice
Krolthy asked.

'Yes, I did,' Jarek said, without batting an eyelid. 'After
my release from police custody, I participated regularly in
the meetings of the directorate, and, as Colonel Kronenberg-Freinitzer instructed me, made copious notes on
everything discussed there. When Colonel Kronenberg's
man contacted me—usually once a fortnight—I gave him
the notes, together with my personal observations and
comments. As a result, eight members of the directorate
were arrested, myself among them, in order to avert
suspicion, the Youth Movement was paralysed and, a few
months later, dissolved altogether.

'In the meantime, thanks to the support of Colonel
Kronenberg and Captain Drazhek, my Sorbonne scholar-

ship was approved. Before I left, Captain Drazhek informed me that the Department's opposite number in the French Deuxième Bureau had been notified of my arrival and would contact me. In Paris, Captain Drazhek said, my task would be twofold. First, I was to keep an eye on our students, most of them Jews who got their scholarships through high government officials being bribed by rich parents; several of them were suspected of leftist leanings and some even of underground activities. Second, I was supposed to infiltrate the university's left-wing organizations passively, seeking information and connections, rather than by direct action. On any other concrete matter, I was to follow the instructions of my French *liaison*.

'I had no difficulty in carrying out those directives. About two weeks after my arrival in Paris, the contact from the Deuxième Bureau called me to a meeting in a bistro on the Left Bank, behind the famous Deux Magôts, and from then on, until I finished my studies and returned home, we worked together.'

Justice Krolthy saw Jarek at the Tricolour Club, lanky and bony, his blue eyes flashing with fury, as he lectured them on his very own garden of earthly delights, so profoundly different from Bosch's landscape of horror which Justice Krolthy had just seen in Madrid. Ah, youth and its boundless conceits! Justice Krolthy wished he could smoke a cigar. Now the chickens had come home to roost. Here was Jarek's garden of delights in its full splendour: the big hall, ornamented with fiery slogans, giant red flags, hammers-and-sickles, partly to cover the crumbling plaster of the walls and ceiling, partly to underline the substance of the trial with the symbols of the Alliance. On Justice Krolthy's left and right, the jurors of the People's Tribunal fidgeted nervously with their pads and pens. They seemed under a spell, incapable of comprehending the farce being played out in front of their eyes, yet aware of the formless menace swirling around them. On the left side of the stage, Dr Urban, the public prosecutor, impatiently waited for his turn. It was rumoured, Irene had told Justice Krolthy only the day before, that Dr Urban had already finished writing his closing speech. It was supposed to last for at least two hours, and to recapitulate in minute detail the activities of the accused and Justice Krolthy shuddered at the thought of having to listen to it. How was he going to survive that? He longed for a cigar.

Beyond the spotlights, microphones, guards, flags, placards—'All power to the people!' 'Death to the enemies of the Alliance!' 'Long live Copass our beloved leader!'— the extras of this second-rate historical epic sat in tense expectation in the growing heat and airlessness of the big hall. Though Justice Krolthy couldn't clearly make out their faces, he could sense the upsurge of hatred in their bodies, as Jarek, with such splendid nonchalance, recited the story of his treachery. They sat there, listening to Jarek's confession, which with every passing minute became more incredible, more ludicrous. To the growing admiration of Justice Krolthy, Jarek made absolutely certain that his confession sounded ludicrous to any sane listener, but this gory little army of zealots did not understand a word of it. They took Jarek's brilliant opening statement as clear proof of his unforgivable infamy; they saw his comic portrayal of the admiral's counter-intelligence operation as a historical drama; they viewed the burlesque of Colonel Kronenberg-Freinitzer and Captain Drazhek as high tragedy. *O sancta simplicitas!* Justice Krolthy remembered Professor Weiskopf's eloquent dis-

course at Major-General Jefferson-Smith's garden party:
they were supposed to be the knights of the apocalypse,
the vanguard of history, but they were only a pack of
bloodthirsty jackals ready to tear Jarek to pieces, ready,
when the word was given, to tear to pieces anybody who
stood between them and the sacred image of their Garden
of Eden!

'It was then,' Jarek went on, 'that, at the order of Colonel
Kronenberg-Freinitzer, I travelled to Prague to infiltrate a
group of volunteers who were on their way from Moscow
to Madrid, intent on joining the Copass Brigade in Spain
to fight Franco's Fascists. Before I left, Captain Drazhek
gave me detailed instructions, a forged passport and some
money. In Prague . . .'

For the first time that morning, as if somebody from
behind the scenes had given them the signal, a sudden
snarl of fury rose in unison from among the jackals.
'Silence!' Justice Krolthy shouted, his gavel raised high.
'Silence in the court! Or I'll have you removed from the
hall. Silence!'

Obediently, the jackals fell silent.

'Please, Dr Jarek, continue,' Justice Krolthy said.

When he first heard rumours about Jarek's arrest, Justice
Krolthy didn't pay much attention. Rumours were the
staple of this town as far back as he could remember, and,
besides, the idea of Jarek's arrest—he was the darling of
the Alliance, idol of the young, hope of the people—made
very little sense, even in the growing madness of a mad
regime. But then one morning Irene came in with her usual
report of gossip and told him that her sources had con-
firmed, and her *other* sources reconfirmed, Jarek's arrest a
few days after the May Day reception. Justice Krolthy

remembered watching Jarek, with tears in his eyes, embracing Copass, as his leader and patron saint. Justice Krolthy looked out to the silent, sundrenched *Sackgasse* behind the Supreme Court, where the balmy spring breezes had revived his sickly little acacias and plane-tree saplings. If Jarek had been arrested he had got what was coming to him, what he truly deserved. The hatred he had felt for him ever since Jarek jilted Eve and married that buxom peasant from Copass's court came back to him with a force doubled by the joy of vengeance. Yet he still didn't believe it had happened.

Then, early that afternoon, Gerogen called. 'Yes,' Gerogen said. 'High treason. General Gabriel has irrefutable documentation. We have all the necessary evidence to hang him. But first, we'll try him in public. And, as chief justice as well as our expert in treason, the unanimous wish of the Secretariat is that you preside over the trial. I said, *unanimous* wish, Adam, yes. No excuses this time, as in the Zenty case. Absolutely none. Later this afternoon you'll get Jarek's dossier. As soon as you've read the stuff, we'll discuss the details. Cheer up, Adam. This is the greatest opportunity for a judge since Tristan l'Hermite tried the Vicomte de Montferrand at the order of Charles VII, and had him hanged, beheaded and quartered, remember? It's all in your book.' Gerogen laughed.

Justice Krolthy remembered Tristan l'Hermite very clearly—as the Royal High Justice, he left a magnificent description of the Vicomte de Montferrand's execution on 14 July 1454 on the common of Poitiers—but he did not remember having heard Gerogen laugh lately, so he understood that the final decision had been made. Frankly, much as he loathed Jarek's arrogant austerity, insolent vanity, pompous pride, he would have preferred somebody else to have tried him, but he knew that he couldn't get out of the noose without hanging himself, so he resigned himself to the inevitable. He knew, too, that it was going to be one of the greatest circus-attractions of all time, but he couldn't foresee its true dimensions.

'Prague, at that time,' Jarek went on, 'was a veritable transit camp between Moscow and Madrid. With my past and credentials, it wasn't difficult to infiltrate those groups—for the sake of security, they consisted of only two or three people—and I was soon able to send important information to Colonel Kronenberg about the volunteers: their names, underground connections, planned routes through Germany and France, etc. Because of the bourgeois democracies' sympathy with Republican Spain, we could move without being molested by the police or any other counter-intelligence organization. After several months, however, Captain Drazhek came to Prague with new instructions from Colonel Kronenberg, who ordered me to go to Spain to join the Brigade.

'I arrived in Madrid in June 1937 and immediately contacted the headquarters of the Brigade. I was named deputy political commissar. My instructions from Colonel Kronenberg were: first, to gather as much inside information about the Brigade, its plans and personnel, as possible; and second, to try to disrupt its activities from within. It was an ideal post for me. I did everything I could to deserve the trust Colonel Kronenberg had placed in me. My wrecking activities became particularly important when, in November 1937, the Brigade was ordered to link up with General Heredia's Eleventh Division at the Guadalajara, then move against Teruel. The surprise attack on Teruel was to have been one of the most important campaigns of the war, and it was planned for three major reasons: first, Teruel was thought to be undermanned; second, its capture would secure the road to Saragossa; and third, the town had come to have a special place in the minds of the Republican forces. But, as a result of my activities, the campaign against Teruel turned into a disaster for the International Brigades.'

Two days after his telephone conversation with Gerogen, Justice Krolthy read in the morning paper a terse press release from the prime minister's office, which informed the world of the arrest on charges of high treason of Dr Ladislas Jarek and his accomplices. From then on, every morning before he walked to his office across the square, Justice Krolthy sat on his balcony, drank his early morning Colombian milds and read the morning edition of the *People's Truth*. It was a dry, hot summer, the sky deep blue, the river bluer than it had ever been, but then, conformity, compliance, consent were the order of the day, and not even nature could escape the command. Justice Krolthy studied the paper with increasing curiosity and amazement. Gerogen's agitprop rogues and Adymester's clever young scribblers had swung into action with feverish enthusiasm.

In cables to the press, letters to the editors, at meetings in factories, farm cooperatives, trade-union cells and military barracks, workers and peasants, professors and students, doctors and nurses, secretaries and soldiers expressed their 'passionate hatred' towards those 'vermin' whose inconceivable treachery, they demanded in unison, must be punished 'forthwith and without mercy'. Gerogen knew what he was doing. Designed to appear as the spontaneous manifestation of the wrath of a people betrayed, it was actually a coldly calculated offering of the scapegoat on the altar of the class war's avenging god, thus purging from the holy body of the Alliance the evil of the bourgeois demon.

After he got Jarek's dossier from the Archangel, Justice Krolthy took it home, though he couldn't bring himself to open it immediately. He found it was a jumbled affair, with names, dates, localities, viewpoints all chucked together in a heap. The first name that caught his eye was Eve's.

Since Jarek had so abruptly broken with Eve and married that peasant wench, Justice Krolthy had never once talked with Jarek about Eve, never even mentioned her name in Jarek's presence. He wasn't quite sure why, but he felt he had to keep Eve's name out of that mess, and somehow talking with Jarek about her would have defiled her. Still, when he visited Jarek for the first time after his arrest, about three weeks before the trial, Justice Krolthy decided to confront Jarek with the question of Eve. But the moment Jarek stood up from his rickety table—strewn with sheets of paper covered on both sides with his familiar, small, dense handwriting—and turned towards him, pen still in hand, his body, despite debasements and humiliations, still conveying power and demanding respect, Krolthy only said, 'I see you're working on your memoirs.'

Jarek must have known that not one word of whatever he was writing now would survive, or if it did—on Gerogen's orders—it would be kept in Gerogen's office safe. Like everybody else, Justice Krolthy knew the story about the memoirs of an old warrior which contained certain unpleasant revelations concerning Copass's conduct in prison and Gerogen's Chekist connections and

manipulations in the Komintern and on the front. After
the old warrior had met a fiery death in an improbable car
crash in Poland, where he was serving as ambassador, his
Warsaw office was looted by Gerogen's minions during a
night-raid, and, according to Bellona Hagen, the ambassador's manuscripts disappeared into Gerogen's bottomless safe. Yet Jarek was working on his memoirs, but then,
Jarek had always been an eccentric, always had strange
ideas about immortality.

'Could be interesting,' Justice Krolthy said.

'Could be,' Jarek said, 'but it's a novel. Ever since I went
to Spain, I've been wanting to write a novel. You see all
kinds of things, and you want to write about them. For
years, I haven't had the time, but now I have plenty of time,
and they let me work on it as much as I please. Compli-
ments of old Henryk, if you want to know. He, of course,
hopes that he'll be one of its heroes. But, in confidence,
Krolthy, he won't be.' Jarek let out a brief, dry laugh, and
sat back at his table.

'Are they treating you properly?' Justice Krolthy asked,
looking around. The cell was small, dirty, dark, but so far
as he could determine, Jarek showed no signs of torture.
'You can tell me, Jarek, you know that.'

'I could read you a few pages, Krolthy,' Jarek said,
grinning. 'It's quite funny. Actually, it's a satire. Don
Quixote at the Guadalquivir in 1937. I'm sure you'd enjoy
it. The don fighting windmills again.' He picked up a sheet
of paper. 'Here, for instance, is an episode I've just finished
about a general who quarrels with the don because the
don has rescued a friend on the battlefield who, according
to the general, is an enemy. The don argues that he's a
friend, because he always fought bravely and was willing
to make sacrifices, but the general counters that he must be

an enemy precisely because he always fought bravely and was willing to make sacrifices, for that was the only way he could conceal his true colours and call their bluff. The don is shocked. The gist of the chapter is how the don realizes—very slowly, poor chap—that he lives in a world where love is viewed as hatred, honour as treachery. Would you like me to read it to you?'

'I'm afraid we won't have time for that today,' Justice Krolthy replied. He wanted very much to hear Jarek read it, but he knew he mustn't let him do it.

'Frankly,' Jarek said, 'I haven't the slightest idea, Krolthy, why you never came straight out and asked me about Eve, but now I'll tell you, regardless. I left Eve because I stopped loving her. To be honest with you, Krolthy, I never really loved her. Of course, she was fun to be with, and she worked well and hard in the Resistance. Still I was never *really* in love with her—you know what I mean, you're a man. When she came to me—and remember: *she* came to *me*—I thought I loved her. I was certainly flattered, and she certainly knew how to butter a man up, how to make him feel on top of the world and give him pleasure in every sense. But after a while she became selfish, demanding. And when I met Susanna, I knew I had to break with Eve. I'm sorry if I hurt her. I didn't mean to. I hear she's all right now, and I hope that's true. You understand me, Krolthy, don't you? I'm sure you're familiar with the experience. You just stop loving.'

'Shut up, Jarek,' Justice Krolthy whispered, trembling with rage. 'Shut up, or I'll have you whipped, so help me!' And instantly, he felt himself reddening with shame.

'Are you telling us, Dr Jarek,' Justice Krolthy said loudly, with a broad gesture of his right hand towards the audience in the hall and beyond, 'are you suggesting that the defeat at Teruel of the International Brigades was the result of your activities?'

'Partly,' Jarek said.

'That is by no means a modest statement, Dr Jarek. And you seem to be quite proud of your achievement. *Are* you proud of it? Do you consider that something to be proud of? A moral triumph, perhaps?'

'I am not proud of what I did, Your Honour,' Jarek replied, 'although Colonel Kronenberg praised me highly for my accomplishments. If anything, I give myself credit for the fact that I hid my activities so well behind a façade of loyalty, devotion and good works, that until now, when the vigilance of our leaders has finally exposed my true colours, nobody even suspected my double-dealings.'

'But while you were yourself a revered leader of our people,' Justice Krolthy raised his voice to a pitch he felt epitomized his disgust and contempt, 'you were secretly proud of your knavery?'

'Basically, what I meant to say was . . .'

'Your duplicity?'

'At the time, I felt . . .'

'Your treachery?'

'I would like, if I may . . .'

'Answer me, Jarek. Yes or no.'

'Yes,' Jarek said. 'Yes.'

'Tell us what happened,' Justice Krolthy said icily. It was an excellent riposte. Jarek looked choleric. Justice Krolthy was pleased. The exchange forced Jarek directly to admit his obliquity, which was what Jarek really wanted to avoid. Gerogen should be delighted. Justice Krolthy had managed to hit Jarek where it hurt him most, the memory of what Jarek referred to as his 'Spanish *experience'*.

'Please, Dr Jarek,' Justice Krolthy said, 'we are waiting.'

'After heavy fighting,' Jarek said slowly, 'Teruel fell towards the end of December. A snowstorm stopped everything except the battle that went on in the centre of the town. Occasionally, the weather cleared, and then the Condors bombed us at least twice daily. They couldn't care less who got hit, rebels or Republicans, but our pilots were also in the air, flying their ancient machines with tremendous skill and bravery. Finally, however, under growing pressure, Colonel Rey D'Harcourt, commander of the Teruel Defence Corps, had to surrender after Christmas. The battle had ended and immediately began anew, but now the attackers were the besieged, prisoners in the town they'd just liberated. Soon, early in January 1938, we found ourselves surrounded by Franco's armies, pounded day and night from the air and the neighbouring hilltops, cut off from our supply lines, and from our headquarters, which, as we were to learn later, had been captured by rebel forces. The situation was desperate. On the northern walls, the Thaelmanns tried heroically to stop the enemy's advance; on the south, the Lincolns fought with ferocious determination; and we were trying to defend the Western Front, though not with great success. Food was scarce, ammunition scanty, the temperature often fell to ten or fifteen below freezing, while our uniforms were like rags. Near their quarters, in what was once an elementary school, the Americans found an abandoned tailor's and turned that to advantage. Soon you could see machine-gun ramparts manned by people dressed in elegant pin-striped suits, and patent-leather shoes, with huge automatics tucked, for emphasis, into their wide trouser-belts: those were the few comic moments in an otherwise tragic situation.'

For a second, Jarek stopped to mop the sweat on his face with his large, white linen handkerchief and Justice Krolthy looked at him with curiosity. What was Jarek up to now? True, the Teruel incident was given a fairly prominent role in Adymester's wobbly script, as an illustration of Jarek's activities on behalf of virtually every intelligence agency in the Western world. But now, it seemed to Justice Krolthy, Jarek was building the Teruel episode into a climactic event of historical importance and far-reaching consequences, a real crowd-pleaser. It wasn't what Jarek said—though he was beginning subtly to change the boring factual narrative of Adymester's banal script by adding convincing details to it, vivid *couleur locale*—it was the way he said it, that made it significant. His head was lifted, his voice softer, his tone mellifluous, almost nostalgic, as though reciting a love poem rather than a confession of crimes against humanity. In an almost imperceptible way, Jarek created a tension in the hall different from the tension of hatred which had, since the opening of the trial, hovered above the audience—a tension of reverence, even grace, which made them pay attention to him.

'In that situation,' Jarek continued, his voice suddenly hardening, 'a new, daring plan was conceived by General Heredia, our commanding officer. The plan—a centralized assault by the Brigades' combined forces on the heart of General Yagüe's headquarters and communication systems which controlled the offensive against Teruel— was a gem of simplicity. Given some luck and a good storm, the plan had an excellent chance of success. I knew that I mustn't let that happen. Somehow, I had to inform Yagüe of the attack, but I had to wait until an opportunity presented itself, when I could do so without arousing suspicions which might have jeopardized my position in the high command.

'I didn't have to wait too long. During a vicious dog-fight between the Condors and our air corps, one of our best pilots, a Frenchman named Sébastien LaCroix, was shot down. As we watched his disintegrating plane fall into the ravines of La Muela, I realized that this was the opportunity I'd been waiting for. I convinced our commander that I could reach Sébastien LaCroix and bring him back, dead or alive, so that we could give him either a chance to recover, or the proper burial he so much deserved. Under the pretext of saving one man's life, I marched towards the hills with a plan of betrayal which, if successful, would cause the death of hundreds, if not thousands of people. But in my arrogant pride and growing hatred against all progressive forces under the leadership of the *Vozhd*, I didn't give much thought to that. On the contrary, I felt delighted to be part of a historical action, the prime cause, one might say, of a great battle. Seething with rancour, I approached the hills of La Muela. I had, of course, been warned that the territory was swarming with Yagüe's soldiers, and that if they captured me, it would mean the end of my life. But before Colonel D'Harcourt's withdrawal from Teruel I'd managed to establish contact with him—we met secretly in an abandoned tavern, where the good wines of Catalonia awaited us invitingly in uncorked bottles—and I gave him information concerning our plans and strengths, which he was supposed to forward to General Yagüe. In exchange he gave me the password which would, in any situation, save my life.

Needless to say that soon after I'd found Sébastien LaCroix's body, mangled but still alive, near the wreckage of his beloved Nieuport, I was picked up by the Guardia Alba and came dangerously close to a painful death. But Colonel D'Harcourt's password did the trick. As quickly as possible, I briefed Yagüe's intelligence chief and deputy chief of staff about Heredia's plans and was then escorted back to where Sébastien's bloody torso and limbs were still convulsed in tremendous pain. He cried and groaned as I carried him back to headquarters, where he died soon after and was buried hastily. Later, I was ceremoniously decorated with the Red Flag of Courage.

'My reputation grew by leaps and bounds, but after a fierce battle, Heredia's surprise attack was defeated and Teruel changed hands again, this time for good. The fate of the Republic was sealed. Undermined by the intrigues and sabotage of the anarchists, syndicalists and social democrats—bourgeois idealists whose fuzzy dreams were actually more damaging to the war effort than the Fascists' rabid realities—the army of the Republic could no longer effectively resist the assaults of Franco's well-fed divisions, armed with modern weapons from Germany and Italy. Though the fighting continued with undiminished ferocity, it was all over. One month after the defeat at Teruel, my contacts ordered me to leave Spain, to take up residence in Paris and try to infiltrate Yezhov's Special NKVD Group, whose main task, my informant told me, was to eliminate the enemies of the *Vozhd* who were once his friends.

'This time, however, I was unable to follow the orders of my superiors. At the border, I was arrested by the gendarmes and spent the next months in camps in Le Boulou, Argèles, St Cyprien, together with a growing flood of refugees from Spain. I had, of course, managed to establish contact with my old friends in the Deuxième Bureau, and through them sent a message to Colonel Kronenberg. While waiting for his response, I was able to get valuable information from the former fighters, especially from the Yugoslav contingent, whose commander, Colonel Kosta Kostič, became a good friend and, after the war, became my direct contact with the American, British and French intelligence services. In the meantime, Colonel Kronenberg's dispatch arrived, and I was ordered to return home, where Colonel Kronenberg was waiting for me with new assignments. And so, after almost two years, I was looking forward to . . .'

In the growing heat Justice Krolthy felt dizzy. He closed his eyes. What Jarek had said was pure bunk. Not one word of Jarek's long recitation of the Teruel episode came from Adymester's script. Except for the rescue of that downed French pilot, Jarek had invented everything. When he realized what was happening, Justice Krolthy should have cut him off in mid-sentence—he knew Adymester's deranged script by heart—but he couldn't do that. Jarek was cataloguing his sins, exactly as he himself had done so many years before. But in his youth, he had done it to prove his guilt; Jarek was doing it to prove his innocence. Adam Krolthy had fabricated those idiotic peccadilloes because he wanted to escape a senseless punishment; Jarek invented those terrible treacheries because he wanted to make his inevitable punishment meaningful. Krolthy had lied because he wanted to hide the truth; Jarek lied because that was the only way he could tell the truth: Krolthy had been a cowardly clod, but Jarek was a brave man.

Justice Krolthy glanced at Jarek in the witness stand, wiping his forehead with that large, white handkerchief, and felt a tremor through his being. He came as close to forgiving Jarek as he ever could in a world which had never forgiven him, nor, for that matter, anybody else in this life.

From the porch behind The Waldhorn, Justice Krolthy had a superb view of the forests and the western hills shimmering in the early afternoon sun. He sat in a wobbly old wicker chair, a small glass of slivovitz in his hand. He marvelled at the fragrance of the slivovitz, at once strong and mellow, dry and juicy, which reminded him of the fragrances that wafted above the hills and valleys of his youth at plum-picking time.

'There you are, Krolthy,' General Wulf said behind him. 'What are you doing here alone? The whole village is inside. You can get some absolutely superb *Apfelstrudeln*, fresh from the oven. And your Esmaralda's just arrived.' General Wulf seated himself and put his bottle of wine on the table. 'It was a nice service, don't you think? I liked that angry young priest a lot. I wonder, though, what our Monsignor is going to say about all those allusions to slavery and freedom, violence and what have you.' He took off his tunic and sat in his short-sleeved shirt, his cap cocked jauntily over his eyes, sipping his wine.

'Henryk,' Justice Krolthy said. 'You're drunk. You shouldn't drink so much. Hasn't Dr Asklep warned you? It's bad for your blood pressure.'

'I'm not drunk,' General Wulf replied. 'But I soon shall be. And I don't care one bloody shit about Dr Asklep.' He filled up his glass and quickly gulped the wine down. 'Do you have any idea, Krolthy, what you're going to say come Friday?'

'Yes,' Justice Krolthy said. 'I'll tell them that if there's such a place as heaven, as our priest talked about so fervidly, I want my balcony on the rue de Liège back, and I want to sit there with Jarek and watch the milk-trains of Saint-Lazare, smoking long cigarillos, slurping Mme Escande's famous vegetable soup with plenty of carrots, *haricots verts* and dill—especially dill!—then go down to the Chaussée d'Antin and watch the whores, perhaps even pick one up, then go back to the balcony and watch the trains again. For all eternity. That's what I'm going to tell them.'

'That's telling them,' General Wulf said. 'That's fucking telling them, all right. And what else?'

'Nothing,' Justice Krolthy said. 'Not one single word.'

ELEVEN

BUT above all,' Father Novak whispered in the rectory's empty reception room, and Monsignor Beck hoped, with a suppressed smile, that the young man he so much liked would not throw Shakespeare in his face, 'above all, Monsignor Beck, you sold yourself to them, body and soul. It wasn't enough for you openly to oppose the cardinal when he was in mortal danger, when everybody knew his arrest was only a matter of time and nobody had any doubt that the fate of the Church was sealed. It wasn't enough for you to accept high government office after the cardinal's trial—and so lend credence or at least tacit support to every absurdity Kral uttered in the witness stand about the cardinal's American connections and foreign-currency manipulations—with such unseemly haste that even your allies found it a little too quick and delayed the official announcement of your appointment as deputy first secretary. No, all that wasn't enough for you, Monsignor Beck, because what you were really after was publication of your pamphlet, the famous *Considerations*, which, of course, became the theological justification of your political activities on behalf of an anti-Christian regime of apostate Jews. "We can take St Anselm's ontological argument one step further by proving—as we shall do subsequently—that the idea of perfection, because perfection cannot exist without being, can only be based on the reality of existence." Yes, Monsignor Beck, I know your book by heart. At the seminary, we were not only required to read it, but we had to venerate it. According to your protégés on the faculty, yours was the most significant contribution to theology since St Paul. We studied it, analysed it, taking it apart and putting it back together, as though we were expecting to find in it the answer to the mystery of the universe.

'But that was beside the point. Your friends in the seminary cared only about the *apparent* and not the *real*. Those latter-day docetists prayed with one eye on your office. They worked for peace, all enthusiastic supporters of your sacerdotal movement, *Opus Operatum*, whose name makes clever reference to the inherent efficacy of grace in the Eucharist, yet they ended up at war. A class-war within the Church! Why, Monsignor Beck, for God's sake, why did you write that essay? Ever since I entered the seminary and first read it, I have wanted to ask you that question, but, alas, I could never get near enough to you to do so; and when occasionally I did, at official functions, I was suddenly struck mute. So I went on wondering: why? *Why?*

'You could just as easily have cosied up to those murderers by submitting to their political demands. They'd have given you everything you wanted, power, a seat in the Parliament; but, of course, that was *not* what you wanted. You wanted your book published! And so, you gave them what they could only have hoped for in their wildest dreams, you gave them the theological argument for the primacy of dialectical and historical materialism, which was exactly what they wanted, what they really needed to consolidate their hold over the spirit of the Church. No wonder they were grateful to you, Monsignor Beck.

'Not many of those who ended up on the gallows cared much for your theological subtleties, but those subtleties certainly helped your bedfellows hang them high, whether or not their political or religious beliefs could be verified, as you argued they must be, by human experience. There we were, literally at the edge of the abyss, and your *Considerations,* Monsignor Beck, gave us the final shove into the pit. In exchange for what, Monsignor?

'I have wanted to ask you all that since I first realized how cleverly you were leading us down the garden path. I wanted to tell you that your arguments were erroneous, your attitude immoral, your work treasonous to the Church, because I felt that it would clear the air, that I'd feel better for it, but here I am, telling you all that, and—God forgive me!—I don't feel a bit better. I don't feel good at all.'

'Frantisek, calm down,' Monsignor Beck said. 'Sit here and rest. You're exhausted. Don't worry. If you need an explanation, I can give you one. I could have given you one a long time ago, but you never asked. Why didn't you come and ask? You and your pals have been whispering *all that* since you left the seminary. Here's a glass of water. Papa Krauss brought it from the well a couple of minutes before you came. He said you looked terrible in church, and he was right. Now, drink it.'

Before the meeting with Gerogen in the library, Monsignor Beck had decided to drive to the village and have a talk with Father Novak, but after Gerogen had finished his discourse, Monsignor Beck knew he couldn't go anywhere, let alone face a long and, in all probability, raging *pourparler* with a recalcitrant young priest. He knelt on the *prie-dieu*—grateful now to Henryk for having sent it—but the prayers revolved empty in his mind. He went back to his cot, lay down and closed his eyes. With its cold sharpness, the silence knifed him.

Though Monsignor Beck knew that most of the mourners at Jarek's burial on Friday would be agnostics or unbelievers, for whom prayer meant little or nothing, the best he thought he could do was to lead the crowd in a short, powerful prayer for Jarek's soul. Prayer worked in mysterious ways even for those who denied its power. If Monsignor Beck decided to comply with Gerogen's orders to speak at the funeral, it was because this time he wanted Jarek buried properly, with the benediction of the Lord. He recalled his violent clash with Gerogen over giving Jarek a Christian burial after his execution. Gerogen wouldn't hear of it, and Jarek had been tossed into a hastily dug ditch somewhere at the edge of the public cemetery on the outskirts of town. Only a small flock of huge black crows watched the rough-hewn pine box disappear into unhallowed ground, or so one of the two grave-diggers, whom Monsignor Beck had known for years, told him in the strictest confidence.

Soon afterwards he and his fellow grave-digger disappeared without a trace, so nobody knew where Jarek was buried. Monsignor Beck wondered if the bones in Friday's coffin would be Jarek's or those of the first corpse Gerogen's hired hands dug up. Not that it mattered; it didn't matter at all. Monsignor Beck, who had had the privilege of being with Jarek the night before his execution, never for a moment doubted that the grace and mercy of the Lord would reach Jarek's soul and bathe him in His *lux perpetua*. Now, Monsignor Beck was ready to meet Jarek for the last time.

He had met Jarek for the first time at the ceremony to

consecrate the site of the new church in his native village. On the advice of Henryk Wulf, Monsignor Beck had invited Jarek because, as the minister of the interior, he had authorized the funds to build the new church. Monsignor Beck wanted to spend some time with his mother and look around the village he hadn't seen since his return from Paris, so he arrived two days before the ceremony. He stood and prayed among the charred remains of the old church where the Virgin had ordered him to look after her Son's people. The fire had been started, Monsignor Beck suspected, by some rabid village enthusiasts in response to a particularly vicious anti-religious campaign by the radio and the press.

By some odd coincidence, the house that had been built by his forefathers had burned down the same day as the church. Fortunately, his mother, who lived there alone, managed to escape the voracious flames that consumed the age-old wooden structure, but she had not been able to salvage anything—not even her favourite photograph album, the last memento of her happy past. Now, frail and mute—since the fire she hadn't said a word—the old lady lived with Monsignor Beck's youngest brother.

Miraculously the fire had left his mother's rose garden and his father's workshop undamaged. In front of the blackened remains of planks, posts, and two-by-fours, the green shoots of roses were already raising their tiny spears, and, as Monsignor Beck entered his father's large, dusty shop, he saw, even in the devious light of April, that here, too, everything remained the same.

Monsignor Beck walked around his father's workshop, touching the empty shelves and the cold kiln. Despite Gerogen's growing impatience, clearly audible on the phone whenever he called him, Monsignor Beck still hadn't made up his mind whether or not to accept Gerogen's invitation to write a pamphlet based on his discarded *Proslogion Two*. It was a tough decision, and he had to make it by himself. There was nobody he could turn to for help or advice. He couldn't rely on his father's experience and wisdom. He couldn't take advantage of his mother's down-to-earth common sense. He couldn't ask his brother Pherencz for his opinion, because with his saintly simplicity, Pherencz would have laughed. And Monsignor Beck couldn't consult his brothers in the monastery either, especially now that Abbot Gregorius had been arrested and they saw a devil in every bush. But it was also true that he couldn't postpone the decision much longer. He prayed incessantly for an answer, but, once again, God wrapped Himself in one of His thunderous silences, remained hidden, and left the decision entirely to Monsignor Beck.

There was much to recommend accepting Gerogen's proposal. To write a short, cogent piece for an audience not only untrained in theological speculation but also downright hostile to metaphysics in general, about the idea of reason as the main instrument for proving God's existence—and, to fire, *en passant*, as it were, a well-aimed broadside against the solipsistic antics of that new French philosopher whose influential book about being and nothingness Gerogen had recently brought back from Paris—would not simply be an intellectual achievement but also a spiritual exercise, a contribution, perhaps his last one, to the general understanding of God's intent and man's purpose on earth. A pamphlet like that might be a masterstroke to cut through the intrigues and machinations of his antagonists; it might show those ecclesiastical bloodhounds and papal lackeys that it could and should be done: a sign for all those who felt that, in lieu of the stale platitudes and complacent rigidities of old Vatican strategists and their young tacticians, a new, flexible approach was necessary to deal with the complexities, anxieties, ambiguities and, above all, tyrannies of the world. It might be an incentive to the faithful and a triumph for the Church—and they both needed it.

On the other hand, a great deal could also be said for rejecting the proposal. The moment, historically speaking, was not exactly auspicious for such an undertaking. The conflict between the Church and the Alliance was growing sharper, arguments were heating up, exchanges becoming more vitriolic. Cardinal Zenty, a rigid man under any circumstances, followed his own path to martyrdom: as his attacks became tougher and more pronounced, the baroque flourish of his rhetoric became less and less effective. Monsignor Beck watched the duel with increasing desperation. Cardinal Gaunilon's prophecy, uttered a year before in the Vatican, was turning into reality. What was needed at this juncture was patience, understanding, courage, but, above all, insight into the historical nature of the moment, and what Monsignor Beck got was choler, bravado, blindness.

All Cardinal Zenty should have done was pick up the phone, or better still, send an emissary to Alliance headquarters with a brief note bearing his seal and signature, and request a private meeting with Copass or Gerogen. Together, they might have hammered out a compromise, which was the only way for the Church to stay alive, to keep moving, however slowly, towards fulfilment of Christ's mission. It could have been done. After all, Copass and his cohorts were not storybook monsters, as they were now portrayed, unnamed but recognizable in the cardinal's speeches and pastoral letters, but human beings who, however deeply they had sunk into the abyss of hell, would understand, if not the transcendent truth of the Church, at least their own strategic and tactical interests. They didn't need a clash with the Church, but they did need the clergy's obedience and public approval: not too steep a price to pay for survival! Such a step would have required genuine courage and deep humility, together with a profound perception of the Church's role in the history of salvation. However, the cardinal was incapable or unwilling or possibly both; he forged ahead towards a showdown with remarkable energy and unshakeable faith—as even his enemies were grudgingly compelled to acknowledge—in his unique destiny as saviour of his country's Church.

To publish a pamphlet now, even if it dealt with an abstract and ancient theological argument, could and would be interpreted by some as cowardly evasion, and by many as downright betrayal of the Church, and, of course, the cardinal, in their fight to the death with a mortal enemy. It might lead to a weakening of the Church's power, or what was left of it; to a Vatican censure; even to his excommunication. Yet, though Monsignor Beck couldn't imagine how he could live outside the protective wings of Holy Mother Church, he could not stop himself from sketching his pamphlet in his mind. More and more intensely, he felt that he had to write it; whether he would be loved or hated, praised or excoriated, mattered less and less. What really mattered to him was the truth, and linked inseparably to it, the fate of the Church. The sympathy he had always felt for the cardinal, despite their acrimonious disagreements, was still there, though it was cooling. True, they were soldiers of the same army, fighting for the same cause, but not in the same way, certainly not with the same weapons. Whose sword was sharper? Whose aim deadlier? Monsignor Beck had little doubt that, in every respect, he was right and therefore he should write the pamphlet; but still, for reasons he didn't clearly understand, he hesitated.

He left his father's workshop, crossed his mother's reviving rose garden where, he remembered warmly, he'd snatched that flaming red rose for Julishka before they went down to the river-bank and made love, then walked towards the Black Swan, the only tavern left in the village, where at midday he was to meet Henryk and his protégé Dr Ladislas Jarek, famous minister and puritan, whispered to be one of the most narrow-minded fanatics among the hidebound zealots. Monsignor Beck wasn't looking forward to the meeting. For two days now, he had been visiting the places of his childhood and youth, which he found enchanting and exhilarating. Much as he intended to talk to Jarek about the suspicious circumstances of the fire that had burned down the church, and even more urgently, about the circumstances of the fire that was threatening to burn down the whole country, he was in no mood to do so. But as so many other times in his life, he couldn't do much about that.

'Dr Jarek,' Monsignor Beck said, pouring wine from a dark-green bottle into a tall crystal glass which bore the Dombinsky coat-of-arms, 'I'm sure you're aware of the fact that the circumstances of the fire are, to say the least, suspicious.' Jarek, sitting opposite him by the window, was watching General Wulf pacing up and down the street talking to the people, dressed in solemn black, who were gathering slowly for the consecration ceremony.

'Everybody is whispering about arson, and I must say,'

Monsignor Beck continued, 'I'm not at all surprised. Your local loyalists are not exactly people I'd trust to uphold the law or, for that matter, to preserve the good name of your Alliance. Yet, almost two months *post factum*, no investigation has been started, no attempt has been made to find out exactly what happened, let alone to punish the perpetrators of this outrage. No wonder our people feel discriminated against by the law of the working masses you so fervently preach all over the country. Don't they belong to that category? Aren't they precisely those simple working men and women you talk about so much in every one of your speeches? Imagine, they say, what would have happened had your headquarters been burned down.

'Slowly it is becoming clear to them—to *us*, Dr Jarek—that it isn't *our* law. It isn't *our* order. So, what is it? It's a farce, as they would say. Well, Dr Jarek, I'm in complete agreement with that sentiment. To have a new church built is a great gift for all of us here, and we are grateful to you and General Wulf for having made that possible. But though it will provide us with a place of worship, it will never replace the old one, which was more than 150 years old and full of relics and mementoes, not to mention irreplaceable traditions. It was the church where I was baptized and received my first Communion, where I also had the first intimations of my vocation as a priest. So, Dr Jarek, could you tell me what you intend to do about all that, both as an enlightened man and as minister of the interior?'

Monsignor Beck looked at Uncle Arnulf and Aunt Amalia, proprietors of the Black Swan, and his cousins, tiptoeing aimlessly around the beer-counter. Well versed in swiftly deciphering glances and raised eyebrows, Uncle Arnulf and Aunt Amalia instantly disappeared into the

kitchen, though Monsignor Beck knew, and knew that
Jarek knew, that they would continue to listen through the
cracks in the door. Everybody was listening everywhere
in the village. But was Jarek listening? He didn't drink the
wine Monsignor Beck had poured for him but ordered
coffee instead. His long face and blue eyes were relaxed as
he watched a group of children playing football on the
common. Suddenly a thin smile appeared at the corner of
his lips, and Monsignor Beck sensed that Jarek was listening in a way Gerogen never would, or could, listen—with
a hint of interest, curiosity, even understanding, which not
only surprised Monsignor Beck but made him both ani-
mated and angry.

'All that, of course, is only the surface, Minister,' he
continued, unable to suppress his resentment. 'Scratch the
surface, and you'll find the real problems beneath. Plenty
of them. I'm sure you know a great deal more about those
than I do. Still, I'd appreciate it if we could talk. I'm in no
hurry, and I hope you have a little time left for us. Yes, I
must tell you, Minister, and you had better listen to me, the
situation is bad, very bad, and it's getting worse.'

Without haste, Jarek finished his coffee, stood, motioned politely to Monsignor Beck to move ahead of him,
then, in a voice as clear and cold as a wintry morning on Mt
Ephialt, he said, 'We'll change it.'

In that instant Monsignor Beck knew he was going to
write his pamphlet.

'This morning,' Papa Krauss said, pouring tea into Monsignor Beck's exquisite porcelain cup, 'I read a good story
in the Talmud. Would you like to hear it, Monsignor?
We've lots of time till the funeral.' They were sitting in the
small breakfast-room of The Waldhorn. Through the open

door to the kitchen they heard the busy noises of Aunt Elsie's small army of helpers preparing for the refection.

'Why, of course, Papa Krauss,' Monsignor Beck said, somewhat absent-mindedly, 'let's hear the story from the Talmud.' The aroma of his favourite Ceylonese camellia tea soothed his nerves, calmed his anger which, after his furious argument with Father Novak, still boiled in his mind. Father Novak was a wall not even God's own battering ram could breach. No matter how Monsignor Beck had proved his case by logic or quotes from Augustine to Heidegger, Father Novak wouldn't budge. Tall, pale, thin, very much like Monsignor Beck had been in his salad days, he just sat unmoved, unmoving, occasionally nodding in agreement with what Monsignor Beck had to say about politics and theology. Then, he stood up and repeated word by word, as if he hadn't heard one syllable Monsignor Beck had uttered, the same argument, with the same inflection and, of course, the same contempt at the corners of his lips. After about an hour of such futile altercation, Monsignor Beck left the rectory in a rage. He had bumped into Papa Krauss, who had invited him for a cup of tea before the funeral, and, grumbling but grateful, Monsignor Beck accepted.

'Once,' Papa Krauss said, puffing on his clean pipe, 'once, as it is written in the *Avodah Zarah*, Rabbi Eleazar ben Simeon met a Roman officer on the street who had been sent to arrest thieves. "How can you recognize them?" the rabbi asked. "What if you're taking the innocent and letting the guilty go free?" "What can I do?" the officer replied. "I must carry out the king's orders." "Here's what you should do," the rabbi said. "Go to a tavern at breakfast time. If you see a man catnapping with a glass of wine in his hand, ask him what he does for a living. If he's a scholar, he probably got up very early to study and is already tired. If he's a worker, he may have risen with the sun to do his chores. If he's a person who works at night, he may be sleeping off the hard drudgery of the nightshift. But if he is none of those, he must be a thief and you can arrest him in good conscience."

'Word of that conversation reached the king's ear, and he ordered the rabbi to carry out his own advice. Rabbi Eleazar immediately began to arrest people who he said were thieves. Rabbi Joshua ben Karhar, Eleazar's venerable teacher, then sent a message to his former pupil. "Vinegar, sprig of wine, sour son of a sweet father," so the message read, "how long will you continue to deliver God's people to the hangman?"

'"My teacher, my friend!" Rabbi Eleazar exclaimed. "Where did I go wrong? I only remove the weed from the vineyard." To which Rabbi Joshua replied, "Let the owner of the vineyard come and remove the weed Himself, if and when it pleases Him."'

Papa Krauss puffed on his pipe. 'That's the story I read this morning.'

'An excellent story, a most edifying one. One would have to assume that Rabbi Eleazar understood its meaning. I always enjoy instructive stories from the Talmud.' Through the open window Monsignor Beck saw General Wulf in full-dress uniform driving a jeep with Simon Wald at his side.

'Perhaps you'd like some of that Ceylon camellia to take home, Monsignor? I have plenty of it,' Papa Krauss offered.

'Yes, I'd love some of the Ceylonese,' Monsignor Beck said. 'I haven't tasted anything like that since I don't know when. How did you know it was my favourite?'

'A good guess.' Papa Krauss smiled under his beard. 'We might as well leave, Monsignor. It's almost eleven-thirty.'

Monsignor Beck took a step or two towards the door, but felt his legs weaken, his head grow dizzy. Then, as though he wanted to reach the small, age-blackened wooden Crucifix above the transom, he raised both arms, but touched only the doorposts before the world went black.

'Father, forgive me, for I have *not* sinned.' From the depths of his long, narrow cell, Jarek emerged, pale and thin, already a ghost. In the crossfire of powerful lights he moved towards Monsignor Beck, his hands outstretched. 'I'm glad you came.'

'I'm glad you called, Ladislas,' Monsignor Beck said. 'Do you want to go to confession? Take absolution?'

'Monsignor Beck,' Jarek said, 'I apologise if my request for you to come at this late hour led you to believe that I needed a priest, or that I'm going through some sort of religious experience. I regret to tell you that's not the case. I do not want to confess, nor do I want absolution. Of confessions, I'm sure you understand, I've had enough for a lifetime, or what's left of it anyhow. Of absolutions, I feel that if God is as merciful as He is reputed to be, I don't need a formal act of contrition. I must be absolved simply on the basis of facts. I'll explain, but first, please sit down. Take the chair. I'll sit on my bed. I don't think I'm going to sleep tonight. I've only three hours left, and it would be a waste of time.'

When Bellona Hagen had telephoned about an hour before and, in a voice more subdued than he'd ever heard her use, told him of Gerogen's message which enjoined

Monsignor Beck to go to Jarek at Jarek's request, and stay
with him as long as Jarek wanted him to, Monsignor Beck
was moved but not particularly surprised. He had always
expected Jarek to return to Abraham's bosom (as Henryk
would have said), if not formally or doctrinally, at least
intellectually, perhaps even spiritually. It would not be
because at one point or another, Jarek would miraculously
be touched by the Holy Spirit, though that wasn't entirely
outside the realm of possibilities, but because, underneath
his rigid dogmas and inflexible convictions, Jarek was a
man of reason and logic, and Monsignor Beck had yet to
meet a man of reason and logic who could ultimately resist
God's truth or deny the final conclusions of the Church.
Monsignor Beck could never forget Jarek's strange, almost
transfigured face and remote eyes at the consecration
ceremony, while Monsignor Beck offered Mass in the
open air—*Per ipsum, et cum ipso, et in ipso:* here, as everywhere, the great doxology revealed its miraculous se-
quelae—when suddenly, out of the blue skies, a mighty
thunderclap rumbled through the village and the white,
silent houses echoed its indecipherable message. Jarek's
conversion hadn't happened, though Monsignor Beck
had never ceased to pray for it. He liked Jarek, felt close to
him, almost as close as to Henryk, though, immediately
after lunch in the new House of Culture, Jarek got into his
huge limousine and drove away at top speed without even
saying goodbye. Later, when Monsignor Beck became
deputy first secretary, he met with Jarek several times at
official functions or private dinner parties at Henryk's or
occasionally at Adymester's, and Jarek was always coldly
correct, shook hands politely, asked about his health, or
whether he needed a car or a new office, but had never
shown any particular interest in him or his ideas, yet

Monsignor Beck still liked him. Invariably, Jarek called him *Mon*signor, with only a slightly irreverent taunt in his voice which always reminded Anselm Beck of Archbishop Gaunilon as the archbishop stood at the door of his dark Nunziatura at the Quai d'Orsay, and before Father Beck could climb into the old, battered Citroën on the way home to Mt Ephialt, whispering into his ear with unforgettable raillery, 'We'll make you a *mon*signor yet, *caro Anselmo*,' and for that droll inflection Monsignor Beck liked Jarek even more.

The only thing Monsignor Beck had ever received from Jarek, apart from the funds to rebuild his old church, was an entry card for the Zenty trial, which he used only once, for once was enough to watch that sick, broken, old man repeat slowly, almost mechanically, the words his tutors had hammered into his head during three months of grilling. But even less than the cardinal's ultimate humiliation, which Monsignor Beck suffered with pity and fury—for it could have easily been avoided had that stubborn old cassock listened to him, or understood Kral's role in that dreadful affair—Monsignor Beck couldn't, without getting nauseated, watch Steven Kral's glorification on the witness stand. Kral talked with passionate eloquence about the cardinal's dealings with the American Secret Service and his contemptible foreign-currency speculations. The selected audience of high functionaries from the Central Apparat and the foreign press corps, crowded into the small courtroom of the Curia, watched that elegant one-man show hypnotized. The son of a poor Lutheran minister from the Uplands, a student of Baron Friedrich von Bamberl, the famous Nazi anthropologist at Berlin University, whose theories about the cephalic distortions of Jewish skulls as proofs of their racial inferiority had gained notoriety even before the Nazis came to power, Steve Kral converted to Catholicism and entered the priesthood just in time to make a meteoric career during the war in that confused and vacillating Gesterom court. Steve Kral's rise to the post of private secretary to Cardinal Zenty was fully in line with his talents: the intelligence, cunning, deceitfulness and treachery of a genuine *éminence grise*. The surprising thing was that Kral didn't go even higher in the hierarchy, though it was widely rumoured that Zenty wanted to make him a bishop. Apparently, however, becoming Gerogen's side-kick offered much greater advantages. And so, again, Pater Kral, as Krolthy called him, infusing Roman perfidy with Byzantine subterfuge, switched roles and turned his coat—from Lutheran choirboy to Nazi anthropologist to Catholic priest to Alliance ideologue. A most convincing performance! Now he was the star witness to the cardinal's abominations. His foxy nose red, his small black eyes gleaming, his left fist pounding the witness stand in righteous anger, Steve Kral gave the most formidable stage-show of his life, and the clearest, most extensive, most scurrilous report of the cardinal's betrayal of the people. The cardinal, who must have been drugged, sat on the bench between two expressionless guards, staring at Kral expressionlessly. Monsignor Beck could no longer bear it. To the consternation of the audience, he stood up and left. The next day he returned his entry card to Jarek, but whether or not Jarek understood the meaning of such a remonstration Monsignor Beck never found out.

'I'm listening, Ladislas,' Monsignor Beck said.

'When I was seven years old,' Jarek said, sitting on the edge of his cot, 'my mother took me to church for the celebration of the resurrection. My mother was a Catholic, and so, nominally at least, was my father, but she wasn't a church-going woman, especially after her marriage to that angry atheist, with the fire of the Devil, as the parish priest, only half in jest, told my mother when he once dropped in at our house. In any case, we went to church that Easter morning to pray for my father's life. He was on the Russian front and we hadn't heard from him for many months. I remember that sparkling spring which turned our small, dark, cold church into a vast cathedral of the sun. I liked that. The colours of the stained-glass windows were more vivid and telling than the stories they were supposed to illustrate and, in that incense-filled air, amid Latin eloquence and Gregorian chants, I discovered my independence from the supernatural. I found, however vaguely and inarticulately, as a seven-year-old boy would, my own way to freedom without God. It was a happy moment. I cherished it all my life. I never needed God to teach me, console me, instruct me, to punish me for my sins or reward me for my good deeds. Later, when I understood the reasons why man invented God as an extension of himself, I also realized that God was nothing but a symbol of the human intelligence which created Him, as Dr Gregory used to say, rather than the other way round. It wasn't, I know, an earth-shaking discovery, but it was a revelation to me, good enough to live and die on its strength. My home was the natural world of man, warts and all, and not—*not*, Father Beck, I'm sorry to say—the empyrean spheres of God. His priests behind the altar promised me eternal life in exchange for love, trust and obedience, but I had no reason to love or trust—not, at any rate, the way He wanted me to—nor did I have any intention of being obedient. I wanted to doubt, to hate, to rebel. Such intimations on that lovely, distant Easter

morning served me well for a lifetime. As for eternal life
and resurrection at the end of time—those fuzzy hopes of
man terrified by the thought of total annihilation—I felt
they were a crutch, a permissible one, for the spiritually or
intellectually maimed, which, of course, most people are.
For me, death was without threat or hostility. In fact, in a
sense, I had always been curious to experience it. To *feel* it,
as it were. This wasn't a death-wish, far from it. On the
contrary, it was simple, genuine human curiosity to know.
What was death like? What did total dissolution mean?
That, by the way, was one of the reasons I have asked
Henryk not to put the hood on me before they string me
up. I want to see everything down to the last detail, yes, to
the very last second and even beyond. Does that make any
sense to you, Monsignor?'

'It makes perfect sense to me, Ladislas,' Monsignor
Beck said.

'Do you think there's any reason why at this late
moment I should change?' Jarek asked.

'None whatsoever,' Monsignor Beck replied.

'I'm grateful.' Jarek smiled. 'I knew I had called the
right doctor, though I might be the wrong patient. But
frankly, that was not why I asked you to come here
tonight.'

'What was it then, Ladislas?' Monsignor Beck looked at
Jarek, all the while praying in the back of his mind.

'You see, Father Beck,' Jarek said, starting to pace the
cell, 'ever since I was a student at the Sorbonne, I've been
toying with the idea of writing a novel. I'm sure it doesn't
come as a surprise to you. At one point or another, everybody wants to write a novel, though most people fortunately never get close to it, and even more never give it a
second thought. Life is mad enough without getting

embroiled in such a fleeting fancy. You must be crazy to
write a novel, to spend solitary years at your desk, face to
face with the paper's void, in order to invent some nonsense whose reality is, at best, dubious, at worst, disput-
able. And yet it always was my favourite fantasy, except
that I had other things to do—to change the reality that
existed, for one thing, instead of inventing an artificial
one—and I could never manage to sit down in that legendary solitary room and listen to the dialogue of non-existent
characters in my mind. Nevertheless, all my life I've
diligently jotted down ideas and emotions I might, somehow, at some point, smuggle into a narrative. My notebooks are full of fragments of dialogues overheard in a
tram or on the battlefield or in jail, or of landscapes I've
seen, or ideas that have hit me in the bath. I wish I could ask
you to go to my apartment and look at those notes, but I'm
sure they no longer exist, because Gerogen must have
made certain that they were destroyed, just as he destroyed everything else in his path. So be it. But I have
beaten Gerogen anyhow, and he can't do a thing. I've
finished my novel. Yes, Father Beck, I've done it, I *have*
done it!' He stopped, triumphantly, in front of his small
table and from its drawer withdrew a manuscript, holding
it high in the air. 'Here it is, Father Beck. Take a look. The
only time I could satisfy my lifelong urge to become a
novelist was when I had so little time left, but old Henryk,
who understood what I hoped to accomplish, made it
possible. I could now sit down, undisturbed, and write it.
True, I had to rush it somewhat, for I was running out of
time; there was a deadline hanging over my head, and if I
didn't hurry, my head would soon be hanging over the
deadline. But by working day and night, I've managed to
overcome that last obstacle. It may not be the greatest

masterpiece, but it is a work that tells you something about the life we tried to live.'

A sly smile appeared in Jarek's eyes and spread over his whole face, as though he had found the key to the door which had been hidden from him for countless years. 'But there is another reason I asked you to see me tonight, Father Beck. Forgive me, I'm using you again, as I've used everybody and everything in my life, but I have very little time to explain or make amends. We must act now. Gerogen knows about the novel, of course. I wouldn't be surprised if he's already read it. Every day when they take me out into the courtyard for a walk, his henchmen could easily photograph the whole thing for him to read.' Jarek's shadow fell on Monsignor Beck's face, a sudden eclipse of the sun. 'What Gerogen doesn't know,' Jarek whispered almost inaudibly, 'is that I have made a copy, in secret. Never mind how. It's done. When I go this morning, I'll leave *this* manuscript on the table, as I always do. Gerogen might destroy it or put it in the safe where he keeps his records and documents. But we still have *our* copy. And you, Father Beck, will take that one out of here. I've made a pouch you can fit easily around your waist so nobody'll notice it. You're the only person they won't search before you leave the prison. Besides, I ask you to accompany me on my last walk. From there, you're free to go. You must hide the manuscript somewhere out of their reach. Preferably on Mt Ephialt. In the monastery. You know that place like the palm of your hand. Your sole obligation to me is to guard the manuscript, preserve it and make sure that my son gets it on his eighteenth birthday, my gift from the other side of Styx. You may or may not be here to give it to him, but my son must have it, read it, ponder it, for he must understand his father. You will do what needs to be done. Do I have your word, Monsignor Beck?'

'Anything to eat or drink, Monsignor?' Aunt Elsie said. 'You look pale to me.'

'Maybe a glass of wine first,' Papa Krauss suggested. 'From the Furmint, of course, Elsie.'

On the porch behind The Waldhorn, Monsignor Beck saw General Wulf finishing his wine, his tunic thrown on the table, his cap on the ground, his shirt unbuttoned. At the end of the garden, where the long row of acacias marked the beginning of the fields, Adam Krolthy stood, a solitary figure, almost aglow in the brilliant light, watching the sun sink towards the western hills.

'Anselm,' General Wulf called, sitting up straight with some difficulty. 'What happened? We heard you got hit by lightning.'

'Exactly,' Monsignor Beck said and took a sip of the wine Sybil Wald had brought him from the kitchen. It was crystal clear, cold, with a faint tinge of sweetness that made Monsignor Beck take another sip. After the funeral and the long, silent walk with Papa Krauss across the meadows and marshes which he took in order to try his strength, he felt better. 'I fainted, Henryk. I've never before fainted in my life. It was queer. You just go down, and the world goes out. You think you're dead.'

'The *Malach Hamoves* wasn't very far, Monsignor. Please, don't tempt him,' Papa Krauss cautioned. 'I heard his wings beating outside the windows.'

'I stand warned,' Monsignor Beck said. 'Papa Krauss brought me back to the land of the living. I'm not sure whether I should be grateful or furious.' From behind a small grove of elms, he saw Peter, Sara and Berti Lucas emerge and walk straight towards The Waldhorn's porch.

'Peter,' Monsignor Beck called. 'Where's your father?'

'I don't know,' Peter said. 'Mother said he's probably gone up to the hut above Cutting 3, which is where he always goes when he wants to be alone and think. Mother said we mustn't bother him.'

'We've been asked to come and help,' Berti Lucas said.

'What's this *Malach Hamoves* business, Anselm?' General Wulf asked. He was very drunk. 'Are you being threatened?'

'Yes, Berti Lucas, I sent for you fellows,' Sybil Wald said. 'You should all go to the kitchen and finish the preparations. Then you can take the candles, the bread and the wine, and ask Father Novak to consecrate them for tomorrow.'

'The angel of death is God's special messenger, General Wulf,' Papa Krauss said. 'A most powerful, angry spirit. You wouldn't want to tangle with him, would you, General?'

'An angry spirit, eh?' General Wulf growled. 'You and your goddamn spirits, Krauss! This whole village is full of goddamn spirits. Like that little old man I saw at the well this morning. Or old Matthias's ghost wandering around his tombstone. As if we were already dead and sent to hell. Fruitcakes! Would somebody get me some more wine, so that I can survive my own death here? I don't know about you, Anselm, but first thing tomorrow, I'm going to be out of here.'

The sun had reached the upper rim of the western hills, the shadows were growing fast. It turned chilly. As far back as he could remember, Monsignor Beck had always perceived death as a passage, a transmutation, a recognition. It was a continuance. But if death was the way he'd experienced it when he fainted this morning, it was different from everything he'd ever imagined. It was unaware of itself, an existence without being, utterly complete, absolutely empty. It was a severance. In the sudden, cold wind of the sunset, Monsignor Beck shivered. He understood that he had never really understood anything.

BOOK FOUR
DEPARTURES

TWELVE

THE closer Simon Wald got to the old house, the better he saw the devastation Andy Shvihak's gangsters had wrought on old Uncle Matthias's hut. The man-high labyrinthine earthwork, carefully planned and constructed to trap intruders and keep the world out, had been levelled to the ground. The small house, with a larger shed attached on its northern side, was wrecked, its door ripped off, its windows broken, its roof smashed in. In front of what once had been a vigorous vegetable garden, the skeleton of a wolfhound lay in the dust exactly as it must have fallen when one of Andy Shvihak's thugs shot it between the eyes. In the kitchen Simon Wald found the wreck of the old iron range, pots and pans, a couple of broken mugs, a few plates, some blackened forks and spoons. In the old man's bedroom the remnants of a bed, a table and chair were heaped on top of each other in the middle, as if someone had begun to build a bonfire but had no time to light it. The walls, once whitewashed, were now stained by time and rain and snow from the leaking roof and smashed windows. Simon Wald walked around the house a few times, looking for something, a book, a letter, an old photograph, anything he could take home to keep as a memento, but he found nothing.

The shed next to the house was undamaged. Inside Simon Wald was assailed by the intense, repulsive odour of tannin, which Uncle Matthias used to treat the hides of the animals he trapped. At the door of old Matthias's workshop, Simon Wald stopped. Around the walls were metal hooks for skinning the animals the old poacher caught on his nightly jaunts into the depths of the forest, where only he dared to venture. As in the house, the beaten-earth floor was dry and grey, but there were large splotches of blood under the hooks, darkly indelible in the early afternoon sun. Though Simon Wald had never been there before, the place was vaguely familiar. Slightly dizzy and feeling vulnerable because the buzzing in his head was growing louder, he felt pain touch his body with invisible fingers. Slowly, he lowered himself and sat under a large rusty hook.

'Welcome, Chief Forester,' Captain Strappado said. 'Welcome home. Good to see you again. Gottlieb and Chortnik will be here in a moment, so together we can begin our celebration of those days when we worked side by side to save our fellow men from disaster. It wasn't our fault that we failed. Still, those were great times, Chief Forester, don't you think? I hope you bear no ill-will towards us. After all, we only followed orders and in our "Pleasure Palace"—as Kopf, a most witty fellow, so aptly named it—we treated our guests politely and respectfully, as they deserved to be treated, men with great minds and great achievements, though we had no illusions concerning their feelings about us. We knew how much you hated us. We knew that you were willing to do anything to make us feel inferior to you. Yes, we knew what you were up to, Chief Forester, we knew everything, except one minor detail. When we brought you to the Pleasure Palace on that memorable night, which I'm sure has remained in your mind as vividly as it has in mine, we had long been aware of your preparations for your "uprising"—or mu-

tiny, as we called it—despite Kopf's admirable penchant
for secrecy and security. Yes, Chief Forester, we penetrated your operation, almost from the beginning, followed its development with great professional and personal interest. How did we do it? I am not at liberty to tell
you. Suffice it to say that when we decided to have a word
with you, we knew everything, except the precise date and
hour of your attack.

'So, I told Gottlieb and Chortnik: now listen, boys,
here's the chief forester, the only one, apart from Kopf,
who knows every detail, but he's a hard nut to crack, so be
careful. We must break him, but we should do it with tact,
finesse and lenience. They nodded, but, frankly, some
misgiving remained in my mind as to whether or not they
understood what I meant. Still, I had no choice but to
assume that they perceived my intentions and would act
accordingly. But when you decided to refuse to answer
our question, their violent nature and the schooling they
had received in prisons and concentration camps asserted
itself most fiercely. Despite my own personal revulsion, I
couldn't hold them back, for, after all, I was responsible for
the well-being of all of us, duty-bound to defend the order
you wanted to destroy. I regretted greatly that we had to
inflict such pain on you—for, personally, I always found
you an intelligent, attractive man. When you began to yell
curses as we hoisted you higher and higher on the hook,
I begged you to speak, to tell us what we needed to know,
so we could stop the pain and take you back to your
barrack, where you could sleep undisturbed for the rest of
the night and remember everything as if it had only been
a nightmare. But you continued to deny us, shouting,
swearing and even spitting at us, at least until your mouth
went dry. I thought it was quite hopeless and that we

would have to go for Kopf, something I wanted to avoid for obvious reasons. But then Chortnik said, "Listen, Major, listen sharp." We listened and between the curses and obscenities we heard some words, some disjointed but very interesting words, though we weren't sure whether we could interpret them correctly. You went on mumbling for quite a while, until you started to laugh and laughed so loud that we were afraid somebody might hear us. Then you fainted.

'If we wanted to spare you, we had to get you off the hook—forgive the pun—which was exactly what we did. When you came to, we gave you some of that red Bordeaux you had refused to drink with us earlier, but now you appeared willing to drink, thirstily, almost gratefully, a sentiment you expressed somewhat vaguely to Sergeant Chortnik as he escorted you back to your quarters. Later, when we discussed the matter, Gottlieb said you had told us everything we wanted to know, but Chortnik countered that you had told us absolutely nothing. He wanted to repeat the exercise, but I decided to take both sides of the argument into account. Therefore, I gave orders to be prepared at all times for all eventualities, and when your gang attacked a few days later, we were waiting with full force. That was how it happened, Chief Forester. But you've known that all along, haven't you? You've always known that. So, there you are. The answer to your question. Now, I must leave. Official business. I'm going to meet my fellow officers to celebrate my promotion to colonel. Isn't that nice? So, sleep, Chief Forester, sleep well. And have sweet dreams. Maybe that's all we have left to us.'

When Simon Wald opened his eyes, he was lying on the ground among the dark blotches of blood in the spreading dusk. He got up and went out to the yard. It was almost dark, but he could still see the thicket at the edge of the forest quiver and part, as if to let somebody through its dense wall. A giant stag appeared, its head raised high, its huge antlers commanding, and Simon Wald felt a lurch of joy in his heart. It was *his* stag. It was alive. It couldn't be killed. Simon Wald approached it, stroked its head, its neck, the tines of its antlers. The stag made a short, low sound. Simon Wald understood. He took off his jacket, his trousers, his shirt and underwear, and when he was naked, the stag turned, entered the underbrush, and Simon Wald followed it.

Justice Krolthy kept asking the mourners about the Countess Julia's small biplane, but no one seemed to know about it. Some said it was just a legend, and legends about the Countess Julia were as abundant around there as leaves in the woods, as Justice Krolthy realized by now. Some, however, remembered the plane flying so low above the tree-tops that it almost touched them. Others insisted that the plane had long ago crashed and burned, or maintained that it had been requisitioned by the admiral's air force to be used as a trainer for pilots before they were sent to the eastern front. A few people seemed to recall that, after the countess's death, the plane was hidden in one of the big barns that dotted the estate, so that nobody could ever take a look at it, let alone fly it. Justice Krolthy wanted to ask Uncle Karol about that, but the old gardener remained at the chief forester's house after the funeral.

Young Eleazar Wald had driven them back to the manor in Henryk's borrowed jeep; Henryk himself was in no condition to drive, and slept in a drunken stupor in the back seat all the way home. Justice Krolthy went directly to the library to consult some of the local maps drawn over the centuries by estate-managers and foresters, but found nothing helpful. There were excellent maps with innumerable references to landmarks, including barns, but none indicated anything about a hidden aeroplane. Angry and disappointed, Justice Krolthy went to his room, slept fitfully and awoke early, which was not his habit.

Though ordinarily he would never wear a suit two days in a row, now he dressed absent-mindedly in the same grey attire he'd worn at the funeral, and was in so much of a hurry that he even skipped breakfast in the green room. As he stepped outside the main portico, he saw his Skoda parked there. Yesterday he had left it behind The Wald-horn, but some good soul had apparently driven it back, he couldn't help thinking with some sly merriment; the good souls that invisibly surrounded him these days seemed to be taking care of everything. But he didn't need his Skoda now. The sun was already climbing, and, re-freshed and excited, Justice Krolthy started his search on foot for the Fokker.

The moment he came upon the barn, grey and dilapi-dated, not far from Crazy Hill, Justice Krolthy knew it was the one he'd been looking for. He stood motionless in front of the big wooden structure as if wanting to delay the joy of discovery. It was a very old barn on the verge of collapse, so when he finally decided to go inside, Justice Krolthy opened the doors, barred but not locked, with great caution. There among bales of hay and rusting tools, he saw the Fokker. Delighted, Justice Krolthy walked around it several times, examining its wings, propeller, fuselage. A German plane with British markings, pre-sumably to show the Countess Julia's unbending Anglo-philia, it was in perfect condition, without a patch of rust on the engine, or the slightest tear in the fuselage. The propeller was oily brown, the wings glittered grey, the windshield was immaculately clean—the work of Uncle Karol, Justice Krolthy guessed. The old gardener had kept the old lady as young as he could, because even now, some twenty years after her death, Uncle Karol still loved the Countess Julia with all his heart. Deeply moved, using an old barrel as a step, Justice Krolthy climbed into the Fokker's cockpit.

The cockpit was narrow and confining, and Justice Krolthy could hardly sit down, let alone stretch his legs. He felt something cold and irritating in his right trouser pocket, and realized he still had Count Széchy's pepper-box Colt, which he'd forgotten to return to the armoury. The Fokker's instrument panel was very simple, with a compass, a few gauges, lights, buttons, but to Justice Krolthy it was a mystifying puzzle, as all motors and machines had been since he was a child. He'd learned to drive a car, but he couldn't tell a clutch from a carburetor, and didn't particularly care to either. Now he was tempted to press one of the buttons to see what would happen—he was certain that everything would work perfectly, because Uncle Karol knew as much about machines as about roses. Instead, Justice Krolthy touched the stick between his knees, which, to his delight, moved with ease and compliant obedience, sideways, forwards, backwards, as tools and servants should invariably do when called upon to perform their duties.

For a while he played with the stick, observing how the flaps moved, the wings quivered in the headwind of his imaginary flight. Through the open door of the barn he could see the airstrip, perfectly straight, clearly defined, separated from the grey autumnal meadows, an unbroken ascent to the skies. Suddenly the warm yellow mid-morning light turned cool and mist descended upon the strip and the surrounding countryside, unexpectedly tinting them silver.

'The red button is the starter,' the Countess Julia said. 'Just press it, and we're off. Oh, Adam! How good of you to come and see my Fokker! I've been waiting for you for so long! And you've been meaning to come for years! Why did it take such a long time for us to meet? But now you're here, I can fly you to places you've never been before. Will you come with me? We can visit my uncle Lord Agravain in Gareth House. There you could find out what's wrong with my sundial—you remember?—you said it always shows half past ten. But perhaps we should just stay above the clouds without ever looking down to earth. Why shouldn't we? Haven't we seen all that? Don't we know everything? Oh, Adam! You're not running away again, are you? Not now, not from me? Running away from love never helped you find love, my dear. And you have always run away—lost so much love, wasted so much time! I know you understand. You *must* understand. Push that button, my sweet.'

Justice Krolthy felt the Countess Julia's fingers caressing his face, heard her voice whisper in his ears. She'd forgiven him, but could he forgive himself? She loved him. But could he love her? He had never loved anyone. He had wasted so much time. He pushed the red button, and the engine roared to life. How miraculous! How unbelievable! How terrible! Slowly, Justice Krolthy took the Colt out of his pocket, brought it up to his temple and pulled the trigger.

When General Wulf awoke it was still dark and he remained in bed, listening to the feeble chirping of birds still half-asleep among the trees. After a wild drinking bout like yesterday's bash at The Waldhorn, he expected a violent *Katzenjammer*, an enormous headache, compounded by a raging storm in his stomach. To his surprise, he felt better than he had been feeling lately, ready to get up and swing into action, but it was too early. He remembered vaguely how last night, on the porch of The Waldhorn, young Eleazar Wald had lifted him on to his broad shoulders and, without any respect for his rank or age, dumped him on the back seat of the jeep. He had no recollection, however, of how he got back to his room, undressed, closed the windows, lowered the blinds, and had the presence of mind to put a glass of water and his vial of Morpholomin on the bedside table. Yet, with absolute clarity, he remembered the moment he understood that his dream of returning to power and achieving total control was closer than at any other time, that he was only one step away from fulfilling his life's ambition. Just when he felt he'd been shoved lower than he'd ever imagined he could be, humiliated more than he felt he could endure!

While Krolthy and Beck were watching the sunset, embroiled in some ludicrous discussion about miracles, General Wulf saw his own sunrise gleaming on the horizon. It was his turn now. Singer was washed up. The road ahead was clear. He must act swiftly, manoeuvre cleverly, deliver the lethal blow without the sort of sentimental shilly-shallying that in the past had often prevented him from striking hard enough. He wasn't going to repeat those stupid blunders now. He knew what he had to do. He still had allies in the ministry and in the Apparat who had survived Singer's purges and were now lying low, biding their time. They would be more than happy to join him against Singer and his thugs, Kral, Vukovič and the others. He could also do a deal with the Archangel: his freedom in exchange for the co-operation of the State Security Forces, and then, by some shrewd ruse, get the Archangel out of the way. It was a good plan whose details he intended to work out on his way back to Lilac Hill, so that by the time he got home he could set things in motion while Singer was in Moscow, provided, of course, that Singer actually intended to go to Moscow and was not merely waiting in ambush behind the scenes, a possibility General Wulf meant to check out as quickly as he could.

By the time he'd finished packing, it was almost six o'clock and he was hungry. Without even a glance at the portraits of the Széchy ancestors, he walked down the great staircase and went straight to the green room, where the table was already set for breakfast. Above the green marble fireplace, between two giant red candles in silver candlesticks, the Countess Julia looked down at him with benevolence, her innocent smile highlighted by the morning sunshine. More than ever before, he hated her. He snuffed out the candles, probably lit for Krolthy's early morning rite of Julia-worship, then sat down to a tremendous breakfast. He ate mounds of scrambled eggs, grilled goose liver swimming in fat, sausages, butter, jam, though there was none of his favourite fresh rye with the crunchy crust. He felt invigorated. He called the lieutenant of the Special Detachment, but the young scoundrel wasn't available, so he ordered him through his duty-officer to report at precisely eleven o'clock with the jeep at the main portico so they could get to Sentelek station fifteen minutes before the first train left for the city. In the meantime, General Wulf decided to take a stroll.

At the foot of Crazy Hill, the path forked, leading

towards the village on the right, the forest on the left.
Without hesitation, General Wulf took the left fork and
entered the thicket. He felt better and better, his heart
pumping with sonorous regularity, as though the clogged
arteries in his chest had suddenly opened to let the blood
flow through and sustain the energy he needed. A few
minutes later he emerged from the brush and stood on the
edge of a clearing. There was the circular pond with the
giant tree in the middle whose existence Simon Wald had
so vehemently denied. It was just as he had seen it the first
time several days ago, except that now the ice had melted
and the tree-trunk had shed its grimy tufts. The water,
reflecting the blue sky, was motionless, mirroring his own
face, and, in its depths, that of Professor Weiskopf. General Wulf stretched out on the wooden bench near the edge
of the pond.

'You see, Professor Weiskopf,' he said, 'this is precisely
what I was telling you when we last met, remember?
About the detours, accidents, coincidences of my life? You
were sceptical, but I knew that my life was meaningful. So,
Professor Weiskopf, let me present you with my response
to the essential question of history, the answer to the
riddle: *control!* Control is the highest gift of the gods, for to
be able to control without being controlled is to harness
the forces that would otherwise keep you mercilessly in
their Procrustean power. I've known that all my life, but I
could never gain full control. Now I have. *I am in control!*
Control is survival, and survival is freedom. It seems
almost as wondrous as the miracles that scoundrel
Krolthy was yapping about at the wake yesterday, but let
me tell you, Weiskopf, it has nothing to do with divine
intervention. It was no chance, no accident. No, it was
sheer endurance, hard work. As a young man, from the

moment I understood the meaning of control, I worked diligently and unstintingly to free myself from the slavery of historical inevitability, the yoke of social importunities. So, you see, Professor Weiskopf, you were wrong, absolutely mistaken. I *was* responsible for everything I have done in my life.'

'True,' Professor Weiskopf said, 'I was wrong. You *were* responsible for all the disasters in your life.'

The climb to the top of Crazy Hill was easier than General Wulf anticipated. Under the leaky roof of Count Francis's gazebo, he stood panting slightly, but in high spirits. The sky was cloudlessly blue, the sun shone warmly, the air was full of a pleasant, sweet effluvium, but below, in the valley, a grey fog swirled over the forests, the meadows, the manor, obscuring everything. His back against the rotting planks, General Wulf waited for the sun to burn off the fog so he could take one more look at his paradise regained.

The pain exploded high behind his sternum, its tremendous force dispersing down to the tips of his toes, and he collapsed on the cold, dry ground of the gazebo. He couldn't breathe, or move his arm to reach for the vial in his pocket. In his life he had faced death many times, in battles, prisons, concentration camps, yet always there was a chance to outsmart the *Malach Hamoves*, to survive, but now General Wulf knew that death was inescapable. Beyond the gazebo he saw darkness, but what lay beyond the darkness? He saw Inge running towards him, but before she could reach him and comfort him, she stopped—or was she halted? He was not forgiven. For an instant, the pain receded, and, between the blueness of the sky and the greyness of the valley, he watched the fog rise, slowly at first, then swiftly, until finally it flooded over him in wet, cold waves.

From the rickety ledge of the Krestur church belfry, with its low wooden railings, Monsignor Beck surveyed the manor, the arboretum, the vineyards and the little brook where almost five hundred years before, thanks to the archbishop's flawed stratagem and Count Széchy's treachery, king and country had been defeated, never fully to recover again. The air was clear, the sky blue, and Monsignor Beck took a deep breath to suppress a cry. He couldn't really blame the archbishop for his miscalculations, or the count for his inexplicable disloyalty. He, too, had his flawed stratagems, his own unpardonable dishonesties, and he, too, had gone down in defeat.

After a sleepless night in The Waldhorn's diverting Bon Ton Room, he had walked over to the church at first light to say Mass. It wasn't easy to face the truth—probably even Christ Himself found it difficult when He suddenly realized the finality of His human fate—but now that Monsignor Beck had faced it during the darkest hour of the night, he had no doubt left in his mind, in his soul, that his punishment must be death. Kneeling, he repeated the ancient prayer, 'Oh Lord, punish me for I have not kept Your commandments, nor have I trodden the paths of justice and truth before You, so now deal with me severely, as I deserve, command my life to be taken away, that I may turn into dust, for it is better for me to die than to live, refuse me not, oh Lord, grant me my death.' In the small, unfamiliar church, where only a solitary candle flickered before the Presence, Monsignor Beck prayed to the Virgin—his summoner, his mentor—hoping that she would appear once more and intercede for him with the Lord. But she didn't, and Monsignor Beck felt close to despair. The longer he prayed, the clearer it became to him that his wish was not going to be granted. He was not going to die, not now, not for a long time, because the punishment for his sins was not death but a life of suffering and penance. It was a terrible judgement, but wasn't that what he deserved? He was condemned to life.

In the grey swirl of the dawn as he walked from The Waldhorn to the church, he had seen Father Novak on his bike, heading south to the Walds' house beyond the little acacia grove. He telephoned him from the rectory and in a voice that brooked no opposition, ordered him to be at the rectory at precisely six o'clock that evening. Sensing Monsignor Beck's resolve, Father Novak was surprisingly compliant and promised to be there. He didn't ask what the unexpected meeting was all about, which was a good sign.

Towards dawn, when objects and ideas take on sharper contours, Monsignor Beck had decided to reveal the secret of Jarek's manuscript to Father Novak and to entrust him with its guardianship. For six years, since Jarek's execution, Monsignor Beck had kept the manuscript, which he had smuggled out of the prison, but he had never read it, never even opened the clever little pouch in which Jarek had hidden it. He had taken it to the monastery, and placed it in the tower above the abbot's office, where the temperature never rose above ten centigrade and where the cold, dry air of the mountain would preserve Jarek's novel for another millennium. After Jarek's re-burial, Monsignor Beck decided, he would take Father Novak up to Mount Ephialt and tell him that it was his obligation to present the manuscript to Jarek's son on his eighteenth birthday, as Jarek had requested. Father Novak would be a good guardian. Whatever happened to Monsignor Beck—whether he lived or died—the fate of Jarek's novel would be safe. Anselm Beck had kept his word.

The sky was cloudless, the brown fields and hills in the distance clear and luminous, the Indian summer curiously unrelenting. The wounded church bell struck noon, and Monsignor Beck watched the bell-ringer—one of Father Novak's altar-boys—leave the keep and hurry towards the school.

'Anselm,' Krolthy had said yesterday at the refection, 'I'm asking you as an official representative and interpreter of miracles: what do we need to do to induce "Our Lord" to perform a miracle that will get us out of here unharmed, alive? Would extra prayers do it? A holocaust on His altar? He used to be fond of that once. Frankincense and myrrh? Consider our situation, Anselm. We've been screwed. How do you think we can get ourselves unscrewed? Let's go for a miracle, Anselm. It's our best bet at the moment. How say you?'

And he should have said, 'Adam, it doesn't matter one way or another, whether we get out of here alive or not, what matters is that we must experience our guilt and God's forgiveness for our guilt. *That* is the greatest miracle. So, Adam, I think we should not be considering our situation but the inexplicable miracle of God's pardon by His grace, the only miracle capable of redeeming us from the misery and absurdity of existence.' But he had remained silent, refused to respond to Krolthy's jaded smugness, and thereby missed yet another opportunity to stand up and be counted for God's truth.

On the main street he saw three children shuffling towards the church, and even from up here on the belfry, he recognized them. Carefully clambering down the narrow, steep steps, he met them in front of the rectory, where they greeted him respectfully.

'Going for a walk?' Monsignor Beck asked.

'No, Father,' Peter Wald said. 'We're going to the rock.' He carried a small, hand-woven basket covered with a red-and-white checked kitchen-cloth. 'Where Uncle Matthias is buried. Do you know where that is, Father?' He took the cloth off the basket, and Monsignor Beck saw a bottle of wine, a fresh loaf of bread and candles laid out on a white damask napkin, with a crystal wine glass and a silver knife.

'No, I've never been there,' Monsignor Beck said. 'A picnic?'

'Oh, no, Father.' Sara Flur giggled. 'This is our offering to Uncle Matthias. I mean, not just the three of us, but everybody's. Father Novak has consecrated them. Every year before All Souls' Day we take bread and wine to the rock for Uncle Matthias. He comes and eats and drinks.'

'Do you believe in ghosts, my dear?' Monsignor Beck asked.

'Oh, yes,' the girl said gravely.

'Don't be daft, Sara,' Berti Lucas said. 'Remember what Dad told us? It's all a big hoax.'

'It's not a hoax, Berti Lucas,' Peter said. 'Uncle Matthias may not come out of his grave, but this is the way we remember him, my mother says. And my mother says we mustn't forget him. Ever.'

'And who was this famous Uncle Matthias who must never be forgotten?' Monsignor Beck asked.

'A poacher,' Peter said.

'A jackass,' Berti Lucas said.

'A holy man,' Sara said.

They all laughed.

Monsignor Beck accompanied them to the edge of the woods, waited until they disappeared into the dense, high shrubbery, then, seating himself on the ground by the culvert, he closed his eyes and turned his face towards the sun.

'Waiting for the mail, Monsignor?' Papa Krauss asked.

'Yes.' Monsignor Beck looked up. 'For an important letter, with a message of great significance.' Papa Krauss was sitting on the form of the big-spoked gig in which, four days ago, Sybil Wald had driven Monsignor Beck to church. He was holding the reins of the same lovely yellow gelding whose fine, long ears twitched nervously, as if it heard something in the woods nobody else could hear. Monsignor Beck stood up and patted the horse's head.

'This is the time for it,' Papa Krauss said. 'If it comes. Nowadays the mail delivery is very uncertain. Sometimes it doesn't come for weeks. Then they dump a sackful of junk on our doorsteps. No important messages for us these days, Monsignor.'

'Anselm,' Monsignor Beck said.

'Anselm,' Papa Krauss said.

'Still, we wait,' Monsignor Beck said.

'But, in the meantime, we can have a cup of Ceylonese camellia at my house, can't we?'

'An idea whose time has come again,' Monsignor Beck replied.

'And maybe play a game of chess?'

'Until the mail arrives?'

'Yes,' Papa Krauss said. 'But before that, if you don't mind, we could visit my best friend and next-door neighbour, Tobias Feld. He's dying. Cancer of the stomach. A few days, that's all he has, poor fellow. Perhaps you might cheer him up a little? Bless him before he goes? He'd appreciate that.'

'And so would I, very much so, Papa Krauss.'

'Raphael,' Papa Krauss said.

'Raphael,' Monsignor Beck said. 'Heal us, oh Lord, heal us.'